Romantic Suspense

Danger. Passion. Drama.

Cold Case Mountain Murder
Rhonda Starnes

Christmas In The Crosshairs
Deena Alexander

MILLS & BOON

COLD CASE MOUNTAIN MURDER
© 2025 by Rhonda L. Starnes
Philippine Copyright 2025
Australian Copyright 2025
New Zealand Copyright 2025

First Published 2025
First Australian Paperback Edition 2025
ISBN 978 1 038 94060 5

CHRISTMAS IN THE CROSSHAIRS
© 2025 by Denise Pysarchuk
Philippine Copyright 2025
Australian Copyright 2025
New Zealand Copyright 2025

First Published 2025
First Australian Paperback Edition 2025
ISBN 978 1 038 94060 5

MIX
Paper | Supporting
responsible forestry
FSC® C001695
www.fsc.org

Published by
Harlequin Mills & Boon
An imprint of Harlequin Enterprises (Australia) Pty Limited
(ABN 47 001 180 918), a subsidiary of HarperCollins
Publishers Australia Pty Limited
(ABN 36 009 913 517)
Level 19, 201 Elizabeth Street
SYDNEY NSW 2000 AUSTRALIA

Cover art used by arrangement with Harlequin Books S.A.. All rights reserved.

Printed and bound in Australia by McPherson's Printing Group

Cold Case Mountain Murder

Rhonda Starnes

MILLS & BOON

Rhonda Starnes is a retired middle school language arts teacher who dreamed of being a published author from the time she was in seventh grade and wrote her first short story. She lives in North Alabama with her husband, whom she lovingly refers to as Mountain Man. They enjoy traveling and spending time with their children and grandchildren. Rhonda writes heart-and-soul suspense with rugged heroes and feisty heroines.

Books by Rhonda Starnes

Rocky Mountain Revenge
Perilous Wilderness Escape
Tracked Through the Mountains
Abducted at Christmas
Uncovering Colorado Secrets
Cold Case Mountain Murder

Visit the Author Profile page at millsandboon.com.au.

And the Lord, he it is that doth go before thee;
he will be with thee, he will not fail thee,
neither forsake thee: fear not, neither be dismayed.
—*Deuteronomy* 31:8

This book is dedicated to Jackie Layton, Cate Nolan and Dana R. Lynn. Thank you for being my accountability partners and for helping me stay motivated and on track as I completed this book. I couldn't have done it without you.

Chapter One

Jenna Hartley folded her hands on the round table in front of her in the tiny bedroom she'd turned into a home office that she used for a podcast studio in her East Tennessee home and leaned forward, as if making eye contact with her listeners. "That's all for today, folks. Thank you for tuning in to *Seeking Justice with Jenna.* Tune in next time, when we discuss the Boxcar Killer trial, shedding light on the crime that rocked the Chattanooga Choo Choo right off its tracks."

She ended with a prayer for comfort for all the families hurting over the sudden loss of a loved one at the hands of brutality. Then she paused for a count of twenty to allow enough time for the rolling credits she would layer into the video during the editing process and pressed the stop button on the video app on the tablet she used for recording. She'd long since given up doing live videos, wishing to avoid reading any negative comments while on the air. Leaning back, she inhaled deeply and then exhaled slowly. After every podcast-recording session, it took her a few moments to steady her heart rate and calm the nervous anxiety. Three years as a true crime podcaster, and it still never got easier to discuss the gruesome details of the numerous murders that had taken place in her beautiful state of Tennessee.

"Lord, please give me strength to keep going with this work. I pray my podcast continues to shine a light on the darkness in this world as I seek justice for my beautiful Becca and for other families who have lost loved ones." She lifted her head and looked at the photo collage that decorated the opposite wall. Photos of her daughter. A smattering of baby photos, school photos and vacation photos, but the ones that tugged at her heart the most were the ones taken in the last months of Becca's life.

Becca holding her acceptance letter to Vanderbilt University in Nashville. Smiling in her senior portrait. Posing with her best friends at a school assembly. Sitting on a bunk bed in her cabin at church camp. And the last photo they'd taken together, one month before Becca died. Mother and daughter standing on the glass-bottomed section at the highest point on the SkyBridge in Gatlinburg, Becca laughing at her mother for holding on to the handrail so tightly her knuckles had turned white, fear plainly written on Jenna's face.

"Don't be so afraid to live, Mom," Becca had said, laughing. Seventeen and fearless. "We only get one life, embrace it. Be adventurous. Don't let fear hold you back."

As a constant reminder of her daughter's philosophy, Jenna had intertwined the photos with the words *Embrace life with an adventurous spirit. Don't allow fear to control you.*

"Oh, Becca, I wish you were here to see me now. I may not have gained an adventurous spirt, but I have definitely stepped way outside my comfort zone," she said aloud to the empty room. Who would have ever thought an introvert like Jenna would become the host of a podcast with half a million followers?

With a sigh, she pushed back her chair and stood. Jenna had skipped dinner, and it was nearing nine o'clock. If she hoped to watch the video she'd just recorded and make notes for edits and still be in bed before midnight, she needed to grab a cup of coffee and maybe a slice of the lemon pound cake she'd baked last night.

Leaving the lights off, she plodded down the hall toward the front of the house where the range-hood light shone like a beacon. As she neared the end of the hall, the large picture window in the living room exploded. Jenna gasped and dropped to a squatted position, wrapping both arms over her head. A thousand tiny fragments of glass rained down, and a large flat block dropped onto the center of the hardwood floor.

Not again. Her podcast anti-fans had gotten out of control, especially in the last two weeks. Someone had slashed her tires. The words *Let Becca R.I.P. or Join Her* had been spray-painted on her garage door. Then she'd found a photo—her head transposed onto a person's body in a coffin. It had been taped to her truck window in the grocery store parking lot.

Now this. Of course, she was used to these things by now. And when people tried scare tactics, it usually meant she was getting close to a breakthrough in one of the cold cases she featured on her podcast.

Oh, how she missed the days of living in a gated community. Things like this would have been less likely to happen if she still lived there. Unfortunately, when her ex-husband, Patrick, had left her for his secretary, Jenna had made the difficult decision to move her and five-year-old Becca back to Barton Creek, leaving Nashville and her cheating ex in the rearview mirror.

It had been hard to uproot her child and move her away from the only home she'd ever known and her friends and classmates, but Jenna had known living closer to family would be for the best. Her mom had provided free childcare, which allowed Jenna the opportunity to finish her degree in education. After graduation, she'd taught high school math while working on her masters in counseling. Then she had accepted the counselor position when it came available. Working in education had given her a schedule that allowed her to attend all Becca's school and sporting events.

She had no regrets over the sacrifices she'd made to give her only child the best upbringing she could, and she would cherish every memory. But if she let her mind wander, she sometimes wondered if Becca would still be alive if they'd stayed in Nashville. While there were no guarantees in life, if they hadn't been in Barton Creek, Becca wouldn't have been near the hiking trail where they'd discovered her body.

Saying goodbye to her beautiful, outgoing seventeen-year-old daughter had been the hardest moment of her life. But that pain had only intensified from not knowing whom Becca had been on the hiking trail with and why they'd killed her, leaving her body to be discovered by thru-hikers on the Appalachian Trail the next morning.

She pushed to her feet. Thankfully, she'd left her running shoes on instead of kicking them off halfway through the podcast like normal. Food would have to wait until she boarded up the window. It was a good thing she'd stocked up on plywood at the building-supply store the last time this had happened three weeks ago. She'd long given up the notion that she needed to report every little incident that occurred. The sheriff's department always did the best they could, but it was a waste of their time for her to keep filing reports when there wasn't any way to prove who had thrown the rock. And really, she doubted it was the same person committing each offense.

People had strong feelings about true crime podcasts, with some cheering her on in her efforts to uncover clues and assist the police in finding murderers, while others criticized her and accused her of planting evidence to fit her theories. It didn't matter that she gathered most of her information from public records and never visited a crime scene until the police had completed their investigation and removed all crime scene tape.

Not wanting her movements to be seen by anyone lingering outside, she left the lights off. Although she doubted the person who'd thrown the rock had stuck around. In her experience, the people who did this type of thing were more about making her life miserable, costing her money and shutting her up—figuratively, not literally—and would never hang around long enough to be identified. Navigating around furniture in the dark, Jenna made her way to the kitchen. Opening the door that led into the garage, she snaked out a hand and flipped on the light. Then she stepped into the small single-vehicle space, thankful there were no windows.

When vandals had first started attacking her home two and a half years ago, she'd set up a mini workshop inside the garage, which was why she parked her Chevrolet Colorado outside. Jenna sighed. After someone vandalized her truck last week, she'd had no choice but to order a utility shed to convert into a workshop. The contractor planned to pour the concrete pad next week, weather permitting, and then they could assemble the shed. The hit her savings account had taken was enormous, but she was afraid if she didn't get her truck back into the garage, the vandals would do more than slash a few tires. And she couldn't afford a new vehicle.

The picture window was eight feet wide and five feet tall, meaning that one sheet of four-by-eight plywood wouldn't be enough to cover the opening. She could split the difference and leave a six-inch gap at the top and bottom, but that would allow all kinds of creepy-crawly critters to come inside. Walking over to the stack of plywood leaned against the garage wall, she hefted one of the two sheets onto the sawhorses. Then she opened the metal cabinet and pulled out her goggles and the circular saw she had bought for herself for Mother's Day almost two years ago. Being a mother and no longer having her child here with her made the holiday extra hard. Typically, she would pick up a salad from a drive-through restaurant and have a picnic beside Becca's grave, giving her daughter a life update.

On that particular morning, she'd awoken to the sound of breaking glass—the first incident of a rock being thrown into her home. The police were called but couldn't do much, since no one saw who threw the rock. After phoning a local handyman and being told it would be a week before he'd be able to get to her house and do the repair, she'd driven herself to the home-improvement store and purchased all she needed to board up her window until the repairman could order and install a new one. When she finally made it to Becca's grave for her picnic, she talked about the supplies she'd purchased at the home-improvement store and laughed that she'd bought herself a saw for Mother's Day. She pictured Becca smiling and saying she would have bought her the exact same gift if she'd been there to celebrate.

Jenna ripped the plywood to the size she needed. She picked up the pink tool belt her sister, Amber, had given her last Christmas and fastened it around her waist, then looped an arm through the ladder so it rested on her left shoulder before she headed out the side door into the yard.

Pausing, she listened. All was quiet. Her nearest neighbor, a retired detective from Atlanta, lived three-tenths of a mile away. Glancing toward his house, she saw a light shining through the trees. If he hadn't made it perfectly clear when he'd moved in six months earlier what he thought of her "little podcast," she might have called him and asked for his help boarding up the window.

She rounded the side of the house and leaned the plywood and ladder against the brick wall. Thankfully, a flower box ran the length of the window, so the plywood could rest on it as she secured each side into place. A shiver ran up the length of her spine. The tiny hairs at the nape of her neck stood at attention. Someone was watching her. Bending as if she were picking something up off the ground, she peeked under her arm, searching. A bright moon overhead illuminated the front yard, but the woods on either side of her driveway were full of shadows, making it impossible to detect an intruder.

The sound of a vehicle penetrated the silence of the night, and she stood and turned toward it. An SUV came around the curve in the road, and the headlights flashed on a figure at the edge of the yard. She gasped and dashed through the garage and raced into the house, slamming the door behind her and bolting it.

Her phone. She needed to retrieve it from her studio and call 911. This meant running past the shattered living room window. Puffing out a breath, she ran as if the imagined boogeyman from her childhood had come to life and was chasing her. Only this wasn't imagined. A real person with evil intent lurked outside her home.

As she drew even with the picture window, a fiery flame hurtled toward her. A scream ripped from her throat, and she dove behind the couch. A Molotov cocktail hit the watercolor painting of a sunflower, which Becca had painted in eleventh grade, that hung on the wall to her left.

A second flaming bottle of liquid shattered against the hearth of the rock fireplace, and the rug burst into flames, quickly blocking her path to safety. The accelerant used in the Molotov cocktails did its intended job. Smoke filled the room. Her eyes watered and her lungs burned. She had to find a way out of the inferno. And fast. Or the police would have another murder to solve when they discovered her charred, dead body.

Sean Quinn pressed hard on the brakes and sharply turned his steering wheel to the left. Fire and smoke plumed out of Jenna's house. Taking the turn into his neighbor's driveway too fast, his SUV's back tires fishtailed on the gravel drive. He eased off the gas and regained control, then pressed the call button on his steering wheel and gave the command to dial 911.

Slamming on his brakes and coming to a stop in front of the garage, he quickly filled the emergency dispatcher in on the situation and rattled off the address. Then he jumped out of his vehicle and ran toward the front door. Someone had shattered the large picture window, and a couple of pieces of plywood were lying on the ground. A vandal had obviously started the fire. Did the plywood mean Jenna Hartley was outside and not in the house? Flames crawled up the curtains and shot toward the roof, making a hissing noise.

Where was she? He scanned the area. No sign of her. "Ms. Hartley… Jenna! Where are you?"

"Sean? Help!" A faint cry came from inside, followed by a fit of coughing. "I'm trapped."

"Okay. I'm coming." He sprinted up the porch steps and twisted the doorknob. Locked. The handle was warm but not scorching, which meant the fire hadn't spread too far into the entryway. Yet. He turned sideways and rammed his shoulder against the door. It didn't budge. *This will never work.*

Sean took a deep breath and released it slowly. *Think. There has to be another way in.*

He'd only been inside the house twice—once for coffee shortly after he'd moved to the area and once to return mail that had accidentally been placed in his mailbox—but he vaguely remembered the door that led into the kitchen from the back deck had glass on the top half. Sean jumped off the porch, grabbed a large rock from the flower bed border and raced around the house. The doorknob was cool to the touch. The fire had not spread from the front of the house. He peered inside. The range-hood light cast an eerie glow over the kitchen, and smoke danced in the archway opening that led to the dining room. Gripping the rock tightly, he smashed the bottom left pane of glass, clearing the tiny shards as quickly as possible, and then stuck his arm through the opening, feeling around until his hand touched the doorknob. Click. He twisted the knob, and the door popped open an inch.

Pulling his arm out of the window, he pushed the door wide and darted inside. Smoke assaulted him immediately. His lungs burned. He snatched the dish towel that lay on the countertop near the sink, turned on the water and saturated the cloth, then covered his mouth and nose with it.

"P-p-please…hur-hurry," Jenna choked out in a raspy voice.

He darted through the cased opening to the dining room.

The French doors that led into the living room stood open, but flames blocked the entrance. The lights were off. He willed his vision to adjust, but the haze of the smoke was working against him. "Where are you?"

A deep hacking cough answered him. "Here," she said. "On the floor. Against the wall. Between the sofa and the side table."

He mentally visualized the layout of the room. "Closest to the dining room or the entry hall?"

"Entry." Another scratchy cough. "The fire is on both sides of me. There were two Molotov cocktails thrown."

Two? Whoever did this had meant to cause the most damage possible. Hoping to get a better view of the living room, where the light from the fire might give him more insight into the situation, Sean moved to his right and immediately bumped into the dining table. Steadying himself, his hands came in contact with a tablecloth. He balled it up in his hands and pulled it off the table. A clattering sound followed, indicating that he'd knocked a vase or something off the table.

"What was that?" Jenna asked, fear evident in her voice.

"Not sure. But hang tight. I'm coming around to the entry."

He raced back to the kitchen sink. Turning on the water once again, he shoved the tablecloth into the sink, quickly soaking it. Guided only by the light over the range, he made his way through the adjoining family room and then stepped into the entry hall. Sirens pierced the night. Help was on the way, but he couldn't wait for them to get there. He had to get Jenna outside. Now. "I need you to talk. Don't stop until I reach you. Got it?"

"Okay. After you cross...the threshold...go about four feet..."

He draped the tablecloth over his head and shoulders and ran through the inferno. Heat engulfed him, and he broke out in a sweat.

"Turn right... I'm against the...wall..."

Sean fought to get his bearings. She sounded like she was to his left. Had he gotten turned around? "Keep talking!"

Silence.

The siren drew closer.

"Jenna! Talk to me!"

A series of coughs. He spun in the direction they came from, stretched his hand out and down in front of him, and walked forward. His hand came in contact with her silky hair. She jumped up and threw her arms around him.

"You found me," she whispered into his neck. "I was so afraid." Sobs racked her body.

"Shh, it's okay. I've got you." He wrapped his arm around her and pulled her under the wet tablecloth. "The fire hasn't reached the entry hall yet. So once we run through the doorway, we'll be on the other side of it. Okay?"

Her head, still pressed against his shoulder, bobbed in agreement.

With his arm clasping her tightly to him, he walked forward until he thought they were in line with the opening and turned to face it. "Okay. Run!"

They raced through the fiery wall and burst into the entry hall just as two firefighters broke through the front door. Jenna collapsed against Sean. He swept her up into his arms and raced past the firefighters into the cool night air. "I need a medic!"

Dear Lord, please let her be okay. Don't let me have been too late again.

Chapter Two

Jenna jolted back to consciousness as an oxygen mask covered her mouth and nose. The sudden burst of air startled her, and she twisted her head, trying to free herself.

"Try to relax. You're going to be okay," a calm female voice asserted. "Thankfully, your handsome neighbor came along just in time to save you. Now, concentrate on taking slow, steady breaths while I get your vitals."

Jenna blinked rapidly, desperate to get her vision to clear.

"Hold on. I'll put some liquid tears into your eyes. I'm sure they're dry from the smoke."

Fingers firmly held her left eyelid open wide, and a drop of cool liquid splashed into it. Then the process was repeated with the right eye. "There now."

She blinked twice. A pretty blond nurse about ten years her junior met her gaze. "Is that better?"

Jenna nodded. "Yes. Thank you," she whispered.

"Try not to talk. Your throat will be sore for a while. Because you passed out, the medics intubated you in the ambulance on transport to the ER." The other woman smiled and slipped a blood pressure cuff over Jenna's upper arm. The cuff tightened as air was pumped into it, then slowly released.

Jenna closed her eyes and focused on her breathing as the woman finished getting all her vitals. The oxygen calmed her burning lungs, and she no longer felt the fight-or-flight sensation she'd felt when she first came to. "What…time…"

"Nearing one a.m. You've been asleep for a while." The nurse slipped the cuff off her arm, folded it and placed it on a cart. "The medics gave you a Schedule 2 sedative in your IV so you wouldn't fight the tube going down your windpipe. Dr. Branson said you must have needed the extra rest for it to knock you out the way it did. But on the plus side, you didn't have to be awake while they ran all the bloodwork and other tests in the ER."

Jenna looked around. This didn't look like an ER room. There was a small straight-backed chair, a recliner and a private bathroom.

"Oh, you're not in the ER now," the chatty nurse said, reading her thoughts. "Dr. Branson moved you into a room. You're on the sixth floor, close to the nurses' station. We'll monitor you overnight. Hopefully, you'll be released tomorrow. Just a precaution, since you inhaled so much smoke and passed out."

Jenna had never passed out before. She had also never been trapped in a burning house before, either. In her forty-three years, this was the closest she'd come to death. And though she'd always believed in God and had spent her youth attending church services in which the preacher talked about the glory of heaven, the thought of dying still terrified her. Maybe because she'd not only shut all her coworkers and friends out of her life four years ago when Becca died, but she'd also shut out God. She prayed at the end of every podcast and went through the motions of being a Christian, but she hadn't opened her Bible or put effort into strengthening her relationship with the Lord. After all, what was the point in going to church and worshiping Him if He hadn't cared enough to protect the person Jenna loved most in this world?

Yet He'd saved Jenna. The thought hit like a bolt of lightning.

Why, Lord? Why save me and not Becca? She had so much to live for. If she'd lived, she would have been in her final year of her bachelor's degree and getting ready to start med school in the fall. Tears burned her eyes, begging for release, and she didn't have the strength to fight them. Turning her head away from the nurse, she allowed the torrent of tears to flow freely down her face.

"I'll let you rest now. Buzz if you need anything," the nurse said cheerfully over the sound of the squeaky wheel on the cart being pushed toward the door.

"How's the patient?" Sean's baritone voice boomed from the hallway.

He couldn't see her like this—weak and crying. She scrubbed her hands over her cheeks and turned to face him. He and the nurse were deep in whispered conversation. The nurse smiled up at him as she leaned against the cart. Were they discussing Jenna? Maybe she should clear her throat to get their attention.

"Ahem." The oxygen mask muffled her voice. She grasped the mask and pulled it down to her chin and tried again. *"Ahem."*

The force of clearing her throat sent her into a coughing fit. Two pairs of eyes turned in her direction. Her cheeks warmed. Well, the attempt to capture their attention subtly hadn't gone as planned.

"Ms. Hartley, you must leave the oxygen mask on." The nurse grabbed a notepad off the cart, stuck it under her arm, and strode back to the bed and positioned the mask over Jenna's nose and mouth once again. Holding out the notepad, she added, "Here. Use this if you need to communicate. Okay?"

Fighting the urge to pull the covers over her head after being scolded in front of Sean, Jenna accepted the notepad with a sparkly pink pin clipped to the front and nodded, keeping her gaze turned to the floor.

"I'm sure Ms. Hartley knows how to follow directions." Sean's voice had a hint of laughter to it. She lifted her head and met his gaze. There was laughter shining in his cornflower blue eyes.

"Alrighty, then." The nurse gave Jenna one more glare before turning to Sean with a brilliant smile on her face. "Don't stay too long. Our patient needs her rest."

He returned her smile with one of his own, punctuated by dimples. "I promise—" he bent slightly to read her name tag "—Bethany. I'll only stay ten minutes."

"Okay. Make sure to stop by the desk and say goodbye on your way out." Bethany giggled and left the room.

Jenna stared after the young woman. What was she thinking, openly flirting with Sean like that? He had to be at least fifteen or sixteen years older than her—practically old enough to be her father.

"You don't have to look so shocked that a pretty woman would flirt with me." Sean pulled the straight-backed chair closer to the bed and dropped into the seat. "I may have gray at the temples, but I'm not ancient yet."

"You—" A burning sensation shot up her esophagus. She closed her eyes and swallowed.

"Use the notepad." He reached across and tapped the small pad in her hand.

She unhooked the pen and flipped open the cover. Then she scribbled. YOU'RE FLATTERED.

His chest shook as a deep chuckle filled the room. "Who wouldn't be? But being flattered by the attention is as far as it goes. I'm not interested. In her *or* a relationship. I enjoy my solitude. Now…" He leaned closer, searching her eyes. "How are you?"

I'M OKAY.

Sean cocked an eyebrow and waited.

REALLY.

"Good. Any idea who threw a Molotov cocktail into your home?"

She scribbled feverishly. NOT ONE. TWO!

Sean nodded. "Yes. The fire chief confirmed there were two. They're testing the accelerant and trying to lift fingerprints off of the broken bottles. But back to my question… Do you have any idea who would do such a thing?"

Didn't he think she would have already said something if she knew who had started the fire? Pressing her lips together, she shook her head. A sharp pain struck behind her left eye. She winced and rubbed her temple.

Sean was at her side in an instant. "Are you okay? Do you need me to call the nurse?"

"No," she replied, more sharply than she intended, and then winced at the sound of her raspy voice. She didn't like the way most medicines made her feel, often preferring not to take anything.

He tapped the notepad.

Making eye contact, she sighed and picked up the pen and paper. I DON'T NEED THE NURSE. I'M FINE. JUST TIRED.

"Okay. I'll get going. Sheriff Dalton wants you to give a statement. I told him to wait until they release you from the hospital so that you can be well rested and clearheaded enough to give him details of what happened."

Heath Dalton complying with his request surprised her. She knew they were fishing buddies, but she hadn't realized they were close enough that Heath would take investigation advice from Sean. She'd known Heath his entire life. Their mothers had been close friends, and Jenna, being ten years older than Heath, had babysat him many times. One thing she learned early on was that Heath didn't like anyone telling him how to do things. That meant he must really respect her neighbor's opinion.

Sean picked up the notepad and wrote on it. "Here's my number. Call me if you need anything."

That's not going to happen. If Jenna needed something, she'd buzz the nurse. Or phone the police if it was something serious. Knowing if she shrugged or shook her head no he'd not leave until she recanted, and not wanting to lie by implying agreement, she looked at him silently.

Sean rubbed the back of his neck and gave a slight nod. "Get some rest." He turned on his heels and walked out of the room, closing the door behind him.

A shiver racked her body as an icy chill enveloped the room. Had she seemed ungrateful? Jenna lowered the head of her bed and sank under the covers. She would have to think of a way to apologize and thank him for saving her life. Maybe a red velvet cake. She giggled. Was that what her life was worth these days? A boxed cake mix and a small amount of time?

He probably didn't eat sweets, though she knew little about his eating habits—or anything else, for that matter. Only that he grew up in Atlanta but had visited his grandparents in Barton Creek every summer as a child. He'd inherited their farm when they passed away in an automobile accident two years ago. After retiring from the Atlanta PD, Sean had moved here to—in his words—"live a simpler life."

She had loved having his grandparents, Jim and Lois Ferguson, as neighbors and had tried to build a neighborly relationship with Sean when he arrived in Barton Creek six months ago. But the only thing he'd wanted was to tell her that her podcast was reckless and she needed to leave crime investigations to the police. *Like they'd done such an excellent job when Becca was murdered.*

Why did Sean have to be the one to save me? Now he'll have even more reason to believe he's right.

Jenna gasped and jerked awake. A dark shadow stood at the edge of her peripheral vision. She couldn't move, her body paralyzed. Soon, the sound of the monitors penetrated her consciousness. Frozen in fear, she forced herself to focus on her breathing. The shadow never moved. Gradually, her body relaxed, and the rhythm of her heart returned to normal. Logic settled over her like a warm blanket. She was in the hospital. Everything was okay. The shadow wasn't a bad guy in her room. This was an episode of sleep paralysis, like she had suffered from as an adolescent and again following Becca's death. Brought on by stress. Her imagination was in overdrive because of the trauma she'd been through. What time was it? She felt as if she'd barely fallen asleep, but the light peeking through the blinds proved it was morning.

Her hand brushed the call button. The nurse had said to buzz if she needed anything. Did that include having someone open the blinds so the sunlight would chase away imaginary shadows? Only one way to find out. She closed her hand around the call button.

A gruff male voice came from the shadow. "No one can save you."

Jenna gasped, and the call button remote slipped from her hand.

The shadow snickered. "I've been watching you sleep. I was afraid you wouldn't wake in time."

She frantically patted around the mattress. Where was the call button? The shadow charged forward, grabbed the cord attached to the button with a gloved hand and dangled it above her head. She reached for the device, and he slung it behind the headboard.

"I'm sorry," the man said in a mock-apologetic voice. "I can't allow you to call the nurse, because then I'd have to kill her, too. And I don't like killing innocent people."

Lifting a shaky hand to the oxygen mask, she pulled it away from her nose, then hesitated. If the mask were around her neck, it would be too easy for him to grasp it and strangle her. She snatched the mask over her head and shoved it behind her, her eyes never leaving the shadow figure.

The man wore dark jeans, a black turtleneck and a white lab coat. A surgical hat and mask covered his hair, nose and mouth. She itched to reach out and snatch the mask off his face but knew it would be a waste of energy. The man was tall, well above six feet. Even if he bent over slightly, she'd never grasp the mask.

"What—" She swallowed in a futile attempt to moisten her throat. "What do you want?"

The man's body quaked, and a soft chortle reached her ears. "I'm sure you know the answer to that question." He pulled a small vial out of his coat pocket and then quickly filled a syringe with the liquid. "After all the torment you've put me through, my only regret is this won't be the painful death I'd envisioned, but at least you woke up in time so I can watch the fear in your eyes." He plunged the needle into the access port midway up her IV line.

"No!" A burst of adrenaline surged through her. Jenna rolled to her left and flipped over the low bed rail, landing with a thud on the floor on the opposite side of the bed from the man. The intravenous catheter in her hand tugged painfully as the IV tubing stretched taut, blood dripping down her arm.

"Sorry, darlin', but that maneuver won't save you." He held up the empty needle, then dropped it onto the bed. "A high dose of Propofol is already working its way into your bloodstream."

"No, no, no," she muttered under her breath, and yanked the partially extracted IV line out.

He rounded the bed with a low, guttural growl. His body shook as he stretched his hands forward. If he got them around her neck, he'd choke the life out of her. She rolled under the bed, scooting as far as she could from the hands that reached for her. The door to her room creaked open a few inches and stopped. She locked eyes with her tormentor.

"Sean, I'm surprised to see you here so early," Nurse Bethany said cheerfully from the other side of the door.

Sean is here! Hope surged inside Jenna.

"I'm an early riser. Thought I'd come see how our patient is doing and hang around to give her a ride home once she's discharged," Sean replied. "If you're headed in to check vitals and things, I can stay out here until you've finished."

"Looks like your neighbor saved you once more. You won't be so fortunate a third time," her tormentor ground out through clenched teeth. Then he straightened and rounded the foot of the bed.

"Sean! Stop him!" Jenna yelled.

The door to the room flew open, and the shadow man shoved the rolling bedside-tray table at the two people standing in the doorway.

Sean pulled Bethany out of the way, and Shadow Man darted past them.

"Check on Jenna. And call security," Sean ordered as he pushed a small backpack into the stunned nurse's hands. Then he sprinted after the man.

Jenna scooted out from under the bed, grabbed the side rail and pulled herself to her feet, her knees shaking.

"Are you okay?" Bethany rushed to her, lowered the bed rail and helped ease her onto the bed.

"Yes, just shaken."

"Your IV catheter came out. I'll get it replaced and then re-connect it." Bethany snatched the call button remote.

"No!" Jenna puffed out a breath, grasped the top of the discarded syringe with the tips of two fingers and held it up. "He put Propofol in the IV."

A male orderly rolled the tray table back into the room. "I called security. Is everything okay?"

"There was an attempt on Ms. Hartley's life. She's okay but understandably shaky. I need to notify the on-call doctor, let him know the attacker may have drugged her," Bethany replied.

"I don't think any got into my system." Jenna dropped the syringe onto the tray and leaned back against the pillow as she blinked rapidly, fighting to keep her eyes open. "The IV came loose when I tried to get away."

Bethany checked her vitals, then made eye contact with

the orderly. "Stay with her." She patted Jenna's shoulder and rushed out of the room.

Jenna turned toward the window. A bright streak of light peeked around the sides of the window covering. "Could you please turn on the light and open the blinds?"

The orderly followed her instructions, and soon fluorescent light mixed with morning sunlight filled the room. The Appalachian Mountains stood proudly in the distance. Their snowcapped peaks were like a soothing balm to her soul. A yearning to hike the numerous trails the way she had many times as a single mother, praying and surrounding herself in God's beauty, washed over her.

Be strong and of a good courage; be not afraid, neither be thou dismayed: for the LORD thy God is with thee whithersoever thou goest. Joshua 1:9—the verse she'd comforted herself with after Patrick had run off with his secretary—echoed in her mind. She'd clung to that verse as a single mom in her midtwenties. But she hadn't given it much thought these last four years. Was God still with her even after all this time?

"Rest, Ms. Hartley, and let us take care of you."

The orderly's words pulled her from her thoughts. Jenna narrowed her eyes at him. He had been quick to show up. Could the orderly be Shadow Man? No. He wasn't tall enough, and his build was too lanky. Besides, he wore light blue scrubs with a long-sleeved white T-shirt underneath his top. He couldn't have changed clothes that quickly.

Her vision blurred, and she felt faint. *No.* Had the drugs reached her bloodstream after all? *Resist the urge. Stay awake. Focus on the sunlight.*

Chapter Three

Sean stepped into the elevator and jabbed the button for the sixth floor. The hospital was eerily silent this time of morning. He scrubbed his hand over his face, then pressed the Door Close button. What was taking the elevator doors so long to close? He pressed the button twice more. Just as they started to close, a hand reached inside and halted them.

The large metal doors opened once more, and a tall gentleman in his early sixties, wearing a suit and tie, stepped into the elevator and pressed the button for the top floor. "Most people don't realize pressing the Door Close button doesn't really speed things up. Because of the Americans with Disabilities Act, federal law requires that the doors stay open long enough for those with crutches or a wheelchair to get in the elevator."

"Then why haven't they removed the button?"

The white-haired man stepped back and made eye contact. "I've asked that same question myself many times." He held out his hand. "Jefferson Price, CEO of Knoxville General Hospital."

Sean accepted the handshake. "Sean Quinn. Nice to meet you."

"Well, Mr. Quinn, what brings you to our fine hospital so early in the morning?"

Sean narrowed his eyes. Could this man be Jenna's attacker? He was the right height and build. No. The man he'd chased wouldn't have had time to change and would surely be out of breath. "I'm visiting a friend."

"Your face is red and sweaty, as if you ran to get here. Is everything okay? You didn't receive bad news, did you? If you'd like, I can have the hospital chaplain visit your friend."

Having spent his entire life in the southern United States, Sean knew some people in the south tended to be overly friendly, but this man's chattiness seemed excessive, especially this early in the morning.

"Everything is fine," he replied, never one to share more information than needed.

Mr. Price reached into his inner coat pocket and pulled out a business card. "Well, if you need anything, or even if you want to file a complaint about the slow elevators, don't hesitate to reach out to my office."

The elevator stopped, and the doors opened. They'd reached the sixth floor. Accepting the business card, Sean stepped out of the elevator without looking back. Even if he liked the practice of small talk, there was no time to engage in it at the moment. He'd chased Jenna's dark-clad assailant down the stairs, losing him somewhere between the second and fourth floors. Now he needed to check on Jenna and make sure she was okay.

The nurses' station was vacant. He glanced at his watch. 7:23 a.m. Shift change typically occurred in most hospitals at seven o'clock—at least according to his sister Marilee, who was an ICU nurse. Maybe the day shift nurses were making their morning rounds. He made his way down the hall to Jenna's room, pushed open the door and froze. Bethany, another nurse and a doctor surrounded Jenna's bed.

He rushed to the unoccupied spot at the foot of the bed. Jenna's eyes were closed, her dark hair splayed across her pillow, framing her pale heart-shaped face. He couldn't tell if she was breathing or not. "Is she okay?" he asked hesitantly.

"Who are you?" The doctor, who had shoulder-length brown hair and looked like he was barely out of high school, looked up, noticing Sean for the first time.

"Oh, he's Ms. Hartley's hero. He's saved her twice—first when he pulled her from the fire and again when he stopped the attack this morning." Bethany smiled and turned to Sean. "We need a few more minutes. Could you wait in the hall?"

He hesitated, unable to make his feet move. Why was he so worried about a neighbor he'd only spoken to a handful of times? It couldn't be because he'd saved her life. He'd saved many lives during his time with the Atlanta PD and had never felt a sense of responsibility like the one that kept him glued to the floor in this hospital room.

"Please." The doctor swept his hand toward the door. "I'll be out in a minute to talk to you."

Sean cast one last glance at Jenna, praying he'd see her chest move or hear a snore—anything. Nothing. He shuffled toward the door. She had to be alive. If she weren't, the hospital staff wouldn't just be standing around. Would they? *Wait!* He pivoted on one foot and craned his neck to look at the vitals monitor mounted on top of a pole with wheels that sat beside the head of the bed. A jagged heartbeat line meandered across the top of the screen. Heart rate: 53 bpm. Blood pressure: 117/69. He released the breath he'd been holding since entering the room. She was alive.

"Sean. Go. Now." Bethany gave him a pointed look, and he turned and slipped out of the room.

A young male orderly and a security guard walked over to him.

"You're the one who chased after the man who tried to hurt Ms. Hartley, aren't you?" the orderly questioned.

"Yes, but I didn't catch him."

"Could you identify the guy?" the security guard asked.

"No. I wasn't able to get close enough." Sean scanned the

ceilings and pointed at a camera. "Can't you zoom in on the security tapes and get a close-up of him?"

"We'll try, but I'm not holding out much hope. One of my guys caught a glimpse of the man as he raced out of the building. Said he wore a covering over his head and face."

"Yeah, that's what I thought, too." Sean shoved his hand through his hair, as had become his habit since letting it grow out after he retired from the police force. "I hope they release Jenna today, but if they don't, could you station a guard outside her door? This is the second attempt on her life."

"We don't normally offer private security, but I'll talk to my boss and see what we can arrange. If she has to stay overnight again."

Sean leaned in and read the guard's name tag. "Thanks, Aaron. I really appreciate it."

Bethany exited the room with the other nurse. "She's going to be fine." She placed a hand on Sean's shoulder. "Dr. Davidson will give you a full update." She motioned for the orderly to follow her to the nurses' station.

The doctor stepped into the hall and pulled the door closed behind him. Sean walked over to him and held out his hand. "Dr. Davidson, I'm Sean Quinn. Ms. Hartley is my—" How should he identify himself? If he said *neighbor*, the doctor might not give him any information. He could say *friend*, but that was a bit of a stretch and carried little weight for getting personal information on someone in the hospital.

"I know who you are, Mr. Quinn. Bethany has made it clear that you are a knight in shining armor." The doctor grinned.

Sean shrugged. "More like a neighbor who was in the right place at the right time."

"Well, that's a good thing for Ms. Hartley." A solemn expression replaced the doctor's smile. "In all seriousness, Ms. Hartley will be okay. But the man who attacked her tried to give her an overdose of Propofol. Thankfully, she managed to pull her IV catheter out so only a small amount actually reached her bloodstream."

"Is that why she's sleeping?" Sean probed.

"Yes. But she's already starting to come back around, and her vitals are strong. We'll watch her a few hours. Then she should be able to go home this afternoon." The doctor turned and crossed to the nurses' station, effectively cutting off any further questions.

Sean met the guard's gaze. "I'll stay with Ms. Hartley until she's released, so no need to worry about posting someone outside her door. But a police report should be filed."

"Yes, sir. We'll take care of that on our end." The guard hurried down the hall.

Sean entered Jenna's room. She stared at him, and her lower lip trembled. Though their interactions had been minimal over the last six months—primarily because he'd opened his big mouth about the dangers of her playing amateur detective—she had never struck him as a woman who was afraid of anything. Fierce. Determined. Justice fighter. Independent. Loyal. Those were the words that described his neighbor. Of course, two attempts on her life in nine hours would justify fear. He could only hope she'd take these attacks seriously, shut down her podcast and let the police handle things from here on out. If not, he'd have to step in and help protect her because there was no way the sheriff's department had a large enough force to assign someone to guard her.

Jenna climbed into Sean's SUV, closed the door and dropped the bag with her smoke-infused clothes onto the floorboard. Then she clicked her seat belt into place as Sean settled into the driver's seat. She folded her hands in her lap and looked down at the extra-large Atlanta Braves sweatshirt and gray sweatpants with the drawstring waist pulled as tight as it could go. "Thank you for bringing me a change of clothes."

"You're welcome." He backed out of the parking space. "I'm sorry they're too big."

"It's okay. They're warm and don't smell of smoke. That's all that matters."

Silence blanketed the vehicle.

Jenna hated chitchat, but the idea of spending the forty-minute drive in awkward silence was worse. "I'm sorry you were stuck at the hospital all day, waiting to drive me home. I could have called a rideshare service."

"It was important to have someone standing guard over you. What if the guy who attacked you came back?"

The question was rhetorical, so she didn't bother to reply. They both knew perfectly well that if the guy had shown up again, she might not have survived.

He paid to exit the parking garage and merged into traffic. "So, what's the plan?"

"What do you mean?"

"Where are you going to live while your home is rebuilt? They contained the fire in the living room, but the damage was extensive. You can't stay there. Do you have a safe place you can go? Somewhere the person after you won't know to look?"

"I haven't really given that any thought." She furrowed her brow. "But I'll figure something out. Just drop me off at home. I'll pack some clothes, grab my laptop and book a room somewhere."

"I know we've not really seen eye to eye on things since I moved here." He pulled to a stop at a red light, turned to her and frowned. "I overstepped. It wasn't my place to tell you to stop your podcast. But my concerns were—" A horn honked behind them, and he turned his focus back to the road.

"Look, I don't want to hear *I told you so*, okay? Unless you've lost someone you love in such a senseless manner, you have no right to judge me."

"Actually, I have. My wife," Sean mumbled. "And I wasn't trying to judge you or your motives. I understood them perfectly. However, I know all too well how civilians with good intentions sometimes hinder an investigation while putting themselves in danger and creating more work for the law enforcement officers involved in the case."

Jenna digested his words and swallowed her anger. She'd known he was a widower, but she'd never heard how his wife had died. A thousand questions raced through her mind. It wasn't her place to ask about his pain. In different circumstances, they might have been able to discuss their losses and maybe even be friends, but she doubted that would ever be possible now. She'd put up too many defensive walls when he'd first moved in and she'd felt judged by every word out of his mouth. It didn't help that he was right.

She *had* created more work for the police department. In the beginning, she'd called them to her house every time someone vandalized her property. She probably made twenty calls to the sheriff's office in three months before realizing the vandals were too smart to get caught. Even installing a video doorbell and cameras outside her home hadn't helped. The vandals always seemed to attack late at night and stayed in the shadows, not offering any identifying clues.

"I'm sorry. I should have realized you spoke from experience." She examined his profile. "Was your wife's murderer caught?"

The vein in his neck twitched. "Yes. Ten months after she... passed."

"I'm glad they solved her case before it became cold." She turned back around in her seat and faced forward. The first few months after Becca was gone, Jenna had held on to so much hope that the police would find the person responsible for her murder. With each passing month, she'd become less hopeful. On the one-year anniversary of her child's death, Jenna had recorded her first podcast. Six months later, she'd walked away from her position as the high school counselor to be a full-time podcaster, desperate to help the police find the clues necessary to solve the case before it hit the three-year mark. The point where, according to the former sheriff Matt Rice, unsolved cases officially became cold cases.

They rode in silence. Forty minutes later, they reached Barton Creek. With a population of twenty-five hundred, Jenna knew how blessed their town was to be untouched by the droves of tourists who flocked to the region yearly, visiting the Great Smoky Mountains National Park and nearby Gatlinburg and Pigeon Forge.

She'd always loved her hometown, situated in the foothills of the Appalachian Mountains. Which was why, after Patrick had left her, she'd moved back with her young child in tow. She had wanted her daughter to grow up in a small town where everyone looked out for one another—which made Becca's unsolved murder all the more torturous.

"We're here," Sean announced, pulling her from her thoughts. "I spoke with the fire chief this morning. He said to caution you to stay out of the room with the damage because he's not sure how structurally sound the roof is on that section of the house and doesn't want it caving in with you inside."

Sean activated his blinker, turned into her driveway and parked. Jenna gasped. She had known there had been a lot of fire and smoke but hadn't been prepared to see the busted-out picture window and soot-stained brick. Exiting the vehicle, she crinkled her nose at the smoldering stench and stared open-mouthed at the damage in front of her. Tears burned the backs of her eyes, but she blinked them away. She would not wallow in grief. Her home could be replaced. However, she wouldn't stop until she found the person responsible. The attack could only mean she was finally getting close to finding her daughter's murderer.

Sean came to stand beside her. "Are you okay?"

She nodded and turned at the sound of a vehicle door closing. Sheriff Heath Dalton walked toward them, concern etched on his face. "Jenna, are you okay?"

"I'm fine, Heath." She offered a forced smile. "I'm sure you're a busy person. You didn't need to drive out here to get my statement. I could have given it to one of your deputies."

"But then I wouldn't have an excuse to check on you and make sure you're truly okay." He searched her face. Seemingly satisfied that she was holding up under the pressure of the attacks, he turned to Sean and clapped him on the back. "How are you doing? I got a call from Knoxville Police Chief Dan Graves. He wanted to fill me in on the incident at the hospital."

"Gotta love small towns and how fast news travels." Sean smiled. "In Atlanta, it could take days to know about related incidences. Usually, there were so many eyewitness accounts and different takes that the actual details of the crime would get complicated."

Jenna examined her neighbor with fresh eyes. She'd spent many an evening sitting on Jim and Lois Ferguson's porch, listening to them speak of their grandson, the big-city detective. Lois had always looked forward to the weekly phone calls with him. While Jenna had known he was a retired detective, she'd never really thought about what pushed him to dissuade her from continuing her podcast. This explained why he'd been so vocal.

"I also heard you risked your life to save Jenna last night when you didn't wait for the fire department to get here."

"Just doing the neighborly thing." Sean pinned her with his gaze. "I may have grown up in a bustling city, but my parents taught me to care about what happens in my community and to look out for my neighbors."

She fought the urge to squirm under his scrutiny. A chill washed over her, and she rubbed her arms. "If you guys will excuse me. I'll go pack some things and then see if I can find a place to stay for the next few weeks."

"Do you—"

"Let me—"

"No. I don't need either of you coming into my home with

me. I am capable of packing my own bags." Sean opened his mouth to speak, and she rushed on. "I promise I won't go into the living room. You've already told me it's dangerous."

"Okay, then."

Heath turned to Sean. "I brought a couple of tarps and a ladder. If you'll give me a hand, we should be able to get the damaged area of the house covered by the time she's finished packing."

"There's a ladder and plywood—" Jenna looked at the front of the house where she'd placed the items last night. "Never mind. Looks like they were damaged in the fire."

"Don't worry about it. We'll get it covered well enough that it's weather proofed," Sean told her.

"Okay. And, since I know you'll both offer, while I'm packing you can decide who'll escort me to my temporary home. But just know, whoever is tasked with that responsibility is only following me to make sure I make it there safely and will not stick around afterward as a guard. I'm an adult woman. And I refuse to have a babysitter."

She turned and made her way into the house as the men talked in hushed tones behind her. Before long, she had packed a small suitcase with clothes that needed to be washed the minute she reached the place she would be staying. They may have contained the fire to the living room, but the smell of smoke had penetrated the entire house and all its contents.

Jenna crossed the hall and entered the room she used as a studio. Opening the closet, she knelt and opened her fireproof safe and removed the documents pertaining to Becca's case that she'd collected over the years. She pulled a backpack off the top shelf and placed the documents, her laptop and recording equipment into it. Then she went over to the wall of photos and removed the one of her and Becca on the SkyBridge and placed it in the front zippered section of the backpack.

One more thing to do. She picked up her phone and bit her lip. Should she call Amber? No. Her sister would insist she come to Nashville to stay with her, but Jenna needed to be in Barton Creek to oversee the repairs of her home. And to continue to untangle the clues to Becca's murder. Maybe Jenna could book a room at the Hideaway Inn Bed and Breakfast, run by her mother's best friend Frances Nolan. No. Jenna couldn't risk leading danger to Ms. Frances.

She could go stay at her parents' house in Maryville until they returned from their Caribbean cruise. Only, if she did that, they'd want her to stay with them until the repairs to her home had been completed. And she couldn't put them at risk any more than she could her sister or Ms. Frances. She puffed out a breath. It might be easier to hide in a tourist area. She'd drive to Gatlinburg and find a hotel with a room she could rent for an extended stay.

Okay, time to go.

She slipped her arms through the backpack's straps and returned to her bedroom. Picking up her purse off the dresser, she dug inside for her keys so she could start her vehicle remotely and allow it a few moments to warm up. For whatever reason, she couldn't seem to shake the chill that had descended on her earlier. The February temperatures could be to blame. But she suspected it was more nerves than anything, as the cold had never bothered her before.

Jenna snagged her down jacket off the hanger on the back of her bedroom door and then made her way to the front of the house. When she stepped onto the front porch, she was amazed to discover that the men had finished their task and were standing beside the sheriff's truck, engaged in conversation.

"Hold on, I'll get your bags!" Sean yelled, and headed across the yard in her direction.

Heath lifted a hand in farewell, settled into his vehicle and started backing down the drive. As Sean climbed the porch steps, Jenna pointed her key fob at her truck and pushed the remote start button. The parking lights flashed, and the engine sprang to life.

A loud explosion, followed by a bright flash of light and a rush of hot air, shook the world around her. Glass and metal rained down on the lawn. Sean dove toward her and pushed her through the open front door. They landed in a tangled heap on the hardwood floor of her foyer.

"Are you okay?" he asked huskily in her ear.

Jenna nodded, unable to form words. Someone had planted a bomb in her truck. *Dear Lord, how many more times can I escape death?*

Whatever it took, she had to stay alive long enough to see Becca's murderer brought to justice.

Chapter Four

Sean grasped the doorframe and drug himself to his feet, then reached out his hand to Jenna. She slipped her hand into his, and he pulled her upward until they stood face-to-face.

"Are you sure you're not injured?" He looked her up and down. Other than a scratch on her face, she seemed unharmed. This time.

"I'm fine." She pushed past him and stepped through the open doorway. "Unfortunately, my truck isn't."

"A vehicle is replaceable. People are not." He picked up her jacket, which had fallen onto the porch, shook it out and draped it around her shoulders. Her body was shaking. Sean rubbed his hands over her shoulders. It would be easy for her to slip into a state of shock, given all that she'd been through. "Why did you use the remote start?"

"Habit, I guess." She shrugged one shoulder. "I always use it during the winter months so the seats warm up before I get inside."

"Are you both okay?" Heath jogged toward them. He'd parked his cruiser at the edge of the road, blue lights flashing. "Do we need an ambulance?"

"There are no obvious physical injuries. But it wouldn't hurt to have a medic come check out Jenna."

"No." She shook her head, frowning at him. "I'm fine."

Their gazes locked, and he searched her chocolate-colored eyes. When she refused to look away, he pressed his lips together and dipped his head.

"Yes or no?" Heath stood a few feet from the porch, staring up at them.

"No ambulance, just the fire department," Sean replied.

"They're already en route."

Turning to look at Jenna's truck—the cab fully engulfed in flames—Sean gasped. "My vehicle! I've gotta move it!"

He jumped off the small porch and raced to his SUV, which sat a few feet behind Jenna's truck. Intense heat assailed him as he drew near. His windshield had a large crack, and the paint on the hood had bubbled. Slipping his hand into his denim jacket, he used it as a makeshift oven mitt to allow him to touch the hot door handle. Then he hopped into the driver's seat, turned the key he'd left dangling in the ignition and, without even shutting his door, quickly backed away from the flames. The sound of sirens rang out as he parked his SUV, close to the sheriff's cruiser.

Jenna and Heath made their way across the lawn to a large oak tree, her luggage in tow. Sean jogged over to them as the first fire truck pulled into the driveway.

"Is your vehicle damaged?" Jenna asked, her eyes wide.

The concern etched on her face made his knees buckle. His wife, Felicia, had had a similar expression on her face when she'd been shot outside their home. Sean had witnessed the shooting, and he'd dropped to his knees beside the woman he'd loved for two decades and yelled for the next-door neighbor who'd ventured outside to call 911. Then he'd held his wife's head in his lap and pressed his hands against her chest, desperate to stop the flow of blood.

"Sean… Sean!" Jenna's concerned voice sounded miles away.

Heath placed a hand on his shoulder. "Are you okay, buddy?"

Shaking his head, Sean pulled himself back to the present. "Sorry." He closed his eyes and counted to three before meeting Jenna's gaze. "Don't worry about my vehicle. The damage is minor. It's drivable."

He turned to Heath. "Does she need to stay here for this, or can I take her to my place?"

"No, I need—"

"Actually, Jenna," Heath said, interrupting whatever she had been about to say, "Sean's right. It would be a good idea for you to wait at his house. There's nothing you can do here."

Jenna looked over her shoulder. "The blue tarp you put up has melted. I need to board up my house."

Heath grasped her shoulders and turned her to face him. "I'm not going anywhere until the fire is out and the vehicle has been transported to the impound lot so the forensic team can go over it. While I'm waiting, I'll call someone to come out and board up the window with plywood. And, before I leave, I'll lock up the house."

"Okay." Jenna's shoulders slumped. "I hate to ask, after you've done so much, but I thought I'd get a hotel room in Gatlinburg for the night. Could you maybe drive me there later?"

Heath frowned. "I don't think that's a good idea. You need to be somewhere we can protect you."

She placed a hand on her hip. "Does that mean you're going to assign an officer to guard me?"

Heath scratched his head. "I'll figure something out. Just wait at Sean's until I'm finished here."

"I'll protect her," Sean interjected. Now, why had he said that? He'd warned Jenna her podcast would make extra work for the sheriff's office, but there was no way Heath had the personnel to assign a guard to watch Jenna around the clock. Sean puffed out a breath and met two pairs of eyes. "You don't have the man power, Heath, and it's not like I'm a novice trying to play cops and robbers."

"Both are valid points," Heath acknowledged, turning to Jenna. "I think it's the best plan."

"I can't stay in a home—alone—with a man. The neighbors will talk."

Sean bit back a retort that her virtue was safe with him. He'd been married to the love of his life; they'd had a beautiful nineteen years together. He wasn't looking to replace Felicia. Being a widowed hermit suited him just fine.

But of course, he also knew she was right. No matter how honorable his intentions were, people liked to talk, especially in a small town. "Look, we don't have a lot of options here. Unless you want to hire a private security firm. I've heard good things about the Protective Instincts office in Knoxville." He raised an eyebrow, and she turned to survey her damaged home and vehicle.

He felt like a heel for pushing her like this, but she had to realize she wouldn't be safe on her own. "You can stay in the house. I'll bunk in my camper."

"Will you be able to hear her from the camper if someone breaks into the house?" Heath queried.

"I'm a light sleeper. Besides, I'll leave Beau in the house with her. He'll wake me."

"Beau?" Jenna cocked her head.

The fire chief ambled over to them. "Sheriff, my men have extinguished the flames, but I'll have a couple of guys stick around for a little while to make sure the fire doesn't reignite."

"I appreciate that, Fred. I'll call the tow truck. Should take them about thirty minutes to get here," Heath replied.

"I'll let the boys know." Fred tipped his head at Jenna. "Ma'am." Then he turned and walked away.

Once the chief was out of earshot, Heath turned his focus back to Jenna. "I can't force you to stay with Sean. But I need you to understand—if you don't take him up on his generous offer, you're being reckless and you could put innocent lives in danger. Whoever is after you is getting more brazen. And the best way for you to stay alive is to let Sean protect you."

She wet her lips and swallowed. Sean hated for anyone to live in fear, but he understood Heath's need to make her realize the seriousness of the situation.

After several long minutes, Jenna nodded. "Okay. Thank you, Sean. I'll accept your offer. And I appreciate it."

Heath hugged Jenna. "Wise decision. Now, get some rest." *Even if it means giving up my warm bed and sleeping in my camper on a cold winter's night.* Felicia would have expected him to help a neighbor in distress, and even if she was no longer around to witness his actions, he still wanted to live his life in a manner that would make her proud. Not only that, but if he could help capture the guy who was after Jenna and solve her daughter's murder, maybe she'd give up her podcast and things would become a little more peaceful around here. *Yeah, keep telling yourself that, man. Don't admit—even to yourself—that you're not doing this for the peace but because protecting innocent people and solving murders is in your blood. You may be retired, but you miss the action and the adrenaline rush.*

Jenna added a scoop of detergent to the washing machine, closed the lid and pressed the start button. "Thanks for letting me do a load of laundry." She crossed into the kitchen, where Sean stood at the stove, preparing omelets. "It surprised me that my clothes smelled so strongly of smoke, since the fire was contained in the living room."

"It happens." He smiled and motioned toward the table. "Have a seat. Your supper is ready."

"You didn't have to prepare me a meal. I can cook for myself." She slipped into a chair at the round table in the breakfast nook.

"I know. But since you don't know your way around my kitchen *and* I also needed to eat, this seemed to be simpler."

He placed two plates on the table—one in front of her and the other in front of the chair across from her—each one with a Western omelet that was big enough for three people to share. "What would you like to drink? I have orange juice, milk or coffee—it's decaffeinated."

She pushed her chair away from the table. "I can—"

"Stay seated. I'll get it."

"Thank you. Coffee, please."

"I'm sorry I don't have any of those fancy flavored creamers, but I have regular cream and sugar." He reached into the cabinet above the coffeemaker and removed two mugs.

"Just cream. Thank you."

He poured coffee into each mug and added a generous serving of cream to one of them. After setting the coffee with cream in front of her, he settled into his chair. "Do you mind if I say grace?"

"Kind and most holy Heavenly Father, we come to You this day to thank You for our many blessings. We especially thank You, Lord, for watching over Jenna and protecting her from the attacks on her life. I pray they capture her attacker, and if it's Your will, that she finally gets answers about her daughter's death. Please watch over us and keep all involved in this investigation safe from harm. Thank You for this food. I pray it's nourishing to our bodies. In Christ's name, amen."

Sean smiled at her, cut a generous piece of the omelet with the edge of his fork and took a bite. "Mmm. Go ahead. Try it." He pointed with the handle of the fork.

She poked at the omelet. Chunks of ham, bell pepper, onion and tomatoes spilled onto the plate.

"Is everything okay?"

Biting her lip, she lifted her eyes to meet his. "Why did you say 'if it's Your will' in the prayer? Why wouldn't God want me to have answers concerning Becca's death?"

Sean put his fork down, placing it on his plate, and wiped his mouth with a napkin. "I want to tell you that, yes, God wants everything about Becca's death to be revealed to you, but no one can know that for sure. I believe, one thousand percent, that He wants murderers to be captured and punished. However, even if you never find out who was behind Becca's death, God knows. And one day that person will face the ultimate judgment."

Jenna chewed on her bottom lip as tears stung the backs of her eyes. Why had she questioned his prayer? For the same reason she'd been questioning God since her daughter died. Because without knowing who killed her beautiful Becca, she needed someone to blame. She looked down at her plate and forked a bite into her mouth. The eggs were pillowy—soft but tasteless. The food went down the wrong way, throwing her into a coughing fit. She reached for her cup and drank a large gulp, the hot liquid burning her already-dry throat.

Sean jumped to his feet and filled a glass with cool water from the dispenser on the refrigerator door. "Here." He placed the drink in her hand.

Jenna guzzled it like a person rescued after a week stranded in the desert.

"Slow down," Sean urged as he patted her upper back. "Are you okay?"

Placing the glass on the table, she felt heat creep up her neck. "I'm fine... Thank you," she said, her voice raspy. "I just took too big of a bite."

He didn't question her logic but raised an eyebrow.

"Really, I'm fine."

"Would you like me to fix you something else to eat?"

"No!" She puffed out a breath and picked up her fork. "No. Thank you. This is good."

He settled back into his seat, eyeing her. She took a few small bites. With each one, the omelet tasted better and better. Before she knew it, she'd eaten the entire thing.

Looking up, she noted that Sean had also cleaned his plate.

She offered him a wobbly smile. "Thank you for the meal. It was delicious."

"You're welcome." The washing machine emitted three short beeps. "Sounds like the clothes are ready to go into the dryer."

Jenna scooted her chair back and crossed into the small laundry alcove, thankful for the distraction. Jenna transferred the clothing to the dryer, closed the door and pressed the start button. Turning back to the kitchen, she saw Sean had already cleared the table and was in the process of loading the dishwasher.

"Here, let me do that. You cooked. I should at least do the cleanup."

"That's not necessary. Besides, I'm almost finished." He placed the last few dishes onto the rack, dropped a detergent pod into the dispenser, clicked the door closed and started up the machine. Then he grabbed a sponge off the sink and began wiping everything down. "I left our mugs on the table. Why don't you pour us both another cup of coffee?"

As much as she'd love to go hang out in the guest room until he went to the camper for the evening, she didn't think it would be polite to argue. She snagged the coffeepot off the warming plate and began refilling the cups at the table.

"Done," Sean declared. "I'll be right back. I want to grab a notebook and pen from my office. Then we can sit at the table and you can tell me everything you know about Becca's murder."

Startled, Jenna glanced up and sloshed coffee onto the wooden tabletop. "Oh, no." She returned the coffeepot and reached for the roll of paper towels she'd seen on the counter, but Sean had already grabbed them and wiped up her mess.

He turned to her with concern in his eyes. "You didn't get burned, did you?"

"No, I'm fine. Just embarrassed." She struggled not to squirm under his gaze.

"There's nothing to be embarrassed about. Accidents happen." Leaning against the counter, he folded his arms across his chest. "If you're not up to discussing your daughter's case at the moment, we can wait and talk about it in the morning."

"Why do you want to go over the details? Do you think you can solve a case that the local authorities haven't?"

"I'm not sure. One thing I know is that I'm a very good detective. I also know the only way we can figure out who is trying to kill you is to solve your daughter's case."

Unable to form words around the lump in her throat, she nodded and settled into the chair she had sat in earlier, wrapped her hands around the warm coffee mug and tried to ward off the chill that engulfed her. Feeling judged and being the brunt of other people's jokes were two things that had always bothered her. While she didn't suspect Sean would make jokes at her expense, she had felt judged by him many times over the last six months when he'd driven past with a frown and a shake of his head as she cleaned up whatever mess vandals and anti-fans had made of her yard and the exterior of her home.

Jenna had longed for someone to discuss the case with, someone who would tell her if they thought she was on the right trail or not and would give her their take on the leads she'd uncovered. But she'd hoped that person would be a supportive friend. She met Sean's gaze and slowly released her breath. "I doubt I'll sleep much tonight anyway, so let's discuss it now."

"I'll be right back." He took off down the hall and ducked into a room at the back of the house.

Lord, please, let Sean figure out what we've all been missing. It's time for Becca's murderer to be put away so he can't hurt anyone else ever again.

Sean crossed to the walnut desk that sat in front of the built-in bookcases in the room that had been his grandfather's office but was now his. He moved behind the desk, rolled the chair aside, pulled open the middle drawer and rummaged around until he found an ink pen. Then he closed the drawer and snatched the spiral notebook off the corner of the desk, knocking over the small black picture frame that housed a photo of him and Felicia taken on their nineteenth anniversary.

He picked up the frame and examined the photo. It was his favorite picture of the two of them. While Felicia beamed at the photographer, Sean had turned away from the camera to smile at his beautiful wife. She had always been his favorite view, and he was thankful she had insisted on having professional photos taken to commemorate their anniversary that year.

He'd tried to persuade her to wait until their twentieth anniversary, since nineteen wasn't a milestone. She'd laughed and said, "Every year I get to spend with you is a blessing, and I intend to celebrate all our anniversaries as if they are the most important day of the year. Because to me, they are."

So he had agreed to an outdoor photo shoot in Piedmont Park. Three weeks later, the day after Felicia had been murdered, the photographer emailed the digital file of the photos to their joint home email account.

"Are you okay?"

He startled at the sound of Jenna's voice and looked up to see her in the doorway. "Yeah. I'm fine."

Jenna walked over to him and craned her neck to see the picture in his hands. "Your wife was beautiful. I don't know if I've ever told you, but I'm sorry for your loss."

"Thank you." He put the photo back on his desk where it belonged. "She passed a long time ago."

"Doesn't mean you don't still miss her," Jenna replied softly.

He didn't want to discuss his feelings over the loss of his wife with Jenna—or the frustration he'd felt over the dead-end leads they'd received on the tip hotline, mainly thanks to all the crime scene investigator wannabes on social media. Sean held up the notebook and pen. "I got what I was looking for. Why don't we go back to the kitchen table so we can be comfortable?"

Not waiting for her reply, he brushed past her and headed

down the hall toward the kitchen. It was nearing eight o'clock. If he hoped to get all the facts straight and retire to the camper before midnight, he needed to keep them focused on the topic at hand. What had Jenna uncovered about her daughter's murder that had turned the killer's attention on her? And if the killer thought the information was enough to convict them, why hadn't the police discovered it already?

He selected the chair next to hers instead of the one on the other side of the table. One thing he'd learned as a detective was that sometimes you had to sit elbow to elbow to get to the nitty-gritty details. Building camaraderie couldn't be achieved if the parties involved in the investigation were standoffish to each other.

Jenna dropped an expandable file folder onto the table with a thud. "These are all my notes. I have everything backed up on my computer, but I like to keep hard copies, too."

Sean picked up the folder. Instead of choosing one that was a generic brown color, she had chosen one with flowers and a hummingbird design imprinted on it. In all his years with the police force, he'd never seen clues stored in such a colorful vessel. He cleared his throat and unlatched the folder, which appeared to be stretched to its limit. "I'm glad you thought to pack this when we stopped by your house."

"There's no way I'd let this out of my sight. I kept it locked in a fire-resistant filing cabinet in my home office." She dropped into the seat beside him and settled her laptop onto the table in front of her. She flipped it open and pressed the power button. "I thought we might want to watch the video from my last podcast recording where I talked about Becca's case."

"What other cases do you discuss on your podcast? Do you stick to cold cases that the police have already given up on?"

"Sometimes I'll touch on a murder that has recently happened." Her fingers flew over the keyboard as she typed in her security code. "I started out just talking about Becca's case, trying to keep it in the news so the police wouldn't forget it—"

"Police don't forget cases, especially ones that involve young people. And I can promise you, murder cases they can't solve plague them." It had always bothered Sean when people thought that because a case wasn't solved, the police didn't care.

"I—" Jenna bit her lower lip. "Sorry. Poor choice of words. I believe, in the beginning, Sheriff Rice wanted to solve this case. But after several months, he hit upon the idea that Becca had committed suicide and, after that, quit trying."

"Where is Sheriff Rice now?"

"He moved to the Gulf Coast after he retired." She sighed. "A high-profile serial killer case happened here the year before Becca… Sheriff Rice never explicitly stated it, but I think when they discovered Becca's body, he was afraid it was another serial killer. Thankfully, no other young women came up missing, so it quickly became obvious that wasn't the case."

As he took a sip of lukewarm coffee, flashes of days gone by flooded his mind—being buried in a case, sifting through clues, and surviving on cold coffee and junk food. It had gotten especially bad after he'd lost Felicia. Sean had hated going home to an empty house and had spent days on end at the station. He'd convinced himself he was the only one who could solve her case, so he couldn't go home to shower, sleep or eat.

Until the day—five months after Felicia's murder—Chief Monica Freeman had told him if he didn't leave the station for a minimum of eight consecutive hours each day, she'd have no choice but to suspend him. He'd said some not-so-nice words in reply and stormed out. Thankfully, she'd understood he was coming from a place of pain and wasn't intentionally lashing out at her. And she'd called her husband—Sean's former high school track coach—and sent him to Sean's house to check on him. When Coach Freeman had arrived, he took one look at Sean and told him to take a shower. Then he'd taken him out for a big steak and a long talk.

It hadn't gotten much easier to go into his home afterward. But that night, Sean had slept better than he had in months, and the next morning he'd packed his camping gear and taken off for a week of intense hiking in the North Georgia mountains, giving him much needed time for prayerful thoughts on moving forward without the love of his life by his side.

He looked from the bulging file folder in his hand to the beautiful woman peering at her computer screen. One didn't have to be a detective to deduce she'd had no one to talk sense into her like Coach Freeman had him—or if she had, she hadn't taken their advice.

Dear Lord, forgive me for not realizing what Jenna needed wasn't someone to tell her to stop her podcast, but rather someone who would help her realize racing through life, putting herself in danger, wouldn't bring Becca back. Someone who would encourage her to take time for self-reflection, so she could develop a plan to move forward and have a full life, even while missing the one she loves the most.

Could Sean be that person for Jenna? Or had he already botched any chance to be a friend she would take advice from? He puffed out a silent breath. Before he could ever hope to be the friend to her that his former track coach had been to him, he'd have to solve her daughter's four-year-old cold case murder.

Chapter Five

Unable to fully turn off his mind and rest, Sean had been up
for hours, pacing and fighting the urge to go inside and look
through Jenna's files in greater detail. He scrubbed a hand over
his stubbled cheek. It was barely past 6:00 a.m., but he couldn't
stand the thought of staying in the camper a minute longer. He
needed coffee and Bible time, and Beau was probably eager to
get outside to stretch his legs and take care of business.

If he tread lightly, Sean should be able to enter through the
back door without waking his guest. He'd let Beau outside,
put on a pot of coffee and settle into his favorite chair for his
scripture reading and prayer time. After that, he'd feed Beau
and dive back into the file Jenna had composed on her daughter's death.

He stepped out into the frosty morning, pulled the camper
door closed and made his way to the back of his farmhouse,
his breath sending small puffs of fog into the air. Playful barking reached his ears, and he looked up just as Beau leaped at
him. "Whoa, boy, what are you doing outside?" He scratched
behind the coonhound's ears and bent close for their usual
sloppy morning kisses.

The smell of coffee and bacon greeted Sean as he pushed

open the back door. Jenna sat at the table, her brow furrowed as she wrote in a notebook.

"Good morning. The coffee is hot, and there's toast and bacon staying warm in the oven." Jenna pushed to her feet. "I'm happy to make you some eggs if you'll tell me how you like them cooked."

He waved her off. "No need. Continue with what you were doing. I can fix my breakfast after I feed Beau."

She settled back into her seat. "I hope it was okay that I let him outside. He was scratching at the back door."

"Yeah, it's fine. He's good to stay nearby, especially when it's feeding time." Sean reached into the dog-food storage container that sat just inside the pantry, scooped up a serving and carried it out to the sunroom with Beau on his heels.

After depositing the food into the metal dish next to the water bowl near Beau's bed, he returned to the kitchen, washed his hands and poured himself a cup of coffee. Then he took a seat beside Jenna and reached for the notepad he had used the night before. Jenna had sketched out a timeline of events of Becca's last day, using cell phone–location records and bank records that she had gathered over the years.

"Have you ever physically retraced Becca's steps from that day?" Before she could answer, he rushed on. "I'm not asking if you have been to the places she visited that last day. What I'm asking is, have you retraced her steps, going to each location in one day, following her timeline as closely as possible?"

"No. I *have* been to the locations, all of them. I questioned the people that worked with her at the library and the people at the café. But I've never retraced her steps the way you're talking about." Her brow furrowed, and she turned to him. "Do you think it would make a difference?"

"I'm not sure. It's just a thought that came to me." Sean took a sip of his coffee, checked the time on the stove's clock and glanced at the paper in his hand. "According to the timeline, Becca left home around seven thirty in the morning, headed to her part-time job at the library, where she worked from eight until two. It's a little after seven now. I don't think that we need to hang out at the library for six hours. So why don't we listen to your last two podcasts and leave here around eleven?"

"Okay. But if it's all the same to you, I'd prefer if we listen to the podcasts separately." She closed her laptop. "I'll go to the bedroom. That way, you can stay in the kitchen and eat while you listen to it on your phone."

"What if I have questions? Wouldn't it be better to listen to it together?" He watched as she continued to gather her things.

"No. The podcasts only last about forty-five minutes each. Since we're only listening to the last two, we'll have plenty of time for a question-and-answer session afterward." Jenna turned and hurried out of the room.

Shaking his head, he pushed away from the table, picked up his mug and went over to the coffeepot for a refill. Then he pulled up the podcast on his phone, hit play and placed the device on the counter beside his mug. The intro music to the podcast started playing as he took eggs, cheese and butter out of the fridge. He felt as if he was at a disadvantage. She could escape his presence, but with her voice filling the room, he couldn't escape hers.

Why hadn't she stayed in the kitchen with him? Was she afraid of what he would think of the episodes? Man, he'd really messed up with his criticism in the early days of their acquaintance. Felicia had warned him many times that his matter-of-fact personality could be off-putting. He should have listened to her and learned to be more tactful.

"Lord, we're commanded to love our neighbor. I never intended to put strife between us. My instinct has always been to protect, and I couldn't get past the thought that she was putting herself in harm's way. Or that she might be hindering the investigation, enabling a killer to remain free. But it was thoughtless of me to tell her she was wrong when we didn't know each other well enough for me to voice an opinion."

Sean cracked an egg into a small bowl and resolved to make amends with his neighbor. The fastest way to do that would be to solve her daughter's murder. Pulling his attention back to the podcast, he whisked the eggs and poured them into the hot frying pan.

Jenna powered off her computer and plodded to the door. Pulling it open an inch, she listened.

"I'm starting to wonder if the letter *T* Becca had written in her datebook wasn't referencing Thatcher Park, where they found her car, but it was the initial of the name of the person she was meeting," her voice echoed in the silence.

It sounded like Sean had approximately ten minutes remaining on the podcast. Good. This would give her a little more time before she had to face him. She silently closed the door, turned back to the room and hefted her suitcase onto the bed. If they were going to retrace Becca's steps, she'd need to change into a warmer sweater.

She chewed her lower lip. Would he, once again, try to convince her to give up the podcast? Did it really matter if he did? Her own mother and sister had told her to give up the podcast and go back to work, but she didn't want to be a high school guidance counselor anymore. The thought of being around all the students—who were the same age Becca had been when she died—preparing to go out into the world and live their dreams made her stomach twist into knots. She couldn't—no, she *wouldn't*—do it. Even after they had solved Becca's murder. There were too many grieving families that deserved closure. Jenna would continue to be their vocal advocate.

There was a light rap on the door.

"I made a fresh pot of coffee. Come on out whenever you're ready," Sean said from the other side.

She moistened her lips. "I'll be right there."

Jenna heard him turn and leave and listened until his footsteps faded. After pulling an emerald green cable-knit sweater out of her suitcase, she tugged it on over her head. Then she sat on the edge of the bed, pulled on a pair of thick wool socks and shoved her feet into her hiking boots. After tying the laces, she took a deep breath and stood. Time to see what clues Sean had picked up on that she may have missed.

"Lord, if You're listening, I'd appreciate it if Sean isn't critical in his assessment." *Ugh.* She shook her head. Why would she even pray for that? God gave everyone free will. He wasn't in heaven controlling people like puppets on a string. The way Sean portrayed his opinions would be his own choice. And the way she reacted would be Jenna's choice. "Lord, we both know I'm rusty at communicating with You. But if You wouldn't mind, please help me to hear Sean's thoughts without judgment and to temper my reaction. Thanks."

Jenna ambled down the hall and into the kitchen. "Sorry I kept you waiting."

"Not at all." He smiled at her. "You were smart to dress warmly for our day."

"Thanks."

"Would you like a travel mug for your coffee?"

She shook her head. "No. I'll just have half a cup before we go. Any more and I'll be wired all day."

He poured some of the hot black liquid into her cup, and she added a splash of creamer. "Thanks."

"You're welcome." Sean returned the coffeepot to the burner. "Thank you for cooking this morning. It was nice having bacon already prepared."

"It was nothing." Jenna fidgeted with her mug. The polite exchanges were wearing thin. "Can we discuss the podcast now? I'd like to know what you think triggered the recent attacks on me."

Sean sat in the chair across from her, took a sip of coffee and then placed his mug on the table. "First, I owe you an apology."

Of all the things he could have said, she hadn't been expecting that. "It's ok—"

"No," Sean cut her off. "It's not okay. I was rude. I judged you, and for that, I'm sorry."

"Thank you. I appreciate that."

He picked up the notepad. "I jotted a few thoughts down. It seemed like you only shared details the police had—I'm guessing—already shared with the public, but with your unique take on the details. Is that correct?"

"Yes." She clasped her hands in her lap. "I never want to do anything that would jeopardize any future court cases. So I shared all clues I discovered with the police before I shared them on my podcast."

"Including the idea that the letter *T* was a person's initial?" He pinned her with his gaze.

"Well, no. But that wasn't really a clue. It was me simply brainstorming ideas. If I had a specific name in mind, I would have taken it to the police before mentioning it on my show. I didn't." She gasped. "You think I'm on to something, don't you?"

He shrugged. "It seemed to be the only *new* piece of information concerning Becca's case in your last episode. It's logical to think it could be what prompted the attacks. Which would mean your idea that *T* references a person wasn't too far-fetched."

If *T* was a person, figuring out a name wouldn't be a simple task. Her heart thundered in her chest. Barton Creek was a small town. Making a list of *T* names would be time consuming but not difficult. However, since Becca had worked in Maryville, a college town, tracking down all the people she had come in contact with would be pretty much impossible.

"Don't feel defeated before we even get started. I know this is an enormous task," Sean said as if he'd read the doubt on her face. "But you're not working alone anymore. You have me to help. And I don't give up easily."

She raised an eyebrow. "After all these months of telling

me I'm being reckless, why are you so willing to help all of a sudden?"

"Because your life is in danger."

"It's my own fault. You warned me that if I didn't stop digging and poking, it would be," Jenna whispered.

"Actually, it's partly my fault, too."

"What?"

"I could have been less blunt with my words. It's a trait I need to work on." He closed the notepad and clicked the pen closed. "If I had voiced my concerns differently, you may have listened. But even if a different approach hadn't deterred you from the course you chose, I could have been a better neighbor by offering to help you solve the case sooner. I can't go back in time and change my bluntness or my unneighborly actions." Sean locked eyes with her and held out his hand. "If you're willing to start over, I promise to be a good friend and a better neighbor. And I will not turn my back on you in a time of need again."

Tears stung the backs of Jenna's eyes, and she fought to hold them at bay. She had tried to convince herself not to take her neighbor's comments seriously in the early days of their acquaintance, but if she were truly honest with herself, she had taken every word to heart. And they had cut deep. Which made no sense, given that Sean was one in a long line of people who'd dismissed her through the years. Patrick turning his back on her, and her mom and sister doubting her ability to earn a degree while raising a child alone, had been just the beginning. Along the way, people had tried to introduce her to potential husbands because being a single mom would be too hard, and even Sheriff Rice hadn't taken her daughter's death seriously. Jenna should be used to doubters by now.

She swallowed past the lump in her throat, nodded and accepted his handshake. It would be nice to have someone working with her to decipher the clues. Who better than one of Atlanta's finest detectives? And maybe once this was all over, they could be real neighbors, who waved in passing and greeted each other in public. But even if this was simply a temporary truce, it would be worth it if he helped her capture Becca's killer.

Chapter Six

Sean unlocked his SUV and opened the door for Jenna to slide into the passenger seat. They had spent the past hour at the library questioning the employees and volunteers but had learned nothing new.

"Thank you," she mumbled, a frown marring her face.

"Hey, now, don't become discouraged yet. This was our first stop. And you knew it was a long shot that anyone would have new information." He closed the door and jogged around the front of the vehicle.

After he settled into his seat and fastened his seat belt, he turned to face her. "Where to next?"

"Reba's Roadside Grill on Highway 33." Jenna flipped open the notebook and consulted the timetable. "But we're a little ahead of schedule. Becca phoned in the to-go order and arrived at two fifteen to pick it up. It's only one thirty now."

He shrugged, turned the key in the ignition and started the engine. "It's about a twenty-minute drive. We'll drive there now, then place our to-go order. By the time it's ready, our timeline should be in sync."

"Okay." She turned and stared out the window, effectively cutting off further discussion.

Sean drove in silence. He couldn't imagine how difficult this task was for Jenna. He'd never had to retrace Felicia's steps the last day of her life. The person who gunned down Felicia had done so in their driveway, in what he had thought was a safe suburb outside of Atlanta, where his enemies wouldn't find him. What he'd failed to factor in was that with today's technology, no one's address was safe from exposure. People with a grudge could always find their target. And the quickest way to exact revenge on Sean and bring him to his knees had been to kill Felicia. Right in front of him.

"Are you okay?" Jenna asked softly, pulling him from his thoughts.

"Yeah. Why do you ask?"

"You just sighed. And it was one of the saddest sounds I've ever heard."

"Oh." He wasn't purposefully trying to be evasive, but how did one respond to something like that?

They continued in silence for several more miles. The passenger seat squeaked as Jenna shifted to turn sideways and look at him. Refusing to squirm under her assessment, he bit the inside of his left cheek and focused on the road ahead.

"I know our truce—or friendship, or whatever you want to call the stage we're in right now—is still new, so I apologize if I'm being pushy or forward…"

"But?"

"Jim and Lois never said what happened to your wife. Just that she died suddenly."

Sean's breath caught, and he waited for her to continue.

"I was wondering…would you share the details of her murder with me?"

It was a fair question. After all, he knew as much about her daughter's death as she did. Except he hadn't spoken about Felicia's murder with anyone other than his superiors and the officers who'd worked on her case. His in-laws, parents and grandparents had only known that she had been killed in a drive-by shooting—not the details. At least, not until the case went to court, at which time his grandparents had already died in a car crash. Sean silently released the breath he'd been holding.

"It was a Saturday afternoon. The day of the SEC Championship football game. The University of Georgia versus Alabama. We had lost to Bama during the regular season, and I was looking forward to the rematch. Felicia wanted to run some errands that morning. She'd asked me to accompany her. But despite her promise that we would be home in plenty of time for the big game, I refused to go."

His throat tightened as he recalled the annoyance in Felicia's voice when she'd accused him of always being too busy to spend time with her. He'd huffed and informed her that no husband would choose to go shopping with their wife that day instead of staying home to watch the pregame show.

If only he could go back in time and redo that one day, he would choose to spend it doing whatever she wanted without complaint.

"I would hazard a guess that ninety percent of the football-watching population would've done the same."

"I know." He clenched his teeth, and his jaw muscle twitched.

"Sorry. I wasn't trying to be flippant. There's nothing anyone can say that will ever take away your pain."

"I imagine you understand the pain better than most. And for the record, I did not take your comment as *flippant*." He wanted to tell her that he knew what had happened to Felicia wasn't his fault, but he couldn't. Because it was. "You're right—most football fans would have probably done the same that day. My mistake was forgetting my choice of career would make both myself and my wife a target."

Jenna touched his arm. "You don't have to tell me more. I shouldn't have asked. It's none of my business."

"You're wrong. You have every right to ask." He spared a quick glance in her direction. "I have asked you to relive every detail of your daughter's death, and I'm even taking you on a road trip to revisit her last day."

"There is a notable difference, though. The details that I've shared are public knowledge. Shared by the police. And myself, on my podcast. I bared my grief to the world. You didn't. It was wrong to ask you to share it with me." She pulled back and clasped her hands in her lap.

Sean realized he wanted to tell her about the darkest day in his life—no, he *needed* to tell her—though he wasn't sure why.

"After she completed her shopping, Felicia picked up snacks for us to enjoy while we watched the big game. She called me when she turned on our street and asked if I'd come outside to help carry in the grocery bags. The game was starting in ten minutes, and she didn't want to miss the kickoff." He stopped at a four-way stop, then turned left.

"I didn't want to go outside in my house shoes, so I changed into a pair of sneakers. By the time I got outside, Felicia was standing behind the vehicle with the trunk open. She pulled out a pizza box from my favorite restaurant, lifted the lid and turned to me with a smile… She'd had the restaurant spell out *I Love You* with black olives. My anger evaporated, and the kickoff no longer mattered. The outcome of a game is a temporary feeling of elation or sadness, and wasn't nearly as important as our marriage. And I was about to tell her so when a car stopped at the curb. I turned to see who it could be. The guy in the passenger seat was a gang member whose wife I'd helped put away for peddling drugs at an elementary school. The instant I saw the glint of the gun barrel, I yelled for Felicia to get down and raced toward her. But before I could reach her, three shots rang out, and she crumpled to the ground in a pool of blood."

Jenna gasped.

"Sorry. I shouldn't have been so graphic."

"No. It's fine," she said, her voice cracking. "I just… I didn't know she had been killed in front of you. I'm sorry."

Sean pressed his lips together. Her words were meant to convey sympathy, but it felt more like pity. Sean *had* witnessed Felicia getting shot in front of him, and he hadn't done anything to prevent it. When she'd needed him most, he failed her.

Reba's Roadside Grill came into view, and he slowed the vehicle. "We have arrived." And none too soon. Sean needed to refocus Jenna's attention to the task at hand—solving Becca's murder and figuring out who was trying to kill Jenna—and off his biggest failure as a husband *and* a police officer.

Jenna took a bite of her cheeseburger, and a combination of grease and condiments slid down her chin. She quickly pulled a napkin out of the white paper sack and wiped the mess away before it could drip onto her sweater. "I don't think there's a graceful way to eat this burger."

"No." Sean swallowed and smiled. "But that's what makes it so good. This is the best burger I've had in a long time. Why hasn't anyone told me about Reba's before?" He took another bite. "Yum."

He was right. It was the best burger for miles around. She'd always thought so. Only today, it tasted like soggy cardboard. She eyed her partially eaten meal, wrapped it back up and placed it in the bag. Then she took a big sip of her sweet tea and scanned their surroundings. Sean had parked exactly where she'd told him they'd found Becca's car. They were in a remote area of the park, near a meditation garden a local doctor had built in memory of his late wife. Most people parked closer to the playground and the walking trail.

"Who could Becca have met here?" she mused aloud. "My gut is telling me it had to be someone important. But why meet here?"

Sean reached for his cola and took a big gulp; then he put it back in the cup holder. "How old was Becca at the time of her death? Eighteen?"

"Seventeen."

"If it was a guy she met that day, I'd imagine she met him here for the same reason any teenage girl would meet up with a guy for an afternoon picnic in a remote area. She liked him."

Jenna gasped. "No." She furrowed her brown. "I'm sure you're wrong. Becca wasn't like most girls. She had a good head on her shoulders when it came to boys and relationships, choosing to go out just in groups. And as friends only."

Sean tilted his head and pinned her with his gaze. "I've never known a teenager who wasn't interested in dating. Not saying they don't exist, but I'd say they're a rare group."

"Becca had a long-term plan to earn her college degree and get firm footing in her career before she married." Clasping her hands in her lap, Jenna found herself once again fighting the urge to squirm under his gaze. Becca was unique, and Jenna would not apologize for discouraging her daughter from following in her footsteps and marrying young. She'd wanted more for her child than to be a single parent in her early twenties. Her wish had been for her to live her dreams without regrets. Jenna had wanted Becca to…live life to the fullest. But now she was dead.

Had Jenna's desperate desire for her daughter to have the *perfect* life pushed Becca into secretly meeting a boy who then killed her? The backs of Jenna's eyes stung. She bit her cheek, but there was no stopping the flow of tears. Turning her head so her long brown hair hid her face, she feverishly scrubbed the tears away with one hand.

Sean pressed a napkin into her free hand. "I'm sorry. I didn't mean to upset you," he said, his voice remorseful.

Heat crept up her neck. "It's not your fault." She wiped her face with the napkin, then quietly blew her nose. Turning toward him, she frowned. "It just hit me that I forced my desires onto Becca. If she secretly met a boy, it was because she didn't think she could be open with me about liking him. It's my fault she's…dead." The dam broke, and tears poured down her face.

"It is not your fault. You can't blame yourself for someone

else's actions." Sean twisted sideways and pulled her into a hug. "Ouch," he mumbled and shifted a little closer.

She pulled back and looked at his face, which was contorted in pain. "Steering wheel?"

"Yeah. Sorry."

"Why? For trying to offer comfort to a crying mother and injuring yourself in the process?" Settling into her seat, she dried the remaining tears and released a shuddered breath.

"I didn't expect to have this kind of reaction coming here today. I don't know what has come over me. Actually, that isn't true." Jenna pulled her left leg underneath her and turned to face Sean. "What you said about Becca meeting a guy… I had convinced myself her decisions about dating and earning a degree first had been her choice, but now I'm not so sure. If I'm the reason for those choices…and she met a guy she liked in secret to keep it from me…then it *is* my fault she's dead."

"Young people sometimes make bad choices. It doesn't mean their parents are bad people. Or that it's the parents' fault. It simply means the person who made the choice wasn't old enough or wise enough to think through the consequences. Sometimes even fully grown and extremely cautious people still get caught up in situations they never planned for." He picked up the take-out bag and dropped the remains of his meal into it before depositing it onto the passenger side floorboard at her feet. Then he pulled his seat belt around him, clicked it into place and met her gaze. "Ready to go to the next stop?"

A lump formed in her throat. The next stop was the hiking trail where Becca's body had been discovered. Jenna swallowed and reached for her own seat belt.

"If you don't think you can face any more today, we can go back to my house."

"And what? Continue to go over the notes in my files like we did last night? That's not getting us anywhere."

Sean dipped his head, turned the key in the ignition and backed out of the parking space. "While I drive, do you want to go over the list of classmates and friends that the police spoke to four years ago? Maybe you'll think of someone they missed."

She puffed out a breath and reached for the notepad, though she'd practically memorized all her notes. "They interviewed every member of Becca's graduating class. All seventy-three students. As well as any students in the other grade levels who had a class with her or interacted with her. They *all* had alibis that checked out."

"Okay, what about the teachers and staff?"

"Do you really think that a teacher is responsible? What would be the motive?"

"That, I do not know. However, if we can find someone who doesn't have an alibi and who someone saw with Becca the day she died, we could uncover the motive."

Jenna pulled a pen out of her purse, clicked it open and started doodling on the notepad. A thought materialized. "What if I've been looking in the wrong place all these years?"

"What do you mean?"

"If your theory is correct, and Becca met a boy for a picnic that day, then we have to consider it might not have been a classmate. Working at the library in Maryville, she could've met anyone. From a high school student to a college student to a much older man. And whoever it was could have moved far away by now." Jenna drew a big question mark on the paper, clicked the pen closed and shoved it along with the notepad back into her bag. "We might never find him."

"You're wrong. We will find him and stop him before he hurts you, too."

The muscle in his jaw twitched, again, and she balled her hand into a fist to keep from reaching out and touching it. Anger radiated off him. Was he that worried about her? Or was he simply upset that she had created this situation, putting him in a position to protect her?

"I… I appreciate all that you're doing to protect me. I'm sorry that my carelessness has caused this situation. If you want to drop me off at a rental-car location, I can rent a car and then you wouldn't need to drive me around."

"That's not happening." He glanced in her direction. "Do you really think I would abandon you now?"

She shrugged.

A frown briefly marred his face before he turned back to the road in front of him. Silence blanketed the vehicle.

Jenna hadn't meant to insult him or his integrity. She'd simply wanted to give him an out. Sure, he had volunteered to be her protector, but it had only been because he'd known the police force was not large enough to offer twenty-four-hour surveillance. And while he'd been great the night before, listening to her retelling of the facts pertaining to Becca's last day as she understood them, she knew he had to be annoyed that she hadn't listened to his advice to walk away from the podcast months ago. It had been her experience that when men found themselves in situations not of their choosing, they looked for a quick exit. Like Patrick had when they'd unexpectedly become young parents.

They arrived at the parking area for the hiking trail, and Jenna reached into the back seat and grabbed her down jacket and quickly slid her arms into the sleeves. Then she grasped the small daypack, which held two bottles of water, protein bars and a first aid kit, climbed out of the SUV and turned toward Sean as he came around the back of the vehicle.

"Are you sure you want to do this?" he asked.

"What's my other choice? I doubt you'd let me stay in the vehicle alone. And by the time we could get Heath or another officer out here to babysit me, the sun will have dropped further in the sky, and it will be too dark for you to see anything." She headed toward the trailhead. "Come on. Like your grandma Lois would say, 'Daylight's burning.'"

Sean jogged to catch up to her, but she did not slow her pace. She might be several inches shorter than him, but she had mastered the skill of taking long, quick strides.

"How did you determine what time of day Becca arrived here?"

"Sheriff Rice actually came up with the timeline. He based it on the autopsy report. We knew what time Becca got off work and the approximate time she picked up the food from Reba's. Based on the digested state of the food in her stomach and how long it should have taken her to hike to Eagle Point, he estimated she arrived here between four thirty and five o'clock. Which would have given her an hour and a half to complete the two-mile loop."

"Was the sheriff able to locate any witnesses to corroborate his theory?"

She shook her head, and a strand of hair fell across her face. Tucking the hair behind her ear, she looked up at him. "It's not uncommon for this trail to miss a lot of the foot traffic from the Appalachian Trail. Even though they're connected, this trail is a little more off the beaten path. I will forever be thankful for the two hikers who actually hiked the trail that morning." She licked her lips. "Without them, there's no telling how long it would have been before her body was discovered."

Jenna faltered a step, and he grasped her elbow to steady her. Anger bubbled up inside, as it always did when she thought of someone pushing her daughter off a cliff and leaving her alone to die in the woods.

Jenna closed her eyes for the briefest of seconds and puffed out a breath, then looked back up at him. "Ready to follow in my daughter's last footsteps?"

"If you are."

She concentrated on walking along the narrow trail. When the curve in the trail came into view, she pointed. "Just beyond that point, we'll come to a Y. If we go left, the trail will take us up to the ridgeline to the outcropping of boulders known as Eagle Point, where Becca fell from. If we go right, the trail will lead us to the spot where they discovered her body."

"Let's go to the ridgeline first. Then we'll circle back around."

Jenna nodded and led the way. While she hadn't been able

to make herself go to the top of the ridgeline before now, she'd been on the lower trail countless times in the past four years. Usually, she brought flowers to leave at the spot where her child had taken her last breath, but she hadn't wanted to seem silly or overly emotional to Sean, so she hadn't asked to stop to pick up a bouquet. She'd bring flowers next time. Today she was on a mission to gain closure on Becca's untimely death and to stop the killer before he killed her, too.

Chapter Seven

"What time of year was Becca mu—" Sean swallowed his words. He was a police veteran with thirty years of service. Why was he suddenly hesitant to call it what it was? A murder. Was it because Jenna had allowed herself to be vulnerable with him today? He'd seen a lot of women cry, but other than Felicia or his mom, none of their tears had tugged at his heartstrings the way Jenna's tears had earlier. He didn't know whether to be thankful or disappointed that the steering wheel had jabbed him and prevented him from embracing her.

Thankful. He *was* thankful. No need to blur the lines of neighborly friendship. While he didn't know if his beautiful, single neighbor was interested in finding a mate, or not, he knew without a doubt that he wasn't. Sean had already been married to his one and only love. She had rolled her eyes at his corny jokes and tolerated his constant stealing of the remote every Saturday. All while wearing a smile and making him feel like the most blessed man in the world.

"Spring."

He shook his head, pushing his thoughts aside. "What?"

Jenna stopped suddenly and spun around to face him, a scowl on her face. "You wanted to know when Becca was murdered. Right? It was in the spring. April 17. Five weeks before her high school graduation." She jerked her head toward the trail on the left. "We're going this way."

"Would you rather lead or follow?"

"Lead." She pivoted and started up the slight incline.

Of course she wanted to lead. Sean didn't know if he had ever met a more independent woman. It was fine with him, though. He could take his time and take in the view of his surroundings without her questioning why he was snapping pictures of various things. He slipped his phone out of his back pocket and accessed the camera app. It wasn't like he expected to find earth-shattering clues four years after the fact, but one never knew where they might find a hint of something that another investigator had missed.

"You said the previous sheriff had unofficially classified Becca's death as a suicide. What were his reasonings?"

"Other than the fact that six months after Becca's death, he still didn't have any clues who the murderer was?"

"Come on, do you really think that's the only reason the idea of suicide came up?" He'd never met Sheriff Rice, since he had retired and moved to Florida before Sean moved to Barton Creek. But he'd heard stories about what a fair and dedicated lawman the sheriff had been.

She maneuvered around a tree branch that partially blocked the trail. "As far as I know, Matthew Rice was a good sheriff. But I don't think he wanted to leave office with an unsolved case. It was easier for him to believe it was suicide."

He understood Sheriff Rice not wanting to walk away from his job with an unsolved murder. But twisting the narrative to fit what he wanted was unethical.

"Did he tell you why he suspected suicide?" Sean felt like a heel for pushing the issue, but he needed to understand every aspect of this case if he hoped to solve it.

"Becca and two of her closest friends had had a falling-out a couple of months earlier. When I tried to talk to Becca about it, she just said that their priorities had changed. When Sheriff Rice spoke to the girls, they told him that Becca had seemed depressed."

"Did you see any symptoms of depression in Becca?"

"No. I saw a child that was working hard to reach her goals. And while I never would've done such a thing while she was alive, after Becca passed away, I read her journal. The falling-out she'd had with her friends was because they were sneaking out of their homes at night and meeting boys they'd met on-line. They were partying and drinking. Becca told them what they were doing was wrong. That it wasn't right to worry their parents and that it was dangerous to meet strangers from the internet. They accused her of trying to be their conscience."

They reached the top of the ridge, and Jenna sat down on the bench at the overlook. "Was she sad and lonely without her friends? Yes. Was it enough to push her to kill herself? No. Her journal was full of her hopes and dreams and how much she was looking forward to college in the fall." A tear slid down her cheek, and she brushed it away. "Before she left for work the day she died, she made me promise that we'd go to the mall after church the next day and shop for her dorm room. That's not something someone contemplating suicide would be concerned with. Is it?"

The desperation in that simple two-word question almost brought him to his knees. He settled onto the bench beside her, his arm brushing against hers. "I wouldn't think so." Sean frowned. "And if it were suicide, why would someone be trying to kill you for poking around in the past?"

She gave a wry grin. "Who would have thought having someone trying to kill me would be a good thing? It proves Becca didn't commit suicide, and it means I'm getting close to the truth."

A bitter, icy wind blew through the trees, and Sean shuddered. The temperature had continued to drop steadily throughout the day. The weather forecast that morning had called for frost again overnight. He pushed to his feet and crossed to the wood-and-rock fence that stood about four feet high, separating the overlook from a rocky cliff that jutted out over the trail below. There were caution signs posted, warning hikers not to go beyond that point and to stay on the path. "Was the fence put up after Becca fell?"

"No. It's been here awhile. I think they built it when I was a freshman in high school. As I recall, there were some students who decided to have a late-night party out here to celebrate winning the state football championship. Two of the players fell off. One ended up with several cracked ribs, a broken arm and a broken ankle. It paralyzed the other guy from the waist down. The father of the paralyzed boy was the mayor, and three days later, there was a crew out here constructing the fence and posting warning signs." She came over to stand beside him and pointed at the sign. "That's another thing that has always puzzled me. The toxicology report didn't show any alcohol or sedatives in Becca's body. If her killer didn't drug her before tossing her off the cliff, how did he convince her to climb over the fence and hike out to the rocks? I can't imagine her willingly going along with that. She was a rule follower. And she was afraid of heights."

Sean didn't want to upset her more than he already had, but he could easily imagine someone holding a young girl at gunpoint—or knifepoint—and getting her to do his will.

Another thought struck. Had Becca's death really been murder? He furrowed his brow. Could it have been an accident? If it had been an accident, why hadn't the person with her come forward? Since Becca had left her car at the park to ride out here with the person she'd met, proving it was murder would have been harder than proving it wasn't. Unless… "I'm sorry to ask this, but were there any signs of forced trauma to Becca's body?"

"No. Thankfully, she wasn't…*violated*, if that's what you mean."

He pressed his lips together and nodded. "You sit here, but

stay where I can see you. I'm going to climb those rocks and see if I can get any insight into what may have happened." He swung a leg over the fence.

She mimicked his move and pinned him with a glare. "I'm going with you."

"That's not a good idea." He searched her face. Her jaw tightened, and her eyes bore into his.

The sun dipped behind the trees, and it felt like the temperature had dropped ten degrees. If they wanted to get back to the car before the sun set completely, they had about an hour to look around and hike back to the lower trail to see where they had found Becca's body.

Lord, arguing with her will only cost me time, and I'm sure it will be a losing battle. Please don't let her stubbornness cause her to be hurt.

"Okay. You can come, too, *but...*" He put a hand on her arm, ensuring he had her full attention. "You must follow my instructions every step of the way. I don't want you to get hurt."

A nervous laugh escaped her lips. "So, you *do* care what happens to me."

He scoffed. "Of course. I can't let anything happen to my grandparents' favorite neighbor. Besides, I can almost guarantee, if you die, the person after you will disappear, and we'll never find out who killed Becca."

"You have pinpointed exactly what has kept me alive and going all these years. I must find Becca's killer. And that is precisely why I'm going to be extremely careful out on the rocks." She climbed over the wood railing. "Are you coming?"

Dear Lord, my words didn't come out right. Of course Jenna's life is valuable. She's Your precious child. Please help her to see her worth so she won't give up on living once we finally solve this case.

A powerful gust of wind blew out of the southwest, and Jenna grasped a white oak tree. Her hair whipped across her face, but she refused to let go of the tree. A few more steps and she'd reach the tip of Eagle Point.

"Can you make it the rest of the way?" Sean placed a hand on her shoulder.

She puffed strands of hair out of her mouth. "The wind is stronger than I expected. I'll make it. I just need to get my balance first."

"Why don't you wait here? I'll go look around and be right back."

She shook her head. The rough bark scratched her cheek, and tears sprang to her eyes. She blinked them away. "No! I can do this."

For four years, this was the one place Jenna had avoided, too afraid to walk across the boulders to the spot where someone had tossed Becca's life away like yesterday's trash. Not today. Today, she would conquer her fears. After all, there was strength in numbers, and for the first time since that fateful April afternoon, Jenna had someone walking beside her. She was not alone.

An image of the cross-stitch tapestry her mother had given Jenna after her divorce came to mind: *Fear thou not; for I am with thee: be not dismayed; for I am thy God: I will strengthen thee; yea, I will help thee; yea, I will uphold thee with the right hand of my righteousness.* Isaiah 41:10.

Was it her own fault she'd walked alone all these years? How many people, including God, had she turned away, preferring to wallow in her grief? No, not preferring, but also not believing anyone could understand the depth of her pain. Every time her sister or mother had tried to tell her she needed to get out of her house and be around people—that she had to have a *life* to truly be alive—she had burrowed deeper into her shell. Then she'd recorded her first podcast and realized she could make a difference not just in her daughter's cold case but others too. Unfortunately, the decision had only pushed her further into her life as a loner. Not today. Today she was part of a team.

"You lead the way. I'll stay close behind." She released her hold on the tree.

Sean looked like he might argue, but then he pressed his lips together and moved ahead of her. "Okay. Hold on to the back of my jacket."

"No. Not that I plan to, but if I'm holding on to you and I slip, then we will both fall off the cliff."

He grasped her hand, his warm, callused fingers wrapped around hers. "I will not let that happen. Now, please, hold on to me."

Grabbing the back of his dark green Carhartt jacket with her left hand, she met his gaze. "Okay?"

"Thank you. Now, follow my steps."

Fighting to stay upright as they inched their way along the uneven surface, Jenna leaned into the wind. Six feet from the edge, she stepped on loose gravel, and one foot went out from under her. She landed on her backside with a thud. "Ouch!"

Almost at the same instant, a gunshot shattered the quiet afternoon, and a bullet hit the tree beside her, bark blasting through the air.

Sean crouched and crawled toward her. "Are you okay?"

"Yes." She shielded her eyes as she looked at where the bullet was embedded in the trunk, about level with where her head had been moments before.

Another explosion of gunfire sounded, this one hitting the boulder they were crouched on. Small bits of rock sprayed toward them. "What are we going to do? There aren't many places to hide out here."

"Follow me."

She followed closely behind him as they made their way to a nearby pine tree. The tree wasn't large enough for both of them to hide behind easily. Sean rolled onto his side, wrapped his muscular arms around her and dragged Jenna against him, her face buried in his chest.

Two more gunshots rang out, one hitting the tree in front of them and the other hitting the ground behind Jenna. She pulled back, and Sean pulled her close once more.

"I...can't...breathe," she said, her voice muffled by his winter jacket.

"What?" He shifted a few inches and looked down at her.

"I couldn't breathe." She puffed out a breath of air. "What are we going to do?"

Unzipping his coat, he reached inside and pulled out a handgun. "You're going to stay here while I try to get a clear shot and stop this guy."

He shifted his body, and she put a hand on his arm. "Be careful."

"Of course. Now, stay here." He pushed to his feet and ran to a boulder a few yards away. Another round of gunshots volleyed in their direction, a bullet hitting the large rock seconds after Sean had scooted behind it.

Jenna flipped onto her stomach and centered her body behind the tree, her eyes glued to Sean. He raised his gun and braced his arm on the boulder, pulling the trigger in rapid succession. And then silence. Several long minutes passed.

"Do—" Jenna swallowed the rest of her words when Sean shook his head, a finger pressed to his lips.

He crouched low and darted back to the tree where she waited. "I could see movement from a little higher on the ridge, but the person shooting was too far away for me to identify. I don't think he was expecting me to return fire."

"Where is he now?" She hoped she didn't sound as frightened as she felt.

"He disappeared in the trees. I think he's trying to get to a higher point so he'll have a better view. We have to get off this mountain."

"How do we do that? You don't know where the shooter is. He can pick us off like flies if we move out into the open. And if we make it to the trail, how can we be sure he isn't waiting for us there?"

Sean put his weapon into his shoulder holster. "Stay here. I'm going to look for another way down."

Jenna watched as he left the protection of the tree once again. She didn't know of any other trails or anything that would get them off the mountain more quickly than the one they had traveled to reach this point. Her heart raced. There was only one way off this rock. Over the edge. Straight down. The same way Becca had left Eagle Point.

They were trapped. All they could hope for was that the sun would set quickly and darkness would conceal their movements enough so they could escape. She didn't even want to think about how dangerous it would be to navigate the uneven ground they had covered to reach the pinnacle of the boulder that jutted out and over the path below in total darkness.

"Okay." Sean rushed back over to her, breathless. "On the other side of the boulder where I took cover, I found a small ledge about ten feet below us. And it looks like there's a narrow trail that winds its way from the ledge to the bigger trail below."

"A ten-foot drop?" she asked, aghast. "How do you expect us to drop ten feet without breaking a few bones?"

"I'm five-eleven."

"So?"

"I'll go first. If I maneuver correctly, the drop will be roughly four feet for me. Once I'm on solid ground, you mimic my steps, and I'll be there to catch you." He grasped her elbow and helped her to her feet. "Come on. Let's hurry."

His confidence did little to soothe her nerves. And she couldn't help but wonder if someone would find them and report their bodies or if they would be left for the wild animals to devour.

Chapter Eight

Sean spied a broken limb on the ground near the pine tree. It was about nine inches in diameter and six feet long. Would it be possible for Jenna to hold the limb over the edge of the cliff while he shimmied to the end of it and dropped to the ledge below? No. His weight would be too much, and the limb could break free of her grasp and swing up and smash her in the face. Maybe he could hang on to the root at the base of the tree and walk himself backward off the edge so he could control his drop. *Lord, please don't let me get injured. I can't leave Jenna in a position where she's not protected.*

"Pay careful attention, and watch my every move so you can mimic it once it's your turn." The fear that clouded her eyes was almost enough to make him tell her to forget it, they'd make a run for it. But he couldn't. If they stepped onto the open trail, they would be easy prey for the shooter. Their only hope was to get to the lower trail and make it harder for the shooter to see their movements. "I know you're afraid, but I wouldn't ask you to do this if I thought we had another option."

She bit her bottom lip. He leaned in. Catching himself, he stopped, his lips inches from hers. *What are you thinking? You almost kissed her. Don't let the thought of not making it out of*

*here alive make you do something you'll regret if—when—you
survive. Get a grip.*

"We *will* get out of here. Alive." he insisted, more confidently than he felt.

Jenna nodded. "Go. I'll be right behind you."

He rubbed his palms on his jeans, squatted and wrapped his hands around one of the larger roots that extended over the ledge below. "I'm going to use these roots to walk myself down the side of the mountain as far as I can. When it's your turn, do the same. I'll be there to catch you."

Jenna knelt beside him and covered his hands with hers. "I'm sorry I've put you in this situation."

"You didn't. The shooter did." He wanted to tell her much more. How he'd been wrong to judge her podcast. And that he regretted not being there for her as a neighbor. But this wasn't the time. "I'll see you at the bottom."

The root extended only about a foot down the side of the mountain, but every inch helped. When he reached the bottom of the root, he swung his legs out and dropped to the ground with a thud.

"Are you okay?" Jenna had lain on her stomach and was looking down at him.

"Yes. It wasn't that difficult." He held out his hands. "Your turn."

Sean watched as she grasped the root and copied his movements. She took two steps backward, lost her grip and plunged toward him. He braced for impact but had barely gotten his arms wrapped around her when they both fell back with a clunk.

Jenna rolled off him and helped him to sit up. "Did I hurt you?"

"No. I just need a...moment... To catch my...breath." He put a hand on his chest and took several slow, deep breaths. "Are you okay?"

She smiled. "Of course. I had a cushy landing."

"Are you calling me soft? I'll have you know, I'm solid mus—" The twinkle in her eye caught his attention. "You're laughing at me."

"No. Not at…" She sighed. "The counselor I saw after my divorce said making jokes when I'm anxious is one of my coping mechanisms. Sorry."

"Don't be. I cope with stress by whistling." He rubbed his jaw. "I've been biting the inside of my cheek to keep from whistling a tune."

A smile lit up her face, but she immediately replaced it with a somber expression. "So, what do we do now?"

"Now we follow that trail—" he pointed to the trail that hugged the side of the mountain where they stood "—and hope it leads us to the trail at the bottom of this mountain."

"I'll follow you."

A shiver raced up his spine. Her words reminded him of his conversation with Felicia when he'd told her he wanted them to move to a small town when he retired. She had insisted she could be happy anywhere as long as she was with him and that she would follow him "to the ends of the earth." Sean shook his head to clear his thoughts. They didn't have time to stand around.

"We need to move. Now." He grasped her hand, and an electric shock shot up his arm. When she tried to tug free, he wove his fingers through hers and held their clasped hands up. "I don't want us to get separated or for you to stumble and fall off the side of the trail." The explanation sounded flimsy even to his own ears, but he couldn't very well say that he was afraid of the shooter catching up with them and that he really needed the comfort of knowing she was safe.

She opened her mouth, then closed it and nodded.

Ducking under a dead vine, he started the slow descent with her at his heels. Fifteen minutes later, they reached the bottom trail. They hiked toward the parking area, and as they neared a curve in the path, a rustling noise to his right drew his attention. He dropped Jenna's hand and reached for his gun.

As they drew closer, they saw two helium balloons rubbing against each other in the wind. And on the ground, propped against a rock, was a bouquet of yellow roses.

"This is where Becca died. Who would leave flowers and balloons here?" Jenna caught the ribbon attached to one of the Mylar balloons. There was a floral image on the balloon, along with the words *I'm Sorry*. On the other balloon, one side read *You Are Loved, You Are Missed, You Are Remembered*; the other side read *Forever and Always*. She gasped. "Who? The murderer? What kind of game is he playing?"

Tears flowed down her face, and he pulled her into an embrace. "I don't know," he whispered against her ear. "I need to get pictures for the sheriff. Then we'll take everything with us and see if they can lift prints from any of it. Okay?"

She nodded. He pulled away from her and quickly snapped several photos. Then he pulled a small pocketknife out of his jacket pocket and punctured both balloons near the base. Once the helium had escaped, he quickly folded them—careful to only touch the edges—and tucked them into his pocket. Then he knelt to get a closer look at the roses.

Seventeen long-stem yellow roses. One for each year of Becca's life. Wrapped in brown parchment paper and tied with a white bow. No card.

"What are you doing?" Jenna asked.

"Trying to figure out how to get these to the sheriff's office without getting my own prints all over the wrapper." He peered up at her. "Empty your backpack and give it to me."

She removed a couple of protein bars, sticking them in her back pants pockets, and then pulled two water bottles from the small daypack. He'd teased her earlier that they were only going on a short hike and wouldn't need the water and snack, but she'd just smiled. Now he was thankful for her foresight.

Jenna handed him the pack, and he slid the flowers into it,

careful to touch only the rose stems and not the paper. Unable to zip up the bag with the long-stemmed flowers inside, he grasped the straps close to the top and stood.

"Do you want me to wear that?" Jenna nodded at the pack, a water bottle in each hand.

"No. I can carry it like this." He reached for a water bottle. "Thanks."

Sean flipped open the top and took a big gulp, then put it into the side pocket on the pack. "Ready to go?"

She glared at the roses peeking out of the backpack. "Yellow was her favorite color. Today was the first time I didn't bring flowers with me to leave at this spot... Why did he... How did he..." Her voice broke, and she pressed her lips together.

"I wish I had the answers. I don't. But we need to get a move on before the shooter circles around and finds us." Tightening his hold on the daypack, he put a hand on the small of her back and urged her along. "What's the fastest time you've ever made it to your vehicle from this spot?"

"I don't know. Maybe twenty minutes."

"Can you shave five minutes off that time?"

"Do you think he's still out there?"

"I'm not sure, but I don't want to stick around and find out." He looked around at the dark shadows that surrounded them. "We're running out of daylight. We need to get to my vehicle."

"Follow me." She took off toward the trailhead, and he fell in step beside her.

They'd only gone a few feet when a gunshot rang out and a bullet hit the ground to their right.

"Run!" He grasped her hand and ran as fast as he dared on the rugged trail.

More gunfire sounded behind them.

"Here!" Jenna yelled, and pulled him off the trail and into the trees. "He won't be able to see us in here."

"True, but do you have any idea where you're going?" Sean inquired.

"Yes." Jenna darted behind a large tree and pressed against it, panting.

"That was smart thinking, running into the trees, but I'm glad we didn't break our necks."

"I know these woods. I've been out here so many times since Becca died. I believe I could navigate this section to the trailhead blindfolded if I had to."

"Thankfully, there's still a little daylight left. But only if we move fast."

He peered around the tree, searching for the shooter.

Jenna pointed. "There."

A shadow figure stood atop the rock overhang close to where they'd climbed down earlier. Sean watched as the figure turned and made his way back to the overlook at the ridge of the mountain. "Looks like he's headed back to the trail. Either he didn't see how we came off the mountain or he decided it was too risky to attempt in the waning sunlight."

"Let's go." Jenna took off at a brisk pace, and he had to jog a few steps to catch up to her.

They made it to his SUV in under fifteen minutes. There were no other vehicles in the area. The shooter must have parked at another location and hiked. Sean puffed out a breath. *Lord, I guess it was too much to hope the guy after Jenna was reckless enough to leave his vehicle in plain sight, but I need a break here. Something that will point me in the right direction. So I can solve this case before Jenna becomes a casualty.*

A sharp pain radiated behind Jenna's right eye and extended all the way to her temple. A migraine. She leaned her head against the passenger-side window, willing the cool glass to numb the pain. They had spent a couple of hours at the sheriff's office, giving their statements and answering questions. She was exhausted. Jenna planned to take pain pills and go straight to bed, when they arrived home. No, not home—Sean's house. She sighed. Would her life ever be normal again?

"That was a heavy sigh," Sean commented.

"I'm just tired. And I—" The words lodged in her throat. How could she complain about a headache and sore muscles? She was sure he was just as exhausted as she was. And she had brought this attack on herself by sticking her nose in police business. Sean hadn't asked for it. He'd simply gotten caught in the middle of it by being in the wrong place at the wrong time.

"That's understandable. You've had a long day." He sped up. "I'll have us home soon. You can relax while I pop a pizza in the oven."

She didn't want pizza. The thought of food made her nauseated but more than that, she was desperate for space and time alone to process the events of the day. Only, how did one tell their host they didn't want to be in their company? Puffing out a silent breath, she rotated so more of her forehead touched the cool glass. Jenna looked out over Douglas Anthony's farm, which was lit only by the full moon above.

They were nearing her house. Oh, how she missed her bed, her recording studio, her comfortable sofa and fuzzy throw blanket she kept nearby. Maybe she could get Sean to stop by her house so she could pick up a few items she found comforting. No. She couldn't ask him to do that. Not tonight. But maybe she could go tomorrow and pick up a few things. She also needed to talk to Heath about finding alternate living arrangements.

Jenna was thankful for Sean and his hospitality, but finding the person who was after her could take weeks, months or even years. She couldn't continue to stay in his house, making him sleep outside in a cold camper. While they were at the sheriff's office, Heath had told her not to get her hopes too high that the fingerprints would come back with a match. Unless the person who'd killed Becca had a record, the likelihood of prints on file would be slim. And if the person was a serial killer, like the one who had shown up in Barton Creek the year before Becca's death, there would have been other murders after Becca's. While the constant dead ends were disheartening, Jenna was thankful no other mother in Barton Creek had lost a daughter the way she had.

Shifting in her seat, she caught sight of her house. Sitting back off the road, with the front window boarded up and no lights, the cozy home she'd tried to build for herself seemed depressing. Maybe it was time for her to consider moving to Nashville and getting a condo in the same complex as her sister, Amber. In a large city, she might remain in the shadows and avoid the person who was after her.

Was that a light inside her house? She forced her eyes to focus on the yellow glow in the guest room window. It was moving. "Stop the truck!"

Jenna turned and grabbed Sean's arm. "I saw a light. There's someone in my house!"

"What? Are you sure?" He slowed. "It could be the moon glinting off a window or something."

"No. Someone is inside my house with a flashlight. I saw it moving." She watched as they passed her home. Why hadn't he stopped the vehicle yet? "We need to catch him."

"If there's an intruder, I need to take you to my house. You can stay there with the doors locked and Beau to guard you. I'll come back alone." Sean sped up.

"But he'll get away. You know he had to have heard your vehicle and seen your headlights, too. Everyone in town knows there's only one house past mine on this road, so even if he can't see your SUV, he has to know we're the ones in this vehicle. He won't stick around and wait for you to come back and find him."

His brow furrowed. Good, he was thinking about her words.

"You have a weapon. And I'll stay behind you and follow your orders. Don't let him get away this time."

"Okay." He reduced his speed and pulled his SUV off the

road, parking at the edge of her property where it joined his. Then he cut the lights, turned off the engine and shifted to face her. "Do you know how to drive a manual transmission?"

Why was he asking her about her driving ability? They were wasting time. She reached for the door handle, but he stopped her.

"You *will* stay inside this vehicle with the doors locked. Or we're both going to my house. Do you understand?"

Her irritation rose. She didn't need anyone giving her orders. She'd been taking care of herself for too many years. Only, he hadn't sounded demanding. Just concerned. Pressing her lips together, she nodded. "I understand."

He leaned close, his brow furrowed. "Can you drive my vehicle?"

"Yes."

"Okay, I'm leaving the keys. I want you in the driver's seat. Get out of here at the first sign of trouble. Got it?"

"Do you want me to call 911?"

"No." He reached up and turned off the dome light, then opened his door. "We don't know if the light you saw was a flashlight beam or not. There may be no one inside."

Jenna bit back the retort that itched to be released. She knew what she saw. But arguing about it would only prolong Sean's departure, giving the intruder a chance to escape. She crawled over the console and settled into the driver's seat he'd just vacated. "Be careful."

"Lock the doors." He dropped the keys into her outstretched hand, turned and jogged toward her house.

She pressed the door-lock button, her eyes trained on her yard. As Sean neared the front steps, a dark figure raced from the back of the house toward the tree line that hid the fence separating her property from Doug Anthony's farm.

Sean would be upset with her, but Jenna couldn't let the guy get away. He had to be stopped so she could move back into her home and live life again, and so she would finally have answers about Becca's death.

Throwing open the SUV door, she shoved the keys into her front pocket and charged into the night.

Chapter Nine

The hairs on the back of Sean's neck stood at attention at the sound of footsteps pounding across the front yard. He palmed his gun and spun around. And came face-to-face with Jenna. She gasped, her eyes wide with fear.

"I thought I told you to stay put," he whispered, slipping the gun back into its holster.

"The guy…" she panted, placing a hand on her chest as if to steady her heartbeat, "…ran out…the back door. Headed toward Doug's pasture."

"Get back to my vehicle and call Heath. I'll go after the intruder." Sean took off around the corner of the house, praying she'd follow his directions, though he suspected she wouldn't.

Lord, please protect her when I can't. The prayer he had prayed for Felicia every time he left for work slipped unbidden to his mind. "Lord, I failed Felicia. Please don't let me fail Jenna, too."

Felicia's smiling face flashed through his mind and was quickly replaced by an image of Jenna, sad and frightened out on the trail today. *Focus.* He pushed the thoughts away and pressed on toward the trees at the back of the property.

Pausing beside a beech tree, he listened. Silence. Where had the intruder gone? A cloud drifted in front of the moon. He desperately wanted to use the flashlight function on his cell phone, but he couldn't risk giving away his location. A coyote yapped in the distance, and a dog barked in response. Had the intruder gone across Doug's pasture? Or was he hiding somewhere in the trees?

Frustration bubbled up. He had to have light if he hoped to capture the intruder. Palming his weapon in his right hand, he activated the flashlight. Lifting his phone, he swept the flashlight beam across the area. The intruder was gone. He'd slipped out of Sean's grasp, again.

Disconnecting the flashlight app, he shoved the phone into his pocket and made his way across the yard. Time to get back to Jenna. He'd make a sweep through the house first and make sure all the doors and windows were locked. Then he'd get Jenna to the safety of his house. Hopefully, she'd followed his directions and called for backup. The intruder was most likely long gone, but the officers would file a report and look around to see if he'd left any clues.

Sean climbed the steps to the back deck and entered the open door, stepping into the laundry room of Jenna's home. He automatically reached to flip on the light switch but caught himself. The electricity company had temporarily disconnected power to the house because of the fire damage.

"There's another flashlight in the drawer next to the refrigerator," Jenna yelled from the hallway.

He crossed to the drawer, opened it and felt around inside until his fingers brushed against the flashlight. Grasping it, he powered it on. "I thought I told you to go back to the truck."

"You did, but…" There was a grunt, followed by the sound of something being dragged. "I wanted to see what the intruder was looking for."

He sprinted around the furniture and down the hall. Jenna shoved a box across the threshold of the first room on the right, pushing it in front of Sean. He jumped out of the way. "What are you doing?"

Jenna straightened and turned back to the room. "Becca never lived in this home. When I walked away from my job in education, I had to sell the home I raised my daughter in and downsize. But I couldn't bring myself to part with her furniture or any of her stuff, so I moved it here and put it in this room."

Sean scooted the box aside, stepped into the doorway and scanned the room with the flashlight's beam. She had decorated the walls with various pictures of herself and her daughter through the ages.

"As you can probably tell, I didn't decorate the room exactly the way Becca had left her old one, but I think you can admit it would be easy for anyone to tell that this furniture and these items belonged to a teenage girl."

The bed had a few stuffed animals resting on the pillows, and there was a jewelry box and several photos of Becca and her friends on the dresser. He nodded. "I would agree."

She sighed. "But what I haven't figured out is why the intruder was in this room. What was he searching for?"

"What do you mean? How do you know he was searching this room?" Sean swept his light around the room once more.

The dresser drawers appeared to be undisturbed, but the closet door stood wide open. Boxes of books and other memorabilia had been dumped on the floor. Several were open and tossed aside. "Did he do that?" Sean fixed the beam of light onto the pile of stuff.

"Yes." She crossed to the closet, settled onto the floor and started placing books back into the boxes.

"Whoa. Wait a minute." He put out a hand to halt her. "You shouldn't disturb a crime scene."

"Seriously?" She dropped the book she was holding into the box, then pushed to her feet. "Do you really think the police will get any clues from this?"

He wanted to say yes, but he couldn't. The only thing the

scene before him proved was that the intruder had been inside this room. And as much as he wanted to argue that they might get fingerprints, he seriously doubted that would be the case. Even the most novice criminal knew to wear gloves when entering a home. "I don't know. But they should at least see it. They may want to take pictures."

Jenna plopped down onto the bed, and her shoulders slumped. He knelt on the floor beside her. "Did you call Heath like I asked?"

She nodded. Her long brown hair fell like a curtain, hiding her from his scrutiny. "He should be here soon. Said he'd come out himself."

Reaching out, Sean swept the hair back and tucked it behind her ear. "After Heath looks at the room, I'll help you get everything boxed up. We can take whatever you want back to my house. Okay?"

A lone tear slid out of the corner of her eye and down her cheek. He brushed it away with his thumb, and she captured his hand and pulled it away. Sean suddenly felt self-conscious about his actions. He'd only intended to offer support and hadn't meant to cross boundaries. "I…ah… I'm sorry."

She shook her head. "You have nothing to apologize for. I'm just—"

"Sean! Jenna! Where are y'all?" Heath yelled from the front of the house.

Sean shoved to his feet and stepped into the hall. "We're here."

Footsteps drew closer, and Heath stepped into the hallway, a flashlight in his hand.

"The intruder got away. But we think he was searching for something in Becca's belongings." Sean moved to the side to allow the sheriff to enter the room.

Jenna remained seated but pointed to the pile of boxes and books dumped in and around the closet floor. "I looked through the rest of the house, but this seems to be the only room touched. Of course, I could have missed something." She shrugged. "It would be easier to tell if there was electricity."

"Well, since that isn't an option at the moment and—" Heath glanced at the box in the hall "—you apparently want to pack Becca's things, I suggest we go from room to room and take a quick look. With three flashlights, we should be able to get a pretty clear visual."

She nodded, stood and swept her hand toward the door. "Lead the way."

Twenty minutes later, they had searched every room of the house. None of the other rooms appeared to be disturbed.

Heath used his cell phone to snap photos of the boxes on the floor of the closet in the room that housed Becca's things. "It seems the intruder was looking for something specific." He turned to Jenna. "I really should load all this up and haul it to the station and have one of my deputies go through it to see if they can pick up on any clues."

"How would they know what they're looking at? They didn't know Becca, and—"

"Agreed. Also, as it has been pointed out many times, we're shorthanded. So…" Heath turned to Sean.

"So you're wondering if I'll be the lead detective—pro bono, of course." Sean raised an eyebrow.

"Hey, you know I'd put you on the payroll in half a heartbeat. All you have to do is say the word." Heath held out his hands, palms upward. "But since you don't want to come work for me, I'm asking you, as a friend, if you can help me decipher the clues in this case."

"You don't even have to ask. I already told Jenna that I'd help her box everything up and take it to my house. We can go through everything once we get it there." Sean glanced at her for verification, and she nodded. He turned to Heath. "If you'll help me, we can get these items loaded into my vehicle."

Sean picked up the box Jenna had shoved into the hall earlier and strode toward the front door. His heart raced as adrenaline surged through him. Why did it feel so good for his detective skills to be needed once again? He'd thought he was way past wanting to put his life on the line to protect civilians. Maybe being a protector wasn't something one ever got over. It was part of their DNA. He'd never intentionally gone out looking to put his life on the line, but solving cases and helping bring closure to loved ones was invigorating. Was that the same feeling Jenna felt when she used her podcast to help solve cold cases? Sure, her daughter's case had prompted her early foray into true crime podcasting—a form of investigative journalism in its own right—but being willing to put her life on the line, not just for her own daughter's unsolved murder but for other families seeking justice for their loved ones, was about more than a mother's love. Maybe he'd been wrong about her.

Jenna dropped the box she was carrying onto the big table that took up most of the space in the dining nook that sat in the corner of Sean's farmhouse kitchen. Sean and Heath trailed in behind her and sat their boxes beside hers. Five boxes in total, all containing Becca's high school memories. "Thanks, guys. I'm not sure what the intruder could have been looking for, but maybe there's something in here that will lead me to the killer."

"I think you mean *us*. Lead *us* to the killer. Remember, you're not in this alone, anymore." Sean dropped an arm across her shoulders, and a warm, protected feeling spread over her.

"That's right," Heath agreed. "You have us now. And I'm truly sorry I didn't look into Becca's death sooner. I should have gone over the file myself when I took office and not blindly accepted Sheriff Rice's assertion that it was suicide."

She turned to face her friend. It was nice to hear him admit he'd messed up, though she couldn't fault him for accepting his predecessor's assessment on cases the department had deemed closed. "Thank you. But we can't dwell on mistakes of the past. We have too much to keep us busy in the present. Learn from it and move on."

A smile spread across his face, and she could see hints of the young boy she'd babysat all those years ago. "You're very gracious."

No. She wasn't. She was simply learning to let past hurts go so they wouldn't fester and spread like a disease and engulf her.

"Okay, I need to get going. I plan to go to the high school in the morning and interview the faculty and staff. See if anyone remembers anything they may not have thought was important four years ago." He searched her face. "I know it isn't standard practice to bring victims' families on these types of interviews, but I was wondering if you and Sean would meet me there. You know the faculty and staff better than I do, and you may be able to tell if they're hiding anything by their body language."

Slowly releasing a breath, she thought of all her coworkers and so-called friends who had faded from her life when she'd refused to give up on finding Becca's murderer. She hadn't faced any of them in two and a half years. Not since over-hearing the conversation in the teacher's lounge the day she'd announced she was quitting so she could work full-time on Becca's case. Not one person supported her decision. They'd all thought she had taken a headfirst dive off the deep end. But that didn't matter now. With Sean and Heath beside her, she could confront the naysayers. "Sure. We'll be there."

"I'll text you in the morning to let you know what time I'll be there." He gave her a quick hug and then headed for the door. "Let me know if y'all find anything of interest in the boxes."

Stopping midway, he turned back to Sean. "Keep her safe. This guy is getting too close. I know you stayed in the camper last night to give her privacy and space, but you may need to sleep inside tonight."

"Agreed." Sean cast a quick glance in her direction, as if he expected her to argue.

Jenna pressed her lips together and stayed quiet. She didn't have any experience with evading killers, having only ever dealt with them from the other side of a microphone and a computer. There was no way she was about to tell these two lawmen how to do their job, especially when the task at hand was keeping her alive.

"Okay. I'll have one of my deputies drive by periodically throughout the night. I'll also have him check on your house in case the intruder goes back there tonight. And in the morning, we'll see about getting someone out there to secure your home a little better to keep him—or any other would-be vandals—out."

"I appreciate that. Tell whomever you call to send me a bill, and I'll see that they're paid quickly."

Heath tipped his head and slipped outside. Sean caught the door before it closed completely and whistled for Beau to come inside. After the coonhound had bounded into the room, Sean shut the door and locked the dead bolt.

Beau came and sat at Jenna's feet, and she bent down and scratched between his ears. "Were you so happy to get to run outside after being locked indoors all day? You're such a good boy."

One of the few regrets Jenna had as a mom was never getting a dog for Becca. She hadn't wanted the responsibility of having to care for anyone else besides herself and her daughter. And living in a condo that lacked a sizable fenced-in backyard meant a dog would have to stay locked inside for long hours each day. It hadn't seemed fair to the animal. So when Becca was eight and started begging for a dog like her friend Patty had, Jenna had listed all the reasons they couldn't own a dog and driven Becca to the pet store and allowed her to pick out an animal that could live in her tiny bedroom and didn't require long walks outdoors. Which was how they'd ended up with a guinea pig named Harry—a pet that was supposed to have had a life expectancy of five to seven years that ended up living nine, dying just two months after Becca had.

A tear slid down her cheek, and she quickly buried her face in Beau's fur. What would Sean think if she kept allowing her emotions to run unchecked? One of her biggest fears in life was appearing weak to others, a leftover emotion from her divorce. Patrick's last words to her as he walked out the door had been, "Run home to your mommy. You'll never make it on your own. You are a weak human being who needs to be taken care of. There's no way you'll be able to raise Becca alone."

And Jenna had done exactly as he'd said. She'd run home to Barton Creek and moved into her mother's house, but only for two years. Once she'd completed her teaching degree and gotten a job, she purchased a condo and started her new life as a single mom.

Sean cleared his throat. She pulled back from Beau and met Sean's gaze, a frown on his face, concern etched in his eyes. Had he seen the tear? *Please don't let him mention it if he did.*

He looked from her to the coonhound and back again. "I put a pizza in the oven. It should be ready in about twenty minutes. If you want to…um…go wash up or relax, I'll feed Beau. Then we can eat before we go through the boxes."

How had she missed him getting the pizza out of the freezer and putting it in the oven? She really needed to get a grip and stay aware of the things going on around her. Jenna had been so oblivious. Lost in her own emotions and thoughts, she'd completely tuned out her surroundings. That the killer could have snuck up on her if this had happened anywhere else made Jenna suddenly nauseated. She nodded. "Okay."

After giving Beau one last pat on the head, she turned and quickly made her way to the guest room. Once inside, she closed the door, crossed to the bed and lay down. If she could close her eyes for just a few minutes, maybe she would stop feeling like her world was spinning out of control.

Some time later, Jenna opened her eyes. Where was she? *Oh, yeah, Sean's house.* She swung her legs off the side of the bed, sat up and listened. The house was quiet. How long had she been asleep? She'd only intended to close her eyes for a few minutes.

What time was it? She didn't know how long she'd slept. It could have been a few minutes or a few hours. Fumbling with the lamp on the bedside table, she found the knob and twisted it. She blinked her eyes repeatedly until they adjusted to the light. Her phone wasn't on the nightstand. It must still be on the kitchen table. Pushing to her feet, she plodded across the carpeted floor and slowly opened the door. Why did she feel like an intruder? It might not even be that late. The kitchen light shone like a beacon in the distance. She headed in that direction.

"You're awake. Are you hungry?" Sean spoke from behind her.

A small scream escaped her lips, and she jumped, spinning around to face him. "You startled me," she accused, clutching her chest.

He reached out a hand and steadied her. "I'm sorry."

"What time is it?"

"Just after ten. You slept for about two hours."

"Why didn't you wake me when the pizza was done?"

"I thought about it but decided you needed sleep more than you needed food." He smiled. "But now that you're awake, how does cold pizza or a grilled cheese sandwich sound?"

Her stomach growled, and she giggled. "Actually, grilled cheese sandwiches are my favorite comfort food."

"Good. I also put on a pot of coffee earlier. It should still be hot." He gently turned her toward the kitchen and escorted her down the hall. "If you're afraid the caffeine will keep you awake the rest of the night, I can always make a fresh pot of decaf."

"Coffee sounds nice. Caffeinated is fine. Since I had such a long nap, it will be okay if I'm awake for a few hours."

They reached the kitchen, and she noticed he had shifted the boxes. There were stacks of Becca's things scattered all over the table.

"Here, I'll move this aside. We can—"

"No!" She reached out and halted him before he could push

a stack of yearbooks aside. "I'll move them. I can't believe you touched Becca's things while I was asleep. Why would you do that?"

"Because I'm searching for her killer and trying to stop you from becoming his next victim," he stated in a calm, matter-of-fact tone. Then he stepped back, crossed to the refrigerator, and removed the cheese and butter.

Her cheeks warmed. She'd had no right to snap at him. He had saved her life four times in the past forty-eight hours and had even opened his home to her so she would be safe. "I'm… I'm sorry. I didn't mean…" Her voice cracked. She took a deep breath and released it slowly. "Did you find anything suspicious?"

He placed a pat of butter into a cast-iron skillet on the stove and watched it sizzle. Then he added the cheese sandwich into the hot skillet. "No. Nothing that jumped out at me as a clue," he replied after several long minutes. "I quickly realized— since I'd never met your daughter—that going through the boxes alone was a waste of time. That's why I was in my office reading and not in here looking for clues when you woke up."

She didn't have a right to probe into his private life, but curiosity got the better of her. "What were you reading?"

He flipped the sandwich in the skillet and reached into the cabinet and removed a plate. Then he turned off the stove, plated the sandwich and placed it on the kitchen table in front of her. She met his gaze. Maybe she should apologize for being nosy. She opened her mouth.

"The Bible," he said softly before she could speak.

Of all the answers he could have given, she wasn't sure why this one surprised her, but it did. Maybe because she hadn't made church or reading her Bible a priority since Becca died. The last time she'd even stepped inside the church building had been for Becca's funeral. Come to think of it, she didn't have a clue where her Bible was. She vaguely remembered packing it when she sold the condo but couldn't recall where she'd put it once she moved into her house. But she knew exactly where Becca's Bible was. She turned and looked at the boxes on the table. Sitting in front of the box labeled *Becca's Prized Belongings* was the red leather Bible with the name *Rebecca Lynn Hartley* stamped in gold lettering on the bottom-right corner.

"Finding your daughter's well-worn, well-loved Bible reminded me I hadn't spent enough time in mine in a while," Sean said from behind her, as if reading her thoughts.

Sadly, Jenna hadn't spent time in her Bible in a while, either. Almost four years. Though she wasn't proud to admit it.

Chapter Ten

Sean scrubbed a hand over his face, the stubble of his five-o'clock shadow scratching his palm. It was nearing midnight, and his eyes felt gritty, as if he'd walked through a sandstorm. He blinked several times, but it didn't help. Pushing his chair back, he crossed to the sink and splashed cold water on his face.

"If you want to go to bed, I'm fine working alone," Jenna said.

He turned to face her and leaned against the counter. They had looked at every memento and piece of paper in four of the boxes. Only one to go. He didn't know if it was best to keep pushing through or if he should encourage her to take a break so both of them could get some rest. Which would enable them to look at the items with fresh eyes tomorrow.

"I'd feel better if you got some sleep, too."

She reached into the last box and pulled out a school year-book. "I'm not sleepy."

He went to stand behind the chair he'd vacated earlier. "I know you want to find answers tonight. But sometimes you have to know when to walk away for a little while. If you keep pushing yourself past the point of exhaustion, you're more likely to miss a valuable clue."

"Really, I'm fi—"

"I know." He gently tugged the yearbook out of her hand and placed it back in the box. "You're fine. But I'm not. And I won't be able to sleep as long as I know you're still up."

Her brown eyes searched his. Then she pressed her lips together and nodded. "I get it. Having a guest in your home disrupts your routine. You won't sleep as well if you're worried about hearing every sound I make anytime I move.

"I'll retire to the guest room so you can get some rest." She stood, and Beau was instantly by her side.

"Thank you." Sean clicked the button to turn on the range-hood light, something his mom did when guests visited her house. Once, when he was eight years old, he'd asked her why she always did that, and she'd told him it was so their guests wouldn't trip over the furniture in an unfamiliar home if they woke up in the middle of the night needing a glass of water. "Come on, Beau. Time for bed."

Jenna scratched the coonhound's head. "If you don't mind, can he stay with me? He slept beside my bed last night. It was comforting."

Beau looked up at him with pleading eyes, as if he knew they were discussing him. Sean liked routine, which meant Beau sleeping in the sunroom. But if the coonhound gave Jenna comfort, how could he say no? Though he was sure he'd have one sad dog on his hands when this ordeal was over and Jenna was no longer there to slip treats to Beau under the table or allow him to sleep with her.

"I guess I can move his bed into your room, for now. Try to get some rest, okay? Remember, we're meeting Heath at the school in the morning." Sean followed Jenna out of the room, snaking out his hand to turn off the overhead light as he passed the wall switch.

Beau let out a loud, drawn-out howl, and goosebumps prickled Sean's skin. Was someone outside?

A bullet shattered the window above the sink and struck the wall just above the light switch.

"Get down!" Sean yelled, and dropped to the floor, regretting his decision to leave the light on over the stove.

"Quickly, get into the hall," he commanded Jenna, who swiftly followed his instructions, crawling on her hands and knees.

Two more bullets came through the dining room window, one piercing the glass front of his grandmother's china cabinet and the other hitting the back of one of the dining chairs.

They reached the safety of the hallway, where there weren't any windows, and Jenna settled against the wall with her knees pulled to her chest and an arm wrapped around Beau—the coonhound barking and straining to get free.

"Beau. Quiet!" Sean commanded. The dog instantly stopped barking and sat, proving obedience training had been worth the time and expense.

"Now what?" Jenna asked.

"Do you have your phone?"

"Yes."

"Call this in. And stay here. I'm going to slip into my bedroom and retrieve my gun."

She reached into her back pocket and pulled out her cell while he headed for his bedroom at the end of the hall. The lights in this part of the house were all turned off, so he prayed the shooter wouldn't be able to follow his movements. The gunfire had stopped, and that made him very nervous. He needed his weapon, and he needed to make sure Jenna was somewhere safe so he could go outside and capture this guy.

Sean reached his bedside table, opened the drawer, pulled out his Glock and stuck it into the back of his waistband. Now, what about Jenna? He couldn't take her outside with him.

"Police are en route," she whispered from the doorway, Beau pressed against her side.

"Great. I have to go outside and try to stop this guy. The hall bathroom is an interior room without windows. I think you'll be safest there." What if the guy breached the house and found her hiding in there? She'd be trapped, and Beau would be no match against a gun. "Do you know how to shoot a rifle?"

"It's been years, but I'm sure I can manage."

Staying low, he went over to the closet and pulled out the .22 hunting rifle his grandfather had given him for his fifteenth birthday. "Be careful. It's loaded, and there's a live round in the chamber."

The bedroom window shattered, and a bullet whizzed past his head, hitting the closet door. Sean dove to the other side of the bed and slid the rifle toward Jenna. "Get into the bathroom. Now!" He propped his arms on the bed and returned fire, thankful she had followed instructions and not insisted on sticking around and helping.

Sean and the assailant exchanged several rounds of bullets. Then the sound of a police siren pierced the night. The shots from outside halted. Convinced the shooter had taken off, Sean pushed to his feet. "You can come out now. He's gone."

Jenna rushed into the room. "Are you okay?"

"Yeah. I'm fine." He looked around his bedroom. Two walls were peppered with holes and would need to be patched, but in the grand scheme of things, that was a minor issue. He was thankful no one had been injured. "Where's Beau?"

"I put him in the guestroom so he'd be out of the way."

"Good thinking."

There was a loud banging on the front door. "Everyone okay in there?"

"That sounds like Deputy Moore." Sean led the way back to the front of the house and opened the door to allow the uniformed officer inside. "We're fine. The shooter took off when he heard the sirens."

"My partner is following him through the woods. But he had a big head start, so I wouldn't hold out too much hope that he's captured tonight." Deputy Moore's phone rang, and he glanced at the screen. "Excuse me. I'll take this outside."

Sean glanced at Jenna, noticing her pale complexion and trembling hands for the first time. Was she going into shock? "I think you and I should wait in the living room."

He slipped his arm around her shoulders and guided her through the open doorway. Once inside, he directed her to sit on the couch. Then he snagged the thick red-plaid throw off the ottoman in front of the fireplace and draped it across her shoulders. "Give me a few minutes, and I can have a fire started."

"There's no need for that. I'm fine. The blanket will be enough." She smiled up at him, her lower lip trembling.

That was his undoing. He instantly settled onto the couch next to her, put his arm around her and pulled her into a warm embrace. All he could think of was that he needed to reassure her that he was there to protect her and everything would be okay. He would do whatever it took to keep from seeing that look of sheer helplessness in her eyes ever again.

The front door opened, and Sean scooted several inches away from Jenna as if he were a teenage boy who'd just been caught kissing. He stood as Deputy Moore entered the room.

The deputy held out his phone to Sean. "Sheriff Dalton wishes to speak with you."

Sean accepted the phone and tapped the screen to place the call on speaker. Otherwise, he'd just have to repeat everything to Jenna. "Hi, Heath. I've placed you on speaker. Jenna's here, too."

"Good. Are you both okay?"

"We're fine," they said in unison.

"I'm guessing I wouldn't be able to convince you to move to a different location, would I?"

Sean looked at Jenna, though he knew her answer before he did. She shook her head vigorously. "Becca's things are here. We'd have to move all the boxes, and my laptop and belongings."

"I can have—"

"We appreciate the offer, but she's right. We can't leave all those things here, and it would be too much trouble to move it all tonight." He rubbed the back of his neck. "We'll be okay. I won't let him get the jump on us again."

A sigh sounded across the line. "I believe you two are equally matched in stubbornness. Okay, but I'll have my men stay. They can stand guard outside overnight so both of you can get some rest. You've had a long day, being shot at twice."

"There's no need for that," Sean protested.

"There is. And you won't argue, or I'll have my men take you into the station for questioning."

"But—"

"You know I can do it," came the stern reply.

Jenna clutched Sean's arm, and he met her pleading gaze. He puffed out a breath. "Fine. Thank you."

"Don't mention it. Just keep Jenna safe. And get some rest. Hopefully, tomorrow we can find a new lead."

Sean handed the phone back to Deputy Moore just as his partner entered the house. The deputy—who introduced himself as Deputy Bishop—said the intruder had cut through the woods to an old, overgrown logging road that was midway between Sean's and Jenna's houses. Then he'd jumped into a pickup truck and taken off before Deputy Bishop could get close enough to identify the make or model, or get a tag number.

"Will anyone ever be able to stop this guy?" Jenna demanded.

"We're sure going to try, ma'am," Deputy Moore replied before Sean could. "In the meantime, try to get some rest. I doubt he'll return tonight, but if he does, we'll be waiting for him."

"Thank you." Sean showed the men out and bolted the door behind them, a strange sensation settling in the pit of his stomach. He was used to being the one doing the guarding, not the one being guarded. The feeling of needing others to help him do the job he'd been assigned to do was not one he enjoyed. Whatever it took, Sean *would* protect Jenna.

Chapter Eleven

Jenna chewed her lower lip. She hadn't seen any of her former coworkers, except in passing, since she'd walked away from her job. The eighteen months she worked after Becca's death had been awkward, and her relationships with both the faculty and the students had been strained. Meeting people's eyes and seeing pity etched in them had made her self-conscious. She would walk up to a group of teachers, and they'd stop talking. Students she'd worked hard to build trust with had stopped coming to her for guidance. When she'd questioned the behaviors, her principal had told her to give it time. He'd said it would only be natural for the students to be hesitant to talk to her about their college plans and their futures when they thought hearing such things would be painful for her, knowing her daughter would experience none of the things they were about to do.

"You're going to make your lips bleed if you don't stop worrying," Sean said, breaking into her thoughts. "If you're this worried about going to the school, I can always drop you off at the sheriff's office."

"No. I'd rather stay with you. Besides, Heath is right. I know these people better than both of you do. They may not be open to discussing things they remember, but I should be able to tell if they're covering up something. You don't work with people for ten years without learning how to read them."

"If you're sure."

"I'm sure."

They rode in silence until they turned into the school parking lot fifteen minutes later. Sean parked beside Heath's green-and-white sheriff's department SUV.

"Let's do this." Jenna opened her door and stepped out, pulling her coat tighter to ward off the stiff wind that ruffled her hair. "Brr."

Sean rounded the vehicle, placed a hand on her lower back and hurried her to the main entrance of the building.

Heath met them in the foyer. "I'm glad y'all could come. Today is a teacher workday. There won't be many students on campus other than the football team and the band students who are having practices."

"That's probably for the best. We wouldn't want to interrupt classes, anyway." Jenna shrugged out of her coat and draped it across her arm. "This year's senior class would have been in middle school when Becca died. I doubt they'd offer much insight into her death."

They made their way to the office where Principal Fisher and the school counselor, Mrs. Hill, waited for them with the school resource officer, Deputy Manning. Jenna greeted each of them. Mrs. Hill, who'd been Jenna's mentor her first year teaching, pulled her into a warm, motherly hug, and some of Jenna's apprehension evaporated. The people at the school were her work family. They had meant nothing when they questioned her ability to do her job after Becca's passing, and if they'd seemed awkward around her, it was only because they were concerned about her and didn't know how to help her through the pain.

"It's so good to see you," Mrs. Hill whispered in her ear.

"I've missed you," Jenna replied, hugging her friend tighter. They pulled apart, both with tears glistening in their eyes.

"I have asked Officer Manning to escort you today. We have

notified the staff that you're on campus and wish to interview them." Principal Fisher pinned Jenna with a stern gaze. "While I'm not sure what you hope to accomplish here today, everyone has agreed to be cooperative and answer all of your questions. Even the ones they've answered before. Multiple times. We all want you to get the closure you are searching for."

Jenna felt Sean stiffen beside her. But she pressed her lips together and nodded. Principal Fisher wasn't known for his tact. He hated when things disrupted his schedule. Quite honestly, he probably would have been better suited to just about any other job than that of a high school principal, which actually required a great deal of flexibility with schedules and routines.

"I appreciate everyone's understanding. Especially since I've reopened the case and plan to do a full investigation myself," Heath said, his tone making it clear he wouldn't tolerate any more snide comments.

Principal Fisher bristled. "I'll be in my office. *If* you need me." He turned and walked away.

Heath and Sean exchanged smiles as if they'd just stopped the schoolyard bully from stealing her lunch money.

Thank You, Lord, for placing people in my life who stand with me and want to solve Becca's murder. Prayer seemed to be getting easier for her. Maybe she'd read in Becca's Bible when she got back to Sean's house.

"If you all will follow me, we'll start in the freshman hall. From there, we'll make our way to the senior hall before looping back through the sophomore and junior halls." Officer Manning led them out of the office.

An hour and a half later, they had spoken to every faculty member except the football coach and his staff. Officer Manning walked them to the football field, stopping just outside the gate. "I'm going to leave you here. I need to get back to the office and make some calls concerning truancy." He glanced at his watch. "Practice is scheduled to be over at noon, so it looks like you have about a fifteen-minute wait. In the meantime, you can sit on the bleachers and watch the team scrimmage. Then Coach Kent will meet you in his office in the field house."

"I need to make a quick phone call. I'll be right back." Heath pulled out his phone and went to stand by the chain-link fence that encircled the field.

Sean swept his hand toward the cold metal bleachers. "Ladies first."

Jenna bounded up the stairs, her footsteps thumping on the metal steps. Reaching the landing, she paused. Coach Kent's son, Tristan, sat on the top row of the bleachers watching the practice. She hadn't expected to see him here. The university was only a few hours from Barton Creek, but still she would have expected the starting quarterback—and projected first-round draft pick—to be on campus, attending classes and finishing up his coursework. After all, graduation was only a few months away.

She started to sit in the closest row, but Sean placed a hand on her shoulder, stopping her.

"Who's the guy at the top?" he asked in a hushed tone.

"Tristan Kent, the coach's son."

"Let's go sit by him. Maybe we can question him."

"It would be a waste of time."

"Why do you say that?"

"For starters, he was a year ahead of Becca, so he was already away at college when she was murdered."

"Doesn't mean he couldn't have heard something when he came home that might lead us to the killer. Did he and Becca have any classes together when he was still in high school? Or maybe have some friends in common?"

"I believe they had a literature class together Becca's sophomore year, and they may have had a math class together her junior year. As far as having friends in common, I don't remember her ever talking about him. I would think, if they attended the same parties and things, she might have mentioned him."

"Let's go to the top."

She glared at him. Wasn't he listening to her?

"I know you think it's a waste of time. But sometimes the people you think know nothing are the best kinds of witnesses. They see or hear things they don't even realize are important, and then they freely share that information. Besides, we have to sit somewhere, so why not near him?" He turned and headed up the bleachers, taking the stairs two at a time.

Jenna went after him. If nothing else, it would be nice to speak to a former student who was doing so well and on a clear path to work in his chosen profession.

As they neared the top row, Tristan stood. "Ms. Hartley. How are you? I didn't expect to see you at Dad's practice."

"I could say the same for you, Tristan." She gave him a sideways hug. "It's good to see you, but I'm surprised you're here in the middle of a semester."

A frown marred the handsome young man's face, and he shrugged one shoulder. "Something came up at home. I'm only here for a quick visit."

"Well, I'm glad I saw you. You're the hometown hero. We'll all be glued to our televisions watching the football draft, cheering for you."

"I'm not a hero, but thank you for your kind words." He looked out over the field. "Looks like Dad just finished up practice. I've gotta go meet him in the locker room."

Tristan made a move to go around her, but Sean stepped into his path. "If you could spare a moment, I wanted to ask you about Becca's murder."

Shock registered on the young man's face. "Why would you ask me about that? I wasn't in high school then."

"I know, but you may have heard someone talk about it. Anything at all. No matter how small you think it may be."

"I don't know what to tell you." Tristan turned to Jenna. "Other than I am sorry…for your loss."

"It's okay, Tristan. I know you and Becca didn't hang out with the same group of friends. So I didn't really expect you to have any information on her death." She forced a smile. "Go on. Tell your dad we had to leave, but we may want to talk to him later."

"Yes, ma'am." He jogged down the steps and ran toward the field house.

"Why did you tell him we'd talk to his dad later? Why not talk to him now since we're here?"

"Coach Kent didn't even know Becca. She wasn't a cheerleader, never attended the games and never had him for a teacher." Jenna sighed. "I have a headache, *and* I'm ready to go. Please." She stepped around him and ambled down the same steps Tristan had just taken. The interaction with the young man had been awkward. For the first time since Becca's death, Jenna felt uncomfortable probing for answers. What right did they have putting innocent people—people who had only known Becca in passing, if at all—on the spot like that?

They reached the bottom step when a frightening idea popped into her head. Jenna spun around to face Sean and lost her footing. His arm snaked out. He caught her and pulled her against him, preventing her from tumbling onto the asphalt track that surrounded the football field.

Her breath caught. Was that his heartbeat or her own echoing in her ear? Muffled words swirled in a fog around her. She pressed her eyes closed and counted to three. Then she pressed her hands against his rock-solid chest and pushed free of his hold.

"Thank you. Um. I'm not normally so clumsy."

"What happened? You spun around so fast…"

The crease in his brow deepened as he studied her, and she fought the urge to squirm.

"It's just… It suddenly occurred to me we could put innocent people in danger by going around asking questions. If the killer sees us talking to someone and he thinks they know more than they do, he could go after them." She wrapped her arms around her waist and hugged herself tightly. Jenna would not be able to forgive herself if she ever were the reason another family had to say goodbye to a loved one.

Sean narrowed his eyes and assessed the woman in front of him. She looked like she might collapse at any moment. He wrapped an arm around her shoulders and headed toward the exit.

Heath came up to them. "Was that Tristan Kent I saw you talking to? Hey, where are you going? We haven't spoken to Coach Kent and his staff yet."

"*We're* headed back to my house," Sean replied without breaking stride. "Jenna's had enough for one day. And no one today could offer any new information. So maybe it's time to take a step back, regroup and assess how to proceed."

Heath walked with them, looking from Jenna to Sean and back again. "That sounds like a good idea. I'll go talk to Coach Kent since I'm already here. But I'll check in with you later. Also, I'm assigning two deputies to watch your house again tonight—"

Jenna stopped in her tracks. "I thought the reason I was staying at Sean's was because you didn't have the personnel to assign deputies to watch me. That he was supposed to protect me."

"Yes, but the shooter got too close last night. So I—"

"And *Sean* protected me. Like he said he would," she replied, in a tone that brooked no argument.

Her fierce defense of him caught Sean by surprise. He wasn't sure if he should be flattered or annoyed. Did she think he needed defending?

Sean pulled back and looked at Jenna. Her face was flushed, and her eyes shone. She'd never looked more beautiful. *Whoa. Where'd that thought come from?* "Look, I—"

"No one said he didn't protect you," Heath said sternly. "If I thought you weren't being protected, I *would* assign officers to guard you twenty-four hours a day. As it is, I'm just sending help for the overnight shift. So you *and* Sean can get some rest knowing someone else is standing watch."

Jenna's mouth formed an O.

Heath's face softened, and he pulled Jenna into an embrace. Sean's gut tightened. He gave himself a mental shake. It wasn't any of his business if the sheriff hugged Jenna. Besides, Heath was at least ten years younger than her. And hadn't she said she used to babysit him when he was a child?

The embrace ended, and Heath met Sean's gaze, one eyebrow arched quizzically. "I'll escort y'all to your vehicle. Take her back to your place. And I'll have my officers out there by nightfall."

Sean hated he couldn't just say no to his friend, but Heath made sense. Sean couldn't protect Jenna if he wasn't rested. Although he knew, even with an officer outside standing watch, he wouldn't get more than a few hours of sleep, it would still be better than no sleep at all. "Thanks, buddy."

A little while later, Sean merged into traffic and headed out of town. "Do you want to tell me what happened back there? Why did you suddenly care if we had officers standing guard again tonight?"

"You said yourself when you volunteered to protect me that the police force was too small for Heath to assign an officer to look out for me. Why, then, would I want the night shift officers to be stuck guarding me? What if something happened in another part of the county that required their attention? It could be a matter of life or death, and they would be delayed because they were babysitting me overnight."

Her behavior was making sense. "Are you still concerned that the killer may have been around today and seen us questioning people on the school campus?"

"Of course I am." She twisted in her seat to look at him. "You're the one that told me when you first moved here that I was putting innocent people in danger with my actions. Yet today, you didn't seem to be concerned if innocent bystanders were being put in harm's way."

A muscle twitching in his jaw. *Choose your words carefully. She is hurt and scared.* "I never should've said that. And I believe I've already apologized for it, so I won't apologize again. But this is a little different. Our actions today were not reckless. Even if the killer saw us on campus today—which, by the way, would mean somewhere in your subconscious, you believe the killer is a member of the school faculty or staff—"

"I never said that. Nor do I believe it."

"Then why would you believe the killer saw us there today? Did you see anyone who didn't belong there on campus while we were walking around?"

She shook her head. "No. I recognized everyone we saw, and they were all employees of the school, except for Tristan."

"Do you think he could be the killer?"

"No."

"Okay, no one should be in danger because they spoke to us. If they were, then the killer we're seeking is one of your former coworkers. And he'd have to have reason to believe someone else knows his secret. If the killer thought anyone could identify him, do you really think that the person would be alive to talk to us?"

She settled back into her seat and turned to watch the scenery go by. He hated being short with her, but he needed her to understand that if Becca's killer did kill someone else, it wouldn't be her fault. *Just like it wasn't her fault the killer was after her.* If Sheriff Rice hadn't decided it was easier to label Becca's death a suicide than to admit he didn't know how to solve the case, Jenna wouldn't have started her podcast. She had only been doing what any good mother would do—fighting for justice for her child. No one would intentionally step into a killer's path, and Sean knew that. So why had he been so harsh with her in the beginning?

No changing it now. All he could do was protect her and help her find the answers she needed.

"We didn't finish going through that last box of Becca's things. Do you feel like tackling that when we get back to my house?"

"Sure," she replied, without looking in his direction.

Dear Lord, please don't let her get swallowed up by her pain and despair. I can't solve this case without her, and I can't protect her if I can't figure out who I'm protecting her from. I know the answer to Becca's murder is somewhere close by. Let me—no, let us—find it soon. And, Lord, please don't let Jenna's fear of an innocent person becoming this killer's next victim because of our investigation become a reality. If that were to happen, I don't know how she would overcome her grief and guilt.

Picking up the blue snowman mug Sean had placed in front of her some time ago, Jenna took a sip of coffee. And almost immediately spit it out again. *Yuck.*

"Do you want me to freshen it up?" Sean asked.

"What?" She frowned at him.

"Your coffee." He nodded at her mug. "It's cold, right? Which isn't surprising, since I fixed it for you an hour ago."

"Really? I didn't think it had been that long." She straightened and rubbed the back of her neck. "Okay, so yeah, I guess I lost track of time."

Jenna picked up her mug, pushed her chair back from the table, stood, crossed to the sink and dumped the contents down the drain. "I'm sorry I wasted the coffee."

"Don't be. I assure you, I've wasted my fair share of coffee through the years. When you're a detective working on a big case, there are a lot of cold cups of coffee involved." He shrugged. "Some you pour down the drain and some you drink because you've not stopped long enough to eat or drink anything else all day."

She looked out the window above the sink. The sun was setting over the Appalachian Mountains. Streaks of purple, gold, red and orange decorated the sky, like paint strokes on a canvas. It was a breathtaking view. One she had often enjoyed from the swing in the backyard of her condo, but one she hadn't taken the time to enjoy since moving into her current house.

Sean came over to stand beside her. "You seem deep in thought."

"Just admiring God's artwork." Her throat tightened, and she swallowed. "I'm ashamed to admit it, but I've not really given my relationship with Him much thought since I lost Becca."

"No need to be ashamed. I understand, probably more than you know. After Felicia died, I spent the next two years in a fog. It wasn't until I moved to Barton Creek that I found my way back to church and rekindled my relationship with the Lord." He leaned over to peer out the window. "I'm thankful to Heath for encouraging me to put in the effort. Of course, I still falter and struggle from time to time, when I let my grief overwhelm me. But I now realize my anger was misplaced. God wasn't the one who took Felicia away from me. Instead of *me* being the one that needed to forgive Him, *He* was the one who had to forgive me. One great thing about our Heavenly Father, He never stops loving us or welcoming us back into the fold."

His words settled over her. Mom and Amber had said similar words to her in the past, and it had always irritated her that they were *pushing* her to *forgive* God. Although she knew their words came from a place of love, somehow she'd always taken it as them being preachy. However, Sean's words hadn't come across that way. Was it because he'd suffered a similar loss? Maybe she should take Becca's Bible to bed with her tonight and reacquaint herself with the Word.

Sean went to the refrigerator, pulled out creamer and turned to her. "Would you like a fresh cup?"

"Yes. Thank you." She handed her mug to him.

He added a splash of creamer to their mugs and then poured

hot black coffee into both of them. She accepted hers and returned to her chair at the table.

"I thought you drank your coffee black." Jenna took a sip of the hot liquid.

"Most of the time, but occasionally, I'll add creamer. Sometimes I'll even add a spoonful of sugar."

Jenna giggled. She had no idea why she thought what he'd said was funny. Maybe the mental exhaustion of the past few days had caught up with her.

Sean's phone dinged. He picked it up and read a text message. "It's from Heath. The deputies standing watch tonight will be here within the hour. And he wants you to know that a couple of off-duty officers have volunteered to be on call and will tend to any issues in the county overnight." He smiled and quickly typed out a response. "Heath's mom is sending over beef stew and cornbread for our supper."

Jenna hated that Marilyn Dalton had gone to so much trouble, but she knew better than to refuse the kindness. "Send my thanks, too, please."

"Already done." He placed the phone back on the table and settled into the chair he'd vacated earlier. "Do you need a break? Or should we keep working until the food arrives?"

"I'm fine. Let's keep going."

There was only one more item they hadn't looked through yet, and that was Becca's senior yearbook. They had been handed out at school two days after Becca's death, so Becca had never even seen it.

Jenna pulled the yearbook out of the box and ran her hand over the cover. Instead of having Becca's teachers and classmates simply sign their name in a guest book to denote their attendance at Becca's funeral, Jenna had requested that they sign Becca's yearbook, leaving comments of memories they'd shared throughout her high school years. She gasped. "This... this triggered the attacks."

Jenna locked gazes with Sean. "I always record my podcasts

five days before I upload them online so I have plenty of time to complete edits. As you know, in addition to the traditional audio version, I also post a video version of me recording the podcast. That way people can choose the format they prefer. At the end of the video version, I display a few inspirational quotes or something as a bonus for the people who choose to watch. When I edited last week's video, it was about ten minutes shorter than usual. Since there was a larger gap of time that needed to be filled, I pulled out this yearbook and shared some of the sweet comments Becca's classmates had written."

She jumped out of her chair. "I'll be right back."

Running through the house, she darted into the guest room, grabbed her laptop bag and raced back to the kitchen. Breathing hard, she plopped onto the chair, settled her laptop onto the table and powered it on. "I took snapshots of the quotes, being careful not to include the names of the authors since I didn't want to infringe upon anyone's privacy, and did a slideshow for the end of the podcast."

Sean scooted his chair closer and leaned in so he could see the laptop screen. "Who wrote the messages you displayed?"

"I don't remember." *Ugh.* If only she'd kept better records and written the names and quotes in one of her notebooks instead of just putting the pictures into a slideshow. "I took the pictures of the messages months ago. I was just saving them until I needed them."

She opened the folder for the podcast from last week and quickly fast-forwarded to the end. The first slide flashed on the screen. Becca, thanks for tutoring me through geometry. It was quickly replaced by another. I will never forget how you were always so kind to everyone. And another. You will forever be missed!

"How many are there?"

Jenna furrowed her brow. "I'm not sure. Maybe fifteen or sixteen. I just kind of threw some random ones in until I thought I had enough."

"Okay, so I guess we need to freeze the screen on each image and then look through the yearbook for the handwriting and wording that matches it."

She reached for a pen and paper. "Or, since this isn't really a two-person job, I can do this while you do something else."

He looked like he might argue, but then he nodded. "I'll feed Beau."

Jenna nodded and opened the yearbook. Her eyes scanned the pages, and she quickly located the first two quotes. After jotting down the quotes and the names of the students who'd written them, she excitedly turned the pages. It didn't surprise her that Becca's closest friends—her childhood friends—had written the first four quotes. Working her way through the book, she located all but one quote. Then, on the inside of the back cover, she spotted it, written in small cursive handwriting with sharp edges. *I will miss your laughter and your smile.*

Whose signature was that? She leaned in and squinted. *Tristan Kent.* Jenna collapsed against the chair. Did Tristan know Becca better than she thought? No. Maybe? Jenna's mind whirled. She pinched the bridge of her nose and squeezed her eyes shut.

"Do you have a headache?" Sean asked from behind her. "Should I get you some pain meds?"

"No." Jenna opened her eyes, looked up at him and shrugged. "I found all of the quotes I shared on the podcast. And I know who wrote them."

Sean rested his hip against the countertop and waited.

She swallowed. "One of them was written by Tristan Kent."

"And the rest of the quotes?"

Picking up the notepad, she held it out for him to inspect. "I've listed all the names."

"Tomorrow, we'll see how many of these people we can locate and question. After we finish, if we still have questions, we'll pay Tristan a visit."

"Do you think he knows more than he let on today?"

"I'm not a mind reader. I'm a detective." Sean frowned. "When we saw him today, Tristan said he didn't know anything. Before we question him again, we need evidence that he is lying. Otherwise, we're not going to get anywhere, and he's going to say we're badgering him and trying to frame him."

Jenna gasped. "I would never do that. And I do not believe Tristan Kent is a killer."

The thought that someone so young could kill and cover it up for so long was terrifying. No. She had to be right about Tristan. Her judgment couldn't be that bad.

Chapter Twelve

Sean opened the front door and stepped out into the cold, bright morning. A crust of frost covered the grassy areas, and the sun glimmered off the ice crystals, making them sparkle like diamonds. The weather the past week had been cooler than normal. But he didn't mind. There was something invigorating about the fresh mountain air on a chilly February day.

A sheriff's department cruiser was parked to the side of the driveway, an officer sitting in the driver's seat, his attention focused on his computer. Sean puffed out a breath and watched as a small fog wafted into the air. Then he headed across the lawn with Beau at his heels. As he approached the cruiser, the driver-side door opened and Deputy Moore climbed out.

Sean held up the thermos of coffee and two disposable coffee cups he was carrying in his hands. "I thought you guys might like to have something to warm you up."

"Thank you." Deputy Moore accepted the thermos. "Chris is doing one last sweep of the perimeter. I'm sure he will appreciate this when he returns."

"Were there any disturbances overnight?"

"No. Everything was quiet. Almost eerily so."

Sean tilted his head. "What do you mean?"

"I'm sure it was nothing. But there were no sounds. All night. Not even movement or night noises of wildlife." The younger man shrugged. "Maybe it was too cold last night, and all the deer and raccoons and things found places to burrow and stay warm."

Sean pondered this. The deputy was probably correct in his assumption, but in all the nights he'd spent on this farm, he'd never known there to be complete silence. But now that he thought back to the evening before, he realized Beau hadn't barked once. And the coonhound always barked when he heard the raccoons and the foxes yapping in the night.

A chilly breeze blew through the trees, and he shivered. "Breakfast will be ready in ten minutes. We'd like it if you both joined us."

"Thank you, but we need to head on back to the station. We still have paperwork to complete and reports to file before we can go home to our families."

Sean understood all too well the desire to get home to a family but having to complete paperwork first, even on nights when there was no action. "Okay. Thank you for being the watchmen last night so I could get some shut-eye."

He tipped his head, then turned and jogged back to the house, lifting his hand to wave at the other deputy in passing.

Pounding through the front door, he inhaled deeply. The smell of sausage frying mixed with the scent of strong coffee, along with the sound of a woman humming as she worked, greeted him. He picked up his pace, joy in his heart. Rounding the corner to the dining room, his steps faltered, and he stopped, staring in disbelief. Jenna stood at the sink, looking out the window. The scene before him brought him crashing back to reality. Felicia was dead. Jenna had been the one humming. Though logically he'd known that when he heard the sound, his heart had momentarily forgotten.

Jenna turned and smiled at him, and his breath caught in his throat.

"Good morning," she greeted him in a singsongy voice.

He frowned. Why was she suddenly so chipper? The smile on her face faded away, and remorse settled over him. Sean cleared his throat. "Good morning. I take it you slept well?"

"Yes. I hope you did as well."

He nodded, unable to tell her yes but also unable to say no. While he had only slept about five hours, he had rested well.

"Will the officers be joining us for breakfast? I was about to scramble the eggs."

"I invited them, but they have to get back to the station." He crossed over to the refrigerator, opened it and removed the carton of eggs. She held out her hand, and he relinquished them to her. No point in arguing over who would cook the eggs, though he had never shared cooking duties with anyone other than Felicia. Even his grandmother had never allowed him in her kitchen—*this* kitchen—when she'd been alive.

"Are you going to tell me what put you in such a good mood?"

She broke an egg and emptied its contents into a bowl and whisked. "I'm not sure how to explain it, but I just feel like we're getting close to a breakthrough. That sounds silly, doesn't it? Considering I don't have any hard evidence to support the idea. But for the moment, I choose to embrace contentment and hope."

He settled at the table and picked up the notebook from the night before. "Are you still convinced Tristan Kent knows nothing about Becca's death?"

She poured the egg mixture into a sizzling-hot skillet, moving the golden liquid around with a spatula. He wondered if she was going to ignore his question as she removed shredded cheese from the refrigerator and added a generous sprinkle to the eggs.

"I know you think I'm being naive or that I'm not considering all options, but I really don't believe Tristan would kill anyone. I know him. He's a good kid." She reached into the cabinet and removed two plates. "A lot of boys would have broken under the pressure that he had to endure growing up. His dad pushed him every step of the way to be the best he could be at football. But Tristan loves his dad and only wants to make him proud."

Jenna plated the eggs, then placed one dish in front of him and the other at her seat. *Whoa.* When had he started thinking of that seat as Jenna's spot? He shoved a bite of egg into his mouth, chewed and swallowed, forcing the food past the lump lodged in his throat.

"He also has a cousin who has special needs," Jenna continued, obviously oblivious to Sean's inner struggle. "I have seen him stand up for her when others wanted to bully and make fun of her. I've also seen him carry books for an underclassman with a broken leg without being asked to do so. A lot of athletes who are viewed as superstars and are almost idolized by their classmates would have acted differently, maybe even joining in on the bullying. They would act tough and above the rules because they would want to fit in with their peers, but not Tristan. He always stood up for his beliefs."

She sat down and seasoned her eggs. "Does that sound like a kid who is a murderer?"

"Killers don't always fit a set stereotype. Several killers throughout history were seemingly good people."

A frown briefly marred her face. She forked a bite of egg and shoved it into her mouth.

There was nothing else to say, so they ate their meal in silence. When they finished, Sean stood and took both plates to the sink. "You cooked, so I'll do the cleanup."

"Sounds good." She drank the last of her coffee and then pushed back her chair. "If you'll excuse me, I need to go to my—the guest room—and work on my podcast."

"Before you go…" He scraped the remnants of the meal into the garbage disposal. "Why do you think Tristan came back for the funeral of an acquaintance? You said he was away at college when Becca died, right?"

"Yes, but it's only two hours away. So it's easy for him to make a quick trip home to Barton Creek, especially when football season is over."

"Do you still think they weren't friends?"

"I have no reason to believe they were more than acquaintances."

"Then explain to me why he would write what he did in her yearbook."

"Because he was in my Algebra I class his freshman year. He was a star student. And when I accepted the counselor's position his junior year, he made a point of telling me he thought I'd be great at the job, and he thanked me for preparing him for college. A kid who has a teacher they feel pushes them to be their best and helps them get into college would want to come and offer condolences at the death of that teacher's child. Besides, several people wrote in Becca's yearbook that they would miss her smile or miss her laughter. She was a joyful person, and people noticed. His comment could simply be a sign of respect."

He placed the last dish into the draining rack. "So do you think the person responsible for Becca's death is one of the other students?"

She offered a half shrug. "I don't know. I'll have to examine that more closely after I finish the edits on my show so I can schedule the upload. It's supposed to go live tomorrow."

"Are you sure that's a good idea?"

"What do you mean?"

"Just that right now, someone is desperately trying to kill you. Is it a good idea to post more content that might enrage him further?"

She raised an eyebrow. "Do you really think if I stopped the podcast today and never posted another episode, never spoke about Becca's death again, that it would make a difference, and the person who is after me would just go away?"

She had him there. He knew as well as she did that it didn't matter at this point what she said or did. The threat would not go away. He clenched his teeth, and his jaw muscle twitched.

"I didn't think so." She turned and walked out of the room without another word.

Lord, I hope she's right about Tristan. She defends him as if he were her own child. It's obvious she developed a strong bond with him when he was her student. I'd hate for her to discover he was involved in this.

Ten minutes later, he dried the last dish and placed it on the shelf where it belonged. Then he turned off the light and headed down the hall toward his office. Pausing outside Jenna's door, he lifted a hand to knock and froze. He owed her an apology for arguing with her over petty issues. But he hated to interrupt her while she was working.

Entering his office, he went over to his desk and picked up his worn leather Bible, then settled into the oversize chair in the corner of the room. Opening the book, he started reading in Ecclesiastes, chapter three, where he'd left off last time.

Sean's phone rang, and he glanced at the ID. Douglas Anthony. Swiping his finger across the screen, he answered and put the phone on speaker. "Hello?"

"Sean. I hate to bother you, but a tree fell on my fence on the south side of the pasture, where our properties join. The missus and I leave tomorrow to visit her folks in Iowa, and I have to get it repaired today. But my ranch hand is in Nashville and won't be back until late this evening, so I don't have any help. Could you give me about an hour of your time? It's really a two-man job."

"Of cour—" He swallowed his reply. He couldn't leave Jenna. Could he convince her to put on a pair of his overalls and lend a hand? "Actually, Douglas, I'm not sure I can. I'm kind of in the middle of something here."

"What are you in the middle of?" Jenna stood in the doorway.

He pressed the mute button on his phone. "You know very well what I'm in the middle of. I can't just leave you here. Unless... Do you want to go out in the cold and help repair a barbed wire fence?"

"I would, but unfortunately, I have to finish my edits. That doesn't mean you can't go."

"I can't *leave you* here," he repeated.

She nodded at the phone in his hand.

"Sean? Sean, are you still there?" Douglas asked, over and over.

So distracted by the conversation with Jenna, Sean had completely tuned out the man on the phone.

He unmuted the device and took a deep breath. "I'm here. Sorry, but I'll get back to you. I won't be long."

After disconnecting the call, he turned his attention to Jenna. She stood with her hand on her hip. He had seen that same stance several times during his marriage, when his wife's opinions had differed from his. No matter. He would not give in to Jenna. Either they both went or neither did.

"Can you take your laptop and work in my vehicle while I help Mr. Anthony?"

"Not really." She relaxed her arms and leaned against the doorframe. "I appreciate that you're trying to keep me safe, but trying to work, sitting in a vehicle, while you and Douglas use a chain saw would be too distracting. He said it would take less than an hour, which means it's probably not a large tree. I can stay here, with all the doors and windows locked. Beau will be here to protect me, and I know where the rifle is if I need it."

"I'm st—"

"And," she said, interrupting his argument, "I'm sure if I call you, you can be back in under two minutes."

They locked gazes, neither speaking for several long seconds. He picked up his phone and texted Douglas, I'll meet you at the property line.

Sean prayed he wouldn't regret his decision to leave Jenna and help his only other neighbor.

Chapter Thirteen

Jenna twisted the dead bolt and then pressed her ear against the door. "Did you hear that?"

"Yes," Sean replied from the other side. "Leave it locked until I get home."

"Just go already. I'll be fine. Beau is here with me. You know he'll do a good job guarding me. And I have the rifle. I'm going to work on my podcast. Bye."

Once she heard the ATV motor start, she went to the guest bedroom and grabbed her laptop bag, her laptop, headphones and cell phone. Then she went back into the kitchen, where she placed everything on the table. Snagging a mug out of the cabinet, she poured a cup of coffee and settled in at the table, ready to work, with Beau at her feet. The house was exceptionally quiet, enabling her to hear every creak and moan as the wind howled outside.

"It's an old house, Jenna. Don't let your imagination run away with you." After opening a new tab on her computer, she navigated to her favorite music-streaming website and pulled up a playlist of soft instrumental jazz. Beau howled.

"Come on, boy. Surely you like good music." The coonhound

laid his head on the floor and covered his face with a paw. She giggled. "Okay, I won't force you to listen to my music."

She pulled her laptop bag closer and dug around inside until her hand closed around her headphone case. Opening it, she pulled out one earbud and pressed it into her ear. She needed the noise to settle her nerves, but she still needed to listen for an intruder. Allowing the music to envelop her, she quickly got to work editing the bonus material she was adding to the end of the video clip.

Forty-five minutes later, she completed the last edit and initiated the video upload to the podcast host site. Standing, she rubbed the back of her neck, then crossed to the coffeepot and poured herself a fresh cup. Her phone rang, and she jumped with a start.

Picking the device up off the table, she looked at the screen. A local number scrolled across the top. She didn't recognize it. Probably a telemarketer. She ignored it and turned to her computer to check the upload progress. The ringing stopped, but then started again almost immediately. The same number. She slid her finger across the screen and answered the call. "Hello?"

"Ms. Hartley, it's Tristan. Tristan Kent. I hope… That is…"

He sounded out of breath, as if he'd been running. Her heart raced. What if he was in trouble because he had spoken to her yesterday? Could the killer be chasing him?

"Tristan, is something wrong? Where are you? Is someone trying to hurt you?"

"No, I'm okay. After I saw you yesterday, I started to think. And I need to talk to you, to tell you what I know."

"What do you mean?" She clutched the phone tighter. "Do you know who killed Becca?" If he knew something, why had he not told her before? She tamped down her anger and released a slow breath. "Tristan, if you know who killed Becca, tell me. They're after me now. My life is in danger."

"I know who's after you," he whispered. "I'll stop him before he can hurt you. I promise to protect you. For Becca." His voice cracked, and a sob came across the line.

"Don't do anything to put yourself in danger, Tristan. Just tell me who it is. I'll call Sheriff Dalton. He can arrest the person and put a stop to this, once and for all."

"No. I'll call the sheriff later. I promise. But I need to talk to you first. I need to explain why I didn't come forward sooner and tell you what I knew. But I need to do this in person. Is there any way you can meet me?"

"Of course. Just tell me where you are. I'm ready to put this nightmare behind me—well, I can't ever truly put it behind me, but I'm ready for answers. So Becca's death doesn't continue to consume me."

"I understand. And I'm ready to release the information I've been holding on to. I just hope you can forgive me for not telling you sooner. I should've told you yesterday, but I was afraid of what he would do if I did."

"Who is *he*?"

"I can't tell. Not yet."

"I won't let him hurt you, Tristan. Tell me where to meet you."

"You pick a spot. It needs to be somewhere he won't think to look for us. I don't want him finding us before I talk to the sheriff... We don't want to put others in danger, but I understand if you want to make it a public place. I know I'm asking a lot for you to meet me."

"Why don't we meet at the sheriff's office? We would be safe there. You could talk to me and Sheriff Dalton at the same time."

"No! Please. I need to explain everything to you first. I'll go straight to the sheriff, afterward, but *please* let me talk to you alone first."

"What if I bring Sean with me? He's the man you met yesterday. You can trust him."

"I won't talk with him. He's a former cop." The sound of

someone knocking on a door came across the line, followed by the sound of a flushing toilet and running water. "I've gotta go," Tristan said in a hushed whisper.

"No, wait!" *Lord, I have to find out the truth about what happened to Becca. Please let Tristan be on the up and up, and don't let Sean be mad at me for leaving the house.* "I'll meet you. Meet me at Thatcher Park. There may be a few people at the playground, but in the back corner, there's a small parking area and a meditation memorial garden few people are aware of. I can be there in twenty minutes." This was the best compromise she could think of for a public meeting place that was still private.

"I know exactly where it is. I'll be there waiting for you."

Jenna disconnected the call and headed toward the door, then stopped. How was she going to get there? For a moment, she'd completely forgotten her truck had blown up. She didn't have a vehicle, and even if she could find a rental place that made deliveries in Barton Creek, there was no time.

Sean had driven his ATV to meet Douglas. His SUV was still here. She could *borrow* it. But where were the keys? *Think.* The first night she'd spent in his house, he'd hung his keys on a hook beside the pantry door. She quickly crossed the room. *Yes!* His keys dangled from a hook. She clutched them in her hand and raced for the front door with Beau at her heels, barking and nipping at her feet.

"Stop it, Beau."

The hound nipped at her again, caught her shoestring in his mouth and pulled, untying her shoes. She swatted him away with her hand and quickly retied her shoe. Then she looped her arm around the dog's neck and hugged him tight.

"It's going to be okay, boy. I promise. I know what I'm doing." He licked her cheek, and she buried her face in his furry neck. Did she really know what she was doing? Or was she being reckless? What advice would she give someone in her position?

She pushed to her feet and went back to the kitchen table. Grabbing the notepad and pen, she jotted down a note telling Sean exactly where she was going and who she was meeting. Then she grabbed a handful of dry dog food, carried it to the sunroom and dropped it into Beau's food bowl. He rushed over to it and ate, and she eased out of the room, closing the French door behind her. He looked up, whimpered and then turned back to his snack. "I'm sorry, buddy, but I have to go."

Jenna turned and raced out the front door. She was finally going to get the answers she had been looking for.

Sweat ran down Sean's neck despite the temperature being a cool forty-seven degrees. He wiped it away with his gloved hand and squinted at the sun. They had been working for almost an hour and a half. He'd been gone much longer than he had expected. While Douglas had been correct and the fence was a quick repair, the job hadn't been small at all. A large fallen tree had needed to be cut away before they could repair the fence. Fortunately, the tree had missed the posts, so it would simply be a matter of pulling the barbed wire taut and reattaching it once they removed the last section of the tree. Hopefully, Sean would be headed home soon.

He turned to watch the chain saw in his neighbor's hands chew through a seven-inch-diameter limb. The bar broke through the wood, and the limb dropped to the ground. Douglas cut the motor on the chain saw, and Sean grabbed hold of the limb and pulled it off the barbed wire. Then both men stretched the barbed wire taut and fastened it into place.

Sean swung the hammer and drove his last fencing staple into place. He dropped the tool into the open toolbox and turned to Douglas. "I hate to leave you with all this cleanup, but I really need to get back to the house."

"I heard Jenna is staying at your place while the sheriff is trying to capture the person who has been attacking her."

Sean knew the older man wasn't trying to gossip or find out

details from him concerning Jenna—it was more a matter of a neighbor showing concern. Still, he would never share the details of an open case with anyone. It wasn't ethical. Besides, even though he strongly suspected Douglas Anthony wasn't guilty of killing Becca, or trying to kill Jenna, he didn't know who was, so it was best to keep silent.

"Well, I'll get going."

"Tell Jenna the missus and I are praying for her." Douglas followed him to his ATV. "Keep her safe."

Sean nodded, straddled his ATV and raced across the field, the small vehicle bouncing over the terraces. He hoped Jenna had finished her podcast edits. He wanted to sit down with her and do some internet sleuthing. Maybe they could find Becca's classmates on social media and find connections between them and Becca, photos and whatnot, from around the time of her death. If so, the information could lead them to the killer.

He pulled the ATV up to the back of the house and parked it close to the patio. Turning off the motor, he dismounted and headed toward the back door. The minute he stepped onto the patio, Beau started howling. He sounded as if he were close by. Sean turned toward the sunroom and could see furry paws reaching up under the closed blinds, scratching at the windows.

The hairs on the back of Sean's neck stood at attention. Why was Beau in the sunroom? Had Jenna put him in there because he was bothering her while she worked? No. Surely not. If that had been the case, she would've let him free by now. His howling and scratching had to be more distracting to her work. Sean jogged to the back door and twisted the knob. Locked. He banged on the door. "Jenna! Jenna, let me in!"

Beau's cries grew louder, as if he were in great distress. Sean had to get inside. Was the spare key still where his grandmother had hidden it years ago? He stepped off the patio and crossed to the garden gnome that stood watch in his grandmother's flower bed. Picking up the figurine, he found the key embedded in the dirt beneath it. Snatching it up, he wiped it on his pants and ran back to the door.

He entered the kitchen. It was empty. Jenna's laptop sat on the table, a screen saver montage of photos flashing across the screen.

"Jenna, where are you? Answer me!" he yelled as he went from room to room.

No answer and no Jenna. Had the killer taken Jenna and locked Beau in the sunroom? It didn't feel or look like a crime scene. Knowing Jenna, if someone had abducted her, she wouldn't have gone without a fight. There would have been chairs knocked over or broken lamps or something. Instead, there was just a distraught Beau looking into the house from the other side of the French doors. Moving through the living room, Sean opened the door, and the coonhound darted out and made a beeline for the front door. Which was locked. A criminal wouldn't have taken the time to lock the house up before leaving. Jenna had left off her own free will. But she didn't have a vehicle. Unless...

He grasped the doorknob and fumbled with the lock. Finally, he unlocked the latch and yanked open the front door. Stepping outside, he looked at where he had parked his SUV last night. It was gone. She had taken his vehicle. But where was she? And why would she leave without telling him?

Sean stomped back into the house and made his way to the kitchen. He sat down at the table in front of her computer. Maybe he could find answers. He clicked a button, and the screen saver went away. But a password prompt replaced it. Now what?

Beau placed his front paws on his leg.

"Where did she go?" Sean asked, peering into the dog's sad eyes. "Too bad you can't answer me. Now, go. Let me think."

The coonhound slunk under the table, and Sean ducked to look at him lying on the floor. "I'm sorry, buddy. I know you're worried about her, too."

Straightening, Sean's shoulder connected with a notebook, knocking it to the floor. He bent to pick it up and was about to place it back on the table when the handwriting caught his attention. It was a note scribbled by Jenna.

Sean, I'm sorry I had to leave without telling you. I've gone to meet Tristan. He knows who the killer is. Said he'd talk to Heath but wanted to talk to me first. Couldn't tell us anything yesterday because the killer was watching him. Meeting at Thatcher Park. Don't worry. I'll be back soon and fill you in. Jenna

He pushed his chair back and jumped to his feet. What was she thinking? How could she have gone without telling him? He knew the answer to that. She'd been afraid he wouldn't let her go alone. And he wouldn't have. Reaching into his back pocket, he pulled out his phone and dialed Heath.

As soon as the phone stopped ringing—before Heath had a chance to speak—Sean blurted, "Jenna's in trouble. You need to send help immediately."

"Is she at your house?"

"No, she went to Thatcher Park to meet Tristan Kent. He says he knows who killed Becca. I have a bad feeling."

"When did she leave? And why did you let her go alone?"

"I didn't. And I don't know when she left. I was helping Douglas with…" He puffed out a breath. "Look, I never dreamed that she would willingly leave to go meet someone. But she did. And she took my vehicle. So please send help."

"I can't. There was an accident involving a school bus on Rudd Hollow Road. My officers are out there directing traffic and dealing with the injured. And I'm on my way back from Sevierville."

Frustration bubbled up inside him. Sean had let down another woman who'd expected him to protect her. "Her life is in danger."

"Listen, Sean, Jenna is a smart woman. If she thought Tristan was a threat, she wouldn't have gone."

Sean didn't care that Jenna had felt safe. Felicia had felt safe, too, in her own driveway in a gated community. Sometimes, no matter the precautions one took, things still went terribly wrong. "How far are you from Barton Creek?"

"Ten minutes."

"Can you swing by and pick me up? I want to go with you."

"Sure. In the meantime, say a prayer for her safety."

Sean disconnected his phone and shoved it into his back pocket. *Lord, let Heath be right. Let Tristan be a good guy, and let Jenna be safe. Please. I beg of You.*

Chapter Fourteen

Jenna pulled Sean's SUV into the same parking space they had parked in two days ago—a green Jeep was two spaces away. There were no other vehicles in sight. Jenna exited the SUV, walked over to the Jeep and looked through the tinted windows. The vehicle was empty. There was a practice jersey in the passenger seat. This had to be Tristan's vehicle. Where was he? Had he gone for a walk in the memorial garden?

"Lord, don't let the person after me find us here. I don't know how I could ever live with the guilt if something happens to Tristan because he's helping me. Please guide my steps and protect us from the danger lurking in the shadows. If something happens to me, Sean will feel guilty, even though it won't be his fault. And, Lord, forgive me for trying to do this all on my own, and for not leaning on You for strength when I lost my sweet Becca. I now know that I can't get through any of life's bumps or heartaches without You."

Her phone rang, the sound piercing the silence. Sean's name flashed on the screen.

"Please don't answer it," Tristan said from behind her.

Spinning around, she saw him standing beneath the arched entrance to the meditation garden. Jenna rejected the call with an automated text saying she couldn't talk right now. Then she pressed down on the small button on the side of the phone to silence it, not wanting to attract attention from others who were enjoying the playground area of the park.

"Okay. I've silenced my phone." She slipped it into her jacket pocket. "Do you want to talk in my vehicle?"

The young man shook his head. Then he turned and walked into the garden.

A calm peace she couldn't explain if she tried settled over her, and she trailed him.

They walked in silence until they reached a short wooden bridge that crossed a narrow creek. Tristan stopped and leaned against the railing, a sad expression on his face. "Becca loved this garden. Did you know she ate lunch here at least twice a month, no matter how warm or cold the weather was? She said that being in this garden brought her a sense of peace and that she thought it was the closest she'd ever get to the peace you felt when you would hike in the woods."

Tightness gripped Jenna's chest. How had she not known this about her own daughter? And why had Becca kept her friendship with Tristan a secret from her?

He locked gazes with her, and the pain she saw in the depths of his eyes chilled her to the core. "You were the person Becca had lunch with the day she died."

"Yes. It was our first and only date." Tears streamed down his face as loud sobs racked his body.

She tamped down the urge to comfort him and tell him it would be okay. Until she knew what happened to her daughter, her maternal instincts would have to remain dormant. "Did you kill Becca?"

"No! I could never have hurt her. I would have done anything to keep her safe. You'll never know how many times I've cried myself to sleep, begging God to turn back time and take me in her place."

If only it were possible to bring back the dead by offering

to exchange places with them, Becca would've returned long ago because Jenna had made the same useless plea to God.

"Were you with her when she died?"

He opened his mouth, then closed it, and the muscle in his jaw twitched. Looking down at his hands, he whispered, "Forgive me, Lord." Then he turned toward Jenna, his gaze seemingly looking straight through her. And an icy shiver shook her entire body.

"It was my first year at college. The football practices and games were so time-consuming that I struggled to keep my grades up. It was Christmas break. I was only home for a few days because we had a bowl game. And I had to get back to campus for additional practices. But I was determined to get a head start on my assignments for the next semester. I was doing research and needed a book. So I came to the Maryville library to see if they had it, and Becca helped me. We'd had classes together in high school, but we never hung out with the same crowds. So I never really spoke to her until that day. She had the most beautiful smile I had ever seen. I flirted with her, and she brushed me off. But I was enamored with her, so every time I came home, I found an excuse to go to the library. I knew she would be there. We started talking and were amazed at the things we had in common. Soon we became friends. We started chatting online, and I asked her out for Valentine's Day. But again, she turned me down. I was hurt, so I stayed away for a few weeks, and I ignored her when she reached out."

Nausea enveloped Jenna. How had she not known about any of this? Why hadn't Becca confided in her? She thought they had been close. That they'd had a relationship that most mothers and daughters could only dream of having. Had it all been a lie?

Her legs shook. "I need a place to sit down."

"There's a bench near the sand-and-rock garden." He reached for her arm. "Here, let me help you."

She dodged his grasp. "No! I can manage on my own."

He looked as if she had slapped him. She immediately regretted the pain she had caused him, but at that moment, her senses were on overload. And she could not bear the thought of him touching her.

They walked in silence. She had the sudden thought that going deeper into the garden with him was just leading her farther and farther away from help. Her steps faltered, and she stumbled on a patch of uneven ground. Tristan caught her, steadying her. She jumped back, his touch making her physically ill.

"I won't hurt you." He held up his hands, palms out, in surrender. "I understand why you don't want me to touch you, but I couldn't let you fall and get hurt. I wasn't able to keep one Hartley girl safe, and the pain and guilt have been more than I can endure. Once I finish telling you the story, I'll go straight to the sheriff. I will also avoid you at all costs in the future so you don't have to see me and I don't heap additional pain upon you."

More than he could endure? What about the pain she'd gone through for nearly four years, not knowing what had happened to Becca? Had he never once thought about that—her neverending pain? Tears burned her eyes, and her throat tightened. She moistened her lips. "Tell me what happened. I will listen and reserve judgment." She walked over to the bench, sat down and scooted to the opposite side, sitting on the edge.

He frowned and sat down, leaving two feet of space between them. "Becca called me and left me a voice message. She said that she really liked me and didn't want to lose my friendship. That she promised you she would get her college degree before she seriously dated. So she mostly just hung out with people in groups, and she was afraid if she allowed herself to go on a date with me, she might not be able to keep her promise to you. If she stopped thinking we were just friends, she was sure she would fall in love...with me."

He picked at the side seam of his blue jeans. "I told her I understood because I was already falling for her."

A cloud drifted in front of the sun, and the shadows deepened in the grove of bamboo to their left.

"We agreed to keep in touch via text and to not see each other in person because the temptation to want to go on a date and see where the relationship would go would be too great."

"Why didn't I see any text messages between you when I looked through Becca's phone?" she blurted out, unable to stop herself.

"My middle name is Jordan. I asked Becca to use that name in her phone for me because I knew if you saw it, you would think the person sending the text was a girl. But we also always texted through an app that deletes the messages as soon as they have been read. I'm sorry."

He grimaced. "My aunt Harriet used to say nothing good will ever come from a lie or a deception. Oh, how I wish I would have heeded her words. If I had, maybe Becca would be alive today."

A twig snapped, and a red fox scurried out of the trees and across the bridge. Jenna placed her hand on her chest, willing her heartbeat to slow. She released a long breath. "What happened that day? Why did y'all decide to meet that afternoon if y'all had previously decided to not see each other in person again?"

"I had—"

"Stop right there, Tristan." Coach David Kent stepped out of the woods, a pistol in his hands. "I told you I'd handle this. Now, you need to get out of here. Go home. Let me take care of things."

"No, sir." Tristan scooted closer to Jenna and placed a hand on her arm, his eyes never leaving his father. "I told you, it's past time for me to own up to my mistakes. It's long overdue."

"But you did nothing wrong. *You* didn't kill Becca," David insisted. "She wouldn't have wanted you to give up your education or your chance at the pros because of her clumsiness."

He was blaming Becca for her own death? An involuntary

gasp escaped Jenna, drawing David's ire. He took a step forward, raising his weapon and peering through the sights.

Tristan jumped between Jenna and his dad, positioning himself so that he shielded her with his body. "I didn't report what happened all those years ago because of *you*. It was wrong. I constantly wonder, if I'd called the sheriff instead of listening to you that afternoon, how different my life would be."

"You're right—your life *would* be different. For starters, you would have lost your scholarship to college. Do you think the university would have held the spot open, waiting for you while you went on trial to defend yourself? Of course they wouldn't have. Which also means you would not be slated to be picked in the NFL—"

"I *will not* be part of the draft, Dad. I'm going to do what I should have done four years ago." Holding his hand out as if he were approaching a wounded animal, Tristan took two steps toward his father. "It's time for me to go to the sheriff's office and come clean about what happened the day Becca died."

"No!" David bellowed. "I've worked too hard to get you to this point. I won't let you throw it away over a reckless schoolgirl and her nosy mother. Now, go home and let me clean up your mess, again."

"Like you *cleaned it up* last time? I don't think so," Tristan said through clenched teeth.

Jenna scooted half-off, half-on the bench and looked around for anything that might be used as a weapon. A large rock the size of a softball lay on the ground just out of her reach. Moving slowly so she wouldn't draw attention to herself, she slipped off the bench and inched toward the rock.

"You'll have to shoot me to shoot her," Tristan said firmly. Hurrying footsteps sounded behind her.

She wrapped her hand around the rock and turned. Tristan shifted, once again blocking her from his dad. Jenna stood, the rock firmly in her hands, not sure how it would be a match for a gun, but it was all she had.

"Move, Tristan. It's time for this to end. Once and for all," David bellowed.

"You're right, it is. But it won't end this way, Dad." The football player she'd enjoyed watching run plays through the years turned and snatched the rock from her hands. Then he whirled around and threw it, knocking the gun out of his dad's hand. The weapon flew into a juniper bush.

Coach Kent dove after his weapon, and Tristan grabbed Jenna's hand, and they ran in the opposite direction, deeper into the meditation garden.

Dear Lord, there's nowhere to hide. Had Sean found her note? Was help on the way?

Chapter Fifteen

"Can't you go any faster?" Sean probed. "I still don't understand why you aren't using your lights and siren."

Heath accelerated as the broken yellow line of a passing zone came into view. "I already told you. I won't run sirens on a curvy two-lane country road unless I know it is an emergency." He glided into the left lane, overtook the older gentleman in the sedan they had been following for the last five miles and maneuvered back into the right lane, well ahead of meeting the oncoming vehicle.

"How is this not an emergency?" Sean bit out through gritted teeth.

"Look, Sean, I realize you've formed a close attachment to Jenna the past few days, but don't tell me how to do my job. She *chose* to leave your home, *borrow* your SUV and *meet* Tristan. The people driving on this road today didn't ask her to do any of those things. The road is curvy, with minimal straight sections, and there are no pull-offs. If I activate my siren, the other drivers are likely to speed up—thinking they are helping me get to my destination more quickly—take a curve too fast and crash. Which means it would take us even longer to get to Jenna, and an innocent person could lose their life."

Sean drummed his fingers on his leg. Heath was right to not take unnecessary risks that put innocent people in danger, but the thought of Jenna being out there alone with a killer… No. He couldn't let his mind go there. Jenna would be okay. She was a smart woman, and she had done a good job of taking care of herself all these years.

It suddenly hit him that he didn't want her to always have to be strong and independent. He wanted to be the one to take care of her. To nurture her. To protect her. To help her solve all the cold case crimes she desired. To love her.

He didn't know how she would feel about his newly discovered feelings, if she would open her heart to the possibility that they could be more than neighbors. If they could see where their budding friendship could lead them. After all, according to Grandma Lois, great love stories always start with friendship. Could Jenna possibly have similar feelings for him? Bouncing his leg, he itched to get out of the slow-moving vehicle and run. Because at the moment, the adrenaline coursing through his body made him feel as if he could fly.

Sean's phone rang, and Jenna's name flashed across the screen. "Thank You, Lord."

He pressed the button to answer and immediately placed the call on speaker. "Jenna, are you okay?"

"No… Sean, help," she whispered, urgency punctuating her words. "He has a gun. He's going to kill me."

"Tristan?"

"No, Coach… I mean David. David Kent." Unintelligible, whispered words sounded in the background. "Tristan, no. Stay with me. Don't go out there. Tristan!"

Accelerating, Heath activated the emergency lights and siren.

Sean gripped the phone tighter. "Jenna we're almost there." Turning to Heath, he added, "How long?"

"Less than five minutes." Heath palmed his radio and called Dispatch for backup.

"Did you hear that? We're almost there."

"Please hurry." The fear in her voice reached out and squeezed his lungs like a vise.

He inhaled deeply and slowly exhaled. "Can you tell me what's happening?"

"Tristan is trying to lead his father away from me. I'm hiding in the gazebo. Sean, please hurry." Her voice cracked, and a sob sounded across the line.

Heath weaved in and out of traffic. "Jenna, stay hidden and stay on the line. And stay perfectly still and quiet."

"Is your phone pressed to your ear?" Sean asked.

"Earbud," she whispered softly.

He smiled. "Smart thinking. I can keep talking to you, and you won't feel so alone. Make sure you have all sounds muted on your phone, though. You don't want a text message or something giving away your location."

Silence settled over the line. He missed the connection to her voice, letting him know she was still okay. But as long as she was silent, there was less risk of the killer finding her.

The entrance to the park came into view. "We're almost there, Jenna."

Heath turned into the parking lot, lights and sirens blaring, and zoomed past the main playground area. Parents grabbed their children and pulled them close, staring at the scene. A deputy's vehicle pulled in behind them. Heath spoke into his radio and ordered the deputy to instruct the families to evacuate the property and then to block the entrance to the back parking lot, not allowing spectators into what was likely to be a very dangerous situation.

Sean wished he had been smart enough to bring his own headphones, but he hadn't. He didn't want to disconnect the call, but he would have to at this point. "Jenna, I have to hang up. I will get to you as quickly as I can."

"I understand." The line went dead. It felt as if someone had reached into his chest and pulled out his heart.

Heath parked, and Sean went to open his door. Heath placed a hand on his arm. "Do you have a weapon?"

"Of course I do." Sean palmed his Glock and exited the vehicle, then rounded the front and met Heath on the path that led to Jenna.

"You know I shouldn't let a civilian be involved in this. If things go haywire, I could be in a lot of trouble."

"Try to stop me."

"That's what I figured. We're going to separate. Head toward the gazebo and get Jenna. I'm going to circle the other way and see if I can find Tristan and his dad. If you see anything, yell. I'll come running. But be aware, as my other deputies arrive, they'll be in these woods as well."

"You forget I'm not a rookie. I've been doing this longer than you have. Now, it's time to find this guy and end this today." They crossed under the entrance archway, and Sean went left while Heath went right.

Sean had never explored the meditation garden. He was reliant upon the signs to point him in the direction he needed to go. His feet crunched on the gravel as he ran, and he moved off the path to the grassy area, racing toward the unknown. *Lord, don't let me be too late.*

Sounds from the parking area reached Jenna's hiding spot, Sirens clashed with the screams of children, and she could only imagine the chaos. Her heart raced, and sweat beaded her hairline. Wrapping her arms around her body, she huddled against the gazebo wall. *Help is on the way. Sean is almost here.* Over and over, she repeated the silent mantra in her head. *Sean will save me. He won't let David get to me first.*

"Dad, it's over." Tristan yelled from somewhere to her right. "Dad, come out wherever you're hiding. Come out and turn yourself in," Tristan pleaded. "I'm sorry. I know I let you down. I wish I could go back four years and undo everything. But I can't. What I can do is stop you from making things worse."

A twig snapped behind her, and she gasped. Clamping her hand over her mouth, she prayed that if the noise had been David, he hadn't heard her. *Hurry, Sean.*

A firm hand grabbed her by the hair and jerked her upward. She cried out and twisted, looking into the eyes of her tormentor.

David threw a leg over the low wall of the gazebo and climbed over to stand next to her, his grip on her hair never wavering. She flailed around, swinging her arms and trying to break free. He pressed his gun to her side, let go of her hair and slid his left arm around her neck. She clawed at his hands. He tightened his grasp, cutting off her airway. Dizziness descended upon her, and a whooshing sound clogged her ears. She was going to pass out. *No.* Jenna couldn't allow the darkness to win.

If someone grabs you from behind, instantly go into the turtle position—neck down, shoulders up. If that fails, execute a drop and flip. A long-forgotten self-defense video clip she'd shared with her viewers in one of her early podcasts suddenly came to mind. Too late for the turtle position. She'd have to try the other maneuver. *Lord, don't let the gun go off.*

Tilting sideways, she dropped to her left knee. David lost his grasp on her throat, and the gun clattered to the floor. Scrambling to the wall, she clawed her way upward as she inhaled large gulps of air, desperate to relieve her burning lungs.

"No!" David grasped her hair, jerked her around and backhanded her across the face. "You will not get away that easily. You and your daughter have ruined my son's life. All my son's dreams have been taken away. All because of a clumsy girl and her ridiculous podcast mom."

Tears stung Jenna's eyes. *Ignore the pain. Focus on escaping.* Blindly, she kicked and swatted at him. He let go of her hair. She landed on her backside. David bent over her and reached for her legs. She drew back and kicked as hard as she could, connecting with the one area that was sure to bring him to his knees. He convulsed in pain and fell against the railing. She scooted backward, never taking her eyes off him. Splinters dug into her palms, and she bit the inside of her cheek. *Don't stop. Keep moving.*

Jenna pulled her knees close, flipped over, her feet flat on the floor, and pushed upward, then leaped off the gazebo, clearing both steps. She raced toward one of the two bridges that connected the small island the gazebo was on with the land encircling the pond.

A gunshot rang out. She startled, missing a step. The toe of her left foot connected with the wooden deck floor of the bridge, and she plunged toward the cold water below.

"Heath, over here!" Sean raced along the trail that wound through the trees in the direction the gunshot had sounded from. He burst into the clearing just in time to see Jenna crawl out of the pond and collapse onto the small island. David Kent stood inches away with a gun pointed at her. Why hadn't she swam to the other side?

Sean raised his Glock. "Drop your weapon, Kent. It's over," he commanded, inching closer to the bridge with small half steps, his eyes never leaving the football coach. He desperately wanted to rush to Jenna. If she wasn't able to get out of the wet clothing quickly and warm up, she would be at risk of hypothermia.

In one swift move, David pulled Jenna to her feet and positioned her in front of him as a shield. "Don't come any closer, Quinn."

Movement on the other side of the pond caught his attention. Heath had made his way to the other bridge. Sean's heart jumped into his throat. One wrong move and David would kill Jenna. *Keep him talking.*

"You don't really want to do this. You're throwing away your career. Do you really want to spend life in prison—or worse, receive the death penalty?"

"Dad!"

Tristan darted past Sean and raced onto the small island. "It's over. Please do as Mr. Quinn asked." The young man cast a quick glance over his shoulder. "Stay behind me."

"Can't do that," Sean replied through clenched teeth. He would not allow someone else to shield him. "I won't have my view *or* my shot blocked."

"Please give me a chance to resolve this," Tristan whispered. He turned back to his father. "Ms. Hartley did nothing wrong, Dad. She simply wanted answers, like any parent would. When I heard about the attacks on her, I knew you were behind them. And I knew I had to stop you."

"You should've stayed at college. You have several busy months ahead of you, with the NFL draft and then finals."

"I've withdrawn from the draft."

Pain etched the coach's face. "No!" he bellowed. "Why?"

Tears streamed down Tristan's cheeks. "Because it was the only way I could stop you and put an end to this. And because it was time—actually, *past* time—to give Ms. Hartley answers. Keeping quiet about what happened that day hasn't been fair to anyone. Not to Becca's memory. Not to me. And not to you."

David tightened his hold on Jenna. Her eyes widened. "You're wrong. What isn't fair is you throwing away everything we've worked for. Why are you throwing your dreams away?"

Heath rounded the gazebo, his weapon fixed on David.

Tristan took a step closer to his father. "Besides teaching me how to be the best football player, you also taught me to be an honorable man. Somewhere along the way, you decided fame and glory were more important than honor. But I don't believe that. I will not dishonor Becca's memory any longer by staying quiet."

Two sheriff's deputies stepped into the clearing with guns drawn.

"Drop your weapon, Coach Kent. You're surrounded," Heath instructed, making his presence known.

The coach turned his head from side to side, taking in the scene that had unfolded, realization dawning on his face. He let go of Jenna, and she collapsed to the ground at his feet.

Tristan went to his father and gently pried the gun from his hands, then handed it to Heath. "We'll turn ourselves in together. Okay, Dad?"

Sean raced across the bridge and gathered Jenna into his arms as Heath and the deputies handcuffed the two men. She shivered. Sean shrugged out of his coat and wrapped it around her shoulders.

"Do…do they have to cuff Tristan? He saved my life," Jenna asked, burying her face in Sean's neck.

"It's okay," Tristan assured her.

Heath jerked his head, signaling to the deputies. "Okay, guys, let's get these two to the station." He met Sean's gaze. "After she's had a chance to change and warm up, I need you to bring her in so she can give a statement."

Sean nodded, then turned his attention back to the woman in his arms. "Do you think you can walk?"

"Yes." She looked up, remorse written in her eyes. "I'm sorry I—"

Her bottom lip quivered. And, as if he were being pulled by an unseen magnetic field, he lowered his head and captured her mouth with his. She wrapped her arms around his waist, the kiss deepening ever so slightly.

When he was completely out of breath, he pulled back and stood. "If we don't get moving, you're going to catch hypothermia."

"Not if you keep kissing me like that," she said.

They had a lot to discuss before they got lost in each other's kisses. But later. For now, Sean had to be the voice of reason. "I'm afraid kisses won't be enough to keep you from catching a cold—or worse, pneumonia. So humor me, and let me get you to my warm vehicle quickly."

Sean kissed the top of her damp head. He placed an arm

around her shoulders and slid the other under her knees. Then he scooped her up into his arms and made his way across the bridge. Closing her eyes, she rested her head against his chest. Their hearts beat in rhythm. After the trauma she'd endured, he couldn't be sure what the exchange meant to her. Did she share his feelings? Or was she simply accepting his embrace because she needed comfort? He'd have to be patient a little longer to find out. There were more important things to deal with first.

Chapter Sixteen

Heath met them as they entered the station. "Are you okay? Do you need to see a doctor?" he asked Jenna, concern in his eyes.

She shook her head. "No. I'll be fine."

"Are they opening up about Becca's death, or have they lawyered up?" Sean asked, obviously ready to get down to business.

"David Kent has called his lawyer. We're waiting for him to arrive so we can continue our questioning. Tristan, on the other hand, wants to tell his story. But he has requested Jenna be in the room."

"No. Absolutely not." Sean shoved his hand through his hair.

"That's my call, don't you think?" She met his gaze and refused to look away.

He puffed out of breath. "Yes, of course. But don't you think you've been through enough? That kid allowed you to live in torment for nearly four years. Do you really want—"

"What I want," she said softly, "is to know what happened to my precious Becca and why she had to die alone in the woods."

"Okay, then, although this is very unorthodox, I will allow you to be in the room during his questioning. Tristan requested a court-appointed attorney. So he will be present during the interrogation." Heath put a hand on her upper back and turned her toward a long hallway. "If you'll come this way."

"I'm coming, too. I believe I've earned the right, being part of this investigation and all." Sean fell into step beside Jenna.

"Not so fast. I know you want to be there, but I can't risk the kid clamming up if you are." Heath paused beside a closed door. "So this is as far as I will allow you to go."

"But—"

"You'll see and hear everything on the monitors. But Tristan won't be able to see you," Heath insisted.

"Sean, I appreciate all you've done and how you've protected me and kept me alive these past four days. I know you want to be there for me for moral support, and I appreciate that." Becca raised her hand, catching herself before she caressed his face, and placed it on his arm. "This is something I have to do without you." She turned to Heath. "I'm ready."

They left Sean standing there. Heath led her a little farther down the hall and into an interrogation room.

Tristan sat at a small oblong table beside a man wearing a button-up shirt and tie with a bored expression on his face. When Tristan saw Jenna, he brightened. "Ms. Hartley, you're here. My dad didn't hurt you, did he?"

"No, I'm fine. How are you?" It felt odd to exchange pleasantries in this small interrogation room with the person who had been with Becca the day she died. But she needed him to feel at ease so he would open up about that day.

"I'm sorry I didn't tell you what I knew sooner. It's my fault that my dad tried to kill you."

The bored-looking gentleman sat up straight. "I told you not to volunteer any information."

"And I told you I'm not keeping secrets any longer. I'll face whatever consequences come my way."

Heath looked to the other gentleman. "May I proceed?"

The man shrugged. "Sure, but I want it noted that my client is answering your questions against my counsel."

"So noted." There was a knock on the door. Heath opened it and accepted two folding chairs from a deputy. "Thanks." He placed the chairs next to each other on the opposite side of the table from Tristan and his lawyer.

The deputy backed out of the cramped space, closing the door behind him. Jenna took in her surroundings, observing a camera near the ceiling in the corner. Was Sean watching, or had he left? No, he wouldn't leave. He'd proven the past four days that he was a loyal neighbor and friend. Heat warmed her cheeks as she remembered the kiss they had shared earlier. She must have seemed like a helpless, lost soul in that moment for him to feel the need to offer her such comfort. And she had most likely cemented that impression when she'd allowed him to carry her in his arms, snuggling in like a child hungry for affection.

"Jenna." Heath touched her shoulder and brought her back to the moment at hand. "Are you sure you're up to this?"

"Yes." She settled into the chair closest to the door and folded her hands in her lap. Nothing would get her out of this room until she finally knew why her precious daughter had been killed.

Sean leaned close and examined the image of the interrogation room displayed on the thirty-inch monitor. Jenna looked as if she might pass out. He knew this was too much for her. He should've insisted on Heath postponing the interrogation until tomorrow, giving Jenna a little time to recover from the ordeal of the morning. Of course, he had no rights to demand anything. And if the cold shoulder Jenna had given him since the shared kiss was any indication, he never would have rights to voice his opinion about what she should or shouldn't do for her own well-being ever again.

He was angry with himself for not reading the situation correctly. Sean should've realized that she was in shock following the near-death experience and falling into the cold pond.

He had always heard hindsight was twenty-twenty. In this case, it definitely was. But he couldn't go back and change things. All he could do was pray that she would allow him to explain and to declare his intentions. He chuckled. Sean could hear his grandpa now. "It's important to not let your wishes and desires lead you around. Always make sure your intentions are honorable."

The door opened, and Deputy Moore stepped into the room. "You look pretty happy for someone watching an interrogation."

Sean shook his head. "No. Just remembering something my grandpa always said to me."

The deputy raised an eyebrow but did not comment.

"Are you here to watch with me?"

"Yes. It's standard procedure. I'm sure you understand."

Sean turned his attention back to the monitor.

"As I was telling Ms. Hartley before my dad showed up…" Tristan slammed his fist on the table and Jenna jumped. "I don't know how I could've been so reckless. I should've known Dad would follow me today, just like he did that day."

"I will not tolerate an outburst like that, young man. Do you understand?" Heath growled angrily.

"Yeah, I'm sorry." The young man turned to Jenna. "Sorry."

"Continue." Heath motioned for Tristan to carry on.

"The day Becca died. We were on our first date. We went on a picnic and had a nice time. Originally, that was all we were going to do, but Becca said her mom was visiting her aunt and wouldn't be home for several hours, so we went hiking. We left Becca's car at the meditation garden. I drove us to my house, where I picked up a daypack, a couple of protein bars and a couple of waters, and then we went to the hiking trail."

"Was anyone at home when you went by there?" Heath inquired.

Tristan shook his head. "No. My dad had taken my mother for a chemo treatment."

Jenna reached across the table and placed a hand on Tristan's. "I heard your mom passed away last year. I'm sorry."

Her ability to be so forgiving and offer sympathy to the person who was most likely responsible for Becca's death amazed Sean.

"Thank you," Tristan replied.

"Back to your story," Heath redirected the young man. "Please continue."

"We reached the hiking trail and hiked the ridge for better views. When we reached the overlook, I wanted to climb out to Eagle Point and see what the views were like from there."

"Didn't you see the warning signs?" Heath leaned closer.

"Yes, sir. But I thought nothing would happen." Tristan shook his head. "How many people have had that very thought right before tragedy?"

Silence descended upon the interrogation room, and after several long seconds, Tristan continued. "Becca didn't want to go out to the end of Eagle Point, and I teased her for being a goody-goody. I told her…" His voice cracked, and tears ran down his face. "I told her I wouldn't let anything happen to her." He lowered his head, and his shoulders shook as he openly sobbed.

Jenna whispered something to Heath, and he pulled out his phone and typed a message.

Deputy Moore's cell phone buzzed. He read the text message and turned for the door.

"What's going on?" Sean asked.

"Ms. Hartley has requested water. I'll be right back."

The deputy left the room, and Sean turned back to stare at the woman who had stolen his heart.

There was a knock on the door. Heath got up to answer it, and Jenna followed him. "Can we talk outside just for a moment?"

He looked at her quizzically and nodded. Then he opened

the door, accepted the bottle of water and passed it to Tristan. "We'll be right back."

They stepped into the hall to find Sean already waiting on them. "What's going on?"

"Jenna asked to speak with me." Heath gave him a pointed look. "In private."

Sean bristled.

"It's fine. You can stay," Jenna said, then turned to Heath. "I know that you've already bent the rules for me—and I hate to ask this—but could you and the lawyer maybe go into the viewing room and let me talk to Tristan alone?"

"You can't do that!" Sean's tone made it clear he didn't approve.

She spun around to face him. "If you want to stay in the observation room and listen, that's fine, but you don't get to have input here."

He looked as if someone had punched him in the gut, and she instantly regretted her words. She knew he meant well, but there was no way he could understand what she had been through the last four years and how desperate she was to have the answers she had been searching for. How much longer could she sit and watch as Tristan cried? She needed to put the young man at ease so he could get the story out quickly. Dragging it out was excruciating.

"I'll allow it." Heath laughed. "If for no other reason, then the fact that I've never seen anyone make my good buddy speechless."

Sean grunted, turned and went back into the viewing room. Jenna would have to mend fences with her neighbor later, or they would go back to the cold, not-so-neighborly relationship they had shared for the past six months.

"Thanks, Heath."

The sheriff searched her eyes. "Are you sure about this?"

She nodded.

"Okay, but I cannot force his lawyer to leave the room. If he refuses, I'm not leaving, either. Got it?"

"Sounds fair."

They reentered the room. Tristan had drunk some of the water and seemed to have regained his composure.

The lawyer sat with his legs straight out, crossed at the ankles, and his arms folded over his chest with his chin tucked in and his eyes closed. Had the man fallen asleep?

Heath gently kicked the sole of the lawyer's shoe, and he opened one eye. "Ms. Hartley has requested to speak to Tristan alone. And I am inclined to allow it."

The lawyer sat up straighter. "I object."

"I don't believe anyone is asking your permission," replied Tristan. Then he jerked his head toward the camera in the corner, near the ceiling on the far wall. "If I'm not mistaken, this room and all that is going on inside is being video recorded."

"That's correct," Heath affirmed.

"Who will watch our conversation?"

"Currently, there is a deputy and Sean Quinn watching the monitor. If you agree to talk to Ms. Hartley alone, your lawyer and I will watch the monitor along with Mr. Quinn, and I will station the deputy outside this door."

"I have no objection to that," Tristan stated.

His lawyer got up and stormed out of the room. Heath hugged Jenna. "If you need me, just give a signal, and I'll be back in here immediately," he whispered. Then he pulled back and followed the lawyer.

Jenna sat across from Tristan at the small table. "I know this is very emotional for you. You've had to keep everything bottled up for so long. You told me you didn't kill Becca, and I believe you." She inhaled deeply and then pushed out the breath slowly. "Did your dad kill my daughter?"

"No. Yes. Ugh." He pressed the heels of his palms against his temples. "His actions caused the accident, but he didn't plan to kill her."

"Why don't you tell me what you know? Then the sheriff can sort everything out." The urge to grasp him by the shoulders and shake the story out of him welled up inside her. She bit the corner of her lip and waited.

"I told you we went out to the rocks known as Eagle Point. We took our time and moved slowly so that we wouldn't fall. And after we made it to the tree, we sat down on the ground with our feet dangling over the edge. We were probably there for about thirty minutes, talking and finding out about each other."

"What did y'all talk about?" Jenna knew that Tristan and Becca's conversation had nothing to do with the case, but she needed to know. It was that simple.

Tristan frowned. "Nothing of significance. Normal things that people discuss when they're trying to get to know each other. Favorite color. Favorite music. Hobbies. School. We discussed my upcoming awards banquet. I asked if she would think about allowing me to talk to you and ask for permission to invite her to attend as my date."

"Her response?"

"She said she would think about it, but that even if she decided it would be okay, not to get my hopes up because you would never allow her to go on a solo date." He fidgeted with his fingernails.

Jenna squirmed in her seat. Sean, Heath and the attorney had just heard how she had failed as a mom, placing her own insecurities and past mistakes on her daughter. *Lord, I'm glad You are forgiving and are able to overlook my shortcomings. Because I'm afraid it will take me a long time to forgive myself.*

"I'm sorry, I shouldn't have told you that," Tristan said softly. "You were a wonderful mom, everyone knows that. Becca never once spoke negatively about you. She loved you, and she wanted you to be proud of her. I know you were... *Are.*"

"Let's get back to what happened to Becca. You said y'all made it out there safely and sat near the tree. Then what?"

"My dad found us. I was supposed to be at the gym with some of my teammates who were also home for the weekend. Dad had taken Mom for her chemo treatment, so I figured what he didn't know wouldn't hurt him. Or me." Tristan pushed to his feet and paced. "I knew he had a tracking app on my phone. It's been on there since I was old enough to drive. He said it was for my protection. If anything happened to me, he would know where to look. But I knew it was so he could keep tabs on me. I was naive to think that he wouldn't check the app since he was busy with Mom, but he did. After he took Mom home from her treatment, he tracked me to the hiking trail. The sun was going down, so we had just headed back and were making our way across the uneven ground when Dad showed up on the other side of the fence and yelled at me. His sudden appearance and tone of voice startled Becca, and she stepped back. Only, when she did, she went over the edge. I tried to grab her, but it all happened so fast."

Tears sprang to Jenna's eyes, and she sucked in her breath. Oh, her sweet Becca. She wiped her eyes, desperate to stop the flow.

The door to the interrogation room flew open, and Heath and Sean burst into the room.

"I'll take over from here," Heath said. He glanced over his shoulder at Sean. "Get her out of here."

Sean gave a curt nod and started toward her.

"One moment… Please. I need to know one more thing." She held up a hand, halting Sean in his steps, and turned back to Tristan. "Why didn't you call for an ambulance?"

"At first, we didn't have cell service. We raced to the spot where she landed. Dad pushed me aside to check her pulse and said it was weak. Then he said he'd be right back and took off toward the parking area. Ten minutes later, he came back and said he had called 911 and ordered me to go home. He said Mom had already been left alone too long after a treatment. I told him I wasn't leaving until I knew Becca was okay. But he promised he'd take care of her and reminded me he was the only one of us certified in CPR. I left… But I only made it a couple hundred yards and turned around. I couldn't leave Becca …" Tristan sank onto the chair he'd vacated earlier. "As I came closer, I saw Dad…twist Becca's neck."

Jenna gasped, and Sean put a hand on her shoulder.

The court appointed lawyer tried to hush Tristan, but he continued as if in a trance watching a replay of the events. "I confronted him, and he said her injuries had been fatal. That she was suffering, and the ambulance wouldn't get there in time. I was in shock, so when he told me, once more, to go home and take care of Mom, I did. It wasn't until late the next day that I found out he hadn't actually reported it and Becca's body had been found by a couple of thru-hikers. When I asked him why he hadn't called it in, he said it was to protect me from a scandal that would cost me my football scholarship and a career in pro football. And to protect my mom from undue stress during an already-stressful time with cancer treatments. He said what happened had been an accident and sacrificing my *life* wouldn't bring Becca back."

Jenna stood, her entire body shaking, and turned to Sean. "I'm ready to go." He held out his hand. She placed her hand into his and focused on putting one foot in front of the other.

"I'm sorry, Ms. Hartley," Tristan whispered. "I'm sorry that I talked Becca into the hike that day. I'm sorry that my dad tracked us there. Most of all, I'm sorry we couldn't do anything to save her."

Grasping the doorframe with her free hand, she turned back to the tormented young man. "That's where you're wrong. She would have survived if only you or your dad had called 911."

"What do you mean?"

"After I received the autopsy report, I reached out to Dr. Langston—a doctor of internal medicine at Vanderbilt. She looked over the report of injuries. And she said *if* Becca's neck had not been broken and she had made it to the hospital within an hour of the accident, she would have had a ninety percent chance of survival. Every hour after that, that treatment was delayed, her chances would have diminished by fifty percent. Until she succumbed to her injuries." Jenna locked eyes with Tristan. "There's a good chance Becca would have been paralyzed from the waist down, but she didn't have to die."

Tristan recoiled as if he'd touched a live wire. "The doctor has to be wrong. Dad said Becca's injuries were fatal. That's why he sent me away."

"He sent you away so he could murder my child and protect you from any fallout from the accident. Nothing—not even a young girl's life—mattered more to your dad than you becoming a pro football player." Jenna frowned and shook her head. Then she glanced at Heath. "Dr. Langston said she'd be willing to testify in court."

Tristan's face blanched. He ran to the trash can and became violently ill.

Sean put his hand on the small of Jenna's back and guided her out of the room. They made their way to Sean's vehicle in silence.

"Would you mind dropping me off at the rental-car place on Wisteria Street?" Jenna asked as Sean pulled out of the parking lot.

He looked as if he might argue, but then he nodded. "Okay."

"Thank you." She looked out the side window. "I thought I'd get a hotel room tonight and then look for a rental tomorrow."

"There's no need for that." He activated his blinker and slowed to turn into the car-rental parking lot. "You can stay at my house until you find a place."

"But I don't need to be protected now, and it wouldn't look right for us to share your home."

"I'll move into the camper until you find a rental." He pulled into a parking space.

"I don't know. It's been a stressful day. I really need time alone to decompress."

"You shall have it. I'll move into the camper before you get back to the house. You won't see me the rest of the evening," Sean promised. "I'll even keep Beau with me."

How could she say no? He would think she was ungrateful for all he'd done. "Okay. Thank you." She smiled. "Beau can stay in the house with me."

Sean's deep, rich laughter followed her as she exited the vehicle, and her heart skipped a beat. She had gotten too comfortable being around him. But she *would* find a new place to live tomorrow. Put distance between her and her handsome neighbor so they could go back to being…what? Acquaintances? Friends? Jenna wasn't sure what their future relationship would look like, but she knew better than to hold out dreams of something more based on one kiss after a near-death experience.

Chapter Seventeen

Sean stretched and massaged his lower back with his fingertips. He really needed to invest in a more comfortable mattress for the bed in his camper, especially since he hoped to convince Jenna to stay in his home until hers was repaired. Although he knew the probability was slim, he hoped she'd hear him out and consider the idea. He wanted to be there for her, to be a shoulder for her to lean on and to ensure she knew, even though they had captured the ones responsible for Becca's death, she wasn't in this alone. If she would allow it, he would be there with her through the court trials and all that would come after that.

What time is it? Trying to be mindful of Jenna's request for space to decompress, he would prefer not to go into the house unless he knew she was awake. He swung his feet to the floor and reached for his cell phone on the small built-in side table. 11:15 a.m. It was almost noon!

Jumping to his feet, Sean scrubbed a hand over his face and went to his tiny closet. He could not remember the last time he'd slept this late—probably not since his college days. He'd had difficulty shutting off his thoughts the night before and hadn't drifted off to sleep until after three, but he'd thought he'd only slept a couple of hours. Grabbing the jeans and long-sleeved pullover he'd hung up the night before, he quickly dressed. Surely Jenna was awake by now.

He shoved his feet into his boots, grabbed his denim jacket off the dinette table and headed out the door. The sun was shining brightly, the temperature warmer than it had been in months. It was going to be a beautiful day.

Whistling a tune, he made his way to the back door. He twisted the knob. Locked. Was Jenna still asleep? Maybe she'd had difficulty going to sleep, too. Sean had promised himself he wouldn't go into the house until he knew she was awake, because he didn't want Jenna to feel like he was hovering. Of course, Beau was probably pacing the floor, ready to go outside and relieve himself. He'd just go inside and take care of Beau, and then he'd slip back outside and enjoy the sunshine until she woke.

He shoved his hand into his pocket and retrieved his keys. Once inside, silence greeted him. Beau rested on the floor under the table. The coonhound lifted his head, looked at Sean with sad eyes, bawled and then lowered his head again.

"What's wrong, boy?" Sean crossed the room, his steps faltering when he spotted an envelope addressed to him on the table. Dropping his keys onto the table, he snatched the envelope and tore into it.

Sean,
Words will never be enough to express my gratitude for all you have done for me these last few days. You provided a safe haven in the midst of a storm for me, and I will forever be grateful. I'm sorry I didn't get to say goodbye in person, but I didn't want to disturb you. I'll be in touch.
Many thanks,
Jenna
P.S. I fed Beau and let him outside to play for thirty minutes this morning.

He crumpled the paper in his fist, pressed it into a ball and tossed it toward the trash can. The shot hit the edge of the can, bounced onto the floor and rolled a few feet from him. With a sigh, he picked it up and dropped it into the trash can. Then he snagged his keys off the table and headed to the front door.

Had he lost his opportunity to tell Jenna how much he cared about her by not addressing his feelings after the kiss? He'd thought giving her space to process everything that happened was the considerate thing to do. Now he wasn't so sure.

Beau barked and raced after him. When they reached Sean's SUV, he opened the door and signaled Beau to hop in. "Let's go, Beau."

Sean wasn't sure where Jenna had gone, but he could not wait around for her to *be in touch*. She might or might not be open to a relationship, but he wouldn't know until he told her how he felt.

For the first time in three years, he felt fully alive, and he wasn't ready to give up on those feelings just yet.

"Lord, please give me the right words to say, and let her hear them with an open heart."

He climbed into his vehicle, reached into the glove compartment and pulled out Beau's restraint, then quickly fastened it on him and tethered him to the seat. Sean fastened his own seat belt and started the engine. "I'm not sure where we're headed, Beau. We may not even find her, but we have to try."

He would call her, but he suspected she'd send it to voicemail like she had yesterday. There was no other option but to drive around and try to find her. Even then, she might reject his affections. But he had to try. He'd lost so much in life already; he couldn't simply walk away from the woman who'd burrowed her way into his heart without at least letting her know what she meant to him.

"Okay, Beau, let's see if we can find Jenna and bring her *home*, where she belongs."

* * *

"I'll order the materials as soon as I leave here, and we'll get started on the repairs next week. Then, barring any unforeseen issues, we should have you back in your home in five or six weeks," Mr. Nabors closed the notebook he'd been making notes in and smiled at her.

"That sounds great." Jenna furrowed her brow. "I called my insurance company. They're supposed to send someone out to assess the damage and let me know what they're willing to pay."

Mr. Nabors, who was an old family friend of her parents', placed a hand on her shoulder. "Don't worry about it, dear. Whatever the insurance company won't cover, I will."

"I can't let—"

"Yes, you can. You've used your podcast to keep our community informed and safe for the past three years. It's our turn to give back to you." He pulled her into an embrace. "Call your parents before someone else notifies them of what's been going on here."

She smiled. "Yes, sir. Their plane should be landing within the hour. I'll text them to call me first thing."

"Good girl." He grinned and ambled down the porch steps.

The sound of Sean's vehicle approaching drew her attention, and she watched as he braked and turned into her drive, Beau sitting in the front passenger seat. The instant Sean opened his door, the coonhound jumped out and ran to her, howling as if he'd treed a wild animal.

"Looks like someone's happy to see you." Mr. Nabors laughed, shaking hands with Sean before climbing into his truck and backing out of the drive.

Jenna dropped to her knee and hugged the animal. "You act as if you haven't seen me in days, but I only left you an hour ago."

"It felt like an eternity." Sean stood at the foot of the steps, looking up at her. "Why did you leave without telling me goodbye?"

Swallowing the lump in her throat, she gave Beau one last hug and shoved to her feet. What could she say? That she had come to depend on him and the thought of not seeing him every day caused an unexpected ache in her heart? Her mom had always told her that when she faced something difficult, it was best to take care of it quickly to keep it from festering and becoming a bigger issue. Removing herself from his presence before her heart became even more invested in him and his loyal coonhound had seemed like the best way to protect herself.

When she was twenty-five years old and Patrick had walked out on her, Jenna had thought it was the end of the world. But she'd had to be strong for Becca, so she had persevered. Then she'd lost Becca and had experienced a pain unlike any other, one that had her spending days in bed, crying and gasping for air. At one point, she literally thought she was going to die from a broken heart. Only sheer determination and a desire to see Becca's murderer captured had kept her going.

She knew she was a capable woman, but she didn't know how many more heartaches her battered heart could stand. So she had to do whatever she could to protect it. If that meant walking away from a man who had made her wonder if there could be a happily-ever-after, so be it.

"I figured you were ready to get rid of me." She laughed. "Besides, when Mr. Nabors said he could meet me at the house this morning, I knew I needed to make it happen if I want back in my home quickly."

She turned, reached around the still-open front door, activated the lock and pulled it closed. "I was just headed to Hideaway Inn Bed and Breakfast. Mrs. Frances has a cabin I can rent until they complete the renovations on my house."

"There's no need for that. You're going to have enough expenses with the renovation. Stay at my house. I'll live in the camper."

"I can't let you do that. But I appreciate the neighborly offer." She brushed past him, but he captured her hand, halting her.

"I'm not being neighborly. I'm being selfish. I want to know you're safe, and I want to take care of you."

"Your responsibilities have ended. David is in jail. He can't hurt me anymore. Heath called and said the judge has denied bail." She bit her lip. "Tristan has agreed to testify against his father in exchange for his part in Becca's death being downgraded to misdemeanor manslaughter."

"I'm not surprised they've offered Tristan a plea deal. While I think he bears some of the responsibility for what happened, he trusted his father. Then his father convinced him that if he came forward at that point, no one would believe him." Sean tilted his head. "How do you feel about the plea deal?"

"I have mixed emotions. He was nineteen years old. He should've called someone, even if his dad said he would handle it. By the time he found out his dad hadn't called for help, Becca was already gone, and he was scared. I feel if he were truly evil, he would've ignored what his father was doing to me, and I wouldn't be alive right now. So I'm okay with the plea deal. I just hope that after he serves his prison time, he will come out and do good in the world." She met Sean's eyes. "I also selfishly hope that he'll choose somewhere else to live. I'm not sure how I feel about the possibility of running into him at the grocery store."

"That's understandable."

"Anyway." She shook her head. "Your responsibility to protect me is over. So, thank you, and maybe if you're up to it after I'm back in the house, you might stop in for coffee sometime." She turned and headed toward her rental vehicle. *Keep walking. Don't let him see you cry.*

"Hey, Jenna," Sean called after her. "What about your responsibility to me?"

Her steps faltered, and she turned hesitantly. "What do you mean?"

He looked her in the eyes and walked toward her unhurriedly. "What about...*your*...responsibility to me?"

"Oh," she gasped. "You're right, I should give you some money for the groceries and things. My wallet's in m—"

"I don't want your money. I want to know what you're going to do to repair my broken heart. Since you're responsible for breaking it."

"I...uh..." She inhaled deeply, then released the breath slowly to the count of ten and willed her heart rate to slow. "How...?"

Sean reached up and pushed a strand of hair away from her face. "Did you think the kiss meant nothing?"

"I thought it just happened. That it was a sign of relief that everything was over." A tear slipped out of the corner of her eye, and he wiped it away. "That I was alive."

"Oh, it was all of those, but it was also pure joy and love. A love that I never knew I could have again." He smiled. "I have experienced relief over a case being solved and a witness staying alive, but I've never kissed any of them or even thought about it."

What was he saying? Did he care about her as she did him? *Lord, am I getting my happily-ever-after, after all these years?*

"Jenna," Sean said softly, pressing the palm of his hand against her cheek. "I don't know the exact moment it happened. Maybe it was when I carried you out of the fire. Maybe it was when I found your note telling me you had gone to meet Tristan and I was so afraid I had lost you forever. Or maybe it was one of a million moments in between. All I know is that I have fallen for you. And I don't want to lose you."

Thank You, Lord. Tears streamed down her face, and she reached up and caressed his cheek. "I have fallen for you, too. But I was afraid to hope that you shared my feelings."

"Darling, Jenna, this is only the beginning. I will spend the rest of my life making sure you know how much you are loved." As Beau barked and ran in circles around them, Sean lowered his head and claimed her lips.

Thank You, Lord, for sending this man to me and for new beginnings.

Epilogue

As he made his way up the walkway to Jenna's front door, Sean shifted the bouquet of red roses into his left hand and slipped his right hand into his suit-jacket pocket, needing reassurance the velvet ring box was still safely tucked inside. His heart raced. He prayed he'd get the response he was looking for, though he was sure Jenna's initial response would be concern for what other people would think about getting married after only dating for a short while.

He'd decided he didn't care much for what other people thought. If the last few years had taught him anything, it was that life was too short. Sean loved Jenna and wanted to spend the rest of his life with her. He didn't want to delay the start of their forever simply because a few people might think they were rushing things, and he prayed Jenna would see it the same way.

Taking the steps two at a time, he bounded onto the porch. The front door flew open as he reached out to press the doorbell.

"You're here." Jenna looked beautiful. She wore a flowy, royal blue dress with a pink-and-white floral print apron on top of it, but it was her smile that took his breath away.

She tilted her face upward, and he captured her lips in the

sweetest kiss. The crinkling sound of cellophane alerted him to the flowers being crushed between them. He stepped back and held out the bouquet.

"These are beautiful. Thank you." She smiled and smelled the roses. "Let me put them in water."

Sean followed her inside and closed the door. He was immediately assaulted by the aroma of comfort food coming from the kitchen. "Mmm, something smells good."

"I called your mother and got her recipes for all of your favorite foods."

"Meat loaf, loaded mashed potatoes, mac 'n' cheese, and..." He sniffed the air. "German chocolate cake."

Jenna laughed. "I hope you're hungry. It's been a long time since I've cooked a meal for two. I may have gone a little overboard."

He followed her into the kitchen. She opened a cabinet, pulled out a vase and filled it with water. After removing the cellophane wrapping from the flowers, she arranged them in the vase and carried them to the dining room table. The table had been set with a lace tablecloth, china place settings and candles. It looked elegant. A smile tugged the corners of his lips. He couldn't have planned a better setting for his proposal if he'd done all the work himself.

"You look happy."

"Oh, I am. Blissfully so." He captured her hand in his and pulled it to his lips.

He'd planned to wait until after dinner, but if Sean didn't propose right then, he felt as if he might burst. "Is everything on the stove fine for a few moments? I'd like to talk before dinner if that's okay."

She nodded. "Sure. We have about ten minutes before I have to take the meat loaf out of the oven."

Jenna led him to the living room sofa. Sitting in the room where he'd saved her from the burning inferno just seven short weeks ago sent a shudder up his spine. If he hadn't been driving along at that exact moment, there was a good chance she wouldn't have made it out alive.

"That's the same reaction I had when I sat in this room for the first time after the repairs. Mr. Nabors and his crew did a wonderful job on the remodel, but I can still see the events of that night clearly in my mind."

Sean squeezed her hand. "But you got out in time. That's the important thing."

"Because of you." Her smile widened. "Nurse Bethany was right. You, Sean Quinn, are my knight in shining armor."

As hard as he tried, he couldn't stop the laughter that flowed out of him, filling the room. "Don't tell me you're still jealous that Nurse Bethany flirted with me."

"Who…me?" She feigned shock and winked at him, a saucy twinkle in her eye. Then she joined in the laughter. Quickly sobering, she smiled. "I will never blame any woman for noticing how attractive you are, as long as they know you're mine."

"I'm glad you feel that way, because I—"

"Wait…please. I have something I want to say first." She licked her lips and smiled. "After my divorce, I was convinced I wasn't lovable."

"That's not—"

Jenna placed a finger on his lips, silencing him. "I now know that isn't true. I allowed someone else's opinion of me to become more important than my own opinion of myself. You have taught me to find the joy in every day. To embrace love. And to silence the naysayers."

Tears sparkled in her eyes. "I know you don't want to take credit for saving me, but we both know, if you hadn't been by my side, I would not be here today."

He opened his mouth to speak. But she shook her head, and he pressed his lips together. *Lord, when it's my turn to speak, help me find the words to let her know what a beautiful, loving woman she is.*

"I can't believe I'm saying this, but here goes." She puffed out a breath. "Sean, if you hadn't saved me, I wouldn't be alive. But being alive isn't enough. I love you, and I don't want to live without you." Tugging her hand free, she reached into the pocket of her apron and pulled out a small box.

His breath caught. Was she really doing what he thought she was doing? He slipped his hand into his own pocket and pulled out the velvet box he was carrying. When she caught sight of it, she giggled.

"On three?" she asked, beaming from ear to ear as she opened the small box she was holding, revealing a white-gold band with a carved infinity-symbol design.

He nodded, opening the velvet box to reveal the one-carat oval-cut diamond set in white gold. "One…two…three!"

"Sean Quinn, will you marry me?"

"Marry me, Jenna Hartley!"

"Yes!" they said in unison.

"I love you." He swept Jenna into his arms and kissed her. *Thank You, Lord, for entrusting me with this woman's heart. I promise to cherish her, all the days of my life.*

* * * * *

Christmas In The Crosshairs
Deena Alexander

MILLS & BOON

Deena Alexander grew up in a small town on eastern Long Island where she lived up until a few years ago and then relocated to Clermont, Florida, with her husband, three children, son-in-law and four dogs. Now she enjoys long walks in nature all year long, despite the occasional alligator or snake she sometimes encounters. Her love for writing developed after the birth of her youngest son, who had trouble sleeping through the night.

Books by Deena Alexander

Love Inspired Suspense

Crime Scene Connection
Shielding the Tiny Target
Kidnapped in the Woods
Christmas in the Crosshairs

Every good gift and every perfect gift is from above,
and cometh down from the Father of lights, with whom
is no variableness, neither shadow of turning.
—James 1:17

This book is lovingly dedicated to
my husband and children—you are my greatest blessings.

Chapter One

"We're losing her!" Chaos erupted as two paramedics shoved a gurney through the emergency department doors at a dead run. One of them called out, "It's Jaelyn Reed. She was attacked."

Jaelyn's heart stuttered. She recognized the voice of her friend and fellow firefighter Pat Ryan. But what was he talking about? She was fine, just finishing up her Christmas Eve shift at the hospital, where she worked as a nurse when she wasn't volunteering as a firefighter for Seaport Fire and Rescue. Since she had no family to go home to, she often worked the holidays.

Footsteps pounded as doctors, nurses, and technicians rushed toward a commotion in one of the nearby cubicles.

She followed the sound of Pat's voice rattling off vitals down the corridor. Why had he said it was Jaelyn? That she'd been attacked? She'd known Pat Ryan since she was a kid, was friends with both him and his fiancée, Rachel, and she'd never heard the slightest edge of panic in his voice. Until now.

She stepped into the cubicle. "What's going on?"

Pat glanced at her then snapped his head back in a double take. "Jaelyn?"

"Pat, what happened?"

His gaze shot to the gurney, where a young woman lay unconscious as the nurses assessed and began treatment.

When Jaelyn followed his stare, her breath caught in her throat. Looking down at the woman's face was like looking into a mirror. The stranger shared the same long, nearly black hair as Jaelyn, though hers was tangled and matted with blood; the same delicate features, at least it appeared so beneath the contusions and swelling; and even the same slim, athletic build.

"I don't understand." Pat frowned and grabbed the woman's purse from the bottom of the gurney. "She looks enough like you to be your—"

"Sister." The one word escaped on a shallow huff of breath. Could this woman be her sister? The sister she hadn't even known existed until a month ago? It'd been almost a year since she'd taken the DNA test—just for fun, something she'd let her fellow firefighters convince her to do to pass the time amid a blizzard that had gripped the area last winter.

Jaelyn had grown up in Seaport, New York, a small town on the east end of Long Island's south shore, daughter of a prominent couple in the community, Dr. and Mrs. Elijah Reed. And she was an only child. The last thing she'd ever expected was to shake loose any deep, dark secrets from the Reed family tree. And then her results had come in…and last month the friends and family app had connected her to her twin. "Maya Barlowe."

"Yeah." Pat held out a slim photo holder with the woman's driver's license. The picture of the woman staring back at her could have been, well, her twin. "That's the name on her ID. Is she your sister?"

Apparently. Since Jaelyn's parents had been killed in a car accident five years ago, she hadn't been able to ask them about her. She had no other family—no one to lean on after her fiancé had left her for another woman while she was grieving—and she hadn't wanted to go to any of her parents' friends. At least, not yet. She'd needed time to process the information first. Jaelyn had yet to decide whether or not to reach out to the woman, try to ascertain how they shared not only the same DNA but the same birthdate as well. Even as she'd debated her options, she hadn't fully accepted the fact it could actually be true, that she could have a long-lost twin sister she'd never known about.

"Out of the way, guys." One of the other nurses shoved past her.

Coming to her senses, Jaelyn stepped aside, careful not to upset the delicate choreography as the doctors and nurses worked together in a desperate effort to save the woman's life.

Pat gripped her elbow and led her out into the hallway. "Hey, you okay?"

Was she? She honestly didn't know. While she hated the thought of seeing anyone suffer, what was she supposed to feel for this woman who might be her twin but whom she'd never met? Confusion was the overwhelming emotion. She shoved a few stray strands of hair out of her face. "Yeah, I guess, but I don't understand what's going on. Where did you find her? And what happened to her?"

"A call came in." With a glance over his shoulder, Pat ushered her farther across the hall so they'd be out of the way. "A couple of kids riding dirt bikes came across her just before dusk in the woods behind the Seaport Bed and Breakfast. She'd been attacked, badly beaten. I'm sorry, Jaelyn, I didn't even know you'd reached out to her. I guess with the holidays and all..."

"No. That's the thing..." Only a handful of people knew about the secret Jaelyn's DNA test had revealed, Pat being one of them. Could someone she'd trusted have contacted Maya? No, not possible. The few close friends she'd told knew that Jaelyn wasn't sure how she wanted to handle the situation yet. None of them would have betrayed her confidence... Besides, she hadn't shared Maya's name with anyone. "I didn't reach out, nor did she contact me. I have no idea what she was doing here. I didn't even realize she knew about me."

"Assuming she's here because of you," Pat pointed out.

"I guess, but according to the information I have, she lives in New York City. What are the chances she just happened to show up a few miles from where I live and work?" Even though plenty of people from New York City visited the south shore of Eastern Long Island, especially around the holidays, most of them flocked to the Hamptons or Montauk. Seaport wasn't exactly a thriving tourist destination.

Pat frowned. "Slim to none, I'd say."

So her sister must have been trying to find her, which begged the question, why hadn't she tried to contact her? Or had she? Jaelyn had been on duty for the past twelve hours and hadn't bothered to check her messages. "My phone is in the locker room. I'll have to see if she tried to reach out."

"The police officers were questioning the kids who found her, but they'll be here any minute." He gestured in the direction of the locker room. "You should probably see if she tried to make contact before they get here. I'm sure they'll want to know if that's why she was in Seaport."

Dazed, Jaelyn paused and glanced into the cubicle where her coworkers and friends worked to save Maya. Should she go in? Try to help? Technically, she was off duty now, but still...

"There's nothing you can do for her in there, Jaelyn. She's being taken care of. It would probably help her more right now to find out if she tried to call you, if she left any kind of message, maybe indicated she was in trouble, anything that would help the police find who did this to her."

She nodded. He was right. "Yeah, okay."

"And Jaelyn..." He turned to face her, rubbed his hands up and down her arms. "I'm really sorry about your sister, but I'm glad you're okay. I'm not gonna lie, when we first arrived on scene and thought it was you, it gave both Jack and me a jolt."

She covered one of his hands with hers. "Thank you, Pat."

"Sure thing." Releasing her, he stuffed his hands into his pockets and started down the hall with her.

"You didn't check her ID there?" Jaelyn asked.

He only hesitated a fraction of a second, but it was a telling pause. "She's in bad shape, Jaelyn. We stabilized her and transported. Plus, like I said, we thought it was you, both recognized you immediately."

She nodded, understanding the urgency of the situation in that moment. Nothing but saving the patient would have mattered to the paramedics.

"I'll tell you what, I'll wait here and keep an eye on her while you go ahead and get your phone. You may as well get changed while you're in the locker room, so you can sit with your sister afterward."

She smiled at him, grateful he understood her need to know how Maya was doing. "Thank you."

"Of course." He squeezed her arm once more, as if needing to reassure himself she was fine. "I'll let the guys know you're okay."

She nodded and started toward the locker room at a brisk pace. Since she was not only a nurse in the emergency room, but also a volunteer firefighter and a member of a well-known family in the community, news of her being attacked would have spread quickly. Especially in the small town of Seaport. It would be good to squash the rumors before they could gain any real traction.

Thankfully, with Pat taking care of that, it was one less thing she had to worry about, and she could turn her attention to her sister. *Sister.* She still couldn't quite wrap her head around the idea. Being an only child was all she'd ever known. She shook off the confusion and increased her pace. None of that mattered now. The sooner she gathered her things, the sooner she could return to Maya and hopefully get some answers.

As she passed the nurses' station, a man's voice brought her up short. "I'm looking for Maya Barlowe?"

Jaelyn turned at the mention of her sister's name.

"Can you tell me if she was brought in—" A bulky man who had to be better than six feet tall shifted his attention from the nurses' station even as he asked the question. As he glanced in her direction, his gaze clashed with Jaelyn's. His expression showed confusion at first, but then it hardened and he straightened.

Jaelyn hesitated, caught off guard by the hostility marring his features.

His focus narrowed on her as he reached inside his jacket and pulled out a handgun.

Her breath caught in her lungs. A dull ache spread through her chest. Fear paralyzed her.

Eyes hard, hand dead steady, the man lifted the weapon toward her.

The chaos of the emergency department receded, and blackness tunneled her vision. It seemed nothing existed but the two of them caught in some deadly stare down. She desperately wanted to believe she was just in the wrong place at the wrong time, but her mind wouldn't allow her to accept that. The gunman's glare was too intense, his attention too pinpointed on her, and he'd just asked about her sister.

"Get down!" another man yelled.

Jaelyn couldn't react. All of her training as a nurse, as a firefighter, had her remaining calm in the face of the weapon. It was the look in his eyes that had her blood running cold. She'd never seen such emptiness, such coldness, such...darkness.

And then someone tackled her from the side, even as the first bullets flew. Sheer terror swamped her.

More gunshots erupted. Screams, crashes, sobs tore through the emergency department as patients and staff ran or dove for cover, trying to protect those who were unable to flee.

Jaelyn landed hard on her elbow. Pain shot to her shoulder and her wrist, and her fingers went numb.

"Go, go, go!" The stranger half-dragged, half-shoved her toward an examination room door, knocking over the Christmas tree in an out-of-the-way corner.

Jaelyn scrambled in the direction she was led, hit the door at a crouch, and tumbled through.

Another round of gunshots pierced the air, too many for just the handgun she'd seen. Had the attacker had another weapon beneath his jacket, or was there a second gunman? Two shots shattered the window in the door.

Jaelyn covered her head and ducked against a row of cabinets.

"Stay down." The man who'd saved her lay a quick hand on her shoulder, glanced through the cracked window into the hallway and looked around.

His strong hand on her shoulder helped ground her. They had to get out of there. People needed help.

The gunman flung the door open and leveled what appeared to be an automatic weapon at Jaelyn.

"Oh, God, please help me." She closed her eyes as she whispered the plea, prayed the attacker hadn't already harmed anyone, prayed he'd leave without killing anyone, then gathered her strength, coiled her muscles, and lunged at him.

A shot rang out beside her.

The gunman's eyes went wide as the bullet struck his chest, as if shocked someone had dared to shoot him, and he crumpled to the floor.

Jaelyn ignored the ringing in her ears, dropped to her knees at his side, and felt for a pulse.

The man who'd saved her caught her beneath the arm and hauled her to her feet. "We have to go. He won't be alone, and no one here will be safe until you're gone."

"What are you talking about?" Falling back on her training, she yanked her arm away and continued to triage, checking vitals, assessing damage.

"Listen to me." He crouched in front of her, lifted her chin until her gaze met his. Turmoil raged in his brown eyes, and his tawny hair was disheveled. "We have to go. Now."

"Look, I appreciate you saving me. Thank you. But I'm not going anywhere with you. I don't even know who you are. And I'm not leaving anyone to die." As she started chest compressions, Pat barreled through the door with his partner, Jack, on his heels.

Pat dropped beside her. "Are you all right?"

"I am, yes." Jack took over compressions, and Jaelyn used her wrist to swipe back a few strands of hair that had come loose from her ponytail. "Is anyone out there hurt?"

"Only minor injuries," Pat replied.

She offered up a prayer of thanks, knowing how much worse the outcome could have been. With Pat and Jack working to save the gunman, she slid out of the way and climbed to her feet, then met her stranger's angry expression with one of her own. "Explain. Now."

Adam Spencer fought for calm. What was wrong with this woman? Why would she argue when he was trying to save her life? Actually, why was he even trying to save her life when he'd had her under surveillance for the past two weeks and suspected she was married to the man who'd killed his wife? The woman who'd meant everything to him.

"Fine." Adam hooked her elbow, started to move toward the doorway. "Walk and talk."

"I will not." She shook him off and stepped back. A spark of indignation flared in her eyes.

Adam was not about to have this conversation right here and now. There was a growing crowd of doctors and nurses moving in to take over the gunman's care and an increasing throng of lookie-loos jockeying for a better vantage point, any of whom might have a camera. And once Maya's picture was plastered all over social media and news outlets, there'd be no saving her, or himself. "Look, Ms. Barlowe—"

One of the firefighters stood and pinned Adam with a curious, not quite threatening stare. "Problem, Jaelyn?"

Jaelyn?

"No, I'm fine, Pat, thank you." She narrowed her eyes at Adam. "I think you might have me confused with someone else."

How could that be? She looked exactly like Maya Barlowe, enough resemblance for them to be twi...uh...oh, no. If this woman was not Maya Barlowe, she might be in even more danger. Not only was she clueless about what was going on, but she'd be considered expendable. He needed time to think, had to figure out what was going on and make a plan to keep both of these women safe. "Um, look, Jaelyn, is it?"

She nodded.

"Okay, listen, I don't expect you to trust me." He dug into his pocket for his ID and a business card, then held them both out to her. "My name is Adam Spencer. I'm a defense attorney from New York City. Please, I can't explain everything right here and now, but everyone in this hospital is in danger as long as you're here."

Her gaze lifted from his credentials. "Me? Why would anyone be in danger from me?"

A second firefighter joined the first. "What's going on, Jaelyn? This guy giving you a hard time?"

"I'm all right, Jack, thank you."

Adam swiped a hand over his scruffy five-o'clock shadow. He needed a shave, and a shower. Neither of which was going to happen any time soon unless he could convince this woman to trust him. He'd obviously come on a little too heavy handed, mistaking her for Maya and figuring she'd jump at the opportunity to escape. That mistake had already cost too much time, and now he had to deal not only with Jaelyn but her two guard dogs as well. "Okay, look, is there somewhere quiet we can talk?"

Jaelyn eyed him for another minute then nodded and handed back his ID. "Follow me."

As she started forward, her apparently self-appointed body-guards flanked her, leaving Adam to follow behind. Great. This was a disaster. A dull throb began at his temples. As he followed them down the hallway, eyes ricocheting around at the carnage—most of it upended equipment and discarded items people had dropped and knocked over in their haste to flee the gunfire—he caught sight of his reflection in a cubicle window.

Yikes, between the rumpled suit, hair sticking up in every direction, four-day-old scruff, and hardened expression, it was no wonder the woman didn't trust him. He wouldn't have gone anywhere with him either. He reached up and smoothed his hair, not out of any great sense of vanity, but because he needed to come across as a professional, someone these people could trust, or they were all going to end up dead.

When Jaelyn entered a cubicle followed by Pat, Jack gestured for Adam to enter then yanked the curtain closed behind him and stood in front of it, scrolling through something on his phone.

Jaelyn leaned back against the counter, folded her arms across her chest, and gave him her undivided attention. The full intensity in her brilliant blue eyes hit him like a sucker punch. In all the time he'd been tailing Maya, he'd never noticed the incredible power her gaze held. Could it be the two didn't share that quality, despite the eerily similar features and build?

"You have five minutes," she said, "less if they need this cubicle or call for help. Thankfully, there don't seem to be many injuries, thanks to your intervention, or I wouldn't even be giving you that long."

He nodded, appreciating her position, even if he didn't like it. Ignoring the other two men, Adam focused solely on Jaelyn. She was the one he needed to convince, and quickly. "Okay, as I said, my name is Adam Spencer, and I'm a defense attorney. I recently lost a client to a hitman known only as the Hunter. During the attack, he tried to kill me as well, but he failed and I escaped."

Barely. Adam had never come so close to death. He'd practically felt the rush of air as the bullet whizzed past his ear as he'd turned to help his client, just in time to avoid certain death. And he was grateful every day for that instinct to turn to help, though he still lived with the guilt of having failed to save the man who'd trusted him.

"The police can't find this hitman," he continued, "the FBI can't find him, and a host of foreign agencies can't find him. No one can identify him, except for one person, my client who was killed a month ago." Adam believed that the reclusive assassin owned Hack Hunters, a multi-million-dollar cybersecurity company—if only he could prove it.

Jaelyn frowned. "So, what does my sister have to do with this?"

He shifted, uncomfortable beneath her stare, and glanced at Pat, watching them closely, and Jack, still hunched over his phone. How much to tell her? Certainly not of the senator's involvement, not in a curtained-off cubicle in the middle of a chaotic emergency department where anyone could overhear. No, for now he'd just go with the basics. "I believe I know who the Hunter is, and who hired him."

She lifted a brow. "Your client didn't tell you?"

"No, he didn't. Just that he knew the Hunter's identity and that he wanted to turn evidence—"

"In exchange for information." Jack held out his phone to Jaelyn. "Your client was going on trial and was willing to testify to what he knew in exchange for immunity from prosecution."

"Yes." Adam's stomach sank. He'd wanted to share the details with Jaelyn himself, wanted to soften the fact that his client stood to gain a whole new life in exchange for the information he was willing to hand over. "But he also maintained his innocence."

Jaelyn looked up from the phone. "Murder charges?"

"Yes," Adam was forced to admit. "But, again, he maintained his innocence."

"And?"

"And I believed him. I think he was framed." After all, Josiah had been accused only recently of a murder that had happened years ago.

She tapped her bottom lip with one short, unpolished nail, a gesture he'd witnessed Maya do on numerous occasions when stressed. Of course, Maya's nails were painted bright red and sharp as daggers. Then again, what would he expect from someone he suspected was married to one of the most notorious hitmen ever known—a man who moved like smoke, one no one knew for sure even existed because he'd never been careless enough to be seen? Now, if Adam could only find a man no one quite believed was anything more than an urban legend and turn him over to authorities before anyone else died.

Jaelyn shook her head, handed the phone back to Jack. "Okay, so I'll ask again, what does this have to do with my sister? And how am I a danger to anyone?"

"I believe your sister's husband, Hunter Barlowe, is the assassin known as the Hunter."

She sucked in a breath, jerked back as if he'd slapped her.

"I've been…" He squirmed, unsure how any of them would react to the fact that he'd had Maya Barlowe under not exactly legal surveillance. "Keeping an eye on your sister for the past few weeks."

She tilted her head but said nothing.

He hesitated, waited to see if she'd balk. When she didn't respond, he continued. "At first, I thought she might be in cahoots with her husband, and I followed her hoping she'd lead me to him, but in all the time I watched her, I never once saw the two of them together. I got the idea I might be able to approach her, convince her to agree to testify against her husband. Then, three days ago, while I was still trying to decide what to do, I trailed her to a bed and breakfast not far from here. I had no clue why she was there, but now, after she was attacked, I believe her husband may have hired someone to eliminate her. While I can't confirm it, I think she decided to run."

"Why would he want to kill his own wife?"

"So she can't identify him."

"Why would she do that?"

"Because my client, the witness who was killed, was your sister's, shall we say, acquaintance." He shook his head. He should have known about Jaelyn, should have realized Maya had family she might turn to. After the research he'd done on her, how could he not have known she had a sister? "I didn't realize Maya might be visiting family, wasn't even aware of the connection between the two of you."

Jaelyn glanced at her friends, then returned her gaze to Adam and spoke quietly. "What is it you want from me?"

"I want to protect you…and Maya, if possible. And I want to find the Hunter and put him away so I can come out of hiding and get my life back, because he won't stop. He doesn't know my client didn't share his identity with me, so he won't give up until I'm dead. And if I'm right, and he's the one who hired someone to kill your sister, he won't give up until she's dead too."

Jaelyn frowned. "If he's a hitman, why hire someone else to kill Maya? Why not do it himself?"

"To distance himself from the crime." Or perhaps it was the senator who'd hired the hitman to go after Maya. But that was a problem for another time. "I'm quite sure he'll have an iron-clad alibi for the time Maya was attacked."

Pat stepped forward. "Jack and I were the paramedics who brought Maya Barlowe in. It didn't appear to be a professional hit." He briefly laid a hand on Jaelyn's shoulder, sent her an apologetic look before turning to Adam. "She was severely beaten."

Adam wasn't surprised. "Probably someone trying to find out what she knew, who she'd told, and what she intended to do next."

"Then why leave her alive?"

"Who knows?" Adam shrugged. He didn't have time for the third degree. "Maybe he was interrupted, maybe he needed the okay from a higher up to complete the job. Whatever the case, the gunman obviously got the go-ahead since he showed up here to finish what he started."

"Okay." Jaelyn straightened and leveled a look at Adam. "So what do you propose?"

Adam's mind raced. He had to get Jaelyn out of there before anyone else mistook her for Maya. At the same time, he had to protect Maya. An idea started to form. "I've done extensive research on Maya Barlowe, had to before I could consider approaching her as a witness, and yet I didn't know about you..."

He let the sentence hang, hoping she'd offer some answer as to why.

Jaelyn heaved in a breath and let it out slowly. "I didn't know about Maya until about a month ago, when the family app from a DNA test I did last year linked me to her profile."

"Hmm..." He chewed that over. Maybe he could turn that in their favor. "Okay, if you didn't know about Maya, there's a chance she didn't know about you. Maybe she just found out as well. If that's the case, whoever's after her may not know about you either. If you'll agree to come with me for now..."

She stiffened.

He plowed on. "I can protect you, and maybe we could keep Maya's identity a secret for the moment. Does anyone else know who she is?"

Pat shook his head. "I honestly thought it was Jaelyn when we brought her in. Then, when Jaelyn walked into the cubicle, I grabbed Maya's purse and we checked the ID."

"As a matter of fact," Jaelyn added, "when Pat came in with her, he yelled that it was Jaelyn Reed. That's what drew my attention in the first place, so maybe..."

"If we let her identity remain a secret, let everyone think it's Jaelyn Reed who was injured, and get you out of here, just maybe I can find the Hunter and keep both of you safe."

"You think Jaelyn's in danger?" Pat asked.

"Even if they don't mistake her for Maya and take her out, once her husband or his employer figure out Maya has a sister, they're going to want to know how much Maya shared with her." But if Adam's suspicions turned out to be true, why had the Hunter's employer allowed Jaelyn to live this long at all? Unless he knew she had no knowledge of her paternity.

Jaelyn shivered.

"How do we keep that from happening?" Jack asked.

Adam shrugged. "I find the killer and turn him over to the authorities."

Jaelyn lifted a brow. "And how do you propose we do that?"

He hadn't said anything about *we*, but he decided to let that go for now. Better to get her to cooperate first, then let her know she wasn't getting involved any deeper in this mess than necessary. "Well, since my best lead is laid up under an assumed identity and unable to answer questions—"

"Stop." Jaelyn held up a hand, then sighed. "If we're going to let everyone believe Maya is Jaelyn Reed, and we look enough alike that even my good friends mistook her for me, why not have me take her place as well. At least long enough to see what, if anything, she left behind in her room?"

Chapter Two

After overruling Pat's and Jack's objections and ignoring Adam's protests, Jaelyn checked her phone but found no messages from Maya. She quickly changed into street clothes while the three men stood guard outside the locker room. With a headache starting to pound behind her eyes, she yanked the band out of her ponytail, shook her hair free, and massaged her temples.

Not wanting to waste a minute, Jaelyn grabbed her bag and slung it over her shoulder, then pointedly ignored her reflection in the mirror. Who knew? Meeting her own gaze might be just what she needed to force her to reexamine this half-baked plan and change her mind about risking her life to possibly save a sister she barely knew and a man who'd barreled his way into her world uninvited.

Of course, he'd already saved her life, so there was that.

Before she could back out, she pulled the door open and stepped into the hallway.

Pat moved into her path, pitched his voice low. "Are you sure you want to do this, Jaelyn? You don't have to go with him to the B&B."

She nodded, trying to project a confidence she most definitely did not feel. "I'm sure. I'll be fine."

He turned on Adam, patted his shoulder once before tightening his grip. His tone, while still hushed, turned forceful. "You keep her safe."

To his credit, Adam maintained eye contact without appearing at all aggressive. "I will. You guys just take care of Maya and let me worry about the rest."

Jack leaned toward her. "We've already contacted Gabe, and he's on his way. You make sure to keep in touch."

Jaelyn nodded, appreciating all their help. The fact that they'd discuss the situation with Gabe, a police officer who also happened to be a close friend, made her feel somewhat better. But they couldn't wait around right now. They had to get to Maya's room before anyone else did. "Tell Gabe I'll reach out once we leave the B&B."

"Here. I grabbed this when they took Maya to X-ray." Jack handed her Maya's purse and stepped back to let them pass.

"Thank you. For everything." She stuffed the purse into her oversize bag and turned her attention to Adam. "You're sure we shouldn't wait and talk to the police first, right?"

He hooked her elbow and started down the hallway toward the exit. "Right now, they may not have Maya's identity. They most likely went with Pat's assertion it was you, and since the paramedics had her bag, they won't have found her ID yet."

"Once Pat and Jack talk to Gabe, that cat will be out of the bag."

"Yup, that's why we need to get into her room as quickly as possible." He kept his head on a constant swivel as he rounded a corner, then guided her back against the wall. "It would probably be best if no one recognizes you leaving and draws attention to the fact that Jaelyn Reed is fine and well."

She couldn't argue that.

Adam reached behind her, caging her between his arms, then lifted her raincoat hood over her head. He took her hand in his, the strength of his grip the only outward sign of his stress, and started through the emergency department. "Stay close to me."

She wouldn't dream of straying so much as an inch from his side. Jaelyn was no stranger to danger—as a firefighter, her life was potentially in danger with every call—but having someone taking shots at you in a crowded emergency room with no care for any innocent bystanders was something else entirely. She kept her head low, face averted beneath the loose-fitting hood.

As they hurried through the beehive of activity, staff rushed to care for and reassure frightened patients that the threat was over, police officers hammered witnesses with questions as they tried to ascertain what exactly had happened, and people assessed damage and tried to restore order. The gunman had already been moved, no doubt into one of the curtained-off cubicles. While there was broken glass, equipment damaged beyond repair, even a cubicle curtain shredded by gunfire, some semblance of order had begun to return. Carts, trays, papers, and a myriad of other equipment had been picked up and returned to their proper places, and the rushed but smooth flow of activity had begun to reemerge.

As she and Adam hit the doors and stepped out into the cold air, she pulled her hood further over her face.

Lightning flashed, followed almost immediately by a long, low rumble of thunder. Rain beat a steady rhythm as the scent of ozone from the passing nor'easter filled the air. Multi-colored lights from the string of Christmas bulbs hung over the ER entrance reflected from puddles on the ground, and she and Adam splashed across the sidewalk and stepped into the road heading toward the parking lot.

A car fishtailed around the corner of the building, its speed way too fast for the current conditions. And it appeared to accelerate as it barreled toward them.

Jaelyn paused, watching in horror as the vehicle closed in. "Adam—"

"Go!" He shoved her out of the way, then jumped as the SUV struck him and he landed on its hood.

Jaelyn stumbled, fell to one knee on the wet pavement, then

regained her footing and whirled back toward him. Run or fight? She couldn't leave Adam hurt.

He saved her having to make the decision when he continued a smooth roll over the roof and tumbled gracefully off the back, then hit the ground running. "Run!"

She turned and fled, didn't look back at the screech of brakes, the slamming of doors, the shouts to stop.

Adam easily overtook her, his stride much longer than hers, and grabbed her wrist. "Go. Left."

She did as instructed, trying to keep a row of cars between her and their pursuers. Stealth wasn't an option as their footsteps pounded against the blacktop, splashing water all the way up to her knees. Jaelyn was a decent runner, tried to hit the track most mornings, but she was nowhere near as fast as Adam. The man could move. For some reason, she wouldn't have expected the lawyer to have such physical prowess.

Adam fumbled a key fob out of his pocket, chanced one quick glance over his shoulder as he hit the button to unlock a dark colored sedan and huffed, "Get in."

She grabbed the handle on the run, used her momentum to yank the door open and swing inside. Her hands trembled as she shoved the seatbelt buckle into the slot, grabbed the chicken stick, and braced herself.

Adam slammed the gear shift into reverse and swung out of the parking spot.

Their pursuers had given up the foot chase and were running back toward their own vehicle.

"Hold on." With barely a glance in each direction for oncoming traffic, Adam yanked the wheel hard to the right as he accelerated out of the lot. The back of the car fishtailed on the slick surface. He battled the wheel to regain control.

Jaelyn's stomach gave one hard roll. A quick glance in the side-view mirror had her heart rate ratcheting up. "They're following."

Barely slowing for a red light, Adam rocketed through the

intersection. The car bottomed out, knocking Jaelyn's teeth together, as he hit a pothole. The narrow residential road was not made for the speed at which they were moving.

Adam checked the rearview mirror. "I don't know the area. Is there somewhere I can lose them?"

The SUV was gaining on them, too close to shake. They weren't going to get away without a confrontation.

"Keep your head low." Adam drove with one eye on the road ahead of him and one on the mirror.

Sliding down in the seat, Jaelyn squeezed her eyes closed, shutting out everything around her as she pulled up an imaginary map in her head. They'd left the hospital from the front entrance, the opposite way she'd usually go to head home or to the firehouse. If they could... She jerked up. "Up ahead. About a mile, you can turn onto a dirt fire road."

A glance in the side-view mirror had Adam mumbling under his breath. "Where does it lead? Will we be trapped in there if they follow?"

She braced for impact as the headlights behind them moved closer. "No. There's a network of fire roads throughout the pine barrens. If they're still passable with the heavy rain, we should be able to lose them."

And if they were already flooded, his sedan didn't stand a chance against the SUV on their tail.

Adam slowed.

"What are you doing?" She wedged her feet against the floorboards, then tried to relax so her legs wouldn't break if they hit something.

"Just hold on."

The SUV barreled up on them, moved into the oncoming lane, tried to pull up alongside them on the driver's side.

Jaelyn held her breath and prayed no innocent civilian would round a curve and plow head-on into the vehicle.

The back window on the driver's side shattered. Gunfire?

Adam held the wheel steady, jaw clenched tight. As the SUV

jockeyed for a better position, he yanked the wheel hard to the left.

The impact jolted through her.

He pulled the wheel back, sending the car into a dangerous swerve, then recovered enough to hit them again.

Losing its traction on the slippery pavement, the SUV spun out and crashed into a tree.

Adam hit the gas. "Where to?"

They'd already passed the first fire road, so Jaelyn recalculated, pointed ahead of them and to the right. "Turn."

He slammed the brakes, skidded, and she was pretty sure took the corner on two wheels. He slowed and checked behind them as he entered the development.

"Head straight through. You can access the fire roads out the back."

He nodded, breath coming in harsh gasps.

"Are you okay?"

He nodded again, slowed as they bounced over a low berm and onto the narrow dirt path through the woods. Pine trees swallowed them up as the road curved. Thick mud shot from beneath the tires, splattered the windows, splashed in through the broken glass.

"So…" Jaelyn slumped against the seat back, working to steady her nerves. Her hand shook as she tucked her hair behind her ear. "Those were some fancy moves back there."

"Thanks." His grin shot straight to her heart, but his expression sobered much too quickly. "Are you hurt?"

"No, no." She sucked in a deep breath, filled her lungs to capacity for the first time since leaving the hospital. "I'm fine. Are you?"

"I'll be fine."

That caught her attention. "You're injured?"

"Not badly."

She shifted in her seat, reached for the interior light, but he lay a hand over hers.

"No light. It's difficult enough to see with this rain."

Rain pounded against the windshield, the wipers barely clearing it, reducing visibility to just about nothing. "There's a gym bag on the floor behind my seat. Can you grab a towel from it?"

She eyed him another moment, just a quick assessment to be sure he seemed coherent and alert, then unbuckled her seatbelt and shifted to unzip the bag. The towel was right on top, and she yanked it out and handed it to him.

"Thanks." He dabbed absently at the left side of his head, gaze firmly locked on the narrow path through the woods, then tossed the towel onto the back seat.

Even with the interior lights off, the dark contrast of blood stood out against the white towel.

Adam used his sleeve to wipe the blood trickling into his eye again. It seemed to have slowed, but the last thing he needed while trying to drive in this weather was anything impeding his vision. The scrape of metal against a tree had him wincing. "How long until we can get out of here?"

Brow furrowed, Jaelyn shook her head. "I'm not sure. It's difficult to tell where we are."

Thick, black storm clouds dumped gallons of rain in sheets over the windshield despite a valiant effort by the wipers to keep it clear. The car bounced in a hole, stuck for a moment as the tires spun and kicked up a wave of mud, then caught and surged forward. "If we're going to try to get into Maya's room, we need to get there before whoever's after her, and us, does. And before the police."

Jaelyn only nodded and chewed on her lower lip. Leaning closer to the windshield, she squinted, then pointed. "There. See that boulder? My friends and I used to hang out there when we were kids. Okay, I know where we are. Just keep going straight for about a mile. After that, you're going to come into a clearing. Follow the road around the field and you'll come out on a back road we can take to the bed and breakfast."

"Okay, good. That's good." Although he'd have liked to get there more quickly, he didn't dare risk increasing his speed. The rain worked against him, distorting his surroundings until the thick stand of trees all blurred together, making it difficult to navigate the narrow, rutted trail.

Jaelyn sat back, took a few deep breaths.

Adam rolled his shoulders, tilted his head back and forth to stretch his neck and ease some of the tension coiled there. He risked a quick peek at Jaelyn, and in that brief moment, he noticed a problem. "You're sure you're okay?"

"I am, thank you." She lay her head against the seat, and her eyes fluttered closed.

Adam allowed her a few moments of peace to collect herself. Unfortunately, they couldn't afford any more than that. He cleared his throat to get her attention.

When she turned her head toward him without lifting it from the headrest, he debated keeping his mouth shut. Then again, keeping his mouth shut just didn't suit him. "Listen, we might have a problem."

"Really?" She lifted a brow. "Only one?"

He couldn't help but grin. "Well, one more pressing than the others."

"Okay, I'll bite, what's the problem?"

"I don't know if you noticed your sister's clothing when she was brought in."

She frowned. "I didn't. Why?"

"Well…" He gestured toward the well-worn jeans and pink sweatshirt she wore beneath her raincoat. "Maya tended to dress a little more sophisticated."

"Yeah?" She looked down at her clothing. "Hmm."

"We might be able to…alter your appearance enough for you to pass as Maya at the B&B. If, that is, no one there knows her or you too well and you don't stop to chat." And if no one had the B&B under surveillance, because one look was all it would take for someone who knew Maya well to know something was off. He could only hope that the B&B staff didn't know Jaelyn, or they'd have wondered why a woman identical to her had checked in under a different name days ago. "If you're going to try to pass yourself off as her anywhere else, we're going to have to do something about your wardrobe."

Jaelyn started to say something, then caught herself and just waved him off. "One problem at a time, and my fashion choices are not a top priority at the moment."

While he begged to differ, he let the subject drop for the moment. He glanced again at Jaelyn and was surprised to realize he found her more attractive in the faded jeans and sweatshirt beneath her open raincoat than he had Maya with her elegant dresses, pantsuits, and strappy heels. There was something fresh about Jaelyn, an innocence Maya didn't possess. Odd, considering how much alike they looked. He shook off the thoughts. What did it matter to him how the two dressed? It didn't.

And Jaelyn could never matter to him in any other way than providing her protection, not after Alessandra's murder. His world had revolved around his wife, and it was his own fault he'd lost her. He tried to shake off the grief, the guilt. They'd do him no good now. There would be plenty of time after her killers were brought to justice to second-guess every decision he'd made that had led to her death. And he had no doubt there was more than one. The Hunter may have pulled the trigger, but Senator Mark Lowell had aimed the weapon.

"Turn up here."

He did as instructed and breathed a sigh of relief when he recognized the gas station on the corner. Only about five minutes to the B&B. "If you roll up your jeans and tighten the raincoat over them, no one should notice."

She shifted to face him. "You really think the way I'm dressed is that important?"

He shrugged, uncomfortable beneath her direct stare. "Look, I'm not the biggest fan of this idea to begin with, which is no secret."

"Nope, you certainly objected strongly enough." She scowled.

He bit back a grin. He had a feeling she might not fully appreciate it at the moment. "But if you're dead set on going through with it, we need to make you as safe as possible."

"What's to say letting people mistake me for Maya is the safest option, considering how she ended up?"

Touché. He couldn't imagine what was going on in her mind. She had to be terrified, having a sister she'd never known existed until recently push into her life in such a violent way, getting shot at when she was mistaken for that sister. Though, Adam had to wonder if the gunman had actually meant to kill Maya or if he was hoping to get rid of those protecting her and snatch her. Either way, he had to give Jaelyn credit. All in all, she was holding up quite well under the circumstances.

Jaelyn turned toward him, swiped a tear that had managed to tip over her thick lashes and roll down her cheek.

While he admired her strength, her sensitivity balanced the scales in a way that made her seem fragile. And yet, he couldn't let the overwhelming instinct to protect her get in the way of finding Alessandra's killer. He wouldn't. Even five years after her death, Alessandra was still his main focus.

"What's she like?" Jaelyn asked softly.

Alessandra? She was beautiful, inside and out. Always so quick to put others ahead of herself. She'd have made a wonderful—

"Adam?"

"Huh? What?"

"Maya? What's she like?"

Oh. He didn't know Maya well, had never actually met her, but he'd been watching her for three weeks, had booked the room down the hall from hers at the bed and breakfast so he could keep her under surveillance, but he'd been careful not to come face-to-face with her. He was, after all, Josiah Cameron's attorney, and she certainly knew Josiah well enough, considering she'd been having an affair with him for the better part of a year. Just because Adam hadn't met Maya didn't mean she wouldn't recognize him.

"She's beautiful, of course." His cheeks burned at the implication, and he hurried past the awkward moment. "And smart. Charming. And extremely powerful."

That seemed to catch Jaelyn off guard. "Powerful?"

"She's the CEO of a multi-million-dollar cybersecurity firm."

Jaelyn huffed out a breath. "Seriously?"

"Yes, the firm technically belongs to her husband, but she's the sitting CEO as he tends to other business interests." In most Manhattan circles, the billionaire businessman Hunter Barlowe was thought of as reclusive, eccentric even. He was never seen in public, and his wife kept up appearances. But, if Josiah's information was correct, which Adam had no reason to doubt, Hunter Barlowe's seclusion had more to do with his second, more lucrative career.

"Wow." Shaking her head, Jaelyn lowered her gaze to her hands resting in her lap. "I don't know what to say. It's weird enough trying to wrap my head around the fact that I have a sister…"

Unfortunately, she was going to have to come to terms with a lot more, but now wasn't the time to bring anything else up. They were pulling up to the bed and breakfast, and there was no time to waste. He hit the turn signal and drove into the small parking lot.

Shrubs ran around the perimeter of the three-story building and its wide wraparound porch, offering a sense of privacy for guests and plenty of shadows to conceal a killer lying in wait, despite the sprinkling of white Christmas lights.

"Let's get this done and get out of here. We can worry about everything else later."

She nodded, swiped her hands over her jean-clad legs. "Do you want me to try to clean that cut up before anyone notices?"

"Don't worry about it." He could deal with it later. "I'll keep my head down. You have Maya's purse?"

She pulled it out of her bag, hesitated only a moment, then opened it and dug through. She drew out a key hanging from a round fob with the number 201 inscribed on it, the same as the one Adam had boasting the number 208.

"Yeah, that's it."

She rolled her pant legs up until they'd be tucked beneath her long jacket. "What about my shoes?"

One glance at the running shoes had him groaning inwardly, but he kept his concern to himself. Nothing they could do about it, in any case, so no point in worrying her. "Don't worry about it. You're just going to go straight through the front door and up the stairs on the right. Hopefully, no one will bother to look down at your shoes."

"Okay." She took a deep breath, let it out slowly. "Let's do this."

Let's not. Let's go on the run, go into hiding, anything but cross that lot and go into that building. But there was nowhere to run. And there was nowhere to hide.

She reached for the door handle, but he grabbed her arm to stop her. "We can't go in together. You go straight in. Keep your hood up and your head down. I'll watch until after you get inside, make sure no one is around, then follow."

"Got it." She nodded.

"And when you walk, try to project a bit of arrogance, put a little sway in your hips."

She simply lifted a brow then smiled and patted the hand still holding her arm. "I'll see what I can do about that."

When she hopped out of the car and eased the door quietly shut, he slumped in the seat. He wanted to turn the ignition off, not draw attention to the fact there was someone still in the car, but without the wipers keeping the windshield semi-clear, he wouldn't be able to see anything at all. Then again, neither would any potential attackers.

While Jaelyn crossed the lot gracefully, keeping her posture rigid—he'd never take her for her sister. Adam could only hope her husband, if he was the one who'd ordered the hit, wouldn't come himself. She might be able to fool one of his henchmen, but Maya's husband would know in a heartbeat that she was an imposter. The senator would not be fooled either, but that coward wouldn't have the nerve to come after her himself.

When Jaelyn reached the front door, she paused for a moment. Light spilled onto the porch from the enormous Christmas tree in the front window covered in enough icicle lights to let anyone watching get a good look at her face.

"No, don't turn around," he whispered.

She glanced over her shoulder, revealing enough of her face for someone to make the ID, and he was not amused. Right now, he just wanted to get in and search Maya's room, get an idea what they might be dealing with before going up against any more goons.

He only waited a minute, scanning the entire area as he hurried across the lot and up the porch steps. He pulled the door open and rushed inside, then offered a smile and a wave to the owner who was arranging poinsettias while Christmas music played softly in the background.

She smiled at him. "Good evening, Mr. Justice."

"Ma'am." He nodded and kept going through the empty lobby to the stairway. Okay, so as far as aliases went, it was probably corny, but it was better than checking in under his real name with a killer's sights set on him. And, while the fake ID he'd made wouldn't hold up under the scrutiny of someone who knew what to look for, it had worked just fine with the sweet older woman who'd checked him in.

When he reached the second floor, Adam released the breath he'd been holding and hurried into the hallway. A man's voice had him skidding to a stop before rounding the corner.

"...playing games, Maya. We both know you have nerves of steel. Now quit fumbling the key—get that door open, and get inside."

Adam peered around the corner. A short, stocky man stood with his back to Adam and a firm grip on Jaelyn's arm. The instant she got the door open, he shoved her inside.

Chapter Three

The door to Maya's room slammed open as Jaelyn's assailant shoved her into the narrow entranceway and followed close on her heels.

She stumbled and braced her hands on the wall to catch herself, then shoved backward with all her strength. Still off balance, she led with her elbow as she swung around and landed a satisfying blow to his jaw.

He went down on one knee, then looked up at her and grinned through his bloodied mouth. "You'll pay for—"

Jaelyn followed through with a hard kick to his chest.

Even as his eyes went wide, he wheezed in a breath and doubled over.

Should she go further into the room and take a chance on the window? No. She might end up trapped. With that in mind, she vaulted over him toward the doorway.

He caught her ankle on her way by, and she belly-flopped onto the floor in the entryway, half in the room and half out.

Her chin smacked hard against the wood floor, and her teeth clacked together, sending a rush of pain through her head. Ignoring it, she rolled onto her back.

The attacker whirled toward her, surged to his feet, and lunged.

Jaelyn lifted both her feet and caught him in the gut as he reached for her, propelling him back into the room.

A flash of movement in her peripheral vision made her falter.

And then Adam was there. He dove over her and went after the guy, plowing a fist hard enough into his face to knock the cocky grin right off it.

Jaelyn rolled and pushed herself up to sit, then froze when the world gave one long slow spin. *Okay. You're okay. Just take a moment, sit still, breathe in and out slowly.*

When everything righted itself, she scooted backward. She had to get up. Adam was still fighting this guy, who she had to assume had a weapon even if he'd chosen not to use it against her. And, while someone clearly wanted something from Maya, Adam was nothing more than a target.

With that thought propelling her forward, she struggled to her feet and staggered into the room.

Adam glanced up from where he was digging through her unconscious attacker's pocket. "Hey, you okay?"

"Yeah." She leaned a shoulder against the wall to keep her rubbery knees from betraying her.

Blood ran down the side of Adam's face and into his eye, trailing into his short tawny hair, disheveled from the fight. Actually, his hair had been disheveled since she'd met him. Maybe he made a habit of running his hands through it. Either way, the fact that he'd saved her life again wasn't lost on her, and it didn't exactly sit well. Sure, she counted on her fellow firefighters to keep her safe, but that was a mutual thing, and she'd known most of them forever. This, counting on a stranger to protect her, made her uncomfortable. Seemed she was going to have to make some time to research the enigmatic Mr. Adam Spencer.

"Hmm...twice in one day, huh?" She swiped a trickle of blood from her chin. "So...what? Do you make a habit of rescuing damsels in distress?"

"Only one damsel, honey." He winked at her.

Jaelyn stood where she was a moment, assuring herself the hitch in her breathing and the gentle roll of her belly were the result of her close encounter with a killer and had nothing to do with Adam's charm or the sparkle of humor in his eyes even in the midst of danger.

Jaelyn's last attempt at a relationship had ended in disaster when her fiancé had betrayed her, turned to another woman for comfort when Jaelyn's parents were killed and she'd withdrawn to grieve. The grief had been unbearable, losing them so suddenly, not having the chance to say any of the things she wished she could say. She'd not had a big family, just her parents and her. But then she'd met Ronnie, and he'd become part of the family. They'd planned to get married, have children. And then, as if losing her parents wasn't bad enough, her dreams had been shattered as well.

She cut the thoughts off ruthlessly. They had no place in her life, and she refused to waste even a moment of her time thinking of him. "Are you okay?"

Adam glanced up and found her assessing his injury. "This? Yeah, fine. This is from earlier, just a graze."

"A graze? From a bullet?"

He shrugged as if it didn't matter and continued to dig through the pockets of the man's jeans. "A bullet, glass, it doesn't matter. I'll bandage it or stitch it when I get time."

The injury didn't appear life threatening. As soon as her legs were steady enough to keep her feet beneath her, she'd take care of the wound. "Who is he?"

"No ID." He shoved at the unconscious guy, clearly frustrated, then grabbed a handgun off the floor. "But I did take this off him."

That was no surprise.

Adam stood, dragged a chair from the corner table to the center of the room. He hooked the gunman beneath the arms and started to haul him up.

Feeling a little stronger, Jaelyn bent on the other side of the man and did the same. "Why put him in the chair?"

Lifting a brow, Adam studied her. "In case he wakes up."

"Oh, right." The sooner they got him where Adam wanted him, the sooner she could tend to Adam's injuries.

Once they had him settled, Adam started searching through the room, then disappeared into the bathroom. He returned carrying a bathrobe belt, two leather belts with decorative buckles, and a long red silk scarf, then went to work securing their prisoner to the chair. When he was done, he grabbed one of the other chairs and slid it out for Jaelyn. "Here, sit. You look a little unsteady."

"Just a bit." She sat, her muscles heavy with fatigue.

He pulled another chair close to hers and flopped onto it, panting heavily from exertion.

At least she hoped it was just exertion. "Do you have any other injuries?"

He shook his head, took a few deep breaths.

Watching him, she leaned back in the chair. Muscles she didn't even know she had screamed in protest. Seemed she must have tensed every last one of them while running and fighting over the past few hours, and they'd knotted up in objection. What she needed was a good, long, hot Epsom salt bath. Her eyelids grew heavy, drifted closed.

The muffled sound of a baby crying intruded, snapping her back to reality and the urgency of the situation. Her eyes shot open, jerking her alert. If the scuffle had woken a baby, it would certainly have woken the parents and possibly other guests as well. And if the fight hadn't, the baby's cries undoubtedly would. They had to get out of there before someone decided to investigate or call the police.

Adam met her gaze, jaw clenched so tightly she wondered how his teeth didn't shatter. "I'm going to try to wake this guy up and get some answers from him. Why don't you look around and see if you can find anything? Then we need to get out of here before any of his buddies show up."

Jaelyn narrowed her eyes at his just a little too innocent look. "By get some answers, you do mean you're going to ask politely and hope he tells you what you want to know, right?"

His answering scowl almost made her laugh. "Yeah, more or less. I'm not going to torture him or anything, if that's what you're worried about."

She lowered her eyes, not willing to admit the thought had crossed her mind. And suddenly she needed to be anywhere else but that room, anywhere she wouldn't have to squirm beneath Adam's intense scrutiny. She shoved to her feet a little too quickly, battled a moment of lightheadedness, then started to search. Of course, it would be easier if she knew what she was looking for.

She took a quick glance around the room, saddened by the lack of holiday festivity, and wondered fleetingly if Maya was as lonely as Jaelyn. What had she been doing staying alone at a bed and breakfast on Christmas Eve? Did she not have any family to celebrate the holiday with either?

She began in the closet Adam must have left open when searching for the belts. She rifled through the mass of designer outfits Maya had hung so perfectly, running her fingers over the expensive fabric. While their taste in clothes might differ tremendously, the need for organization seemed to be something they shared. She felt through pockets, checked the shoeboxes neatly arranged on the top shelf. Nothing but shoes. How long had Maya intended to stay, anyway? Jaelyn wouldn't pack that amount of clothes for a year. And she didn't own half that number of shoes.

Shifting the clothes aside, she looked in the bottom of the closet. Stuffed in the back corner, lost in shadow, was a briefcase. She yanked it out. Locked. No time to try to open it now. Shoving aside the pang of guilt, telling herself it wasn't stealing since she was taking it to try to protect Maya, she set the briefcase on the perfectly made bed.

The nightstand held only a well-worn Bible, and she took a moment to run her fingers over the gold embossed cover, wondering for a brief moment if Maya shared her faith.

A glance under the bed turned up nothing but a few dust bunnies, so she turned her attention toward the bathroom. When she walked through the short, narrow entryway, a door with a clasp and padlock stood to her right. The baby's cries were louder now, and she assumed the locked door must lead to the next room. Anxiety spurred her to move faster. They were already on borrowed time.

Perfume, makeup, toiletries, all lined neatly or arranged in three drawers. How could any one person need this amount of cosmetics? In the cabinet beneath the sink, she found a first aid kit. She set the kit on the counter and opened it, then breathed a sigh of relief that it was well stocked. When she found a box of ammonia inhalants, she briefly wondered what need Maya had for them, then dismissed the thought. What did it matter as long as she had what she needed? Ignoring the niggle of concern, she carried everything out to the bedroom and held a capsule out to Adam, who'd so far had no success rousing their victim. "Here, try this."

"Thanks." He held the capsule under the man's nose.

The man's head snapped back. He shook it as if to clear the cobwebs, then immediately struggled against his bonds. For a brief moment, Jaelyn thought he'd succeed in breaking free, then he stilled.

Adam stood back, carefully out of range if the guy should manage to escape. "All right, buddy, time to have a chat."

The attacker spit at him.

Jaelyn lay a hand on Adam's arm. "Why don't we just go?"

He shook her off. "Did you get what you needed?"

She gestured toward the bed where the briefcase sat. "That's it, and I didn't find the key to open it."

"Maybe it's in *your* purse." Adam held her gaze rigidly with his own.

Jaelyn hadn't thought of that, had already forgotten she was supposed to be Maya. Apparently, it was going to take time for her to get used to this whole cloak-and-dagger thing. Hopefully, she'd master it before she got one of them hurt…or worse.

The attacker studied her, frowned. "You know you can't escape, right… *Maya?*"

Uh oh. Had she just blown her cover?

Adam turned his attention back to the gunman, pointing the man's weapon at him. "Who hired you?"

The man grinned, baring a broken front tooth.

Adam's grip tightened on the weapon, and for a moment, Jaelyn thought he'd fire.

"Look, guy, all I want to know is who hired you. After that, you can go."

Something flickered in the man's eyes. Hope maybe? Then his expression hardened, and he tipped his chair onto the back two legs.

"Fine." Adam took out his cell phone. "If you won't talk to me, you can talk to the police."

Hands bound, the guy simply shrugged.

Jaelyn held her breath, her attention riveted on Adam. "We should get out of here."

He continued to stare the man down. His hands began to shake.

She took the phone from his hand, dialed Pat's number, then walked into the bathroom—where she hoped the gunman wouldn't be able to overhear her—to tell him what had happened and find out if he'd spoken to Gabe.

"Jaelyn, you okay?" Pat asked the instant he picked up.

"I am, yeah. But we need a place to lay low for a little while, regroup."

"I guess you didn't find anything in Maya's room?"

"I wouldn't say that." And she told him about the gunman,

careful not to refer to Maya just in case. "I don't think we should wait around for the police, so I thought maybe you could get ahold of Gabe and get them out here while we take off."

"Sure thing. Remember when Jack and Ava were having those problems, and Missy needed to be kept safe?"

Jaelyn remembered well, had taken a few shifts as bodyguard herself at the small house by the beach in Montauk. "Yeah."

"Head out that way, and I'll set the rental up in my name and have the agent leave a key under the mat for you after I talk to Gabe."

"You think she'll do it tonight?"

"Yeah, she's a friend. She'll do it. It won't be freshly stocked or anything, but she'll run over and leave the key for me."

A wave of relief washed over her, threatening to drop her where she stood. "Thanks, Pat."

"Sure thing. By the time you get out there, it should be done."

She disconnected, rubbed her eyes, and turned to find Adam standing in the doorway.

"Well?"

"Time to go." She hung up and held the phone out to Adam, then held her breath and waited to see if he'd go along with her plan. When she'd finished filling him in, silence descended as they stood staring at one another. "The police are on their way. We should go before they get here."

Still, he remained motionless. Then he frowned, tilted his head, and glanced toward the locked door. "Did you check in there?"

Confused by the sudden change, Jaelyn shook her head. "There's a clasp and padlock. I assumed it was a connecting door to the next room."

Adam's scowl deepened, and he studied the clasp and lock, then muttered, "This is new."

Her heart thundered in her chest, drowning out whatever

he said as he bolted into the bathroom and began to rummage through drawers.

He returned bending a bobby pin, then went to work on the lock. "In my room, which is the exact mirror of this one, this is a closet."

Jaelyn leaned closer on tiptoes, held her breath.

When the lock popped open a moment later and he eased the door open, the baby's cries echoed through the room. On the floor of the closet, secured in an infant seat, a baby stared up at them, tears shimmering in its eyes, streaming down tiny cheeks red and raw from crying.

"No way." Rage poured through Jaelyn as she muscled her way past Adam to reach the infant.

She needn't have bothered, though, as Adam staggered back out of her way, pale as the white blanket tucked around the child.

Even as she unbuckled the seat and lifted the baby into her arms, she whirled on him.

His mouth hung open, his gaze unfocused.

"I thought you said you were watching her?"

"I didn't know." He shook his head, then seemed to come to his senses, and his expression turned to granite. He looked over his shoulder toward the man they'd secured. "Later. Is the baby okay?"

The infant's sobs had lessened upon being lifted out of the seat. The little mouth opened as the baby turned into her. "She needs a bottle, and I have to do an exam."

"Yes, but not here. As long as there's no immediate danger, we have to get out of here. Now." He bent and grabbed the infant seat and the diaper bag lying on the floor next to it. He dropped the seat on the bed. "Secure the baby, and let's go."

She bristled at the order, but he was right. They weren't safe there. They had to get to safety, do a thorough exam, and notify the police.

While Jaelyn cooed gently and resecured the infant in the

seat, Adam took one last look around the room, grabbed a pair of leggings and a sweatshirt that were folded on a chair and stuffed them into the diaper bag. At least she'd have something clean to put on if they ever got out of this mess.

Jaelyn shoved the briefcase at him, praying it contained something that would help them, tucked the first aid kit beneath her arm and grabbed the baby's seat. "You ready to—"

"Shh..." He held up a finger, cocking his head to the side, and inched closer to the door.

And Jaelyn heard what had caused him to go on alert—muffled footsteps in the hallway, followed by the hushed sound of men's voices.

Adam bolted for the window, caught their captive's smirk and ripped the heavy drapes apart. He flung the window open, dropped the briefcase into the bushes, and whirled to call to Jaelyn, only to find her at his side. "Drop into the bushes and stay low."

She thrust the baby's seat at him as he turned and aimed the gun at the door.

As soon as she dropped, Adam lowered the baby to her carefully, tucked the gun back into his pocket and followed. He dropped into the thick shrubbery and landed with a splat in the mud.

"Which way?" Jaelyn's voice held a sense of urgency that made it difficult to think.

The baby cried softly. Fearing the cries would give their position away, he had to decide fast.

Try for the parking lot? Or into the dark woods and circle around? Yeah, better to fall back and assess. "Left, go for the woods."

Hunched over the seat to protect the infant as much as possible, she scrambled in that direction before he'd even finished his sentence.

He stayed right on her heels, running in a half crouch, half crawl while twigs and branches caught at his face and mud seeped into his shoes, sucking at his feet with every step. Finding the infant had knocked him off stride, thrown him completely. How could he not have known about the baby? Where had it come from? He'd never seen Maya with a child, not once.

Just before he reached the corner of the house, he heard a door slam open, followed by the gunman he'd held captive screaming they'd gone out the window. He should have put a gag in the guy's mouth, but there was no time to second-guess. "Go, straight across the yard and into the woods."

Jaelyn ran, a full-out sprint despite the slick conditions and the awkward bundle she carried.

A single gunshot startled Adam. He only spared a quick glance back before turning and taking off, the echo hounding him across the neatly manicured lawn and into the thick stand of trees surrounding the B&B. He swallowed the guilt, knowing if he hadn't left their attacker tied up, he might have had a chance to fight back instead of having just been executed. Adam couldn't change that, but he could make sure Jaelyn didn't end up like her sister had, or worse. He would with every breath in his body fight to defend her and this infant.

When he reached the tree line, he crouched beside Jaelyn, sucked in two deep lungsful of the wet air, then shoved his hair out of his face. "Circle around."

"Do you think we left footprints they can follow?" Jaelyn's teeth chattered as she spoke. Despite the almost knee-length raincoat she wore, her hair was soaked, her feet and legs caked with muck. At least the baby had stopped crying.

He looked back across the lawn. "I doubt it. It's pretty flooded, but it won't be too difficult to guess. We can't flee on foot with an infant, especially in this weather." He gestured toward the thick woods to the right. "It would be shorter to circle around the other way to the lot, so we'll go this way instead."

She nodded, yanked her hood up over her head and followed his instructions. Keeping low, they circled around through the

mud and brush. They'd made it about halfway around the building when the first shot rang out and a bullet ricocheted off a
tree a foot from Jaelyn's head.

"Get down." He pulled her to the ground and ripped the
car key from his pocket then pressed it into her hand. "Belly
crawl. Go."

She muttered something he didn't catch but started forward
at an awkward crawl over the carpet of pine needles, leaves,
twigs, and rocks strewn over the boggy ground, keeping her
body between the infant and the gunmen as she dragged the
seat along beside her.

Adam slowed, crept forward in a crouch, hopefully drawing
their attention long enough for Jaelyn to escape.

A shot rang out, whipped through the bushes far too close
for comfort. He went down on one knee, took aim at the first
of two figures coming across the lawn toward them at a fast
clip, and fired.

The man went down instantly, his partner dove for the
ground.

Leaving them to worry if he'd take another shot, he took off,
moving as stealthily as possible so as not to alert them to his
position. When he reached the far side of the parking lot, he
searched for Jaelyn. He had no way of knowing if more men
waited for them on this side of the building.

He stood, using a large pine tree for cover, and peeked
around the trunk into the lot.

Headlights moved toward him, too fast to be a guest return-
ing. The car fishtailed to a stop in front of him, and Jaelyn
swung the door open just before she scrambled over the center
console into the back seat.

Adam tossed the briefcase onto the passenger seat as he
climbed in, was already accelerating as the door swung shut.
"Hold on."

"Go." She turned around to look over her shoulder as he shot
out of the lot and onto the road.

With the streetlamps casting enough light for him to see by, he turned off the headlights, navigating the familiar road with little trouble. "Are you hurt?"

"I'm okay. You?" She flopped back into the seat, lay her head back, sucking in greedy gulps of air.

"Yeah." He glanced in the rearview mirror. No one following that he could see.

"Head east toward Montauk."

"All right." Not wanting to stay on the road they'd expect him to follow, Adam made a few random turns, weaving through the neighborhood, then headed for the highway. He lifted the diaper bag over his head as he drove, then dropped it onto the floor behind the passenger seat. "Did Pat say if Maya was doing any better?"

"He said she's still the same."

At least her condition hadn't worsened. "Is the baby okay?"

"I'm checking." She already had the baby out of the seat, examining every inch of its body. Quick glances in the rearview showed her rummaging through the bag and then putting on a fresh diaper. "She's fine. Doesn't appear to be hurt."

Pain threatened to crush him as he slowly released the breath he'd been holding, unsure he could once again live with the guilt of failing to protect a baby as he had his own unb—

"She's okay, Adam." Jaelyn leaned forward, squeezed his shoulder in a gesture of reassurance she could have no idea would mean so much to him, would pull him back from a precipice he couldn't hope to retreat from on his own.

"Good." He nodded, swiped at the tears that had run down his cheeks. "That's good."

The storm had finally let up some, reduced to nothing more than a cold drizzle, as Adam drove toward Montauk. Running wasn't the best idea, but with nowhere to hide and an infant in tow, what choice did they have? Jaelyn's house could be compromised if their pursuers found out about her, and Adam's room at the bed and breakfast was most certainly out of the question. Well, at least he'd had the presence of mind to take his bag when he'd left that morning, so he had all of his belongings with him.

As soon as Jaelyn finished examining the baby, she buckled her back into the car seat then weaved the seatbelt through the back of the car seat to hold it in place as best she could. It wasn't ideal, but it was their safest option.

She hummed softly as she screwed a nipple onto a bottle of formula and fed the baby, rocking her seat gently, soothing her. "It's okay, little one, you're safe now."

If only that were true. "I didn't know about the baby, Jaelyn. I would never have left her there if I'd known."

She nodded, staring at him in the rearview mirror. "I know. And I'm not making an accusation, just wondering, how did she get the baby in without you noticing?"

He shook his head. He'd beaten himself up with that question ever since he'd first realized what must be hidden behind that locked door. What if they hadn't found her? He shoved all of the possibilities ruthlessly aside. He didn't have time right now to indulge in what-ifs. The time for that would come later, would intrude at the quiet times, in the dark, in his dreams. A fact he knew all too well from firsthand experience. "How old is the baby? Can you tell?"

"Maybe two months, give or take."

"Okay." The first breath of relief shot from his lungs. "So, if she's Maya's, she had her before I started surveillance. It would have been easy enough to hide her when Maya left her house to come out here, since she packed up the car on gated property, and I couldn't see very well. I tended to follow her whenever she left the property, and I would have tried to get a better view if anyone had visited her, which they didn't."

"What about when you arrived at the B&B?"

He reconstructed the scene in his mind. "I saw her get out of the vehicle, but once I was sure it was her and she was going inside, I circled around, watched for a tail, waited to check in a bit after her so as not to be recognized."

"So, it's possible she could have gotten the baby inside without you knowing."

He nodded, met Jaelyn's gaze in the mirror. "It's possible. I didn't watch her every minute, obviously, or I'd have seen her leave earlier today and she wouldn't have been injured. By the time I heard a woman had been attacked in the woods out here, she was already on her way to the hospital. But we still don't know the infant belongs to Maya."

Jaelyn blew out a breath, ruffling her damp hair, then slumped in the seat and looked down at the child. "No, we don't."

Adam tuned them both out, had to if he was going to be able to think straight. Whatever the situation with the baby, all he could do was keep her and Jaelyn safe. Figuring out who the child belonged to would be up to the police. Unless… maybe there were some kind of documents alluding to the child's identity.

The briefcase they'd taken from Maya's room sat on the passenger seat, calling silently to him while Jaelyn smoothly held the bottle for the baby to drink and rummaged through the well-stocked first aid kit with her free hand.

Jaelyn held a gauze square out to him. "Here, put some pressure on that so it'll at least stop bleeding."

He took the bandage and pressed it against his head, then winced at the sting. "Thanks."

She smiled at him in the rearview mirror, and it tugged at his heart.

"Are you all right?"

"Yes, just a killer headache." She shifted in the seat, groaned. "And maybe a few aches and pains."

Adam grinned. "If I'm being honest, I have to admit to a bit of soreness too. But I'll deny it if you share that with any of your firefighter buddies."

She laughed, the sound filling the warm interior and easing some of his tension. Then she sighed, cuddled closer to the baby. "We're a mess."

He raked a hand through his hair, no doubt making it stick up even worse than it already was. He needed a shower, and about ten hours of sleep, neither of which was going to happen any time soon. "How long does it take to get to Montauk?"

"About an hour, usually." Once the baby finished with her bottle and fell asleep, Jaelyn stuck the briefcase on the floor and scrambled over the center console to the passenger seat. "I secured the seat the best I could for now, since we don't have the base, and covered her with a blanket, but she'll need a better car seat. And we need to cover that shattered window with something."

"I'll take care of the window when we stop. Once we notify the police, we can ask that they bring a car seat when they pick her up."

Something he couldn't read flickered across Jaelyn's features, then she turned away from him. She flipped down the visor, opened the lighted mirror, and started to clean the cut on her chin. "It'll probably take less than an hour to get there at this time of night with no traffic. When we arrive, I can take care of cleaning that wound for you."

He nodded. Then he remembered she was in pain. "No pain relievers in the first aid kit?"

"Nope."

He hit the turn signal and switched to the right lane. Aside from the gash on her chin, small scrapes and cuts marred Jaelyn's face and hands, and mud covered just about every inch of her. No doubt he looked the same, with the addition of a deep, nasty cut on his temple, one that was most likely full of dirt at the moment. "Will you be okay until we get to Montauk? If there are no pain relievers at the house, I'll run out after I get cleaned up and won't draw so much attention."

"Sounds good, thanks." When she'd finished tending her

chin, she flipped the visor back up, dropped back into the seat, and turned her head to study him.

The weight of her stare had him shifting uncomfortably. What did she think of him? The way he'd forced himself into her life? The fact that he was all but stalking her sister? The fact that, despite having been stalking her sister, he'd missed Maya having a child and also missed her leaving the bed and breakfast and being beaten up by someone?

Jaelyn probably viewed him as incompetent at best. In his defense, he rarely made a mistake in the courtroom, but it seemed investigating an elusive hitman while running for your life required a bit of a learning curve. Plus, he was only one man working alone. He couldn't watch Maya twenty-four seven. The thought didn't ease his guilt in the least. As much as he wanted to redeem himself, now wasn't the time. At least, he was trying to convince himself it wasn't.

He inhaled deeply, his breath catching at the instant stab of pain in his ribs. The guy who'd attacked them had managed to land a solid blow, though he didn't think anything was broken. At least, he hoped not. It was probably not a bad idea to take a moment to regroup, figure out where to go next, bring Jaelyn up to speed on the entire situation. And what would she think of him then?

"Penny for your thoughts." Jaelyn's voice jarred him.

"Huh?" He glanced at her, furrowed his brow, stalling since he had no intention of sharing the thoughts coursing through his head just yet.

"You seem…distracted."

"No. I mean, I'm fine." He sighed, relaxed his shoulders, and tilted his head back and forth to ease the tension coiled in his neck. "Sorry. I was just wondering if the police picked up the guy who attacked us yet, got an ID on him."

She took her cell phone out of her jacket pocket, checked her text messages. "Nothing from Gabe or Pat yet."

He studied her expression, then nodded, chewed on the inside of his cheek. Hopefully, whoever was after them bought the Jaelyn as Maya ruse. As long as no one realized Maya was still laid up in the hospital, they would continue to follow him and Jaelyn. If he could just lure them out, he might have a chance of ending this. But was that the best option now that they had an infant in tow? And what if they found out about Jaelyn? He'd do well to keep in mind that Maya might not be expendable—yet—but Jaelyn was. "The guy who attacked us at the B&B...he didn't buy you were Maya."

She lowered her gaze to her hands in her lap.

"If they hadn't shot him—my guess is, for letting us get away—your cover would have been blown. As it stands, we may still have a chance to pull this off."

"Pull what off? I'm not sure what we're even trying to accomplish."

He watched her, her face illuminated each time they passed beneath a streetlamp then plunged into shadow each time they emerged from the puddle of light. He was sorry for her role in this, sorry she'd been dragged from her peaceful life into a dangerous game that might well cost both of them their lives. "At the moment, I'm just trying to keep that baby, you, and myself alive. But the time will come, and soon, that we have to stop playing defense. We're going to have to go on the offense if we're going to put an end to this."

"What *this*?" Her calm, rigid control snapped. She flung her hands out, pinned him with so much anger he figured she probably hated him, and he couldn't even blame her. Especially when he told her what would come next, the only logical step no matter how much he didn't want to take it.

"I know, and you're right. I'm sorry I haven't had time to be more forthcoming about everything."

She stiffened.

What could he tell her? He couldn't divulge any information about the senator's possible involvement yet, considering the man was gearing up for a presidential run and Adam had no actual proof of his involvement. And he didn't dare open up about Alessandra. He couldn't. He barely held himself together sometimes as it was.

"The client I told you about earlier..."

"The one who was supposed to turn over evidence of that assassin you were talking about?"

"The Hunter, yes." If only Josiah had handed over the hit list he'd promised before he was killed. At least he'd have a way to seek justice. "My client said he knew of a hit list and was supposed to turn it over to me the day he was shot."

"You said he never told you who he suspected the killer is?"

"No, he didn't, but I was able to come up with Hunter Barlowe as a suspect based on some of the information he did give me and Hunter's connection to a high-profile client my informant was also associated with. But I still need to find proof."

"And how do you figure you're going to find that evidence?"

Wasn't that the million-dollar question.

"And what does Maya have to do with all of this? You think she knows or suspects her husband is a gun for hire?"

"I believe she may have information about the assassin's identity, although she may not even realize it." Of course, the fact she'd gone on the run made him believe she knew something, but he refrained from sharing that. Jaelyn could come to that conclusion on her own.

She pursed her lips, studied him for another moment, then turned to look out the passenger window as the three lanes merged down to two. Businesses replaced the woods lining the road. Church bells rang from a beautiful old building, signaling the start of midnight mass. That moved something in him that had been dead for five long years, since the day God had abandoned him and taken Alessandra. He lifted his foot off the gas as they passed.

"I'd like to attend mass." She stared longingly at the building, with its grand steeple, historic architecture, and the lighted Nativity scene out front. "When my parents were alive, we attended mass at midnight every Christmas Eve, a lovely tradition I'm sorry to say I didn't keep up after they passed away."

"You believe in God?" He caught himself too late to keep the words he'd been thinking from popping out of his mouth.

"I do, yes." She looked at him, narrowed her gaze. While he read curiosity in the look, he saw no judgment. "Don't you?"

"I don't know what I believe." This wasn't a conversation he could have right now. "And I'm sorry, but what purpose could you possibly have for going into a crowded church looking like you just went ten rounds in a mud pit with a heavyweight, carrying a child that for all we know was kidnapped, with a pack of killers on your heels?"

She tilted her head, lifted a brow. "Can you think of a better time to pray?"

Well—he huffed out a breath—she had him there. And he could probably have spoken a little less harshly, but this whole mess was getting to him. He gripped the wheel tighter and returned his focus to the road ahead of them.

"I believe God guides us, leads us to where we're supposed to be," she said softly.

He wanted to believe that, had grown up believing it, and then Alessandra had been taken from him, despite every desperate prayer he could utter. "I want to believe in an all-loving God, but I don't understand how some of the atrocities, some of the carnage I've seen, could happen if God influences the minutiae of our lives."

"God isn't responsible for the horrible, unfair things people do to one another, Adam. God teaches us, He guides us, He stands by us, He even forgives us when we mess up royally. At the end of the day, it's our own free will, our own choices, that lead some of us down a darker path. We have to come to God by choice, have to choose to embrace His teachings, choose to allow Him into our lives, into our hearts." She paused a moment. "It's up to us to allow His love to flow through us and touch the people around us. Not everyone makes that choice." She stopped speaking then, and the sense of loss within him increased.

"I'm sorry, Jaelyn. Sorry for all of this."

"It's okay. It's not your fault, and I'm not some delicate person who can't handle stress."

An ironic chuckle escaped before he could stop it. "No, you don't appear to be."

In that moment, the intensity in her gaze, the determination hardening her expression, the strong-willed defiance evident in the lift of her chin and the stiffening of her posture reminded him of Alessandra. His wife had contained the same strength, the same loyalty, the same inner spark that allowed her to embrace whatever life threw at her. And she'd loved him, fiercely, with everything she had, and that loyalty had gotten her and their unborn child killed. Most likely by the same men who hunted him now, though for different reasons.

He'd bumped up against these men before, in another investigation, one that had led him on a five-year mission after the Hunter and the senator had killed his wife to get him to back off. That mission had been brought to an abrupt halt a month ago when Josiah had been killed. "As soon as we get to the safe house, we'll see what the police have to say, and we'll get that briefcase open and see if there's anything in there that will help us."

"Okay." She nodded and turned to look out the window.

And if there wasn't, he had no clue what they'd do next, because these men would not stop until they killed everyone in their way.

Chapter Four

As Adam navigated the rutted dirt driveway that led to the small bungalow, Jaelyn tried to recall the layout. Living room in the front, kitchen behind it, short hallway to the right, with a bathroom at the end and a bedroom on either side. Surrounded by woods on three sides with a narrow stretch of ocean behind. The bungalow would provide a secluded, private retreat for them to get themselves together and come up with a plan. Of course, the downside of all that seclusion was that there was only one way in and out by vehicle. If their pursuers somehow managed to find them, they'd be in a tough situation, especially with an infant in tow.

She dismissed the thought as Adam pulled up the circular driveway and stopped beside the cobblestone walkway that led to a wide front porch. They'd just have to cross that bridge if they came to it.

Adam shifted into park and peered through the windshield at the house. "Why don't you go ahead and take the baby in? I'm just going to do a quick perimeter check."

She nodded and reached for the door handle, then paused. "You don't think they could have found out where we were going, right?"

He shook his head. "No, not yet. But I want to get an idea of what's around us if they do."

"Oh, that's easy…" She shot him a grin as she flung the door open, desperately needing to stretch after going on the run then spending the better part of an hour in the car. "There's pretty much nothing around us."

Not that she blamed him for wanting to make sure. Leaving him to his reconnaissance, Jaelyn unhooked the baby's seat, grabbed the diaper bag, and started up the walkway to the front door. Thankfully, the key was already under the mat, despite the ridiculously early—or late, depending on how you looked at it—hour.

She opened the door to the scent of pine cleaner and flipped on the light. The coastal interior boasted a large, cream-colored sectional. Antique crates served as coffee and end tables, and a massive stone fireplace was bracketed by bookshelves, which were accented with fisherman netting, candles, and seashells. As much as she longed to grab one of the blankets thrown over the overstuffed couch and curl up before a fire, she turned toward the kitchen instead. Relaxing was not an option at the moment.

She hung the diaper bag over the back of a stool and set the infant seat on the floor beside the couch.

The baby sat, brilliant blue eyes wide open, one pudgy fist trying to find her mouth, and seemed to watch Jaelyn.

While she couldn't know for sure the baby belonged to Maya, those eyes were unmistakably theirs. The same ones that looked back at Jaelyn in the mirror each morning. Could this baby really be her niece? Could she truly have gone from having no family to having a sister and a niece in no more than a heartbeat? Her hand shook as she knelt beside the seat and brushed her fingers over the infant's soft, dark hair. "I don't know how this will end, but I'll keep you safe, little one. That's a promise."

"You're right."

Startled by Adam's voice, she jumped to her feet and spun around. Apparently, it hadn't taken him long to check the perimeter and reach the same conclusion she had.

"There is pretty much nothing around."

"Lots of trees, sand and water, but not much else," she agreed.

He set the briefcase and first aid kit on the center island, then stared out the window over the sink at the darkness.

Jaelyn studied the locking mechanism on the briefcase. If she hoped to keep the contents intact, she was going to need a key. Hopefully, Maya kept the key in her purse. She shivered, the cool interior hitting her damp hair and clothes, bringing a chill. But first things first, she needed something warm to drink. She shrugged out of her raincoat and hung it on the back of another stool, then searched the cabinets and came up with hot chocolate and a bag of mini-marshmallows.

At the sight of the cut on Adam's temple caked with mud, she put the briefcase out of her mind in favor of the first aid kit. "I'm making hot chocolate if you want some. Otherwise, there's coffee."

"Hot chocolate sounds perfect. I'm hoping we can get at least a few hours' sleep before we head out."

"Head out where?" She checked the fridge for milk but found it mostly empty. Apparently, the owners stocked the cabinets but didn't keep perishables. She filled the teapot with water and set it on the stove, then turned to find Adam sitting at the counter, frowning down at his clasped hands. "You okay?"

"Huh? Oh, yeah." He scrubbed his hands over his head and stretched his back. "Sorry, a lot on my mind."

That she could sympathize with. "So, you said you wanted to sleep before heading out—where do you plan on going?"

He lifted his hands to the sides, then let them drop back onto the counter. "I have no idea, but the first order of business is to get this briefcase open."

"No." After setting two oversize mugs on the counter and

pouring the contents of two hot chocolate pouches into each, she checked on the baby.

She'd fallen asleep, head tilted to the side, mouth open, her soft breaths giving Jaelyn hope she was sleeping peacefully.

Comfortable that the infant was as content as could be under the circumstances, Jaelyn opened the first aid kit. "The first order of business is cleaning that wound before you end up with an infection."

He studied her in that way he had, head tilted, eyes narrowed. It made it seem like he viewed everything with suspicion. Who knew? Maybe he did. But at least he didn't argue as he swiveled the stool to face her.

She moved closer to examine the cut. It had mostly stopped bleeding, though it would surely reopen when she started cleaning the spattered grime out of it. "This is going to sting a little."

His laughter startled her, lit his eyes—eyes she'd been so sure were brown but now realized held a kaleidoscope of browns and greens highlighted by flecks of gold. Who was this man who'd burst into her life so suddenly, bringing so much chaos and fear? What was she supposed to think of his quiet, somber moods, the way he sometimes lost himself in some thought or another? She knew nothing about Adam…well, except that he was willing to risk his life to save a stranger. She did know that, so she should probably reserve any kind of opinion until she got to know him better. She set to cleaning his wound. "Ready?"

He nodded, and his jaw clenched.

"This could really use a few stitches, but I think I can make do with what I have here. It's going to leave a scar, though." It wouldn't leave the only scar on his face. A small crescent-shaped one curved around the corner of his right eye, and a long, faint, barely noticeable mark ran along his jawline. Between the scars, the agility he'd shown while running, and his fighting skills, she had a feeling Mr. Tall, Tawny, and Brooding didn't spend all of his time sitting behind a desk or defending his clients in a courtroom. "You seem to be in good shape for a lawyer."

He frowned at her for a moment, then laughed out loud. "What? Lawyers aren't supposed to be athletic?"

Heat burned in her cheeks. She didn't even know how she'd let the comment slip out. She must be overtired, something that tended to make her lose her filter. "I didn't mean... I just meant it doesn't seem like you sit behind a desk all day."

The tea kettle's shrill whistle interrupted the awkward moment, and she hurried to grab it before it could wake the baby. Once she'd turned off the burner and filled the mugs, she stirred the drinks and added a generous amount of marshmallows, then brought them both to the counter and set Adam's in front of him.

"Thanks."

"Sure thing." She finished cleaning and bandaging his wound in silence. At least that might keep her from putting her foot in her mouth again. "There you go. Good as new."

"Thank you." He held her gaze. "Listen, there are things we need to talk about, things I need to tell you, but for now, I have no idea how long we might be safe here, so why don't we see what's in this briefcase and then take showers and get some sleep?"

She nodded. Considering the fact she'd just come off a twelve-hour shift before going on the run for her life, she was about ready to fall over. And technically, she was supposed to be back on in six hours. She had a feeling she wasn't going to make her 7:00 a.m. start time. "I'm going to have to call out of work."

Adam glanced at her, frowned. "I'm pretty sure, since everyone thinks you're laid up in a hospital bed, they'll assume you're not coming in."

True. She hadn't thought of that, but it still didn't sit right. She texted Pat, asked him to take care of letting her supervisor know she needed the day off, then pulled Maya's purse out of her bag and dug through until she found a key ring with four keys. One was obviously a car key, and one was smaller than the rest. The briefcase key? She said a quick prayer as she stuck it into the keyhole and turned, and an equally quick thank-you when the lock released.

Before she had a chance to open the case, her phone dinged with a text. Reluctantly, she shifted the briefcase aside in exchange for her phone. To his credit, Adam didn't immediately dive on the case when she set it aside. She'd be lying to herself if she didn't admit she probably would have if their situations were reversed. She opened the text and frowned.

"Something wrong?"

"Huh?" She glanced up to find Adam's eyes intently focused on her. "Oh, sorry. It's from Pat. He says they found a body tied to a chair in Maya's room. Gabe is freaking out because we left the scene, though Pat says he explained everything to him, and they want to know if we killed him."

"Who's Gabe?"

Jaelyn shook her head. "Gabe, uh, he's a friend...and a cop."

"Which first?" Adam held her gaze.

"It doesn't matter." She typed a quick answer back to Pat.

"Does anyone really think you'd have executed a man who was tied up and not only didn't pose a threat but couldn't even defend himself?"

She glanced up at him. "They know I didn't kill him, but they don't know you at all."

He nodded and lowered his gaze. "Fair enough."

When she checked the baby again, she found those intense infant eyes open and staring at her. It brought an unexpected surge of wonder. If she truly was Maya's, this child was some of the only family Jaelyn had left. She suddenly felt fiercely protective of the girl. She wanted to keep the child close, love her, care for her, protect her...but first she had to make sure that she was actually her niece. "We have to do something about this baby."

He lifted a brow. "Like?"

"Find out who she belongs to, for starters."

He frowned, shook his head, and finally chanced a quick glance toward the seat before averting his gaze. "You don't think she's Maya's?"

"I don't know." Jaelyn started to pace now. "But we can't assume she is. We can't assume anything. We need some things from the store. She's going to need diapers and formula before too much longer, and we need some way to take her footprint so we can send it to Gabe in the hope of identifying her."

"And if she is Maya's and that identification throws up a red flag that puts her in more danger?" He crossed an ankle over his knee, lifted his hands to the sides. The fact that his argument made sense only served to annoy her. "Besides, we're going to have to make do with the supplies that were left in the diaper bag, since there's not much open on Christmas Day."

She opened her mouth to argue with him, then stopped. How could she have forgotten it was Christmas morning? Her mind was frazzled, her nerves shot. She really did need sleep.

"I'll tell you what." He lowered his foot to the floor, leaned forward with his elbows resting on his knees, hands clasped together. "Notify Pat about the baby, have Gabe look into it. As soon as we hear something back from him, we can decide how to handle it. If he doesn't find any missing person reports matching her description by tomorrow, we'll either go the footprint route and try to identify her, or turn her over to social services. In the meantime, we'll go through the documents in the briefcase more carefully and see if we can figure out who she is."

Oh, how she hated the fact that he was right. "If it turns out she's Maya's, do you think I could get emergency custody?"

She wasn't sure why she'd asked that. But she knew what it was like to be alone in the world and didn't want that for this baby.

Adam's gaze shot to hers and the compassion in his eyes anchored her.

"If she doesn't have any other family members to take her in, of course." The fact that she didn't even know if her own sister had family weighed heavily on her.

He nodded slowly, raked a hand through his hair. "Yeah, I could probably do that, under the circumstances. There is one way we may be able to determine if Maya's her mother fairly quickly."

"Oh? And what's that?"

"See if we can get a look at her medical records. Do you know anyone at the hospital who might be able to do that without a court order?"

"Hmm…maybe." Hope surged through Jaelyn. She hadn't realized until that moment how badly she wanted the baby to belong to Maya, not only because the thought of her sister possibly being a kidnapper shot daggers through her, but because if the baby belonged to Maya, Jaelyn might have some hope of remaining a part of her life. Which brought her to the next pressing thing.

Jaelyn pulled the briefcase toward her, then paused. There wouldn't be much time before she needed to tend to the baby again. "Why don't you go ahead and jump in the shower while I feed and change the baby, then I'll take a turn? After that we'll sit and go through the briefcase." She ran her hand over the top of it, wondering what it held but nervous about what they'd find. "I could use a few minutes to gather my wits before we try to make a plan. Because the stakes just got a whole lot higher with the addition of the baby. No matter what we decide to do, her safety has to be the priority."

"That we can agree on." He nodded and stood. "I'll only be a few minutes."

That was fine, because she really needed to have this whole mess behind her, needed to learn the truth about her past so she could move on with her life, and she most definitely needed to put Mr. Adam Spencer behind her before he snuck past her defenses and she allowed him to get any closer.

They took turns showering and he donned a cleanish pair of jeans and a long sleeve pullover he'd hurriedly rolled up and stuffed into his bag that morning. Since Jaelyn had kept the baby with her while she showered, it had saved him having to watch her—however much of a coward it might make him. Even though he'd give his life to protect the baby, he wasn't yet ready to have the responsibility of being left alone to care for her.

He'd already walked the perimeter once more while he waited, and the lack of an exit strategy bothered him. There was literally no way out of the safe house if they were found. And it wasn't like someone would need an army; with one attacker positioned on each side of the house, the only means of escape would be either the narrow driveway or by water, and they couldn't very well swim in the waning storm with the baby in tow.

While there should be no way anyone could know where they'd gone, he couldn't help feeling like a sitting duck. The wall of windows overlooking the expanse of ocean at their backs was a security nightmare. With the exception of the small clearing the house sat amid, they were surrounded by thick woods anyone could sneak through.

Supposedly, not many people knew where they were, but the senator's reach was far and wide. The instant the senator learned of Jaelyn's existence, if he didn't know about her already, he'd have people searching under every rock for even the tiniest tidbit of information on her. He'd know within minutes of her connection to Seaport Fire and Rescue where she was a volunteer firefighter, and soon after he'd know everything there was to know about anyone and everyone even remotely connected to the place. Including where Pat might recently have rented a bungalow at the last minute on the very night one of his goons was killed and Jaelyn disappeared.

And if he did already know about her and had let her live this long, it was only because she was blissfully ignorant of the situation. Once he found out Maya had shown up, that would no longer be the case.

Of course, if they could find the killer and bring him down, escaping would no longer matter.

Jaelyn wandered into the kitchen with the baby, wearing the sweatshirt and leggings he'd grabbed from Maya's room. She gestured toward the briefcase he'd somehow managed to keep from rummaging through without her. "Do you want to go through it in the living room?"

"Sure." He did as she suggested, not caring where it got opened as long as it did.

She curled up in the corner of the couch with the baby in her arms, kissed the top of her head, and Adam sat beside her and set the briefcase on the coffee table.

The way she gazed down at the little girl who'd wrapped one tiny hand around Jaelyn's finger made him wonder if she'd really be willing to give her over to anyone else. She was getting too attached. When Jaelyn simply looked up and grinned at him, it shot straight to his heart. "Let's see what we have here that might help us out of this situation."

Adam shook his head, shifted his gaze downward toward the briefcase to hide the smile he wasn't ready to share. He wasn't kidding when he'd said Jaelyn was something, and she'd piqued his curiosity.

He cut the train of thought off immediately. Just because her self-assured grin touched him at a moment when he was feeling down, just because her matter-of-fact attitude was refreshing, just because she was a beautiful woman who seemed to always put others first, didn't mean he was attracted to her.

His focus needed to be on finding the men who were after

them. Besides, Alessandra was the only woman who mattered to him, the only woman who could ever matter.

"You know, I was thinking about something," she said.

Still distracted, he turned to her. "What's that?"

"You said earlier that the police and the FBI and a number of other agencies weren't able to find this guy. Why not?"

"What do you mean?"

"Why can't they find him? If you could figure out who he is, why couldn't they?"

"Because they didn't have Josiah Cameron. If he hadn't come to me, hadn't given me a place to start looking, I wouldn't have any idea who he was either." But once Josiah had told him about the senator's connection, it was easier to follow the dots to Hunter Barlowe. "Josiah worked as an aide for a high-profile senator, one he suspected employed the Hunter to get rid of anyone who stood in his way."

"Stood in the way of what?" She kept her voice low, gently rocking the baby as if it was the most natural thing in the world to her.

"Of getting anything he wanted." And he'd stop at nothing. "Josiah said he had proof, said he could provide a coded hit list that proved the senator had paid for certain murders."

"You suspect my sister's husband is the assassin you're looking for, but how could that be? It's hard to believe a regular guy can just run around killing people and not get caught."

"Hunter Barlowe is far from a regular guy." At least, according to the surprisingly little information Adam had been able to dig up. "He is the reclusive billionaire owner of Hack Hunters, a cybersecurity company. A lot of people think he's so good at security because he's paranoid, keeps to himself because it's safer that way."

"But you don't?"

"I think it's a convenient cover. I think he leaves the day-to-day running of his business to others so he's free to roam the world fulfilling obligations for his real career."

"As an assassin for hire."

"Exactly." He understood it was a lot to process at once and sat back to give her a minute, see if she had any more questions. "And who is there to notice he's missing? No one. The perfect alibi, really."

She chewed on her lower lip for a moment, as if trying to decide whether or not to ask something.

He suspected he knew what she wanted to know, but he'd wait for her to decide if she was ready for the answer.

When she did finally ask, she spoke so quietly he could barely hear her. "Do you think she knew? Maya? Do you think she knows what her husband is, what he does?"

His heart ached to hold her, to ease some of the pain this was surely causing her. But he couldn't. All he could offer her was the truth. "I think she found out. And when she did, I think she told Josiah. He came to me determined to take down not only the Hunter but his clients as well, at least one of them—the senator."

She nodded as tears tracked down her cheeks.

Adam lay his head against the back of the couch, let his eyes fall closed. He took a few deep breaths. They needed sleep, both of them, if they were going to be able to think clearly, but they needed to go through the briefcase first, see if there was anything to help them, to give him something to think about while he tried to rest after.

When the baby fell asleep, Jaelyn stood and lowered her into the seat then buckled her in. When she returned to her spot on the couch, she shifted the briefcase closer and opened it.

He looked over her shoulder and caught the scent of strawberries from the shampoo she'd used.

She let out a low whistle. "Wow. I've never seen that much cash. How much do you think is in here?"

Adam shifted his attention to the pile of money sitting in the case. He lifted one of the bundles, thumbed through it. "If they're all hundreds, there's got to be at least a hundred thousand in here, probably more."

Jaelyn lifted the cash out and set it on the coffee table beside the case. "Do you think it's real?"

"Oh, it's real all right." But he held one bill up to the light, checked it thoroughly. "Or an amazing counterfeit."

"Why would she have so much cash in a briefcase?" She picked up a folder, then gasped at the sight of the two handguns lying beneath it.

Adam removed the guns, checked to see if they were both loaded—they were—as Jaelyn opened the folder and leafed through the contents.

"If I had to guess, I'd say she was going on the run. She must know something, must have suspected someone was after her." It would make sense, all things considered. As much as he'd like to spare Jaelyn from learning about Maya's indiscretions before having the chance to meet her and see what kind of person she truly was, he couldn't leave her in the dark. It was too dangerous. "Jaelyn, there's something you should know. About Maya and Josiah."

"They were lovers?"

He nodded. "Yeah. I'm sorry."

"It's not your fault. Besides, I don't judge people based on one action. Whatever Maya's reasons for betraying her marriage vows, she didn't deserve to end up beaten unconscious."

"Has she woken yet?"

"Oh, yeah, sorry. I forgot to tell you, when I texted Pat, he said she hadn't."

"Do they expect her to?"

Instead of answering, she massaged the bridge of her nose between her thumb and forefinger, then tossed the folder she'd been perusing back into the briefcase when the baby gave a demanding cry. So much for sleeping.

She lifted her from the seat, cradled the small bundle against her, and sank back onto the couch. "They expect her to, but who knows. I'm not there, so I don't know the full extent of her injuries. I've been a little busy with everything else."

Adam perched on the edge of the couch so he could face her. "Hey, you okay?"

"I don't even know at this point. There's so much going through my head, and I don't know what to make of any of it." She bounced the baby in what seemed like an automatic gesture, reducing her cries for the moment.

The contents of the briefcase called to him, begged him to search for answers that might point him in the Hunter's direction. He ignored it. "Do you want to talk?"

She shook her head, then stood with the baby, took one of the prepackaged bottles from the diaper bag, and screwed on a disposable nipple. "I wouldn't even know where to start. My entire life was a lie. My parents are gone, so I can't ask them anything. I have no other family. I lost Ronnie, my fiancé, when I couldn't move past my grief. And now…now, I have a sister I never knew about, who may or may not be married to a notorious hitman, who may or may not be trying to kill her. And me. Add in an infant that may or may not belong to said sister, and where does that all leave me?"

Actually, holding up quite well, all things considered. "I'm sorry for all of this, Jaelyn. All I can tell you is I'll do my best to help keep you, Maya, and the baby safe and try to find the answers you're searching for."

"Right now, there's only one question burning a hole in my gut." She laughed, but it held no humor. "I can't imagine why my parents would have given her up, and they're not here to give me the answers I need."

Given her up…? Ah, man. Now what? Should he keep the information to himself? Let Maya be the one to tell her she was adopted, so it would at least come from family, even if it was family she didn't know? No, he couldn't let her continue on blind. Not only would it hinder her search for answers, it might well prove deadly. "Listen, Jaelyn, I'm sorry to be the one to tell you this, and I wish there was a gentler way to say it, but your parents didn't give Maya up."

She frowned, kissed the baby's dark hair, and gazed down at her. "What do you mean? Was she abducted?"

He shifted to the edge of the cushion, uncomfortable no matter his position. "Maya was adopted when she was an infant, when her birth mother gave her up."

"Her..." She paled. "What?"

"I'm sorry. I didn't know about you, so I don't know why you weren't placed in the same home, but when you're ready, if you want, I can pull some strings and try to find out. The one thing I do know is that your mother was from New York City, lived and worked in Manhattan." That wasn't the full truth. He knew who her biological dad was but didn't dare say...not yet.

Her expressions ranged from pain to grief and every emotion in between as she rocked back and forth with the baby clutched close, crying softly as she sank further into the cushions. "Thank you for being honest with me."

He leaned back, giving her a moment to process what little he'd been able to tell her.

It didn't take her long to pull herself together and return her attention to the briefcase. She took out the folder she'd been looking through and a few others then handed them to him. "These appear to be documents regarding the cybersecurity firm, but I can't make anything from them."

He took the folders, allowing his gaze to linger on her raw cheeks and puffy eyes for a moment. She needed rest. "I'll look through them. Why don't you go ahead and get some sleep?"

"Thank you, Adam, for everything. And don't worry. I'm far from fragile. I might take a few minutes to wallow in the confusion, but I bounce back pretty quick." She stood and set the bottle aside to change the baby's diaper. Once she had the baby settled back in the seat, she returned to the couch, set the seat beside her and absently stroked the baby's hand. Then she gave him a smile.

"Come on. We'll go through the rest of this quickly together then get a little shut-eye and start out fresh in the morning."

Her smile left him with a feeling of relief and admiration, though he was reluctant to dwell on that last one. Instead, he turned his attention to the contents of the briefcase. There had to be something there to help them find answers before their attackers could track them down again.

He leaned forward and shuffled through the folders. The first contained financial information from the business.

"What is it?"

"Bank accounts, copies of stocks and investments, and a flash drive labeled tax returns taped to the inside cover." Without a computer at his disposal, he'd have to accept that's what it really was for now, but he'd confirm at the first opportunity.

He turned the folder over on the coffee table and grabbed the next, which contained lists of names, dates, and account numbers. Clients, maybe? The Hack Hunters logo was at the top of each page in the thick dossier.

Jaelyn frowned. "Why would she have taken off with financial information from her husband's company?"

"Good question." Although, she was the CEO of the company, so it was possible she was working from the road. But he didn't believe that for a second.

"Do you think it's possible she knew you were tailing her?" Jaelyn asked. "Maybe she mistook you for an assassin and fled?"

"Huh. I hadn't thought of that. I tried to be careful, but I suppose it's possible she spotted me."

"Especially if she had reason to believe her husband might be trying to kill her and had already murdered her lover."

Since he couldn't argue with her logic, he paged through the document, skimmed over the names, then backtracked when he recognized the name Mark Lowell. *Well, what do you know. Good ole Senator Lowell just happens to be a client.*

He ran a finger along the lines following his name and let

out a low whistle. Seemed the senator had doled out a fortune for cybersecurity. A list of dates, amounts, and letters were detailed beneath the senator's name. Then one date jumped out and gripped him by the throat, threatened to choke off his air supply. He wheezed in a deep breath, his hand shaking as he followed the line of data with his finger. The date—a date from five years earlier, the same date his wife had been killed—was followed by the amount of two million dollars and the letters AS. Her name eased out on the softest whisper. "Alessandra."

The hand he shoved through his hair shook violently. Was he looking at the hit list Josiah had told him about? Was that line the hit on his wife? Coded, Josiah had said. Could it simply have been disguised to look like a Hack Hunters business document? Had Maya found the list? Planned on giving it to Josiah before he was killed?

"Hey." Jaelyn gripped his arm. "You okay?"

He couldn't talk about this right now, was barely keeping it together with all the questions pounding in his head.

Jaelyn lowered her hand, offered a tentative smile. "Well, if that's how you react when someone figures out something you hadn't thought of, this partnership is doomed."

"I'm sorry." He stood abruptly, needing to get out of there. Then he spotted the small tracking device set in the corner of the briefcase. Had Maya place it there in case someone stole the briefcase? Or had the bug led the Hunter's men to Maya at the B&B?

Fear for Jaelyn's and the child's safety had him hoping it was the former. Alessandra was already lost. While he'd do everything in his power to see she had justice, he couldn't sacrifice any lives in the pursuit of that goal. "Sorry. I guess I'm jumpier than I realized."

"Don't worry about it. Believe me, I understand."

No, you really don't. "Get the baby's things together. We're leaving."

"Leaving? I thought we were going to get some sleep?"

"Yeah, well, so did I, but plans change." He cringed at the harshness in his own voice, and yet he couldn't help himself. His insides were twisted into knots. Rather than say anything he'd come to regret, he gestured toward the mess of papers on the coffee table. If he returned to them, he'd never be able to walk out. His conscience wouldn't allow it. "Can you put that stuff back together in the briefcase, please?"

She frowned but only said, "Sure."

Leaving her confused and seemingly a bit wary of him, not that he could blame her, Adam headed for the bathroom for a moment alone and to hide the tracking device. If their pursuers thought they were remaining at the house for the night, they might wait until later, when they could be fairly sure everyone was asleep to attack. If he destroyed it, they might come on the run.

Once the door was shut behind him, he purposely unclenched his hands, lay the device on the counter, then rested his hands on either side of it.

He had to get control of himself. Going off half-cocked wasn't going to help anyone, nor would it get Alessandra the justice she deserved. If the papers Maya had secreted in her locked briefcase were what he suspected—not a Hack Hunters client list, but the Hunter's hit list, with names, dates, and amounts all neatly outlined beneath the client who'd ordered the hit—he might finally have the ammunition he needed to take down not only the Hunter but also his clients. If he could stay alive long enough to see it through.

Chapter Five

Sitting on the couch, with her feet tucked beneath her and the baby cradled snuggly against her, Jaelyn inhaled deeply the scent of the baby wash she'd used on the infant earlier. She listened to the girl's soft breaths as she slept. Jaelyn probably should have left her sleeping in the seat while Adam was in the bathroom, but since he seemed fully intent on going on the run again, she had no idea how long the little girl would have to be strapped in. Better to keep her close while she could.

She shifted so she could look down at the infant sleeping against her chest. How could Maya have left her alone? What kind of woman would do that? A desperate one. So what had she gotten herself into? Was the baby even hers? Or had she taken her from someone? Was there a desperate mother searching for her child even as Jaelyn sat holding her?

She sighed. That wasn't fair. She had no idea what was going on with Maya. She'd probably done the only thing she could to keep the baby safe from whoever had hurt her. Either way, they had to deal with the situation as soon as Adam returned. Taking the infant with them to keep her from immediate danger was one thing, but keeping her in temporary custody was something else entirely. "I'll take care of you, little one. One way or another, I will keep you safe. That's a promise."

With a renewed sense of determination, Jaelyn scanned the papers Adam had been reading. Finances weren't really her thing, but whatever he'd seen had seemed to upset him. She tried to make sense of the lines, names and random letters. When a headache started to brew behind her eyes, she gave up and stood, careful not to disturb the baby, then stuffed the documents back into the folder. Mr. Bossy had told her to pack everything up so they could get out of there, and while she assumed he had his reasons, she definitely planned on asking him if he ever came out of the bathroom.

She returned the baby to the infant seat and strapped her in, then set the carrier on the floor. She hadn't found any kind of coat in the diaper bag, so she had to settle for tucking the thin knit blanket back around her. Once she had the girl settled, she scooped up the remainder of the folders Adam had set aside, tapped them against the coffee table to align them, and started to put them in the briefcase. Then the name Jaelyn caught her eye, printed neatly with a Sharpie on one of the folder tabs. She stuffed the others into the case, put Maya's purse back into her own bag, and set the briefcase, her bag, and the diaper bag all beside the front door next to Adam's bag. With that done, she was ready to go. She flopped onto the couch with the folder and propped her feet on the coffee table.

And a second later, she lurched upright. What in the world? The folder contained a copy of Jaelyn's birth certificate. Why would Maya have a copy of Jaelyn's birth certificate? Jaelyn had never seen this copy, which listed a birth mother whose name she didn't recognize, issued from a hospital in New York City that she'd never heard of. No father was listed. Her own copy contained the names of the only parents she'd ever known. Even stranger, the folder contained a Montana driver's license in Jaelyn's name—odd, considering she'd never set foot in Montana—and several credit cards in the name Jaelyn Reed.

A niggle of fear crept up Jaelyn's spine, settled at the base of her neck, and began to throb. For some reason, the sister she hadn't known existed until a month ago had a bagful of forged documents in Jaelyn's name. How was that even possible? And for what purpose?

"Ready?"

Jaelyn jerked toward the doorway, putting a hand over her chest. "What are you trying to do?" she asked him. "Save whoever's after us the trouble of killing me by scaring me to death?"

Humor lit his eyes and she noticed they were puffy and red as if he'd been crying. He shrugged.

"Mmm-hmm. Well, for now, sit down for a moment. We have a few things to discuss before we leave here."

When he simply stood staring at her, she acquiesced.

"Please."

"We have to get out of here, Jaelyn, and I prefer to do so before we lose the cover of darkness."

His sense of urgency tweaked her radar, especially since some of the problems she had rattling around in her head seemed more important to her than leaving a place where she felt fairly safe. "What aren't you telling me? We've only been here a few hours. It won't even be light out for another hour or more. Why not get some sleep before we go?"

He seemed to look straight through her then. His expression softened, and she saw a gentler side of him, a side he seemed to keep hidden most of the time. The moment didn't last long before he clenched his jaw. "There was a bug in the briefcase."

She struggled to bring her thoughts back to the conversation. "A bug?"

"A tracking device. I left it in the bathroom so it will remain stationary, as if we're still here. I'm hoping whoever's following the case will figure we've decided to stay put and we can slip out undetected before it gets light."

A range of options flickered through her head in an instant before she reached the same conclusion. They had to go. If he could navigate the long driveway through the woods with the lights off, maybe they could escape unnoticed. She glanced at her watch. Which told her they didn't have much time. She stood and took a last look around to make sure she hadn't forgotten anything.

Adam walked through the house, methodically checking each window, keeping to the side as he glanced out from every imaginable angle. He was so determined to keep them safe, her and the baby. Two strangers.

And something in her changed, opened, allowed room for both him and the baby to pull out feelings she'd thought long buried. Instead of being comforting, the newfound emotions only confused her. For years, Jaelyn had been able to keep the wall around her heart well-fortified, keep from trusting anyone enough to even consider the temptation of a relationship. No way would she allow this rugged stranger who'd barreled uninvited into her life so aggressively to get to her. No thanks.

He glanced over at her, then paused and frowned. "Is everything okay?"

"What?" She hadn't even realized she stood so still, watching him, tears slipping down her cheeks. She wiped them away. He'd been honest with her so far, from what she could tell. Didn't he deserve the same in return? "I'm sorry. I was just thinking about my parents. And Ronnie."

Giving up on the surveillance for the moment, he walked to her but left some distance between them. She blew out a breath. "When my parents were killed, I was engaged to a man I thought I'd spend the rest of my life with. I had a hard time dealing with their loss." Memories of that time—of the crushing grief—came back to her.

"I couldn't eat, I couldn't sleep, I was…just…sad all the time. And Ronnie, well, I was lonely one evening, needed company, so I knocked on his door. When he didn't answer, I tried the doorknob and it was open. His car was in the driveway, so I walked in, started to call out, when I heard a woman's voice." The pain punched a hole through her once again, and five years melted away in a single heartbeat. "He was cuddled on the couch with his arm around another woman. He told me he was in love with her and asked me to leave. And my heart shattered."

"Ah, Jaelyn. I'm so sorry." He started to reach for her then seemed to think better of the idea and lowered his hand.

She was grateful for that. Her emotions were too raw. She needed the strength to finish telling him without falling apart, and that would be easier without the warmth of his hand enveloping hers.

She swiped at the tears that had begun to fall, anger creeping in to battle some of the sadness. She'd come to terms with Ronnie's betrayal long ago, was glad in a way that she'd found out exactly what he was before she married him. "It's okay. At least, it is now. But since then, I've never taken the risk of needing someone again, learned to rely on myself, on my friends, but I never let anyone get too close."

"I can understand that."

The fact that he'd simply understand without offering advice or launching into a rant about what a terrible person Ronnie was brought a wave of relief. He'd offered exactly what she needed, simple understanding. "Anyway, there's no time for this…"

"I'm glad you were able to trust me enough to talk to me." He did reach for her hand then and led her toward the door when she put her hand in his. "You're right, we do have to go now."

They'd already used up enough time.

She returned her attention to getting out of there and grabbed the car key. "I'm going to go warm up the car for the baby."

"I'll do it." Adam held out his hand for the key.

"Please, let me…" How could she explain how confused she was, how parts of her warred with each other? She couldn't. At least, not right now. She didn't even know who she was. Why had her parents not simply told her the truth? "I need a moment."

"Okay, sure." He looked out the front windows, then gestured her forward. "I'll grab the bags and follow you out. Just start the car, though, and come right back in for the baby."

"Got it. And Adam…" She paused, waited for him to look at her. "Thank you. For everything."

"You bet."

She lifted her raincoat from the back of the chair and took it out the front door with her without putting it on. When she reached the porch, she shook and wiped as much of the mud off as she could before shrugging into it.

Her thoughts shifted from Ronnie's betrayal to her parents. How could she explain to him how deceived she felt? How painful it was to realize her parents, the two people she'd trusted most, should have been able to trust above all others, had kept something so important a secret from her? Especially when they'd always been so honest about everything else? At least, she'd thought they had. What if they'd kept other secrets too? Ugh… What if Adam was keeping secrets from her? Because she was pretty sure he hadn't told her everything.

She sighed. It wasn't fair to blame Adam when he seemed to have her and the baby's best interests at heart. Her parents had had her whole life to explain she was adopted. Adam had been in her life for less than twelve hours. All of which they'd been on the run for their lives. And he needed her to trust him. Well…she couldn't give him her full trust just yet—he'd have to earn that—but she could cooperate.

Adam stepped into the doorway with the bags and gestured her forward.

She smiled at him.

His answering smile had some of the ice melting from her heart. They'd get through this. They had no choice, really.

While he stood watch, she hurried down the steps and walkway, swung the car door open and got in. Scanning the immediate area for any threats, she stuck the key in the ignition and turned. It clicked but didn't turn over. Her heart stopped in that instant, and she dove from the car.

"Get out!" Adam tossed the bags back into the house and bolted toward her.

The world behind her exploded. A wall of heat slammed into her back and threw her against the porch railing. She hit it hard and dropped. Darkness crept in, tunneled her vision. The odor of singed hair followed her into oblivion.

Adam reached Jaelyn an instant after she dropped to the ground. He lifted her over his shoulder and carried her inside. He slammed the door shut behind him with his foot, lowered her to the ground beside the bags he'd dropped, and turned the deadbolt. "Jaelyn, get up. Now."

"Huh?" Her eyelids fluttered open, her eyes dazed and unfocused.

"You have to get up." He eased her up, hooked the diaper bag cross body, then got her to her feet. "We have to run. Now."

She nodded, clearly not fully aware of what was going on around her. Under any other circumstances, he'd have left her where she fell and called an ambulance while administering first aid. But these weren't other circumstances. Whoever had planted the car bomb was most likely lying in wait somewhere on the driveway, had probably watched her narrow escape. Bile burned the back of his throat at the memory, the instant he'd realized why the car didn't turn over.

Jaelyn staggered toward the couch, scooped the infant seat from the floor over her elbow.

Adam grabbed the briefcase. Since it had a weapon in it as well as the evidence he'd need to get Alessandra's killer, he couldn't leave it behind. Then he grabbed Jaelyn's bag so no one could ID her. He'd have to leave his own bag. It didn't matter. His wallet with his ID was in his pocket, so they couldn't identify him through the bag. He shoved one of the guns he'd taken from Maya's briefcase into Jaelyn's hand. "Do you know how to use this?"

She stared at the weapon and shook her head. Then she clutched his arm in a vicelike grip as her eyes started to roll back.

"Hey." He shook her, once, tapped her cheek. "Look at me."

When her eyes refocused, he grabbed the hand she held the gun in. "You just point and shoot. Got it?"

"Yeah." Rather than nodding, she kept her head perfectly still.

"Okay, I'll go first, then you follow." He started across the house toward the back. No way could he chance running into the woods without knowing how many assassins might be lying in wait or where they were positioned.

"Where are you going? There's nothing out there but ocean."

"We'll head for the woods." If they could make it down the beach without getting killed. Their only advantage was the fact that their pursuers would probably waste time searching the house before coming after them. "Go to the right."

He flung the back door open, gave one quick look around, then bolted.

To her credit, as dazed and disoriented as she was, Jaelyn kept pace, the baby's seat clutched tightly against her. Maybe he should have taken the seat? No. He needed to be able to drop everything and get his hands free at a moment's notice in case he had to fight.

In some part of him, deep inside where he didn't dare look too closely, he knew he was lying to himself. Knew the real reason he couldn't carry the child, could barely even look at her, was because she reminded him too much of what he'd lost. Even as he ran, the memory plowed into him—Alessandra, her cheeks glowing, eyes filled with tears of joy, as she told him the news, shared that he was going to be a father.

Senator Mark Lowell had denied him that privilege when Adam had gotten too close to the truth, and the senator had ordered the hit on his wife, months before his child would have taken its first breath. His throat closed. Rage surged through him, begged him to turn and confront their pursuers.

"Adam." The fear in Jaelyn's voice tugged him back. "They're following, coming around both sides of the house."

The flashlight beams made their pursuers easy enough to spot, but did he really want to risk a shoot-out with Jaelyn half out of it and an infant to consider? Or would it be better to try to disappear under the cover of darkness the thick stand of pine trees would provide?

He reached the shelter of the woods a step before her, then braced himself to shoot, to cover her retreat with the child. He waited until she was behind him then whirled on the men moving across the beach toward them. When one of them yelled and gestured in their direction with his light, Adam fired off two warning shots.

The beams scattered as their pursuers dove for cover.

Jaelyn paused and glanced back over her shoulder. "Aren't you coming?"

Violent tremors tore through him. With the diaper bag across his body, Jaelyn's bag over one shoulder, the briefcase in his hand, and the closely spaced, mature pine trees closing in on him, he felt like he was going to suffocate. He wanted desperately to go back out onto the beach, to confront the coming threat, to demand answers as to why his wife and child were taken from him.

"Adam?" Jaelyn lay a hand on his shoulder.

No way could he risk two lives. They had to run, had to hide, no matter how badly he wanted to make a stand. If they could keep ahead of their pursuers, gain some kind of lead, they'd be home free. Maybe.

"Go." Letting go of the past, for now, he stuffed the gun into his pocket and followed Jaelyn deeper into the woods. It was the best...the only...option they had. "Don't go straight."

She angled toward the beach instantly. It was probably a

smart move, since their pursuers would expect them to try to reach a road. Jaelyn moved fast, weaving between trees and brush, despite the cumbersome infant seat. She stayed just inside the tree line with the beach in sight.

Again, Adam agreed. If they headed deeper into the woods, there was a good chance they'd end up lost before they could find help.

"What about the men coming after us?" Jaelyn's teeth chattered.

"Ignore them. They'll either catch us or they won't." They'd deal with it if the time came. In the meantime, hopefully, he and Jaelyn could move fast enough to disappear into the cover of darkness. The increasing storm could work to their advantage, muffle their footsteps, provide an additional layer of protection.

The wind picked up, whipping through the pine stand, driving the ice-cold rain into their faces. The rumble of crashing waves, one after another pounding against the shore, drowned out all other sound, so he had no idea how close their pursuers were, only that they would come.

Jaelyn tilted the seat toward her body, ran hunched over trying to protect the baby from the worst of the storm.

Then the child let out a cry, long, loud and distressed.

Jaelyn stumbled, went down hard on one knee.

Panic assailed him. When he reached her, he fell to his knees by her side.

She was breathing hard, soaked from the rain.

The baby continued to cry, deep, wracking sobs. Even the cover of the storm wouldn't be able to completely drown out the sound. They had to get her out of the seat.

Jaelyn's hands shook as she tried to unbuckle the strap. She needed help. Even if she could manage to work the buckle, she was in no condition to carry the little girl. He was going to have to take the baby from her.

Jaelyn had asked him earlier if he believed in God, and he'd said he didn't know, which was true enough. He wasn't sure if

God didn't exist or if He'd simply abandoned Adam when he'd begged for Alessandra and his child to be saved. But if God did exist, then it wasn't true what they said—that God didn't give you more than you could handle. Because of everything that had been asked of Adam over the past five years, this was the one thing he couldn't do. How could he bear the responsibility for this child when he'd failed his own child so completely?

He couldn't.

His breath came in short gasps as he struggled for air, sucking in deep gulps of salt and brine.

"Adam!" Jaelyn managed to free the baby. "We have to go! Now!"

"Wait." He lay a hand on hers to keep her from lifting the child from the seat, then thrust her bag toward her and handed her the briefcase. "I'll take her."

"Are you sure?"

"Yeah." He nodded, about as far from sure as he'd ever been about anything in his life, and lifted the tiny bundle into his arms. "Just go."

She focused on him for another moment, studied him while he kept his expression carefully neutral, then staggered to her feet. She took off her raincoat and wrapped it around the baby, then lay a gentle kiss on top of her head before she turned and started forward again.

"God help us," he whispered and, tucking the baby tighter against his body, he started to move.

The little girl cried beneath Jaelyn's raincoat, deep, racking sobs he'd do anything to soothe, and yet, the sound brought comfort with the knowledge she was alive. It also brought fear that her cries would give away their position. How could he fight now with the baby in his arms? He began to second-guess his decision to carry her, then watched as Jaelyn tripped, fumbled the briefcase, and barely managed to regain her footing. No, he had no choice, but God help him, he would not lose this child. He would find a way to protect her somehow.

They moved through the woods as night inched closer to morning. He kept a firm hold on the child, his fingers a mass of pins and needles before going blessedly numb. The rain finally gave up its relentless pounding, but the cold seeped all the way through him.

When the baby's cries finally eased, he sucked in a deep breath and glanced over his shoulder. Darkness swallowed the woods, surrounded them, cocooned them in its embrace. Silence descended.

Then he uttered the first prayer he'd said in five long years, "Thank you for saving us, and please let this baby be okay."

Tremors shook his hand as he lifted the corner of Jaelyn's raincoat.

The infant looked up at him, eyes wide and red rimmed, filled with fear. But she was safe.

He closed his eyes for one blessed moment. "Oh, God, thank you."

They trudged on as hints of gray teased the horizon, as the sun struggled to peek through the thick cloud cover onto the endless expanse of ocean.

The baby remained quiet and still, so he peeked at her again and had a moment of panic when he found her eyes closed, but a quick check showed she was breathing. Exhaustion from crying, fear, and the smooth rocking motion of his walking must have lulled her to sleep. He covered her again, to keep her as warm and dry as possible, but they needed to get to help. None of them were dressed for the weather, especially since they were soaked through.

Though he could see the outline of the beach through the trees, make out the silhouettes of homes that lined the shore, he had no idea how far they'd traveled, nor if the homes he could see would have residents or be uninhabited at this time of year. It didn't matter. He'd break in if need be. "We have to get to help, Jaelyn."

She nodded, her attention fully riveted in front of her as they finally emerged from the span of woods.

Once he reached the dunes that were barely holding back the higher-than-normal tide, he wrapped the raincoat around Jaelyn's shoulders, unzipped his jacket and tucked the baby inside, close to his heart for warmth. Then he collapsed to his knees. When Jaelyn fell to her knees on the sand beside him, he gathered her close, cradling the baby between them, and rested his cheek on her head.

He had no idea how they'd made it, where they'd found the strength or the courage to keep on going, but he offered a prayer of thanks. Then he did what he should have done five years ago and wasn't able to do after losing Alessandra and the baby, he prayed for his wife and their unborn child, prayed they were safe and happy with God and that he'd one day see them again. While the ocean raged, and a flock of seagulls screamed and dove, he closed his eyes and wept.

Chapter Six

Jaelyn drifted in some strange place between sleep and wakefulness, between consciousness and unconsciousness. Snuggled against Adam, with the baby between them, she was no longer cold, no longer shivering. Some deep part of her screamed a warning, but she couldn't quite grasp what was wrong, and her eyes fluttered closed.

"Hey!"

Though she could make out the word, she had no idea who was speaking. A male voice. Adam?

"Hey, there!"

No, not Adam. Too far away. Adam was beside her. She could feel the weight of his arm across her back, feel the warmth emanating from him.

"Are you guys okay?" That voice again, impatient, insistent.

She struggled to open her eyes, managed to get one barely open, and found an older gentleman bent over, hands on his knees, inches from her face.

"Oh, man, thank God. I thought maybe you guys were, you know…dead or something."

Jaelyn lifted her head to look at Adam, and every muscle in her body screamed in protest.

A hand gripped her arm, gentle but insistent. "We have to get you inside now. My wife, she's waiting for me to come back in. She wanted to call nine-one-one, but I told her I'd check things out first."

At the mention of calling the authorities, her eyes shot open.

The man straightened. "If I'm not back in a few minutes, though, she won't be able to resist the urge."

Jaelyn tried to tell him they were okay, that they didn't need the police, but all that came out was a harsh rasp and then she started to cough. Pain racked her body.

The man pounded on her back.

When the fit subsided, she wheezed in a breath and lifted her gaze to Adam.

He shifted, looked into her eyes.

And in that one moment, she was so grateful they were alive she wanted to grab the sides of his face, yank his mouth down to hers, and plant a great big kiss right smack on him. Thankfully, she came to her senses before she could follow through. Instead, she lay a hand against his cheek. "You okay?"

"Yeah, but we have to get up, need to get somewhere dry and warm." And safe. Though he didn't add that in front of the new arrival, she could read it in his eyes. He tilted his face into her hand for just a moment, closed his eyes.

And there was so much she wanted to say to him. She wanted to reassure him they'd make it through this, wanted to thank him for keeping them safe so far, for not abandoning her, or Maya, or the baby. She wanted to ask if he was really okay. He seemed fine physically, alert, coherent, but shaky. Shaky seemed to fit his emotional state as well. But now wasn't the time for questions. They had to move.

Every instinct she had begged her to trust him, and yet...

She lowered her hand, struggled to her feet with the help of the stranger who'd come to their aid.

When her legs threatened to buckle, she willed them to stay strong, to stop shaking, and she held her arms out for the baby.

Adam handed her over.

And the stranger gasped. "Oh, my, you need to come with me right now."

Jaelyn hugged the baby against her, kissed the top of her head, covered her ice-cold hands with one of her own.

"I'm Hank, by the way." He reached out a hand and helped Adam to his feet. If he had any opinion about the two of them being out on the beach with a baby in tow, soaked to the bone, he kept it to himself. "You folks in some sort of trouble?"

The man's southern accent was enough to tell her he wasn't a local but probably came up north to spend the holidays in his summer home. At this point, that would have to be reason enough to trust him.

"We're okay." Adam braced himself for a moment, then straightened and lifted the briefcase. "But we'd really appreciate it if we could use your phone to call a friend to pick us up."

"Sure, sure."

"Thank you," Jaelyn said. If they could just get off the beach, maybe no one would know where they'd gone.

Hank looked out over the ocean then clapped Adam on the back. "Come on then. I can do even better than just the phone. I'll wrangle up a nice hot cup of coffee for each of you while you're waitin' on your friend. Could be Martha might even be talked into cookin' up some breakfast."

"That would be amazing, thank you." The thought of a nice warm mug to wrap her hands around almost made Jaelyn weep.

"Sure, thing." He winked. "Oh, and Merry Christmas to ya."

"Yes, Merry Christmas." Jaelyn hugged the baby closer, reflecting on the hours they'd spent struggling on the run and so thankful they'd survived the night and had been found by someone so willing to offer help. She'd witnessed the worst side of humanity over the past twelve hours. It was refreshing to now witness the best.

Adam took her hand as they trudged up the beach, and she

was grateful for the gesture of support, for the warmth, for the sense of camaraderie his touch evoked.

Hank led them across a wide expanse of back deck that boasted an incredible view of the beach, then through a small back door, and into the mudroom of a cozy bungalow. The scent of cinnamon and sugar filled the air, and Jaelyn's stomach turned over.

"Oh, my." An older woman dressed in black slacks and a red blouse rushed in carrying a stack of towels. Her gray hair was tied into a neat bun at the back of her head, and she wore red ball ornament earrings, despite the ridiculously early hour. "Here you go. Get dried off now, and we'll try to find something for you to wear."

"Thank you." Jaelyn took one of the towels she offered and wrapped the baby. After a moment's hesitation, she handed her to the woman so she could dry herself off. "Do you have somewhere I could change the baby? I want to get her out of these wet clothes as soon as possible."

Despite the fact she'd been covered by the raincoat for some of the night, enough water had still seeped in and soaked her blanket and pajamas.

Adam held out the dripping diaper bag, and she noticed he still clutched the waterlogged briefcase in a white-knuckled grip. The fact that he'd maintained a death grip on the briefcase with one of Maya's guns still inside it wasn't lost on her. Her own bag, however, with Maya's purse and Jaelyn's cell phone and ID inside must have been lost.

She remembered him handing it to her when he took the baby from her, but she couldn't recall what had happened to it. She must have dropped it somewhere along the way. Great. Now if the gunmen searching for them found it, they'd know about Jaelyn—if they didn't already.

She took the diaper bag from him, slung it over her shoulder, and took the baby back from the woman. "Thank you."

"Of course, of course. Come with me." She started out of the room, a whirlwind of motion, probably brought on by nerves. "I'm Martha, by the way."

She paused, waited.

Jaelyn glanced at Adam as they followed the woman through a large living room. A Christmas tree stood sentinel in one corner. The pile of gifts beneath it, many wrapped in children's paper, combined with Martha's guest-ready attire, renewed Jaelyn's sense of urgency. If these people were expecting guests for the holiday, they had to get out of there. The fewer people who saw them, the better. If their attackers somehow found them, she didn't want these people who'd shown them such kindness put in a killer's crosshairs.

"I'm Jack, and this is Suzie." Adam gripped Jaelyn's hand, squeezed. "We're very grateful for your help, ma'am. We're not from around here, were just visiting for the holiday and had a minor accident during the night. The storm had let up, so we thought we could just walk down the beach until we came to a town, but we got caught up in a squall."

Jaelyn just smiled. While she understood Adam only sought to protect the people who'd so graciously opened their home to them, she didn't like the idea of deceiving them any more than she liked the thought of putting them in harm's way. They really needed to go.

"And this is our little girl, Carly."

"Oh, she's a beauty," Martha cooed. "But the poor thing must be half frozen."

"I know. I feel awful about that. I don't know what we were thinking." Despite the fact the story Adam wove was mostly fiction, the regret in his voice struck Jaelyn as sincere.

"Here you go." Martha gestured toward a small bedroom with two twin-size beds, a couple of dressers, and a door that led to a connecting bathroom. The lack of any personal effects told Jaelyn it was probably a guest suite. "You go ahead and change the baby, then look in the dresser drawers for something dry for yourself. My daughter leaves clothes in there for when she visits, and there are more dry towels in the linen closet in the bathroom."

"Thank you so much, Martha."

"Sure." She started to close the door behind her, then turned. "Oh, and I have a batch of cinnamon rolls coming out of the oven, so you'll share breakfast and coffee with us, I hope."

"We'd love to, thank you." Adam lay a hand on Martha's back, then led her into the hallway and pulled the door shut behind them, leaving Jaelyn alone with the baby.

She quickly stripped off the baby's wet pajamas, dried her with a towel, and did a fast but thorough exam. She seemed okay, quiet but responsive. Once she had her diaper changed, she took a blanket from the bottom of the bed and wrapped her, then set her against a pillow in the middle of the bed where she'd be safe. She was suddenly struck by the realization that she didn't even know if the baby could roll over on her own yet, though she doubted it.

With her little ward warm and secure, Jaelyn unzipped the bag, prepared a bottle, and used one of the towels Martha had left with her to prop the bottle so she could drink. As much as she'd love to snuggle the baby close, she had to get dry first.

But, before that, she pulled the gun Adam had given her from the back of her waistband. It had to be soaked, but since she knew nothing about weapons, she had no clue if that meant it wouldn't still work. She set it aside on the dresser.

A quick search through the drawers unearthed a pair of black leggings and an oversize pale pink sweatshirt, which she donned quickly along with a pair of thick pink socks once she'd dried off. Since there were no shoes to borrow, she'd have to put her wet ones back on when they left, but she was grateful for the warmth of the dry clothes and the feeling beginning to return to her extremities.

She began to shiver and wrapped a blanket from the bottom of the second bed around her shoulders, then sat beside the baby. She ran a hand over her soft, dark peach fuzz. "I'm sorry you were frightened, little one. I'll try to do better to keep you out of danger, but no matter what, I promise I will keep you safe."

She wiped the tears that tracked a steady stream down her raw cheeks—there was no time to indulge—and pulled the diaper bag closer. Daggers shot through her fingers as she emptied the bag onto the bed in search of dry pajamas and to take stock.

Thankfully, Adam had had the sense to zip the bag and it seemed waterproof. While some water had managed to seep in, almost everything was dry. They should have enough bottles to last the day and night, but they'd have to find a way to restock the next day. The same went for diapers. She searched through a handful of pajamas for the warmest pair, then set them aside. Once she had herself somewhat organized, had regained a sense of control she had no doubt was nothing more than an illusion, she took a deep breath. She'd just dry out the bag, tuck the gun beneath the baby's things, and get back to Adam so they could get out of there.

Using the towel she'd dried herself with, she soaked up what water had seeped into the bag, then lifted out the bottom piece to dry underneath it. Her breath caught. In the bottom of the bag lay a small leather journal. Jaelyn lifted the book, opened the first page.

Written in neat cursive was the name *Leigha Barlowe* followed by a date two months earlier and the numbers 7-6 19. Another date? Could be. Or could it mean seven pounds six ounces? Nineteen inches? She flipped through the remaining pages, what seemed to be a detailed log of Maya's pregnancy on cursory examination.

If this could be used as proof that Maya had given birth to the child, perhaps Adam could find a relative to care for her until this was over. But would she be safe with someone else? Safer than she was with Jaelyn and Adam? Jaelyn didn't know if Maya had family. What if they could only find a paternal grandparent? One who might turn the baby over to the Hunter?

Maybe the best thing to do would be to turn the baby over to Gabe, or at least see what options he could offer.

On the last page was a detailed recounting of her delivery, at home, with a midwife in attendance and no complications. But something intruded on her optimism. It began as a small niggle at the back of her neck. Something wasn't right. Where was the baby's birth certificate? Surely, Maya would have secreted it with the journal. She checked the inside of the front and back covers. Nothing. Holding the book open over the bed, she turned it upside down, thumbed the pages, shook it. A folded piece of paper fell out.

Jaelyn's hands shook as she lifted it, opened it. It was the birth certificate she'd been hoping to find, but instead of the name Leigha Barlowe as she'd expected, it read Leigha Reed. Jaelyn's name was listed as her mother. And no father was listed.

The room did one slow, stomach-pitching spin. She dropped the book and the document and splayed her hands against the bed, bracing herself to keep the world straight. She sucked in a few deep breaths. What was going on? Had Maya hoped to contact Jaelyn and ask her to keep the child? Had she expected Jaelyn to take the baby and go on the run?

The baby's cries tore her attention from the chaotic whirlwind her mind had become. After pausing for a moment to be sure the vertigo had passed, she lifted the child into her arms, stroked a finger along the side of her cheek. "Hush now, little one. We're going to find Adam, and I'll take care of you."

She cried louder.

Jaelyn was still shaky, whether from the ordeal they'd suffered through the night, the implications of the journal she'd found, or the fact that according to the document lying facedown beside her on the bed, this child belonged to her, she didn't know. She leaned back against the headboard, picked up the bottle that had rolled off the towel, and cuddled the baby close. The instant Jaelyn put the bottle back into her mouth, she sucked greedily, wrapped one tiny fist around Jaelyn's pinky. "It's okay, Leigha, rest now. Aunt Jaelyn will take care of you."

When she glanced down at the journal lying on the bed, back cover open, her gaze settled on the final entry, and a chill raced through her.

Time for Leigha to disappear.

Adam stuffed his wet, pretty much ruined clothes into a small garbage bag he'd found beneath the bathroom sink. Like many of the summer homes dotting Long Island, this one boasted mostly suites, with each bedroom having its own bathroom and sitting area for guests or families' convenience.

He cinched the belt Martha had given him one notch tighter. She had a good eye for size and had said her son-in-law's jeans would only be a little big on him, and she'd been spot on. The long-sleeved Henley and flannel shirt he wore over it fit perfectly. Unfortunately, he'd have to stuff his feet back into his own waterlogged shoes when it was time to go—he glanced at his watch—which needed to be soon.

While he didn't want to linger too long with Hank and Martha, desperate to keep danger from coming to their door, they had to wait for Pat to arrive. Before changing, he'd used the landline to call Seaport Fire and Rescue. Thankfully, Pat had been there and was supposedly on his way after a quick stop to pick up a car seat for the baby.

His heart stuttered at the thought of the infant. He'd had such a difficult time with her in the beginning, couldn't even look at her. Not because he didn't like children—he actually did—but because he'd been so afraid to fail her. Every time his gaze landed on her, it was a reminder that she might die on his watch, that he might not be able to protect her. But now, all he wanted was to get back to her, see her, touch her, assure himself she was safe. The fact that they'd almost walked out of Maya's room before they'd found her knotted his gut. What would have happened to her?

He did a mental head shake to clear his mind, had to if he was going to think clearly enough to function and get them out of this mess. Though the guilt he suffered had him shouldering the blame for their current situation, he knew it wasn't all his doing. Or was it? If he hadn't gone after the corrupt senator five years ago when a junior partner at Adam's firm had insisted she believed he was hiring hits, after the same woman had been accosted, would any of them be in the position they were in right now?

Would Alessandra and his child still be with him? He had no way to know that. No way to know what might have become of them under different circumstances. He'd done what he felt was right, and Alessandra had supported him completely, had encouraged him to do the right thing and try to stop the senator from hiring out any more hits. Neither of them could have anticipated the outcome…that she'd end up at the top of his list.

Perhaps it was time to stop dwelling on a past he couldn't change and start looking toward his future, a concept he hadn't dared consider for five long years. He'd been alone for all of that time, had pushed away his friends, his coworkers. Even Alessandra's family, who'd so kindly reached out to him, embraced him, offered their forgiveness and their love. And he'd been without God. He'd never been overly religious, but he'd believed in God, prayed regularly, maybe not traditional prayers, but more of an ongoing conversation. And then, when he'd shut everyone else out of his life, he'd turned away from God too, and had lived with silence.

Well, he wouldn't turn Jaelyn away, nor would he abandon the child before he saw them safe. And to do that, he needed answers. He picked up the phone on the bedside table to make a call, then winced when his paralegal, Carrie, answered with a cheery, "Merry Christmas."

How could he have forgotten? He apologized profusely, but she'd been with him a long time, knew the case he was working on, so she'd understand. He asked her to do the research he needed, the next day, of course, wished her a Merry Christmas, and ended the call hoping the research would pay off. And in the meantime, it was time to get moving.

He raked a hand through his still damp hair. He'd already checked the contents of the briefcase, found everything to be surprisingly dry, including the weapon still inside. He hadn't asked Jaelyn if she still had the gun that he'd given her as they'd fled. He wrapped his own in a plastic bag and put it in the briefcase, then tucked Maya's remaining handgun into the waistband of his jeans. He checked in the mirror that his flannel shirt covered it. Satisfied that no one would notice the weapon, he closed and locked the briefcase then grabbed it and the bag containing his clothes and walked into the kitchen.

Martha pulled two trays of cinnamon buns from the oven and turned. She smiled when she saw him. "Be a dear, would you, and grab me one of the platters from the cabinet above the stove?"

"Sure thing, ma'am." He did as she asked, set the platter on the butcher block countertop beside the stove while she started loosening the buns with a spatula. "I just wanted to thank you again for taking us in this morning, for everything you've done for us."

"Of course, dear. I'm quite sure under similar circumstances you'd do the same for us." She paused a moment to pat the back of the hand he'd left resting on the counter. Something flickered over her expression that had him wondering if she truly bought their cover story or if she suspected there was more to it. His gut told him it was the latter.

"I would, yes, and if there's ever anything you need from me, I'd be more than happy to help." Of course, once he walked out without giving Hank and Martha his real name, they'd never be able to contact him even if they did need help. When this was all over and it was safe to do so, he'd return to the house on the beach and bring back the clothing they'd borrowed, and then he'd tell them the truth, let them know just how much their generosity had meant to him, that their kindness had saved all of their lives. But for now, well, remaining anonymous was the kindest thing he could do for them.

She smiled knowingly and returned to piling oversize cinnamon buns on the platter. "I've already set the coffee out in the living room. I thought it would be nicer to sit in there with the fire to keep us warm. You go ahead and make yourself at home, and I'll be right along with these as soon as I frost them."

"Thank you." Adam scanned the empty beach through the French doors then did as instructed. He found Hank already sitting in an oversize chair, one ankle propped on his knee, sipping coffee, his ruddy complexion made more flushed by the fire and the hot drink.

Cozy seating arrangements dotted a homey room meant for entertaining. A bar in one corner held coffee and tea machines along with baskets filled with individual-sized snacks. Adam's stomach growled, and he lay his hand against it, suddenly realizing he was starving.

"Don't just stand there, boy, come on in and take a load off." Hank gestured to the chair beside him. "Grab yourself a mug of coffee."

Adam grinned. He'd never had a close family. His mother had lost her parents when Adam was a child and he'd never known his father's parents, since his father had walked out on him and his mother when he was too young to remember. If he'd grown up with grandparents, he'd have wanted them to be just like Hank and Martha. "Thank you, sir."

"Sure, sure." He waved him toward the chair. "And you can stop with all the sir and ma'am—we're just Hank and Martha."

Adam took a mug from the tray on the coffee table, filled it with coffee from the urn, inhaled deeply the rich aroma, and sat with Hank.

The older man studied him for a moment then set his mug down and sighed. "I'm not one to pry, son, but I can't help gettin' the feelin' you and your missus are in some serious trouble."

Yikes. He lowered his gaze to the steam wafting from the mug cradled between his hands. While he might have enjoyed having a grandfather like Hank, having him as a dad would have been rough. Adam had a feeling his kids didn't get away with much.

"Now, I won't ask what it is, but I will say, before the women join us, if you need help, you've only to ask." He gripped Adam's wrist, squeezed in a gentle offer of support, then lifted his mug. "And that's all I'll say about that."

Adam found himself wanting to blurt out the entire story, unburden himself on this man he had a strong suspicion would simply sit and listen, then offer some sage advice that would answer all his questions, alleviate all his doubts. Instead, he looked Hank in the eye and nodded. "Thank you. I can't tell you how much I appreciate everything you've already done."

"Of course." His pale blue eyes sparkled when he smiled. "What better day to be blessed with the ability to help another?"

"Cinnamon buns are ready." Martha walked into the room carrying an overloaded platter, and Adam jumped up to take it from her and set it on the coffee table. "Thank you, son."

It wasn't lost on him that Hank and Martha continuously called him son or boy, anything but the fake name he'd given them when they'd met. No, not much snuck past these two.

"Now sit, eat, enjoy. I'm just going to knock on the bedroom door and let your woman know breakfast is here if she's hungry."

"I'm here, Martha." Jaelyn walked in looking refreshed. She set the diaper bag beside a love seat, along with a plastic bag he assumed contained her wet clothing, then she sat in the corner of the love seat with the baby cradled close. "Thank you."

"Here, let me get you coffee." Adam set his mug on a side table and stood, poured Jaelyn a mug, then handed it to her. He leaned close and whispered, "You okay?"

She nodded, her cheek soft against his, and whispered back, "Leigha."

His gaze shot to the baby in her arms, snoring softly as she slept. The name suited her, soft, beautiful, delicate. He smiled into Jaelyn's eyes as he pulled back.

As they all sat there, Martha beside Jaelyn where she could keep stealing glances at Leigha, occasionally stroking a hand over her dark hair, Adam had a moment to envision Hank and Martha sitting in this room with their own children while their grandchildren ran and played. He had no doubt theirs was a home filled with love and joy, and for just a moment, he coveted that, even wondered if this was Jaelyn's dream. And then he came to his senses.

What was he thinking?

He scrubbed a hand over scruff that had long ago passed five o'clock shadow and shook his head to rid himself of the vision.

As they shared cinnamon buns and coffee, Hank and Martha entertained them with stories about their children, their grandchildren—all thirteen of them and the two on the way— and asked not a single question about Adam or Jaelyn. And he couldn't be more grateful to them.

Footsteps intruded on their conversation, loud, more than one set, and coming from the back deck.

Jaelyn stared at Adam, her eyes wide and filled with fear.

Adam went on alert. He lurched to his feet. No way Pat would come around the back. Plus, it was too soon for him to have arrived. "Are you expecting company?"

Hank stood, his gaze narrowed on Adam. "Not until later when the kids come out from the city."

Jaelyn surged to her feet, clutched the baby tightly against her, looked around the room as if searching for an escape route.

But there was no escape. They were caged, like cornered animals. Adam strode to the front windows, peeked out the blinds.

A black sedan sat in the driveway, and two men beside it scanned the area.

"Two on the back deck, peeking in the windows," Hank said from right behind him.

If they'd settled in the kitchen for breakfast, they'd all probably be dead already. As it was, maybe they'd live long enough to feel the terror of knowing they were about to die.

Chapter Seven

Jaelyn stood where she was, trapped. Claustrophobia assailed her. They had to get out, but there was no way out. If they moved from where they were, they'd be visible through the back windows to whoever was creeping around the back deck. She never should have stuffed the gun Adam had given her in the diaper bag, should have kept it with her instead. Even the illusion of safety would be better than the sheer terror she now experienced. Maybe she should hand the baby over to Martha and go for the weapon.

She looked down at Leigha, so serene in sleep, her features so delicate, the dark peach fuzz a sharp contrast against her nearly translucent skin. No. She couldn't do it, couldn't hand her over to anyone else.

Adam reached behind him for the gun stuffed in his waistband.

Hank lay a hand on his arm. "Just wait."

Adam hesitated, looked Hank in the eye. "I'm sorry for this. Sorry we brought trouble to your door."

"Did the two of you do anything wrong?"

"No, sir, we did not."

"Well then, seems you didn't bring the trouble, now, did

you?" Without waiting for an answer, he gestured for Adam to stand beside the front door, then pointed to Jaelyn and Martha on his way out of the room. "You two ladies get down behind the couch, try to keep the baby from waking up and crying if you can."

Jaelyn nodded, crouched behind the couch ready to spring up at a moment's notice if necessary, and willed herself to calm down, to ease her grip on Leigha before she woke her.

Martha ducked beside her and threaded her fingers through Jaelyn's, held her hand in a firm, steady grip.

Grateful for the support, Jaelyn gripped her hand back, lay her head against Martha's for just a moment, then shifted Leigha into Martha's arms. Jaelyn kissed the baby's head. There was no choice. She needed her hands free in case she had to fight. And she would fight, to the death if necessary, to save this child and the people who'd so kindly taken them in. To save Adam, who—despite the secrets he clearly harbored—had repeatedly risked his life to save them. She whispered to Martha, "If anything happens to me, take Leigha to Seaport Fire and Rescue. Explain what happened and tell them Jaelyn sent you. They'll take care of her."

Martha nodded. The woman sat with her back against the couch and kissed the baby's head, then hunched over her to shield her.

Someone knocked on the front door, brisk, insistent.

When Jaelyn peered over the couch, her gaze met Adam's. A million things passed between them—fear, regret, determination. She eyed the diaper bag, not so far and yet a million miles away. Her entire body vibrated as she crouched, held her breath, waited.

And then, Hank was back. He hurried across the room and shoved a shotgun into Adam's hands, then held up a hand for him to stay behind the door.

Jaelyn dropped back below the couch as he opened the door. "Good mornin' to ya," Hank greeted.

"Morning."

Jaelyn held her breath, prayed Leigha wouldn't choose that moment to wake and cry.

"I'm sorry to bother you this morning," a man began, "but we're looking for a couple, a man and a woman, who are wanted in connection with a murder and escaped custody this morning. We have reason to believe they headed this way, and I noticed footprints on the stretch of beach out back, leading straight up to your back door. We just wanted to check and make sure everyone here is okay and there are no problems."

It wasn't lost on Jaelyn, and certainly wouldn't be on Hank, that they had not offered ID, nor had they identified the agency they supposedly worked for.

"Well, thank you, sir," Hank said. "Mighty nice of you to check in on us, but we've had no trouble here. My wife and my son and I just walked out to enjoy the sunrise, what there was of it anyway, what with all the gray and clouds."

If Jaelyn didn't know better, she'd believe him.

"Didn't see anyone, couple or otherwise, while we were out there. Sorry I couldn't be of more help, but if you want to leave a card, I'll be happy to get in touch if I do see anyone. Always willing to do my civic duty, after all."

Silence descended.

Jaelyn squeezed her eyes closed, willed the tremors coursing through her body to still. *Please, let them believe him. Please, let them believe him.*

"If you see them, lock your doors and don't open them. These two are armed and more dangerous than they look."

"I'll be sure to do that. Thank you again for the warning. I hope you find them."

At the sound of the door clicking closed, Jaelyn's breath shot from her lungs. She swiped her hands over her cheeks, shoving away tears she hadn't even realized had spilled over. And then Adam was there.

He held out a hand and helped her up.

Hank peered through the curtains until the men were gone, then took the shotgun from Adam, took a step back, and leveled the weapon at his chest. "Don't move."

Adam froze.

Martha gasped, then quickly looked down at Leigha sleeping in her arms.

"Martha, you bring that young 'un over here right now." He spoke without ever shifting his gaze from Adam's.

Frowning, first at her husband, then at Jaelyn, she did as he'd instructed, and Hank held out a hand to guide her behind him.

When Adam slowly lifted his hands to the sides, Jaelyn did the same, shifting a few inches to the right to allow both of them space if a fight was needed, though she desperately hoped they could defuse the situation without one.

"I hope you understand. I don't know who those men are, 'cept to know they're not who they're claimin' to be, but I don't know who either of you are either, and until I do, I can't in good conscience let you take this here baby out of this house."

"Hank…" Martha lay a hand on his shoulder from behind him.

"Don't you worry none, dear." He used the gun to gesture Adam toward the couch. "Now, as I see it, you have two choices. You can sit right down and give me the abbreviated version of why you had this infant out in the middle of the winter with those goons after you, and I'll do my best to help you out and see you safe, or you can take your woman—provided she'll go willingly with you—and walk out that door and Martha and I will see to the child's safety."

Adam kept his gaze leveled on Hank. "Listen to me, please. You're right, we're not who we claimed to be when we came in here, and I do apologize for deceiving you. It wasn't out of any malicious intent, that I can promise you. We just hoped to keep you safe and figured the more you knew, the more danger you'd be in."

"Well, now, while I do appreciate your concern, why don't

you come clean and let me and the missus decide how much risk we're willing to take?"

"Fair enough." Keeping his hands where Hank could see them, he shifted toward the couch. "Can I please reach into my pocket for my wallet so I can show you my ID?"

He nodded once. "Slowly."

While Adam dipped a hand into his pocket, Jaelyn's heart pounded wildly. Blood rushed in her ears, drowning out the sound. They didn't have time for this. And she needed to get Leigha from Martha just in case those men returned and they had to make a run for it in a hurry. No way was she leaving the baby with a stranger, especially when their attackers had already found them. Who was to say they would follow Adam and Jaelyn? They could instead kill these people who'd so kindly taken them in and steal Leigha. And then an idea struck. "Please, if I may go to Leigha's diaper bag, I can prove she's my child."

Adam's shocked inhalation threw her for a moment, and she hoped Hank didn't notice.

He didn't seem to, as he nodded once. "But no games."

"No, sir. Thank you." She moved slowly, as Adam had, unzipped the bag, and for one instant she thought about grabbing the gun. What if Hank or Martha could tell the documents were forged? She shoved the thought ruthlessly aside. Grabbing the gun would be pointless. Not only might it be too waterlogged to work, but what was she going to do—shoot Hank? Martha? Instead, she slid the forged birth certificate out of the journal and held it out toward him. "My driver's license is in the briefcase, but Adam has the key. So if you don't mind him reaching into his pocket for it, I'll get that too."

Hank narrowed his gaze at her but nodded again.

While she quickly rummaged through the briefcase in search of the forged Montana driver's license, Adam held out his own ID for Hank's inspection.

He pursed his lips as he studied the documents, then gestured again toward the couch.

This time, Adam sat.

Jaelyn stood behind him and lay a hand on his shoulder. "Please, Hank, we appreciate you helping us so much, and I understand and appreciate your concern for Leigha, but the men who are after us already put my sister in the hospital, and they're coming for us. You have to let us go, and we must take Leigha with us or they will come for her."

With no choice if they wanted to get out of there without any violence, Adam gave him a quick recap of the past few days' events.

When he was done, Hank eased his grip on the shotgun, lowered it to his side. "Martha and I saw that mess at the hospital on the local news this morning. They said the gunman was going to recover but they didn't give any information about who he is."

Jaelyn inched forward and held her arms out for the baby.

When Martha glanced at Hank, he nodded, and she handed Leigha to Jaelyn.

Jaelyn tuned out everything going on around her, shifted her focus fully to the bundle in her arms. Though she ached to understand the truth of the situation that had sent her entire world into upheaval, the only thing that mattered in that instant was having Leigha back. Everything else could come later, and at that point, she had every intention of getting to the bottom of this whole mess. Starting with why her parents had never told her she was adopted and that she had a twin sister. Out of everything, that was the betrayal that stung the worst, even worse than Ronnie cheating on her when she'd needed him most.

"You folks need to get out of here before they come back." Hank set his shotgun aside and held a hand out to Adam.

Adam shook the man's hand even as he gripped Jaelyn's elbow and guided her toward the door. "I don't know how I can ever thank you for helping us, Hank, and I can't tell you how sorry I am that trouble followed us here."

Hank waved him off, peered around the corner so he could see out the French doors onto the back deck. "Don't worry about it. I'm just glad I found y'all when I did. And I hope you understand I needed answers before I could let you take that child outta here."

Adam turned to make eye contact with him, held his gaze. "I not only understand, but I appreciate your concern and your desire to do the right thing by her."

"Well, then, that's settled. Now we need to get you out of here. You can leave the bags with your wet clothes, just take what you need and come back for the rest another time when maybe we can sit out on the deck and you can share how this all turns out."

Adam nodded. "You bet we will, and thank you again."

Jaelyn hooked the diaper bag over her shoulder. "I'm so sorry, Martha."

The elderly woman swiped back a strand of hair that had come free from her bun then fussed over Leigha for a moment, tucking the blanket tighter around her. "Don't you worry about a thing. You just keep this little one safe."

"Thank you. For everything A firefighter we know should be here any minute to pick us up. We just need to get out of the house and slip into the woods unnoticed."

"Okay, then." Hank nodded and held his hand out to his wife. "Come on, Martha. What do you say to a walk on the beach before the kids get here, draw the attention of anyone who might be watching?"

Her smile held such warmth when she looked at him, slid her hand into his, that Jaelyn's heart tripped. The memory of her parents came unbidden, her father holding a hand out to her mother, then his other out to Jaelyn—the picture-perfect happy family. How could they have kept the truth from her? Had they meant to tell her one day but had just run out of time?

Pain tore through her. She'd trusted them so completely—would the sting of betrayal ever lessen?

She didn't have the answer to that, and probably only time would tell, so better to move on to more immediate problems, search for answers they could find. She had an idea how to get whoever was after Maya to come after them again, under controlled circumstances, but she had to make sure Leigha was somewhere safe before she mentioned it to Adam. And she needed time to compose her argument so he'd agree to using her as bait. They would lure the Hunter out of hiding and bring him and all of his associates to justice.

Adam held a branch aside for Jaelyn to pass with Leigha. The way she hovered protectively over the child touched him in a way nothing had for a long time. The sound of an engine running made him pause and listen. He lay a hand on her shoulder and gestured for her to duck behind a tree with the baby and wait for him to return. He leaned close to her and whispered against her ear, "If anything happens, run with the baby."

She nodded, her expression grim, and he wondered for a moment if she'd do as he asked or stay and try to fight if the need arose.

Leaving her to wait, he crouched low, crept closer to the edge of the wooded lot. A black Jeep idled at the curb, windows cracked, though not enough to see inside. The sun's glare blocked his view of the interior.

A light touch against the back of his shoulder had him practically jumping out of his skin.

"Sorry, I didn't mean to startle you." Jaelyn smiled apologetically. "It's safe. The Jeep is Jack's."

"You're sure?" He rubbed his chest where his heart thundered.

"I should be—it's new and he loves it. He's spent the past few weeks showing it to everyone who'd go out and take a look." She started to stand, but he gripped her wrist, held it.

"Please, wait here a minute with the baby. Just let me scope out the area, make sure it's Pat, and check that no one's got him under surveillance."

She frowned and looked around, snuggled the baby closer, and nodded.

With one deep breath to convince himself they'd be safe for a moment or two, he stood and inched forward, scanning the deserted street as he did. When he emerged from the tree line, the Jeep's passenger side door opened, and Pat climbed out.

Since the Jeep's brake lights remained lit, Adam assumed Jack had remained behind the wheel with his foot on the brake, ready to peel out of there the instant anything appeared off.

Pat jogged toward Adam, his gaze darting continuously up and down the street. When he reached him, he held out a hand. "Jaelyn?"

"Safe." Adam gestured for her to come forward even as he shook Pat's hand. "Thank you for coming, man."

"No problem. We have a safe house set up for all of you." He nodded, kissed Jaelyn's cheek when she emerged from the woods, and ran a finger over Leigha's cheek as he assessed her condition. Then he grinned. "This time, we didn't rent it in my name."

"Good choice." Adam laughed, and for the first time since they'd left the hospital, he felt like they might actually get a few hours of rest before they reassessed the situation and figured out how to move forward from there. As much as he was loath to admit it, he needed that time. Needed to rest, to catch his wind, to figure out his next move.

They headed toward the car, and as Adam opened the back door, he held his breath and scanned the area again.

Jaelyn slid in with the baby in her arms, and Pat shut the door behind her.

By the time Adam rounded the vehicle and hopped into the back seat behind Jack, Jaelyn already had the baby buckled into a car seat. "You're sure you weren't—"

A big, black dog leaned his head over the back seat from the cargo area and nudged Jaelyn's shoulder.

She laughed and wove her fingers into the thick fur around his neck. "Well, hello there, Shadow."

"Who does this handsome fellow belong to?" Adam petted the Bernese mountain dog, a beautiful animal with an equally incredible temperament if his behavior with Jaelyn was any indication.

Pat turned in his seat as Jack pulled away from the curb. "That's Shadow. He's my search and rescue dog, works with me at Seaport Fire and Rescue. Since the landline you called from came up private and I couldn't get back in touch with the two of you, I figured it best to bring him in case you had to take off before we could meet you at the rendezvous point."

Shadow rested his head on the seat back beside Jaelyn, and she leaned into him and closed her eyes. The woman had to be exhausted. She'd said she'd been working since seven the morning before, so it had been more than twenty-four hours since she'd slept. She needed rest. They all did.

"Which reminds me…" Pat held two cell phones out to Adam, along with a charger. "You said yours was damaged and Jaelyn's is gone, so at least these give you a way to reach out if you need help."

Adam nodded, touched by the amount of help these men were willing to offer, not only to Jaelyn, who was their friend, but to him, a complete stranger. "Thank you."

"No problem, man."

Adam looked down at Leigha, brushed a finger along her cheek. She was so soft, so delicate, so fragile—how would they ever keep her safe? As much as Jaelyn needed rest, he was going to have to disturb her because, unfortunately, they needed a plan more.

"I'm not asleep." Jaelyn stared at him, her eyes clear, fingers absently stroking the dog's fur.

He smiled at her. "How'd you know I was about to wake you?"

"You think really loud." She grinned back at him, and the barrier he'd erected around his heart cracked just a little.

Seemed Leigha wasn't the only one sneaking past his defenses. Flustered, he ignored emotions he was far from ready to deal with and pushed on. "We have to rest for a few hours, and then we have to figure out what we're going to do."

"Jack and I have a suggestion...regarding the baby..." Pat shifted so he could study Adam. Since Jaelyn was directly behind him, he couldn't see her. So he missed the subtle stiffening of her posture, the hardening of her expression. "Jack and Ava offered to take her for a while, keep her until you get some of this sorted out."

A vise gripped Adam's heart, squeezed.

"No." Jaelyn's gaze shot to Adam, captured his and held. "I want to keep Leigha with me. For now, at least."

He wanted to protest, wanted to remind her they had killers on their heels, wanted to beg her to see reason, to turn the baby over to someone more able to look after her, and instead, he said nothing. He simply sat, staring at the child who'd somehow become so important to him that he didn't want to give her up, even for a little while.

He tore his gaze away from Leigha, forced himself to look out the window, commit their path to memory in case they once again had to flee, anything other than look upon an infant who should have no importance in his life other than to see she wasn't killed. And the best way to do that would be to let Jack and his wife take her.

And still he remained silent. He didn't want to disappoint Jaelyn, didn't want to hurt her by asking her to surrender the child.

Liar.

Bad enough he'd lied to Hank and Martha, who'd been nothing but open and kind to them, but now he was lying to himself as well. He opened his mouth to speak, to say all the things he knew in his mind he should say, yet he couldn't get the words past the lump clogging his throat.

He cleared his throat and turned his attention to the conversation still going on around him. Though it seemed he'd missed some of it, he caught the gist quickly enough—Jack and Pat would drop them off at the safe house. There was a car they could use in the garage, but the house wasn't stocked. Firefighters from Seaport Fire and Rescue would take turns on stakeout duty, while their police officer friend and a detective they knew quietly looked into who was coming after them. Though Adam suspected they'd never find a trace of anything to connect the men who'd come after Maya in the hospital and the B&B to the man pulling their strings or his hired hitman.

But he wasn't about to sit there and discuss that with a group of strangers. "How's Maya doing?"

Jack eyed him in the rearview mirror. "Her prognosis is good."

"Is she awake yet?"

"No, not yet, but they're hoping soon."

"Okay, that's good." Because he needed to ask her some questions, needed to determine if she'd be willing to turn over any evidence she might have and testify as to the identity of the Hunter.

His gaze shot once more to Leigha.

Or he could just let her go, allow her to disappear with her child and find peace instead of ending up like Josiah.

By the time Jack pulled up in front of a small, inline ranch house, Adam was on the verge of a full-on migraine. He got out of the car, breathed in the salty scent of the nearby bay. Blackness encroached, tunneling his vision, and he closed his eyes for just a moment, closed out everything…everyone.

"You okay?"

When he opened his eyes, Jaelyn stood face-to-face with him, concern marring her features. She lay a hand against his cheek as she had before, in a way that made him want to lean into her touch, take whatever comfort she offered.

"I'm okay. Just a bit stressed. Nothing a hot shower, a few hours of downtime..." *And confessing the truth about who Josiah Cameron was charged with killing* "...won't take care of."

He forced a smile and stepped back from her touch.

She let her hand drop to her side. Although she studied him for another moment, she made no further attempts to reach out.

His disappointment at that fact only served to annoy him. "We shouldn't be standing out in the open. Why don't you get Leigha inside while I do a quick perimeter check?"

She nodded, but if the grim look in her eyes was any indication, she probably suspected his perimeter check was only half about security and more to get alone time. And she'd be right about that. But, instead of being honest, he took the coward's way out and turned his back on her.

As he strolled along the sidewalk with his hands in his pockets, a deceptively casual pose to the unaware observer, he surveyed every house, road, alleyway, yard, vehicle, even the sky above them for any sign of possible surveillance. He found nothing but a middle-class neighborhood on a quiet Christmas morning, like a thousand other such neighborhoods dotting Long Island. He had to admit, Seaport was a charming little town where residents probably spent their weekends attending community fairs and church picnics. Undoubtedly, a wonderful place to raise a family.

He stopped short. What on earth was he thinking? He didn't have a family. They'd been taken from him in the most vicious attack. He was too overtired, couldn't focus, didn't have his head in the game. And that was dangerous. For everyone.

With a renewed sense of determination, he stopped procrastinating and strode up the walkway, waved to Pat and Jack, who sat across the street in the Jeep to keep an eye on things, and walked into the house.

Jaelyn had already curled into the corner of the couch with the baby in her arms, feeding her a bottle and humming softly.

As much as he hated to intrude, it was time. Unfortunately, the memories this conversation would conjure would be painful for him to deal with, but there was no choice. Not for him. But for Jaelyn, well, there were other things she didn't need to know just yet, things that would only hurt her once she did. And, as he watched her brush the baby's cheek softly with a finger, he knew he'd be keeping those things to himself. For now, anyway.

He sat on the ottoman, facing her, leaned forward and rested his elbows on his knees. He clasped his hands together and met her gaze. "We need to talk."

She nodded and shifted the baby, giving him her full attention.

Leigha's gaze shifted as well, and he squirmed beneath both sets of dazzling blue eyes.

"Isn't she too young to pay attention like that?"

When Jaelyn smiled, a full-on genuine smile, it was as if she shook off the weight of the world. "She's not really paying attention to anything, just reacting to the sound of your voice, but she is very alert."

Adam smiled at the little bundle. He couldn't help himself. The child was going to be a beauty, with dark hair and brilliant blue eyes. Just like her mother—and like Jaelyn. He lifted his gaze to hers. A dull ache began in his chest, squeezed his heart. "I need to tell you about my wife."

"Your wife…the one you lost?"

"Yes. Alessandra was killed five years ago, along with my unborn child, in retaliation for my allegations of corruption against…" *Your father.* The words almost slipped out, but he caught himself. No need to burden her with that truth just yet. There'd be plenty of time to hurt her with that one later on. "Senator Mark Lowell."

Tears sprang up in her eyes. She shifted Leigha so she could scoot forward and lay a hand over his. "I'm so sorry, Adam. I can't imagine the pain you must have gone through, must still be going through."

"No." He lowered his gaze to their hands, had to if he was going to get through telling this story without falling apart. "No, you can't. No one can, I guess, unless you've suffered that kind of loss."

She squeezed his hand, a gesture of support when there were no words that would bring comfort.

He blew out a breath. He supposed the worst of it was behind him, the admission his wife and child were gone because of him. Now there only remained the facts. "The witness who was killed, the one who was going to turn on the hitman in exchange for immunity from prosecution, was charged with Alessandra's murder."

Chapter Eight

"You were defending your wife's killer?" The instant Jaelyn blurted out the words, she wished she could take them back. She cringed. "Sorry, I didn't mean—it just caught me off guard. Clearly, you believed he was innocent, and you've already said as much. I was just surprised, is all, that you'd have given him the chance to explain."

"No, it's okay. And you're right." Adam rested his elbows on his knees, lowered his face into his hands, and paused. He stayed that way for a moment, and Jaelyn was afraid he'd changed his mind about confiding in her, not that she would blame him after she'd shoved her foot so insensitively into her mouth.

"No, I'm not right. And I am truly sorry, sorry for what I said, and so very sorry about your wife and child." Losing her parents had left an emptiness in her heart. Turning to the man who was supposed to love her and finding out he'd been unfaithful had filled some of those empty places with bitterness, with a hardness that had kept her from feeling anything for anyone else, from allowing anyone to get too close. That had been the most difficult time in her life, and she'd built a shell around her heart to keep from ever suffering that kind of pain again.

But what Adam had gone through, losing his wife, his unborn child, and obviously shouldering a tremendous amount of guilt for what had happened…well…what would something like that do to a man? And yet, here he was, risking everything to save Maya and her child and Jaelyn. She wanted to reach out to him again, offer comfort, support, even just a shoulder to cry on, but she resisted the urge. She'd give him a few minutes, let him have the space he so clearly needed.

Then he stood, raked a hand through his hair, and crossed the room without saying anything.

"Well, I certainly blew that one." Jaelyn looked down into Leigha's eyes. "I think he needs a moment to himself."

The infant looked up at her, then gripped her finger and smiled.

A flood of joy flowed through Jaelyn. Though she'd cared for the child, protected her, connected with her on some basic level, this was the first time she'd just taken a moment to revel in the sheer delight of her. "You are so precious, little one."

Leigha cooed, waved her pudgy fist, taking Jaelyn's finger back and forth with her.

Jaelyn laughed, and for just an instant the weight of the world receded until there was nothing left but the two of them.

And then Adam returned to her and lay Maya's briefcase on the oversize ottoman, a stark reminder of the mess they'd gotten themselves into.

When Adam opened the lid, a tidal wave of anxiety crashed back over her. She wished so badly she'd met him under other circumstances, any other circumstances. She worked to steady her breathing, clutched the baby closer as Adam took a folder out of the briefcase.

"See this? Josiah Cameron was supposed to turn over the Hunter's hit list to me. He said it was coded but easy enough to understand if you knew what it was." He seemed to have reinforced whatever wall he'd erected to protect himself from the pain of the past. Adam held out an open folder and pointed to

Senator Mark Lowell's name. He ran his finger across a line of numbers and letters, stopping at each to let her know what they meant. "I believe the good senator paid Hack Hunters the sum of two-million dollars to eliminate my wife, Alessandra Spencer, on this date five years ago. The same date my wife was shot and killed."

Jaelyn studied the information, tried to draw the same conclusion Adam had from the row of numbers and letters following the senator's name. While she couldn't deny the fact that it was possible he was reading the information accurately, she also couldn't help thinking the data could also mean something else. She had no idea what it meant, but it could be anything. She skimmed farther down the list, tried to make sense of the orderly lines of numbers and letters. There was no denying the date, the senator's name, even the dollar amount, but AS didn't have to be someone's initials. Sure, it was a mighty big coincidence the date happened to be the date Alessandra was shot. But still, there was no proof Maya had been carrying evidence her husband had killed anyone. And yet…

Could it be possible? Did Maya know her husband was a killer? Was she planning to turn the evidence over to the authorities? Or maybe blackmail him with it, exchange her silence for the lives of herself and her child? She needed to talk to Maya, needed answers that only she could give.

And then her gaze skimmed a few lines down and fell on another date from five years ago, followed by a set of initials. A chill raced through her, raising goose bumps. She lay a shaky finger on the line. "Here. This is the date of my parents' accident followed by the amount of three-million dollars and the initials DER plus one. Dr. Elijah Reed plus one." The chances of two coincidences lining up so perfectly, with dates and initials that matched *three* deaths that they knew of, were slim to none. "My mother didn't even rate her own initials, just plus one—an afterthought. And if he charges two-million dollars a hit, as it seems from the other numbers, my mother was not even worth the full amount."

"Jaelyn, I—"

She surged to her feet, dropped the folder, scattering the pages across the floor, and shifted the baby into Adam's arms. She ignored his shocked sputtering and bolted for the door. Better to take her chances a killer was lying in wait somewhere out there than to sit in this room with the claustrophobia threatening to suffocate her for even another second. She yanked the front door open and strode out onto the front lawn.

But where could she go? There was nowhere to run, nowhere to hide, nowhere she'd be safe, nowhere she could escape from the certainty that not only was Adam right about having found a copy of the Hunter's hit list in Maya's possession, but that her own parents had not died accidentally. They had been deliberately murdered.

She bent, propped her hands on her knees, and sucked in deep lungsful of the cold, damp air. The ache in her chest begged for relief. She coughed, as sobs began to rack her body.

How could that be? They had to be reading the list wrong. Why would Maya's husband or the senator have had any reason to kill Jaelyn's parents? Everyone loved them. Elijah and Allison Reed were outstanding members of the community. Her mother had volunteered at the church, the hospital, the PTA, and anywhere else she was needed.

And then Adam was beside her. He rested a hand on her back, circling her arm with his other hand. "Come on now, Jaelyn. It's not safe out here."

"Where's Leigha?"

"I buckled her into the seat. I didn't want to bring her out here and expose her to whoever might be watching." Adam lifted a hand, waved to whichever firefighter had drawn the short straw and was spending Christmas Day on stakeout duty to let him know everything was okay.

But it wasn't okay, and it might never be okay. Her gaze

shot to his, and she searched his expression for answers, for hope, for something…anything…that would help her understand what was happening to her and why. "I don't understand what's going on, why my entire world has just been turned completely upside down."

"I know." He rubbed a circle on her back, guided her toward the house, ignored everything else that might be happening around them to keep his attention firmly on her. "And I promise you we're going to figure it out. I'm sorry this is all happening, sorry you didn't know any of it before now."

She appreciated that, but it didn't ease the pain or uncertainty, didn't change the fact that her entire life—even her parents' deaths—had been a lie.

"Hey." He lay a finger gently beneath her chin, tipped her face toward him. "Listen to me. I promise you we'll get to the bottom of this. I will not rest until I have the answers you need."

She nodded and let him lead her inside, settle her on the couch. Since Leigha had fallen asleep, she left her in the seat and felt the baby's absence from her arms more painfully than she was willing to admit, even to herself.

Adam sat on the ottoman facing her, gripped her hands in his. "Are you okay now?"

Was she? Actually, she had no idea. A short burst of laughter blurted out.

Adam simply stared at her for a moment and lifted a brow, then he grinned, the gold flecks amid the browns and greens in his eyes dancing with humor.

She shook her head and sighed. "We're a hot mess."

"Ah, well…" He laughed then, and relaxed, the stiffness in his posture easing. "I can't really argue that, but I can't think of anyone else I'd rather be in this mess with."

Jaelyn studied him as he frowned, seeming confused that he'd allowed the sentiment to slip out. Then she squeezed his hands. "No, me neither."

And that was true. It had been so long since she'd allowed

anyone to penetrate the shell she'd created. She didn't count her friends and coworkers, because that was different. This, though—whatever this was between her and Adam—well, she was beginning to think God had completely upended her life and then thrown Adam into her path to test her. And so far, she was failing miserably. Although, they *were* still alive, and Leigha was safe—she slid a finger into the baby's tiny fist—so maybe she hadn't completely botched it.

Adam fidgeted with her fingers, cradling her hand in both of his. "Okay, I think we've both dealt as best we can with the most difficult emotional parts of all this. Now we have to lay it all out and come up with some sort of a logical plan."

She nodded. The rest could be dealt with later, when they were safe. She'd definitely need some time to reassess her priorities, determine where she wanted her life to go from here, but now wasn't the time. "Fine, so let's go over what we know and figure out what to do next."

He released her hand, pulled back to sit up straighter.

She told herself the disappointment was only because she felt safer with him near, then immediately dismissed the thought.

"Okay. Josiah Cameron was not only Maya's lover but Senator Lowell's most trusted aide. In addition to pointing the finger at the Hunter, he was also set to testify that the senator himself had hired the hitman to commit the murder Josiah was arrested for, the murder of my wife, which Josiah was then framed for."

"But why frame Josiah?"

Adam shrugged. "Who knows? Maybe Hunter Barlowe figured out Josiah was having an affair with his wife. He could have seen Josiah sentenced to prison for the rest of his life, then waited a while and done away with Maya. Or maybe it was his way of punishing Maya, as the senator punished me by killing my wife."

"Or…" Jaelyn reviewed the timeline in her head. "How long were Maya and Josiah having an affair?"

"Years."

"And Leigha? Presumably Josiah is her father?"

He spread his hands wide, shook his head. "I can only assume so, since I didn't know of her existence before last night."

"Hmm…" She chewed it over. "Maybe Hunter found out his wife was pregnant and the child wasn't his? He could easily have gotten rid of Josiah by framing him, throwing suspicion off the senator after you'd accused him of being corrupt. That would eliminate Josiah as a problem. Plus, even if Josiah did point a finger at Hunter Barlowe, even if he did accuse him of being a hitman, even if he could come up with some kind of proof, like the documents we have here, who'd believe him? Hunter could say Josiah was lying to get him out of the picture so he could have Maya, or that Maya and Josiah planted the evidence pointing down a trail toward her husband as a gun for hire."

"I suppose any of that is possible."

"You know for sure Lowell is corrupt?"

He scoffed. "That man is as low as they come. He uses bribery, blackmail, intimidation, anything to get his way. He uses women one after another then pays them off to keep their mouths shut. Those who won't accept payment in return for silence disappear."

"And you have proof of this?"

"No, not really, just a long list of people—including a junior partner at my firm who was accosted by the senator then tossed aside—who knew exactly what kind of monster that man is. Of course, when it came time for any of them to come forward and testify before a grand jury, to put up or shut up, Alessandra was killed." He scrubbed a hand down his face. "Maybe to punish me, maybe to distract me, maybe as a warning to those set to testify. Either way, suddenly, all of my witnesses had a mass amnesia attack. Even the junior partner. She cried uncontrollably when she told me she couldn't remember anything and wouldn't be testifying. Of course, I understood. How could I not? She had family too."

She reached out to him, wove her fingers through his. "We'll stop him, Adam. We'll get justice for Alessandra and your child. I'm sorry it couldn't be more, sorry it's coming too late to save them."

He nodded, kept his gaze locked on their intertwined fingers. "I'm sorry about your parents, Jaelyn. That they were killed, and sorry they didn't live long enough to explain the truth to you."

"Yeah. Me too." An ache throbbed deep inside her heart, where she could do nothing to alleviate the pain.

"But I have to think that they had their reasons for keeping quiet." He tilted her chin up to catch her gaze and hold it captive. "The child they raised is a beautiful person, one who risked her own life without hesitation to save a stranger. One who has dedicated herself to helping others, both as an ER nurse and a firefighter, and one who took in a stranger's child amid all of this confusion and tended to her with love and affection. It seems to me they would have been close with their daughter, honest with her at all costs."

"And until yesterday I'd have sworn that was true." Would have believed it with every last ounce of her being.

"Then trust them."

She frowned. "What do you mean?"

"Trust that if they didn't tell you about the adoption there was a reason for that. If they didn't tell you about Maya, maybe they didn't know about her. I've asked my paralegal to look into the situation and see what she can find out."

Jaelyn only nodded. As much as she wanted answers about the adoption, they needed to focus on the situation at hand first. Too many lives were at stake for her to indulge in a personal campaign.

"When did you take the DNA test? And when did you find out about Maya?"

"I took the DNA test last winter. There was a blizzard and the guys were sitting around the firehouse, bored, and had a bunch of DNA tests they were all taking. They asked me if I wanted to do one too, so I did. Why not, right? A look into my past, a way to see where my family came from…an attempt to feel close to them once more even though they were gone." And for that one fleeting moment, she'd been able to hold onto them again. But instead of bringing her family back to her, the knowledge of her past had driven a wedge between them.

He nodded for her to continue.

"Then the results came back telling me where I was from but not much else. But then there was a friends and family app you could join to connect you to long lost family members. I figured maybe there was an odd cousin or other distant relative I'd never heard of."

"And Maya's name came up?"

"No." She remembered that clearly, no one else had come up and she'd been slightly disappointed, hadn't even realized she was hoping for some family connection to ease some of the loss. "It wasn't until a month ago that Maya's name popped up."

"But you didn't reach out to her?"

"No, I was too confused. If it had been a cousin, an aunt or uncle, I'd have reached out, but a sister? A twin, no less? At first I thought it was a mistake or something, but then I just set it aside to stew for a while and hadn't decided what to do about it yet when Maya was brought into the ER."

"Okay, but she knew about you—had to have, if she was going to forge all those documents. She had to have known months ago if Leigha's birth certificate is to be believed."

Jaelyn nodded slowly. "Or she forged that within the past few weeks as well, along with all the other documents."

Adam held the cell phone Pat had given him out to her. "Can you access the app on here? I'm curious if it will tell you when Maya's information was added to the site."

"Okay." She took the phone to log in. She didn't remember any notice of when Maya had first shown up in the app, but honestly, she'd been so blindsided by the whole thing, she hadn't bothered to look. An error message popped up. "Hmm...it says my account doesn't exist."

"Did you enter the right username and password?"

Irritated, she shot him a glare. She might not be a computer whiz, but she could enter a username and password. She re-entered the information, careful not to hit the wrong buttons while she typed. "Still no account registered with these credentials."

"Can you search for Maya's name? See if her profile is there?"

She tried it. "It won't let me access that information without an account."

"All right, don't worry about it."

Why would her account suddenly be inaccessible? "Do you think Maya deleted my account so no one would find me?"

"It's possible. She'd certainly have the knowledge and ability to do so."

But why? The question hung heavy in the air between them.

Jaelyn rested her elbows on her knees, lowered her face into her hands. A stress headache beat at her.

Adam folded his arms across his knees, leaned forward until his forehead pressed against hers. "We're not going to find answers to any of that, not yet anyway, probably not until Maya is released from the hospital and can answer questions herself."

"So what do we do now?"

He frowned. "Well, the way I see it, all we've been doing is reacting."

And too emotionally, at that. He was right. They needed to set all feelings aside and develop a logical plan.

"We need to move ahead with what we can do something about," Adam said. "Getting the senator's goons to come after us again. We draw them out, this time with the police waiting to apprehend and question them, and get some answers that way."

Although Jaelyn seemed surprised her account was missing, Adam wasn't. Whether Maya knew about her husband's career choice or not, she was a cybersecurity expert. Hacking Jaelyn's account and deleting it along with her own would have been child's play. And he was beginning to think Maya had a plan in mind all along, one that didn't include leaving hers or Jaelyn's DNA lying around for anyone to find.

If she'd known she had a twin, she might have been searching for her. Without knowing the circumstances of Jaelyn's adoption, it was possible she hadn't been able to find her twin no matter what mad cyber skills she possessed.

Either way, that was a problem for another time. Right now, he had to decide whether to tell Jaelyn the very killer who'd ordered the hits on the parents she remembered, the ones she'd been so close with, the ones who'd raised her to be the warm, caring, incredible person she'd become, was actually her biological father.

He thought back to the punch of shock he'd felt when Josiah Cameron had first walked through his office door.

Adam hadn't known the whole story at that time, only that the senator's aide had been arrested for Alessandra's murder five years after the fact. Since Josiah had such a close connection to the man Adam knew had orchestrated the murder, he'd had no reason to doubt that Josiah was the killer he'd been searching for. He'd been so sure about it that the first thing he'd done when Josiah walked into his office requesting his help was punch him square in the jaw, knocking him out cold.

He rubbed his knuckles, sore at the memory.

But after Josiah had regained consciousness, he'd begged Adam to listen. Adam had listened, and he'd believed. Every word. There would be plenty of time to tell Jaelyn about her real father. For now, he'd let her struggle with the memory of the only parents she'd ever known, with the betrayal she was battling, with the sister Adam wasn't sure had her best interests at heart.

Maya might have put Jaelyn's name on the baby's birth certificate to hide her from the senator or Hunter. She may have been determined to continue where Josiah left off and turn over the evidence in her possession that the Hunter was Senator Lowell's hired gun. In which case, Maya was ready to sacrifice herself to protect her child and a sister she didn't even know. Could the woman possibly be that selfless?

He glanced at Jaelyn, studied her as she looked down at the sleeping baby, rubbing her thumb back and forth over the hand gripping her finger. Yes, maybe she was. Maybe the two shared the same selfless traits. If so, they must have gotten it from their mother.

Because if Maya was anything like her biological father, it was more likely she forged documents in Jaelyn's name so she could assume Jaelyn's identity and go on the run with the baby herself.

Jaelyn cleared her throat, interrupting his thoughts and saving him from contemplating further.

"I had an idea."

"Okay." But he was still distracted, his thoughts ricocheting scattershot around his skull.

"I think I might know a way to get the hitmen to come after me."

A ball of dread curdled in his gut. While he wanted the men to come after him, couldn't think of any other way to get the answers they so desperately needed, the thought of them anywhere near Jaelyn or Leigha turned his stomach.

At the same time, these were the men responsible for Alessandra's death, for their child's death. Didn't he owe it to them to use any and all means at his disposal to bring their killers to justice? "How?"

"When I was going through Maya's briefcase, I noticed she's on the same thyroid medication as I am."

That didn't surprise him, considering they were twins.

"I lost mine when I lost my bag, and I took one of Maya's this morning so I wouldn't miss a dose." She looked at him.

"So, I was thinking, what if I call a local pharmacy and pretend to be Maya, tell them I lost my medication."

Adam scooted closer. She might be onto something. "They'd have to submit it through the insurance company."

Jaelyn nodded. "I mean, Maya could pay cash for it, but either way, the pharmacy would have to get the prescription from the doctor, even if they didn't get approval from the insurance company. If the senator has connections, or if Hunter Barlowe is a cybersecurity expert, surely they'd be monitoring any and all of Maya's accounts."

His body rocked in rhythm with the pounding in his head, bringing a sudden wave of queasiness. Motion sickness, nothing more, and nothing at all to do with the fact that Jaelyn wanted to set herself up to be used as bait. After all, hadn't they done the same at the B&B? But that had been before he'd gotten to know her. "Maybe."

"I figured, since she used a midwife to deliver Leigha, she might expect her husband or the senator to be monitoring her doctor's calls as well, or hacking his records. Is that possible?"

"Hmm…" He played it out in his mind. It was possible, he supposed. And they had nothing to lose by trying. "It's a good idea, and it might work, but I think we can tweak the odds in our favor."

"Oh? How's that?"

"Get in touch with Pat. Find out if Maya had a cell phone in her possession when she was brought in. It wasn't in her bag or we'd have found it, so maybe it was on her person. It's a long shot, considering Maya most likely wouldn't have been using her own phone, but it wouldn't hurt to ask. If we can get that phone, and you can make the call from it—"

"You think they've got her cell phone tapped?"

"I don't know, but it's possible, and if nothing else, it gives them one more way to track her. So, we use her phone, call her doctor's office… Is the pharmacy a chain?"

Leigha let out a loud cry, startling him. When Jaelyn reached for her, he lay a hand on her arm. "I'll get her this time."

She arched a brow but said nothing, simply prepared a bottle while he lifted Leigha from the seat and cradled her in his arms.

He held her gently, afraid he might inadvertently hurt her. "She seems delicate enough to break."

"Don't worry, she's not that fragile." Jaelyn handed him the bottle then leaned over Leigha. "Are you? I think you're stronger than any of us know."

Just like her aunt. The thought brought a flare of heat to his cheeks, along with a wave of gratitude that he'd managed to keep from saying it out loud. He rubbed the tip of the bottle against Leigha's lips as he'd seen Jaelyn do, and she opened her mouth and started to drink.

"Where were we? Oh, right, the pharmacy." Jaelyn returned to her seat. "Yes. The name was on the label, and there's one nearby."

"So we have the prescription called in to them and try to put it through her insurance. Even if they decline it because it's too soon to renew, anyone monitoring would pick it up."

"And then?"

Some of the churning in his gut had begun to turn to anticipation. "Then, you have them charge it to whatever card she has on file. I have no doubt they'll pick up on that."

"But would Maya make a mistake like that?"

"Who's to say it's her mistake?" He grinned, finally seeing an end in sight. If they could pull this off… "Maybe the pharmacy just ran the card on file like usual. It doesn't matter if it's likely, only that whoever might be watching believes it could be plausible. Either way, if her credit card gets used, they'd have no choice but to follow up."

"And then what?" She tilted her head, studied him in that quietly observant way she had. "Do we go to the pharmacy? Hope they show up?"

"No." She wasn't going to like this part, but he'd have to convince her, because there were no other options. He wouldn't get justice for his wife and child at the expense of an innocent woman. "I talk to Pat and Jack, and they can get in touch with your friend, the police officer..."

"Gabe," she supplied.

"Yes, Gabe. And the police can net anyone they find lingering outside the pharmacy."

She was already shaking her head. "It's not going to work. They'll be waiting for me, I mean Maya, to show up. Chances are they won't make a move until she does. The police can't arrest them for hanging around outside a pharmacy. They have to actually do something first."

She was right, though he was loath to admit it. "Okay, all right, we'll figure it out. In the meantime, we have to find out if the gunman from the hospital ever regained consciousness."

"He hadn't the last time I spoke to Pat to check on Maya." She frowned. "Neither had Maya."

"Okay. All right." His thoughts raced. "I'd like to talk to Gabe, see what he thinks. Are you okay with that?"

"Yes, I'll set up a meet."

"Don't have him come here. I'll go out and meet him somewhere else, anywhere that's convenient." The fewer people they had coming to the safe house the better, since they had no way to know who might be followed. He looked down at the baby still drinking the bottle in his arms and found her staring back at him with those innocent blue eyes filled with wonder. Besides, he needed a breather, some space away from Jaelyn and the baby he was starting to grow too attached to. He had to clear his head of them if he was going to think straight.

She nodded absently as she lifted the phone and made the call.

They had a little time, anyway. Since it was afternoon on Christmas Day, the pharmacy and the doctor's office would be closed. The soonest they could move would be the next day, which gave him plenty of time to go over the plan with Gabe and make sure Jaelyn's safety was a priority.

"Pat said they can meet with you now in the diner parking lot in town."

Her voice startled him. "Huh? Oh, right."

"Do me a favor?" With her attention on the baby, she didn't seem to notice his distractedness.

"What's that?"

"Pick up diapers on your way back if you can find anywhere open."

He laughed at the mundane request, as if they weren't in the midst of contemplating a life-and-death situation. "Yes, dear."

Her gaze shot to his, humor lighting her eyes. "Thanks, hon."

He sobered almost immediately, then stood, set the bottle aside and reluctantly handed Leigha over to her. "Make sure you stay inside and keep the doors locked. I'll stop by and check with whoever's on stakeout duty out there and let them know I'm leaving."

She nodded. "Sure."

"Hey." He met her gaze, willed her to know he considered her safety a priority, though he couldn't bring himself to make the admission out loud. It felt like too much of a betrayal to the wife he'd lost only because of her loyalty to him. "Are you sure you're okay with me leaving? If not, we can work something else out."

The thought of that brought a little too much relief.

"No, it's okay, I'm fine. It's safer for Leigha if I stay here with her." She searched his gaze, looked deep into his eyes, and seemed satisfied with whatever she found there. "Just be careful."

"I will." He pushed a few strands of loose hair behind her ear, gave a little tug. "I'll be back in no time."

She smiled, lay her hand over his where he still held her hair, and leaned her cheek into his palm for just a moment. Tears shimmered in her eyes but didn't fall, and then she stepped back and looked away.

Adam turned and walked out before he could change his

mind. After stopping to speak to two of Jaelyn's friends, volunteer firefighters from Seaport, he jumped in the SUV Pat and Jack had mentioned was in the garage, turned on the ignition, then just sat there. Were they really safer there alone then they'd be with him?

There was a high possibility Seaport Fire and Rescue would be under surveillance and someone could follow Pat when he left, since they'd already connected him to her. Taking Jaelyn anywhere would be dangerous for everyone involved. And yet...the thought of leaving her alone sat like a brick in his gut. His growing feelings for her—

He had no feelings for her, growing or otherwise. His only thought was to keep the woman and infant safe and get justice for his wife and child. Beyond that...well, there was no beyond that. He'd resume his life in New York City, return to his role as a defense attorney, though the thought didn't bring as much satisfaction as it once had. He might be able to return to defending those who were falsely accused, but what of those who weren't? Did he really want to spend his life getting criminals a free ride? But then some people, like Josiah Cameron, were innocent and deserved justice. Weren't those the ones he'd wanted to save and the reason he became a defense attorney in the first place?

He shook off the thoughts. There would be plenty of time to contemplate whatever path his life would take after he saw Senator Lowell and Hunter Barlowe behind bars. And right now, it was time to take the first step toward accomplishing that goal.

Chapter Nine

Jaelyn paced the confines of the small living room feeling caged. She bounced and rocked Leigha, who'd been crying for the better part of an hour, as she strode back and forth, her back on fire. "Shh…baby. Shh. It's okay."

She hummed softly, hoping to soothe, but nothing worked. She'd fed her, changed her, rocked her, sang to her. Nothing she did consoled the poor child.

Added to her concern for Leigha, Adam still hadn't called or returned. He'd been gone for hours. Surely, they had to have worked something out by now. What if he'd taken off, given up on her and Leigha and gone after the senator on his own? Would he betray her that way? Maybe, but she didn't think so. And even if he had, she was dead certain it would only have been for her and Leigha's protection.

She warred with herself over calling Pat, then vetoed the idea. What if they were somewhere he could be overheard? Besides, it felt like a betrayal, as if she didn't trust Adam. She'd thought of going outside and asking whoever was on stakeout if they could check in, but that didn't seem any better.

She paused to massage her throbbing back, told herself she was simply concerned for Adam's safety, nothing more than that. But was that true? Because somewhere along the line, she feared she'd begun to develop something for Adam that she hadn't been able to feel for five long years...trust. And the thought scared her nearly as much as the killers on their heels.

Leigha let out one long wail, stiffened her body, and threw herself back.

Jaelyn fumbled at the unexpected move but caught the back of her head. "It's okay, little one."

The baby's face turned bright red as she continued to wail.

"Okay, sweetie, let's try something else." Because Jaelyn needed to sit for a minute, ease the ache in her back. She perched on the edge of the couch, lay Leigha on the ottoman where Adam had sat facing her only a few short hours earlier. She dug through the diaper bag and came up with a small stuffed giraffe and shook it gently. "How about this, huh? Do you like that?"

The cries tapered off for a moment, while Leigha seemed to study the rattling sound, then resumed.

"Oh, Leigha, I don't know what to do for you." She lifted the baby's legs, pushed them toward her stomach, eased back, then repeated the process. "There now, honey, don't cry."

The cries eased off to soft sobs and sniffles. Her eyes fluttered closed.

The front door opened, and it startled Jaelyn.

Leigha let out a long, loud cry.

Jaelyn turned to find Adam standing in the doorway, two bags clutched in his hands, frowning. "Is she okay?"

Jaelyn stood, lifted Leigha into her arms again, and held her close. She refused to acknowledge the relief pouring through her at his return. "I think so. At least, I can't find anything wrong, she just won't stop crying."

Adam set the bags on a small cabinet in the entryway and crossed to her. He studied the baby, ran a finger over her cheek. "It's okay, Leigha, I brought you a surprise."

Jaelyn glanced at him and lifted a brow. "I guess you found diapers?"

"No, well, I mean, yes. I did find a convenience store open and was able to get diapers, but that's not the surprise."

Leigha turned her head toward the sound of his voice. Fat tears shimmered on her bright red cheeks.

"I have to run out to the car for it." With that, he turned and fled.

Jaelyn couldn't help but laugh. He seemed so distraught. It was the first time she could recall seeing him so lacking in confidence. "Seems you bring out the softer side of our hero, doesn't it?"

She caught herself. Hero? Is that what Adam was to her? No, not really, but not so far off either. After all, had he not shown up at the emergency department when he did, Jaelyn would surely have been killed by the gunman and who knows what would have happened to Leigha.

She turned away from the thought, couldn't stand to think what might have happened to Leigha, and clutched her closer.

When Adam returned, he carried a small, scrawny Christmas tree decorated with miniature coffee cups, an assortment of candy bar ornaments, and a few red and green balls.

Warmth radiated through Jaelyn. "Where in the world did you find that?"

"It was sitting on the counter in the convenience store, and I got to thinking, well…" He paused, set the bag down, then put the tree on a side table in the living room and plugged it in. The colorful lights flicked on. When Adam turned to her, with the lights from the tree washing over him in a rainbow of color, he grinned. "No matter what's going on right now, it is Leigha's first Christmas, and I thought she should get to celebrate."

With a lump in her throat she had no hope of swallowing down, Jaelyn simply nodded and shifted the baby to face the tree.

Tears shimmered in Leigha's eyes, darkening her lashes, but

the sobs lessened as her gaze focused on the blinking lights. She waved her arms, bounced her legs, and babbled.

"Looks like she likes it." Adam smiled from ear to ear.

"Yes, that was a really thoughtful thing to do, Adam."

He shrugged it off. "It just struck me is all, when I was standing there in the store, scanning the lot for any potential threats, that today is a day that should be celebrated regardless of whatever else might be going on."

She reached for his hand, gripped it in hers. "Yes, you're right, it is."

"Besides, when I saw the tree, it stirred something in me, something I haven't felt in five years. Faith." He squeezed her hand. "For the first time in so long, I felt not only a return of faith, but of hope as well. As if maybe welcoming God back into my heart has eased some of the pain and grief I've lived with for so long."

She smiled softly. "I'd say God has answered more than one of our prayers in the past hours."

"Yes. Yes, He has." His gaze fell on Leigha as he brushed a hand over her hair, then turned to Jaelyn, his expression serious. "I have a gift for you too."

"For me?" Surprise ran through her, along with a sense of disorientation. Seemed Adam had a way of throwing her off balance.

"Yes, but for now, while Leigha seems mesmerized by the colorful lights, why don't we sit down and eat something?"

Leaving her to settle the baby, he returned to the entryway and grabbed the bags, then set them on the ottoman.

Jaelyn buckled Leigha into the borrowed seat and turned her to face the blinking lights.

The baby put one fist in her mouth, her attention riveted on the tree.

"Sorry, this is the best I could do." Adam unpacked premade sandwiches and soft drinks.

"Are you kidding me?" She lay a hand over her rumbling stomach. "This is perfect. I'm starved."

"Me too." He dragged an armchair across the room and set it beside the ottoman, then sat across from her, using the ottoman as a table. He handed her a sandwich. "Eat while I tell you what's going on."

She nodded and unwrapped the sandwich, trying to ignore the anticipation of whatever Adam was going to say. Was it news? Could they have found a way to stop Hunter Barlowe and Senator Lowell? She ate slowly while Adam outlined the plan for the next day between bites. Things would pretty much go as they'd planned, with Gabe and a detective he knew setting up to take whoever showed up to grab her into custody. The consensus was they'd still try to take Maya alive rather than kill her, since they seemed to want something from her.

Jaelyn struggled to pay attention to the logistics of the plan, while her mind betrayed her and ran through all the things that could possibly go wrong. What if they were ready to just eliminate Maya? What if they figured out it was Jaelyn and not Maya? Would they simply kill her? All the officers in the world surrounding her wouldn't stop a sniper shooting from a distance. Then again, Seaport sat close to sea level on a flat stretch of land. There were no high-rise buildings around for a sniper to settle in and wait for her to show up, and—

"...pick up Leigha."

The baby's name yanked her from her thoughts. "Wait. What?"

"Jack and Ava are going to pick up Leigha first thing in the morning, before you call the pharmacy and set the plan in motion." Done with his sandwich, Adam balled the paper wrapper and dropped it into one of the empty bags, then opened a bag of chips.

"Why are they picking her up so early?" Although she understood she couldn't take Leigha with her, the thought of handing her over to anyone else had the few bites of sandwich she'd managed weighing heavily and threatening to rebel.

"We have to be ready to move at a moment's notice."

She nodded, couldn't argue with his logic, but she didn't have to like it. With her appetite gone, she rewrapped her sandwich and set it aside.

"You okay?"

"I am, yes." Surprisingly so, all things considered. At least now they had a plan in place and hopefully an ending to this whole mess in sight.

"Good, then." He cleaned up and set their garbage and the remainder of the food aside, then sat on the ottoman facing her, elbows resting on his knees, hands clasped together. "There's something else I want to tell you about, the gift of sorts I mentioned earlier."

She swiped her sweaty palms on her leggings, suddenly nervous. She checked on Leigha, who'd finally fallen asleep amid the glow of the Christmas lights.

"I didn't expect my paralegal to get to anything today, but apparently, she had some time this afternoon and made a few phone calls, rousted a few people from their holiday festivities."

"Wow, I'm surprised she went through the trouble on Christmas."

"Yeah, well, the junior partner I told you about is a good friend of hers. While Carrie wasn't able to talk her into testifying, she did say she'd drop anything anytime if I needed help with this case. Anyway…"

Jaelyn held her breath, waited.

"Eventually, she ended up speaking with a Dr. Vance Sajak…" He let the name hang between them, seemed to be waiting for some response.

"He was a good friend of my father's, worked with him at the hospital." A good man Jaelyn remembered fondly, though he was often too busy to attend functions, and she hadn't seen him in years. He was one of the people Jaelyn had considered

contacting when she'd found out the truth about Maya. If anyone would know about her adoption, it would be him.

And suddenly she wanted to beg Adam to stop, to keep whatever he'd learned to himself, because once he said it out loud,
once she knew the truth, there would be no going back, no return to the safe little lie she'd lived most of her life.

"You and Maya were both put up for adoption by your birth
mother as newborns," Adam relayed gently. "You were supposed to go to the same parents, but you were sick when you
were born, and they didn't expect you to make it. The couple
who adopted Maya, well…"

Was there a kind way to say they didn't feel like dealing
with a sickly infant? Didn't want to risk getting attached and
then losing a baby they'd paid good money for? The thought
had been turning over like a ball of grease in his gut since he'd
learned of it. "They weren't able to take on a newborn with the
complications you had. So, they only took Maya."

"What?"

He almost stopped there at the hurt in her eyes, but the Reeds
had been amazing people. And if the person she'd become,
based on what little he knew about her, was a result of their
upbringing, she'd gotten the better end of the deal. The story
of her adoption was the one good thing he could give her. "The
doctor who was taking care of you, Dr. Reed, fell in love with
your strength, your courage, your tenacity, and he told his wife
about you. She went to the hospital, sat beside you for hours
on end, cradled you in her arms, and decided no child should
be without a mother, no matter what the outcome would be. So
he and his wife adopted you."

Tears shimmered in her gaze, deepening the blue of her eyes,
darkening her thick lashes. They then tipped over and rolled
down her cheeks. "Vance knew all of that?"

"He did, yes." He reached for her hands, found them shaking and cold. "And you recovered, grew strong with them at

your side. As to why they never told you, Vance said that was part of the deal with your birth mother, that they'd raise you as their own, never tell anyone else the truth of it all. Since Vance was there at the time, he knew all of it. He said your father confided in him that your birth mother seemed frightened. He figured your father was abusive and she was trying to protect you from him."

Which was true enough. Mark Lowell was not only abusive but a killer—even if he'd only requested the hits. If the list they'd found in Maya's briefcase was what they suspected, he'd known about Jaelyn, about the couple who'd adopted her, so why did he wait so long to have them killed? Had he only just found out about her at that time? And what about Maya's adoptive parents? Had they been killed on his orders as well? He needed to look more closely into the couple who'd died in a freak boating accident just after Maya had turned nineteen.

Too many thoughts crowded his mind, all begging for attention, for answers he just didn't have.

"Thank you, Adam, for finding out what happened and for letting me know." She slid her hand from his, tucked her hair behind her ear, and stood. "I think I'm going to try to get some sleep now. Tomorrow promises to be a long day."

While that was true enough, he suspected her retreat had more to do with taking time to process all he'd told her than it did with trying to rest. But he let her go anyway, resisted the urge to pull her close, to hold her in his arms and promise everything would be okay. The last time he'd made that promise, it had turned out to be a lie. A lie that had haunted him for the last five years and surely always would.

She took Leigha with her into one of the bedrooms and closed the door softly, leaving Adam alone with his thoughts.

Unfortunately, they were not good company. He sat on the couch, propped his feet on the ottoman, and ran through the plan again. Jaelyn would make the necessary phone calls first thing in the morning, although, as he'd suspected, they didn't find a cell phone in Maya's pockets. When she arrived at the pharmacy, the police would already be in place, with under-cover officers inside the pharmacy and others surrounding the parking lot.

If anyone came after Jaelyn when she arrived, they should be able to apprehend them. So why was his stomach in knots? What hadn't they anticipated that could go wrong?

That thought followed him into a restless sleep, chased him through nightmares, and hounded him when the first rays of light peeked through the windows the next morning.

By the time a knock sounded on the door an hour later, he was as ready as he was going to get.

Jaelyn still hadn't emerged from the bedroom when he opened the door to Jack and Ava, whom he'd met at the diner when he'd gone to speak to Gabe. They were accompanied by a beautiful little girl with a mass of blonde curls and big blue eyes that held far more cunning than her age should allow.

Jack shook his proffered hand. "Adam, this is Missy."

Missy, who couldn't be older than four, held out a hand to him and smiled. "It's nice to meet you."

"It's nice to meet you too, Missy." He ushered them inside, scanned the quiet neighborhood, and shut the door. Everything in him wanted to tell them to leave, that he'd changed his mind, that he'd go on the run with Jaelyn and Leigha until they could come up with a better plan that didn't put either of them in the crosshairs of a killer.

Ava held out a cup carrier with two coffees and a plastic bag. "We figured you probably haven't had breakfast yet."

"No, we haven't. Thank you." Though he took the bag and cupholder from her, he doubted he'd be able to get anything down until after this was done. "Why don't you guys have a seat in the living room while I get Jaelyn and Leigha?"

He left them, headed for her bedroom door, and knocked softly. "Jaelyn?"

"Come in."

He opened the door, poked his head in, not sure what kind of mood to expect, then leaned against the doorjamb. She seemed okay, though dark circles ringed her eyes. He had no doubt she hadn't slept much. "Jack and Ava are here with Missy."

She smiled. "Isn't she a sweetheart?"

"She sure seems to be, but I'm reserving judgment. I've heard stories." He grinned, hoping to lighten her mood.

"I bet you have if you've hung out with Jack for more than a few minutes. Don't let those baby blues fool you. Missy is a handful and a half."

He laughed, happy she seemed okay.

She took one last look around the room, slung the diaper bag over her shoulder and handed him the journal and forged documents. "Can you put these in Maya's briefcase with the rest of the documents, please?"

"Sure thing." He took them from her and lay a hand against her arm when she started past him with Leigha, who was already bundled into her seat. "You trust Jack and Ava, right?"

She inhaled deeply, let out a slow, shaky breath. "I trust Jack with my life on a regular basis. But this, trusting him with Leigha, well…let's just say I find trusting anyone difficult. But if I have to trust someone, I guess Jack and Ava are about as loyal as they come."

He nodded, relieved and yet…he didn't want to let the baby out of his sight. He couldn't imagine what Jaelyn must be going through. Thoughts of what might happen in the future tortured him. Jaelyn had become too attached to the baby, especially considering they had no real understanding of the circumstances or what was going on with Maya. What if Maya took off with her after this was all done, and they never saw her or the baby again? How would Jaelyn handle that? If the shadows surrounding her red-rimmed eyes were any indication, she'd spent the night tossing and turning, probably contemplating something along those same lines.

He shoved the thoughts aside. They'd have to deal with whatever came later, when the time came. He kissed Jaelyn's temple. "Come on. Let's get this done."

She sniffed, nodded, and moved past him into the hallway.

Adam followed her into the living room.

The instant she walked in with the baby, Missy let out a delighted squeal. "Can I hold her?"

"Not right now, honey, but you can later on if you listen really well, okay?" Ava said.

"Uh huh." She clasped her hands together against her chest and bent over Leigha. "Hello, baby."

Leigha smiled.

Ava took the seat from Jaelyn, rubbed a hand up and down her arm. "I promise we'll take good care of her, Jaelyn. Missy and I are going to spend the day with my friend Serena and her kids somewhere safe."

Jaelyn squeezed her eyes closed and nodded. "Thank you."

"Any time." Ava gave her a one-armed hug, then turned. "Come on, guys, let's get out of here so Jaelyn and Adam can get on with what they have to do."

Missy held Leigha's hand and walked beside the seat, chattering away about singing songs together in the car.

"I'll be at the pharmacy once I see these guys safe." Jack hugged Jaelyn, then shook Adam's hand. "Don't worry, we've got this part. You two just get this done so that baby will be safe."

"Thank you, Jack." Adam clapped him on the back then watched them all climb into Jack's SUV and pull out of the driveway. Once they rounded the corner and were no longer in sight, he stepped back, guided Jaelyn back inside and closed the door. "Come on. The sooner we get this done, the sooner you'll be back with her."

She nodded.

"Jack and Ava brought breakfast sandwiches and coffee. Why don't you call the doctor and the pharmacy then we'll sit down for breakfast? You barely touched your food last night, and you need to eat something to keep up your strength."

"You're right." She patted his arm. "I'm okay, really. Just a little sad that the baby has to be going through all of this, that we had to traipse through the woods with her in the freezing cold rain..."

He gave in to the urge and pulled her close.

She buried her face against his chest and cried. "It hurts so much that a poor innocent child is in so much danger, that we may not be able to keep her safe, that Maya was so afraid for her life that she locked her in a closet and..."

He didn't know what to say, couldn't offer any reassurance, didn't dare utter the words she probably needed to hear—that everything would work out fine—because he had no idea if they were true.

She paused, stepped back from him.

"Why do you think Maya left her?" She turned to face the front door, seemed to look through it. "After only a couple of days I'm having a difficult time sending her with friends for a little while, and she's not even my child. What kind of danger do you think could have forced Maya to leave her alone?"

"I don't know." The thought of what would have happened to Leigha had they not found her had chased him in and out of nightmares since they'd found her. "The only thing I can figure is that she knew they'd found her, so she hid the baby and took off. Maybe she hoped they'd follow her and not search the room and find Leigha. I have to wonder if she planned to lose them and make it back to the bed and breakfast, or she assumed someone would hear her crying and investigate. Just because I didn't know she'd checked in with a baby doesn't mean the owner of the bed and breakfast didn't know."

She nodded, sucked in a shaky breath. "You're right. Sure. Maybe she figured the owner would hear her crying."

He rubbed a circle on her back, soothing himself as much as her. While he wanted as badly as she did to believe that was true, he just couldn't wrap his head around it. Maya had obviously gone to great lengths to keep the baby a secret. "Come on. Let's make these calls and eat something so we can get out of here."

His gaze fell on the Christmas tree he'd bought the night before, and a sense of sadness descended. Suddenly, he wanted to be anywhere else but that cold, dreary room.

Chapter Ten

Jaelyn counted slowly as she inhaled, held the breath for another count, then steadily exhaled. She sat in the driver's seat in a random parking lot a few miles from the pharmacy, Adam at her side. Gabe had provided a borrowed SUV, and Jaelyn sat behind the wheel, her hands slicked with sweat.

Everyone had told her she didn't have to go through with this—rather insistently. Gabe said they could have a police officer impersonate her sister, but they had none who shared Maya's same slim build and dark hair. If anyone who knew her was watching, they'd make out the undercover officer in an instant and back off.

So, Jaelyn had insisted on going. It was her plan, after all, and she was going to see it through.

"Jaelyn…" Adam brushed her hair back from her face and tilted his head to study her. If the deep lines marring his handsome features were any indication, he didn't like whatever it was he saw.

"Please, don't say it, Adam." If one more person asked if she was sure she wanted to do this, she just might run screaming for the hills.

"Okay, but you know I'll be close, and you remember what to do, right?"

She lifted a brow at him. "Park in the middle of the lot with easy access to an exit, walk briskly, but not too rushed, without looking around. If I make it inside, lower my sunglasses a little to show my face as if I'm searching for something before putting them back in place, then go straight to the counter. And do all of it while ignoring the giant bull's-eye painted on my back."

He shot her a grin. "Yup. That's it in a nutshell."

She had the plan down pat. That part wasn't the problem. The real problem was knowing that somewhere along the way, her plan would most likely be thwarted by an attempt to kidnap or kill her. Hopefully, the officers Gabe had stationed all over would be able to prevent them from succeeding.

Ah, God, please walk with me through this. Help me save my sister and her child. Let Adam find the justice he so badly needs for his wife and unborn child so he might begin to heal.

And what about her? Would she ever heal from having her life completely upended? Probably. Unless Maya walked away with Leigha and didn't allow Jaelyn to be a part of her life. Well, she'd just have to make sure that didn't happen, make sure Maya understood she wanted to get to know her better, wanted to understand the decisions she'd made, wanted to develop the relationship they'd been denied their whole lives. A twin. She still couldn't believe it.

"By the way, I heard from Carrie again this morning—my paralegal—and apparently you own a ranch in Montana."

Jaelyn laughed out loud. Whatever she'd been expecting him to say, that had not been it. "So, what do you say when this is all over, we take a vacation?"

The words were out of her mouth before she even realized what she was going to say. She winced, wishing she could take them back and refusing to examine what part of her subconscious had betrayed her so completely.

"And not only that, you also have a valid Montana driver's

license, from everything she could dig up. Not a forgery as I suspected."

Caught somewhere between embarrassment that she'd invited him on vacation and disappointment that he'd ignored it, she turned her head to look out the windshield. "Huh...what do you know?"

Adam must have sensed her discomfort, because he reached for her hand, which only made matters worse, so she slid it away to brush her hair behind her ear before he could take hold.

"Jaelyn, please. It's not that I don't feel... I don't know what...but something for you. It's just...if we had met at another time...under other circumstances... If...maybe before..." He slouched back into the soft leather seat, stared down at his hands in his lap as if they held the answers he sought.

She wanted to say something—anything—but no words came. What could she say to him?

"I'm damaged, Jaelyn. When Alessandra died, and our child with her, a part of me died with them. Alessandra was my world. She stood by me, encouraged me to pursue the case against the senator, actively involved herself in my investigation... She was strong and brave and loyal, and it got her killed." He paused as he battled to control his emotions.

Jaelyn tried to put herself in his place. When Ronnie betrayed her, she'd been able to hold onto anger at him, and that helped to ease some of the worst heartbreak. But Alessandra had been Adam's world, and she'd done nothing wrong to him. Quite the opposite, she'd been more than supportive. And she'd been ripped away from him.

"Please, Jaelyn, understand," he went on. "I care about you, and if we'd met at a different point in my life, it might have been something more. Maybe we could have gone on vacation together. Maybe we could've had lots of vacations together. You're an amazing person, an incredibly beautiful and kind person. I just can't ever allow myself to feel that strongly for anyone again." He looked at her, and the struggle was plain in his eyes. "As it is, I'd like to keep in touch when this is all over, maybe be friends. And for me, that's more of a commitment than I've made to any other person in the past five years, and it's all I have to give. Can you understand?"

Could she? Yes, actually. And hearing him say it put all of her feelings into perspective. She breathed a sigh of relief. The heightened emotions running through her were clouding her judgment. He'd touched something deep inside her that was better left alone. When this was done, she had to work on her relationship with her sister, work on building a relationship with her niece whom she'd already come to love, work on resolving the feeling of betrayal about her parents.

She lay her hand on the console between them, palm up. "I'd like to be friends when this is done, Adam. Like you, I have my own baggage to deal with before I could even think about being something to anyone else. When I said let's go on vacation, it wasn't an invitation to further our relationship, just a knee jerk reaction to escape the reality of our current situation." She grinned, hoping to lighten the mood.

He smiled at her, closed his hand over hers. "Well, that makes perfect sense."

Relieved the awkward moments had passed, she squeezed his hand, then glanced at the dashboard clock and sat up straighter.

A voice in the earpiece Gabe had insisted she wear told her they were ready to go. "It's time."

"Be careful, Jaelyn, and if anything at all seems off—"

"Don't worry." She offered him a genuine smile. "I'm really just a big chicken at heart. If something seems off, I'm outta there."

He reached for the door handle, hesitated. A variety of expressions ran over his features before his jaw clenched, his eyes hardened, and he opened the door and got out.

Pushing all thoughts of Adam out of her mind, knowing he'd be safe sitting in the parking lot with Pat and Jack, who'd returned after dropping Ava, Missy, and Leigha off with their friend, Jaelyn drove the few miles to the pharmacy. She kept watch for a tail.

Her emotions battled each other within her. Anticipation, fear, acceptance, all vying for the uppermost position in her thoughts. She quelled them all. She'd learned while fighting fires, going on rescue missions, how to detach herself from her emotions. It was more beneficial to react from a place of logic than of feelings. And so, she forced all of her feelings into a box and buried it deep, put every ounce of her focus into what she was about to do.

She scanned the lot as she pulled in, double-checked each of the officers was where they were supposed to be. She hadn't anticipated the crowd. She should have, the day after Christmas when they'd closed early on Christmas Eve and completely on Christmas Day.

She shoved that thought aside as well. The officers would work to keep everyone safe, and since this was like work, she had to trust them to do their jobs properly so she could focus on her part.

She backed into a parking spot toward the far end of the lot, close to the exit, as she expected Maya would probably do under the same circumstances, knowing she might have to escape in a hurry. Was that what she'd done at the bed and breakfast? Escaped in a hurry, been forced to go on the run without having time to implement whatever plan she may have had in place for Leigha?

She couldn't answer that question, and it would distract her when she needed to concentrate. She scanned the lot again, then emerged from the car, shifted her dark sunglasses tighter against her face. What would Maya do now? Would she linger, search for potential trouble? Or would she cross the lot with her head lifted and determination in her stride? Jaelyn had no idea, because the woman was a complete stranger to her.

A voice in her ear prodded her to move. She recognized the detective who'd helped Gabe set this up. She didn't acknowledge his order to start walking, simply started forward, adding a bit of confidence she didn't feel to her walk just in case whoever might be watching knew Maya better than Jaelyn did. Sweat dripped down her back, despite the near-freezing temperature. Though she'd worn dress slacks paired with a bulletproof vest beneath a winter coat, she'd drawn the line at the high heels Maya seemed to favor, opting instead for a low boot she could run in if necessary.

She was more than halfway across the lot and convinced their plan was doomed to fail when a tingle began at the base of her neck and slithered upward. The feeling of being watched overwhelmed her, nearly had her turning on her heel and running. Instead, she kept moving forward, staring straight at the front door, her expression neutral. She was bait, nothing more. Her role was to lure their pursuers into the open so the police could apprehend, then get out of the way as quickly as possible.

She clutched her purse with a fake ID in Maya's name against her chest, just in case she had to go inside and actually pick up the medication. Her breath came in shallow gasps that burned her lungs, a small waft of steam escaping with each forced exhalation. She was almost through the lot—just had to cross the lane between the pharmacy and the parking lot and she'd be on the sidewalk and entering the building. Torn between wanting something to happen, needing for all of this to end, and hoping no one would attack her, she almost missed the squeal of tires as a black sedan skidded into the lot, fishtailed around the first row of cars, and barreled toward her.

Jaelyn froze as the world erupted in her ears. "Go, go, go!"

Then someone slammed into her from the side, shoved her down between the cars and covered her head as gunfire shattered windows and car alarms wailed. Screams, cries, pounding footsteps, shouts and more gunfire ricocheted around the parking lot.

And then silence descended. For just an instant, there was

no sound at all, like a vacuum had sucked her in, and the rest of the world sat suspended in time for that one moment.

"Jaelyn, are you hurt?" Gabe crouched beside her, glanced over his shoulder, then returned his attention to her. "Are you all right?"

"I am, yes." She assessed. A scraped knee, her heart racing like she'd just run a marathon, and the slacks she had on were torn and covered in wet gravel. She could live with that. "I'm fine. Did you guys get them?"

He pressed a hand against his ear, lowered his head for a moment.

She held her breath, waited, strained to hear the conversation through his earpiece, but couldn't make out anything but a sense of urgency.

Then he stood, held a hand out to her, and grinned. "We did. We got them. Both of them."

Instead of reaching for his hand, Jaelyn sat on the ice-cold blacktop, rested her back against the nearest car, which had an alarm blaring at full volume, and closed her eyes. They'd done it. If the men they'd apprehended answered their questions, this could all be over within the next couple of days. Leigha would be safe, Maya would be safe, Jaelyn and Adam could return to their... With suspects in custody who might well testify against Hunter Barlowe and Senator Lowell in order to save themselves, Adam would return to New York City and resume his life...alone.

Her heart ached for him, for the pain he'd already suffered. It would probably be difficult for him to go home to the silence without having the fight for justice to keep him from having to deal with the worst of the pain. Perhaps that pain would come now. Or perhaps he would heal. She truly prayed it would be the latter.

She sensed Gabe ease away, which was good. She needed some space, needed to breathe deep breaths of cool air. And she really needed to get this bulletproof vest off. Who knew it would be so heavy and cumbersome? She opened her eyes, and Adam was there, crouched in front of her.

He smiled. "We got them. Thank you, Jaelyn."

"Any time." A feeling of peace overtook her, the sense that everything had fallen into place. Not that they had all the answers they needed yet, but they were at least headed in the right direction. The two men they'd arrested for coming after Jaelyn would be questioned, and hopefully they'd talk, rattle off a list of names in exchange for a lesser sentence. Did that bother her? Not really. They needed the people at the top, Hunter Barlowe and Senator Lowell, or the two of them would just keep coming, or keep sending goons.

The joyful peace she'd been enjoying turned icy cold. What if they couldn't get the men to talk, to give up their employers?

"Hey." Adam reached out, tugged her hair in a friendly gesture she'd miss. "You all right?"

"Yes, I was..." She didn't want to spoil his good mood, but at the same time, were any of them really safe yet? "I was just thinking..."

"Don't worry about it. I'm going in with Gabe to observe the questioning once the two of them are processed. I'm figuring they'll talk right about the time they realize the severity of the charges that will be brought against them. Hopefully, we'll get enough information out of them to arrest and charge the senator and Hunter Barlowe."

"All right, then. I'll come with you. Will they let me observe?"

"Actually..." He held out a hand and helped her up. "You have somewhere else to be."

"Oh?" She quirked a brow at him. Where could he possibly think she'd rather be than seeing this through?

"Maya woke up. She's asking for you."

Adam walked her to Pat's SUV. He'd go with Jack to the police station, and Pat would take Jaelyn to the hospital. As much as he wanted to go with her, to offer his support while she spoke to her sister for the first time and hear what Maya had to say, he needed to follow up on the two men they'd just arrested. It would take a little while to get them processed and into an interrogation room, but in a town as small as Seaport, it probably wouldn't take long enough for him to go to the hospital with Jaelyn first.

He opened the car door for her. "I'll meet you at the hospital as soon as I'm done."

"Sure. That'd be good." She nodded but avoided his gaze.

"Hey."

She paused, glanced at him before climbing into the front seat beside Pat.

"I'm sure it's going to be fine. You and Maya certainly have a lot to talk about, a lot to say to one another. The other questions can wait." Hopefully until he got there, at least.

"You'll come, though? Because if you're sure, I'll wait for you to ask her about testifying against her husband and the senator."

He cradled her cheek in his hand, kissed her forehead. "I'll be there as soon as I can."

"Okay. I'll see you later."

He watched Pat drive away, saw Jaelyn glance in the side-view mirror, and waved. Although he second-guessed himself about a million times, envisioned himself running after the SUV and yelling for Pat to stop and wait for him, he had to see this through. He knew more about the situation with the Hunter than anyone in the department, and even though he'd brought the small task force Gabe had assembled up to speed on the major points, they could well miss something Adam might catch. Besides, Gabe had a patrol car following them, and there would be officers stationed outside the hospital room door. If anyone tried to get in, they'd be stopped.

They couldn't afford to botch this. If they did, Jaelyn might spend the rest of her life looking over her shoulder. Besides, she and her sister should be able to have some privacy to meet and get to know each other before he gave Maya the third degree and tried to convince her to turn against her husband and father.

Everything in him stilled. What if Maya told Jaelyn the truth about the senator being her father? Did Maya even know? All right, so he probably should have thought of that before sending Jaelyn off on her own to meet with her sister.

"Hey, man." Jack clapped a hand against his shoulder. "You gonna stand there all day, or do you want to head into the police station?"

"Oh, sorry." He shook off any misgivings. For all he knew, Maya didn't know who her father was any more than Jaelyn did. But the chance of that was slim—Maya knew about the adoption, and her husband worked closely with the senator. If she told Jaelyn who their father was, well…he'd just have to deal with that when the time came. But one thing was for certain, as soon as he got to the hospital and had a moment alone with Jaelyn, he was going to tell her the truth.

He hopped into the passenger seat of Jack's SUV. "Thanks for seeing this through, and for hanging around and giving me a ride."

"No problem. How are you doing? Okay?"

"Yeah, just wiped out." Wasn't that the understatement of the century. He couldn't remember the last decent night's sleep he'd had. Plus the physical activity, escaping from their pursuers, had used muscles he didn't even know he had. He needed to rest. And he needed to be able to go to the cemetery and tell Alessandra they'd finally stopped Senator Lowell.

He rolled his shoulders, tilted his head back and forth to ease the stiffness in his neck from sleeping on the couch all night. "Have you heard from Gabe?"

Jack looked in the rearview mirror and hit the turn signal then headed toward the police station. "Yeah, he called right before you got in the car and said neither of the two gunmen had any form of ID on them."

"What about the car? It had to have been registered to someone." Though he doubted Hunter Barlowe or Senator Lowell would be foolish enough to have registered it in their names.

"He didn't say. I'm sure they'll figure it out."

Yeah, but would they? No matter what obstacles got thrown into Senator Lowell's path, he seemed to be able to overcome them. Every time Adam had found someone who was willing to say the senator was responsible for blackmail, bribery, or intimidation, they either suddenly backed out of testifying or they disappeared. The senator was shrewd, knew how to manipulate people, maneuver them in the most painful way possible into doing exactly what he wanted them to do.

When Adam had gone after him, he hadn't killed Adam to stop him, and that would have been an option. A good option. But what pain would it have inflicted on him? None. So what had he done instead? He'd gone after Adam's family, killed them to hurt him. And he was apparently arrogant enough to think he'd covered his tracks well enough that when Adam made it his mission in life to stop him, he'd still walk away free and clear.

Well, not this time. As long as Adam had breath in his body, he'd keep coming until he'd taken the man and his supporters down. And then…

And then what? Where did he go from there, once he could go to his wife and assure her Lowell was behind bars and would never hurt anyone else? What kind of life would he have? He'd been so caught up in seeking justice, so obsessed with his mission, he hadn't given any thought to what would come next.

The jolt of pain came hard and strong, pierced his heart with its jagged edge. Because once his vendetta was over, once his goal was achieved, he'd have nothing of Alessandra and his child left to hold on to. They would forever be a part of his past. And his future? His future was an endless expanse of emptiness.

Jack's phone rang, and Adam shut down his current line of

thinking. It didn't matter right now. All that mattered was putting an end to Senator Lowell's reign of terror.

"It's Gabe." Jack hit a button on the dashboard screen and answered on his Bluetooth. "Hey, what's up?"

"Is Adam with you?"

Jack glanced over at him and frowned. "Yeah. Is anything wrong?"

"I just wanted to let him know we fingerprinted the two gunmen, and their prints aren't on file anywhere. We're running a facial recognition program, but the tech isn't optimistic."

"So, no ID, no fingerprints on file for any reason?" Jack asked.

"Nope, nada. It's as if these two don't even exist."

How was that possible? Everyone left some kind of paper trail nowadays. It was early, and they hadn't had time to do much more than start a preliminary search, but still… "What about the car they were driving?"

"A guy paid cash for it last month from a seemingly random stranger who'd left it in the train station parking lot in Ronkonkoma with a For Sale sign in the window. The tags were stolen from a black sedan of the same make and model."

"No way that can all be coincidence." Adam's mind raced. They had to get something, anything from those men. It was their only lead. Without any kind of connection, the Hunter and the senator would go unpunished…again.

"No, I wouldn't think so." The call started to cut in and out.

And there was one thing Adam needed to know before it dropped. "Hey, Gabe, did you get a chance to question them yet?"

"Not officially, but I can tell you…not a word…not even… for a lawyer."

With the connection pretty much lost, Jack let Gabe know they'd be there in about fifteen minutes and then disconnected. "What do you make of it?"

Adam massaged his temples where a dull throb pulsed. "Honestly, I'm not surprised."

Senator Lowell was a master at covering his tracks, and he'd expect nothing less from those in his employ. And Hunter Barlowe was a tech genius and a cybersecurity wizard. Perhaps he handled more for the senator than just killings.

But something was nagging at him. A niggle at the base of his spine was urging him to figure it out. He was missing something important. There were too many questions, not enough answers. He'd been hoping the two gunmen they had in custody would provide at least some of those answers. He needed to be at the police station, needed to hear what they had to say.

How had Lowell managed to erase any sign the two men ever existed? Did they even work for him? Or had Hunter Barlowe hired them? As a cybersecurity expert, he'd surely be able to hack and delete any records.

A jolt of terror rocketed through him. "Stop the car."

Jack hit the brakes and pulled to the curb even as he frowned at Adam. "What's wrong?"

"Was Pat going to stay with Jaelyn at the hospital?"

He was already shaking his head. "She wanted to talk to Maya alone, said she'd be fine. And there are officers posted at the hospital."

"Go to the hospital." He couldn't explain why, but he had a strong feeling he needed to get to Jaelyn.

"What? Why?" Jack hit the turn signal, looked over his shoulder, and swung a U-turn.

"It doesn't make sense for Senator Lowell to have sent anyone after Maya or Jaelyn." Or did it? He'd obviously paid for the hit on Jaelyn's parents. Had he had Maya's parents killed too? For what purpose? Unless the hit list was a fake. Maybe Hunter was setting the senator up. Once Adam had discovered the list with the senator's initials after so many hits, he'd gotten distracted, lost focus, shifted his attention to the senator as the ringleader. And yet... "It makes more sense to me that it's Maya's husband, Hunter Barlowe, the hitman known as the Hunter, who's been trying to get at her. And now she and Jaelyn are alone in that hospital room."

Chapter Eleven

Jaelyn stood outside Maya's door. She'd sent Pat home. There were police officers down the hall, and Pat had already missed enough of the holidays with his family because he was helping her. Besides, she needed a few minutes to collect herself before meeting her sister for the first time. What did you say to the twin you never knew existed? Should she introduce herself? That seemed weird, considering Maya already knew who she was.

Enough worrying already. Surely she'd figure out the right thing to say when she came face-to-face with the woman whose child she'd already come to care so much for. Whatever was said now, she prayed Maya would allow her to remain a part of Leigha's life.

She blew out a breath and eased the door open, peeked her head into the room.

Maya was sitting up in the bed, staring toward the window where the blinds had been drawn closed.

"Maya?"

She turned her head to face Jaelyn and reached out a hand. "Thank you for coming."

"Of course." Jaelyn crossed the room to her, gripped her

hand. The resemblance was incredible, like looking into a mirror. It was definitely going to take some getting used to. "How are you?"

"I'm okay, thank you, but there's something I have to ask you." Her eyes were swollen, red-rimmed, as if she'd spent hours crying.

"Of course."

Pain twisted her features; tear tracks stained her cheeks. "I left something in the closet at the bed and breakfast where—"

"She's fine." Jaelyn caught Maya's hand in both of hers and kept her voice low. "I have her."

"Oh, thank you." She dropped back against the pillows, squeezed her eyes closed. "I was worried sick. I'd made arrangements for someone to pick her up if he didn't hear from me by a certain time, but when he got there, she was already gone. He was able to find out you'd been there, in my room, but I didn't know if you'd been the one to take Leigha."

The fact that Maya had made arrangements for someone to get Leigha brought an instant sense of relief. She still had a million questions, like why she'd gone on the run, but the most important one in Jaelyn's mind had been answered. She hadn't abandoned her child, only hidden her to keep her safe. "I'm sorry, Maya. I wasn't sure what to do when I found her there, but I couldn't leave her when one of the men trying to find you was already in the room."

"No, no. Please, you did the right thing. Thank you. If you hadn't…" She shivered and sat up straighter. "Well, I don't even want to think about what might have happened if someone else had gotten to her before my guy did."

With that out of the way, Jaelyn didn't know where to start. There was so much she wanted to know. Who were their birth parents? Where were they now? Had Maya known about Jaelyn all along? What kind of trouble was she in, and how could Jaelyn help?

"Where is Leigha now?" Maya tucked her free hand beneath the blanket. "I need you to take me to her."

Keeping Maya's hand in hers, Jaelyn sat beside her on the edge of the bed. She could certainly understand Maya's desperation to see Leigha, but she was in no condition to leave the hospital. Instead, Jaelyn would bring the baby to her. "I don't think they'll release you yet, considering your injuries."

She yanked her hand from Jaelyn's. "I'm getting out of here and going to my daughter. Now."

The woman needed reassurance. "Okay, just hold on a sec. I understand how upset you must be and how desperate you must be to get to her, but I promise you she's safe. She's with friends of mine, friends I know I can trust to watch out for her. I can ask them to—"

Maya narrowed her gaze, and some of the warmth slid away to reveal a cold emptiness in her eyes. "What friends?"

A chill raced through Jaelyn. Why was Maya looking at her like that? Did she think Jaelyn would try to keep Leigha from her? She stood and reached for the button to call the nurse before Maya could get any more upset, or worse, pull the IV line out on her own.

"I said…" Maya lifted her other hand from beneath the blanket and aimed a handgun with an attached silencer at Jaelyn. "What friends?"

Jaelyn gasped. Her hand froze midway to the call button. "Where did you get the gun?"

"My guy wasn't only responsible for retrieving Leigha. He monitored me and brought it as soon as I woke up." Maya grabbed her wrist, and when Jaelyn tried to pull away from her, she maintained an iron grip.

"What's going on, Maya? I wasn't trying to keep her from you. I just wanted to keep her safe from whoever was after us until you recovered. I was going to ask my friends to bring her here to you."

"Well, I'm recovered enough, so you and I are going to get

out of here and go get my daughter." She spoke with a deadly calm. "Then you're going to give me the briefcase and diaper bag you swiped from my room, the briefcase I took a beating from the senator's men to keep hidden, and I'm going to disappear. Now, step back. And don't you dare breathe a word about the gun to anyone, or you will die." She released Jaelyn's hand, threw the covers off, and swung her feet off the bed, all while keeping the gun steady. "The only reason you're still breathing right now is because you have that child. If not for her, you'd already be dead in this bed, and I'd be taking your place."

What was she talking about? The senator was after Maya? But deep in her heart, Jaelyn suspected she already knew that. "The guy who attacked me when I went to your room at the bed and breakfast, he belonged to the senator?"

"Yes, seems Senator Lowell wasn't happy when I took off."

So it wasn't her husband who'd been hunting her down. "And the guys who killed the senator's man, the same ones who tried to kill me at the safe house, they didn't belong to the senator, did they? They belonged to you."

"Good to see smart runs in the family." It all came crashing down on Jaelyn—all this time, they'd been hunted by two sets of bad guys. The senator's men after Maya, and Maya's guys after her. "Now, let's go."

Could she stall Maya? What would the woman do if someone came in? Adam had said he'd meet her here. Maybe she could keep Maya talking long enough for him to show up. But then what? She didn't want to put him in danger. But she did want him, desperately. She wanted him to cocoon her in his arms as he had on the beach, she wanted the chance to tell him she'd been wrong, that she did have feelings for him. Very strong feelings that scared her half to death. "You wouldn't get away with switching places with me," Jaelyn said. "People would know it was me, not you, who died."

She shrugged. "Maybe, but it wouldn't matter. You'd have been beaten as severely as I was and left in the bed. If anyone had reason to suspect it wasn't me, they'd run into a problem identifying the corpse since all records of my existence have already been wiped. And soon yours will be wiped as well and replaced with those I've forged before I leave for Montana, where I'll start a new life with my husband and child as Jaelyn Reed."

"Your husband?" Jaelyn's blood ran cold. If she was going on the run with Hunter Barlowe, with all of the documents she had in her possession, then she had to know who and what he was and must be okay with it. Jaelyn didn't know why that surprised her, especially knowing Maya had already sent men to kill her.

She had to think. She was in trouble—real trouble.

Already dressed, Maya stood and slid her feet into her shoes. "You and I are going to walk out of here. You will smile, nod, say you're taking me for a walk to stretch my legs, say or do whatever it takes to get me out of this hospital without anyone stopping me. Do you understand?"

She simply nodded, since her mouth had gone too dry to speak. She'd go along, cooperate with Maya for now, until she could find a way to take her out.

Maya yanked the tape from her arm and the IV, which she'd already removed, came free. She gestured toward the door with the weapon. "Walk."

Jaelyn turned toward the door, struggled to ignore the wave of emotions threatening to drown her so she could think clearly.

Maya came up beside her, gripped her elbow. She held the weapon in her other hand, secreted in her pocket, no doubt aimed at Jaelyn. "I will not hesitate to kill anyone who tries to stop me. You included."

At her nod, Jaelyn opened the door. Her heart raced frantically, her pulse pounding in her ears. All she had to do was walk out. They just had to make it into the elevator at the end of the hallway and then out of the hospital. And then what?

"Where are we going?" Jaelyn let Maya set the pace, which

was not nearly as slow as Jaelyn would have expected, considering her injuries.

When they reached the elevator doors, Maya stopped. "First floor."

Jaelyn pushed the button, waited. So many things flew through her mind. Leigha. How could she send that innocent child off with this woman and her hitman husband? How could she bring this woman to Ava and her little girl after they'd been so kind and taken her daughter in? Would she kill them as well? She'd have to, wouldn't she? She couldn't leave any witnesses.

The ding of the elevator arriving pulled her back to the moment.

Maya smiled at an elderly gentleman emerging then guided Jaelyn inside.

Jaelyn held her breath while the doors closed, praying no one else would get on with them. When the doors finally shut, she asked again, "Where are we going?"

"We're going to pick up my daughter, and then my family and I will be leaving for our ranch in Montana."

"If you're in trouble, Maya, I can help you. You don't have to do this. I have friends who can keep you and Leigha safe."

"Oh, do you now?" She scoffed. "Safe from whom exactly?"

How much should she say? Should she admit to knowing the truth about her husband? What did she really have to lose at this point? Since there was no way she could bring Maya to Ava's, Jaelyn was already as good as dead. "I know about your husband. I know Hunter Barlowe is the hitman known as the Hunter."

Maya laughed out loud, a deep rocking laugh that had tears running down her cheeks. "Oh, honey, you know nothing. My husband isn't the Hunter."

"But I saw the documents with the hit list, the amounts paid...my parents' names."

"Oh, right, sorry about that." The elevator doors slid open, and Maya yanked her out into the busy lobby. No one seemed to notice the two women passing through. "But that one's not on me. That was dear old Dad who insisted the Hunter get rid of them."

"Dad? What are you talking about?"

Maya crossed over the threshold and onto the sidewalk, then stepped to the side and stopped. She looked Jaelyn straight in the eye. "Our real father, Senator Lowell, hired the Hunter to kill your adoptive parents so they would be out of the way before he runs for president. Anyone who knew the truth about us, that his mistress gave birth to us and put us up for adoption, had to be eliminated. Just as our mother was eliminated right after we were born. He'd have killed you too, had people tailing you and everything, but when he realized you never knew you were adopted he developed a soft spot and let you live."

She spat the words with such bitterness, such jealousy, Jaelyn almost felt sorry for her.

Jaelyn's head spun, not because she couldn't wrap her head around the whole situation, but because it made a sick sort of sense. "How do you know all of this if your husband isn't the Hunter?"

"Because, dear, my husband, Hunter Barlowe, met his end years ago, once he'd served his purpose and was no longer needed to keep up appearances. Since then, he's only existed on paper, a persona I created to take the fall when I decided to retire. I'm the Hunter."

Adam spotted Jaelyn and Maya standing on the curb when Jack pulled up. "What are they doing out here?"

Jack looked in the direction he indicated then shifted into park. "Do you want me to wait here?"

"Yeah, would you mind? Just give me a minute to find out what's going on?"

"Sure, man, no problem."

Adam hopped out of the SUV and started toward Jaelyn.

The instant she spotted him, she stiffened. She cast a glance toward Maya then shook her head once.

He paused, glanced back to where Jack still sat watching him from the SUV, then back at Jaelyn. Something was wrong.

A Jeep pulled up to the curb, and Maya kept hold of Jaelyn's elbow as she urged her forward.

Adam ran back to Jack. "I don't know what's going on, but call Gabe and follow that Jeep without letting them know they're being followed."

He didn't wait for an answer, hoped Jack would do as he'd asked, but no way was that woman getting Jaelyn into that vehicle alone. He forced a smile and waved as he hurried toward them. "Jaelyn, hey, hold up."

Thankfully, Maya averted her gaze and didn't see him, probably not wanting to have to stop and explain why there were suddenly two Jaelyns.

Jaelyn stopped, waved back. "Hey there…uh, sorry I don't have time to chat right now. My sister just got released from the hospital, and I'm taking her home."

Sweat beaded on her forehead; despite the chill in the air, it snaked along her hairline. Though she'd schooled her expression, she couldn't hide the sheer terror in her eyes.

"That's okay." He moved closer, was almost within reach of her. "I won't keep you long, I just had a quick question."

The man driving the Jeep reached across the passenger seat and shoved the door open. "You're going to have to take him too, Maya."

Adam's heart stopped. "Josiah?"

"Climb into the back seat." Maya nodded toward the Jeep. "Now. Or I kill her."

He did as she said. Then, with his full attention focused on the dead man in the driver's seat, he slid across so Jaelyn could climb in next to him. "I don't understand. How are you alive? I watched you die."

"You saw what we wanted you to see." Maya slammed the

door behind them, then climbed into the passenger seat and leaned across the console to kiss Josiah. "We faked Josiah's death so we could start our new life together in peace with no one the wiser. Drive, dear."

Rage poured through him. He'd shouldered the guilt for this man's death. "How?"

Josiah offered a cold smile in the rearview mirror. "Maya was the shooter, and the gun was loaded with blanks. I hit the blood pack under my shirt and then just played dead." He shifted into gear and started through the parking lot. "When she kept shooting, you had to run. Maya's associates picked me up and she hacked the medical examiner's office to close out my case, death from a gunshot wound to the chest. And there you have it. Josiah Cameron no longer exists."

All of the emotions he'd held at bay over the past years threatened to boil over. These people had no regard for anyone, simply manipulated whoever they had to in order to get their way. "But why come to me in the first place if you were going to fake your death all along?"

"Actually, that wasn't part of the original plan." Josiah's expression turned sour. "We had the whole thing set up so perfectly. We left enough circumstantial evidence to get me arrested so I could come to you and provide real evidence against the senator and then watch him burn. Just the thought of outwitting him, of watching him spend the rest of his life in prison knowing we were the ones to put him there, was joyous." He sighed. "The plan was for the senator to go down for hiring out the hits, for Hunter Barlowe to disappear and become the stuff of legends, and for us to find our happily ever after." He glanced at Maya next to him. "But it didn't work out that way. When Senator Lowell ordered a hit on me, we knew we could never find peace as long as he was alive. Or as long as we were." Josiah smiled, then turned his attention to the road ahead and pulled out. "Which way?"

"My dear sister was just about to tell me that, weren't you,

Jaelyn?" Maya turned to point the gun at Adam between the seats.

"I'm sorry, Adam." Jaelyn slid her hand into his and gripped it tightly. "Make a right when you leave the parking lot."

He forced the fury down. It would do neither of them any good. He had to get a grip on himself and stall, because there was no way he was watching the woman he felt so much more for than he'd been willing to admit die. He'd been a fool to ignore his feelings for her, to suppress them to keep from risking his heart again. Now he just had to live long enough to tell her he'd risk his heart or anything else for her, and ask her to take that same chance. "What's going on here, Jaelyn?"

Maya met Jaelyn's gaze and smirked. "Oh, feel free to fill him in. It's not like either of you are going to be talking to anyone else once we get where we're going."

Adam resisted the desperate urge to glance behind him to see if Jack was following. He had to trust the other man would get them help.

"It seems we were wrong about who the Hunter was." Jaelyn's voice shook wildly, and he wanted desperately to pull her into his arms, comfort her, shield her from danger. "Hunter Barlowe no longer exists. He's *her*... Maya is the Hunter."

His mind raced to put the pieces together. Once he did, his stomach sank. No wonder he'd never seen her with her husband. The man was already dead.

"But why, Maya? I don't understand," Jaelyn said.

"That's because you went to a loving family who doted on you and gave you the best of everything." The bitterness in her voice turned Adam's stomach and made him fear for Jaelyn even more. "I, on the other hand, went to Daddy's dear friend, the dear friend he liked so much, he had him killed the day I turned eighteen. At that time, he offered me his job."

"As a hired gun?" Jaelyn's voice had gone from terrified to shocked.

"Of course." Maya seemed to ponder something for a moment, then turned toward the front and met Jaelyn's eyes in the rearview mirror. "Come to think of it, that was probably his intention all along, to have me follow in my adoptive father's footsteps. He never trusted that man, not fully, and he had him start training me from the time I was old enough to handle a weapon. Then, as soon as I was trained and at a suitable age to take his place, he got rid of him."

Adam squeezed Jaelyn's hand, willing her to keep the other woman talking. If she shifted her gaze from Jaelyn, she might well spot Jack or a police officer behind them and kill Jaelyn here and now.

"So, why are you running now? Why are you stealing my life and going on the run?" Jaelyn asked.

"When I found out I was pregnant, I knew Lowell would never allow me to go off and live my life in peace. And if I killed a sitting senator, no matter how tempting, I would be hunted to the ends of the earth. While getting beat up by Daddy's thugs didn't factor into my plan, faking my own death after pretending to eliminate Josiah did. This way, Daddy Dearest thinks I'm dead, he thinks Josiah's dead and that I followed orders. And we're free to live our lives."

"But why take *my* life?" Jaelyn's voice lost all of the tremor, went icy cold. "You could be anyone."

"You're right, I could have invented any alias I wanted and left you alone, but why should *you* have gotten the good life? Why did *you* get to grow up in a nice little town, with loving parents, friends…you probably even had a golden retriever, for crying out loud." Maya whirled on her, and the viciousness in her eyes had Jaelyn shrinking back and Adam going on alert.

The short burst of a police siren sounded from behind them, and Maya lifted her gaze out the back window.

Adam didn't turn around, didn't dare shift his attention from the irate woman sputtering in the front seat.

"What did you do?" she screamed and lifted the gun toward

Jaelyn, her eyes filled with so much hatred Adam had no doubt she'd kill her.

He grabbed Maya's wrist, shoved her arm up, yanked his own weapon from the back of his jeans and pointed it at Josiah's head. "It's over, Maya. Don't move."

He couldn't help the tremor in the hand holding the gun. He wasn't afraid, but he was holding onto the woman who'd killed Alessandra and their child, the woman who'd tried to kill Jaelyn and Leigha. He had every reason in the world to shift his aim and end her here and now to ensure she never killed anyone else. And one very big reason not to. He forced his weapon to hold steady.

Josiah slammed on the brakes. The SUV skidded to an abrupt stop as he jammed it into Park, shoved the door open, and dove out.

With the threat to him removed, Maya lunged toward Adam, raked her razor sharp nails down the side of his face as she struggled to free her gun hand.

He jerked back, faltered his own weapon in a desperate attempt to hold onto her.

Before he could regain his hold on the gun, Jaelyn shifted onto one knee, grabbed the seat back and swung like a champion, landing a solid blow to Maya's chin.

Maya's eyes rolled up.

With his weapon recovered, Adam held it aimed at Maya and prayed she'd stop fighting. Because he didn't want to have to pull the trigger, didn't want to see her die at his hand. She'd go to court, as was her right, and hopefully be convicted not only for Alessandra and their child's murders, but for all the others she'd committed as well. And that would have to be enough. "Josiah?"

"The police have him." Jaelyn lay a hand on his arm. "It's over, Adam."

And, as police officers led by Gabe swarmed the vehicle and

took Josiah and Maya into custody, he knew that Jaelyn was right. It finally was over.

He had to get out of the car, needed air. He shoved the Jeep door open and climbed out. Chaos surrounded him, but he ignored it all.

"Hey, man, you okay?" Jack lay a hand on his back.

Adam only nodded. In the moment he'd looked into Maya's eyes and knew she was about to pull the trigger, a realization had flooded through him. He loved Jaelyn with all his heart, couldn't be without her.

She slid into his arms, wrapped her arms around him, and lay her head against his chest.

"I love you, Jaelyn," he said. "I'm sorry I didn't realize sooner, didn't tell you—"

"You're telling me now. And I love you too, Adam." She looked up at him and smiled, then stood on her tiptoes and pressed her lips to his.

And with that, the bleak future he'd envisioned suddenly seemed so much brighter.

Epilogue

Jaelyn rocked lazily back and forth on the porch swing, Leigha snoring softly beside her, her head resting in Jaelyn's lap. She lay a hand on her still flat stomach where a new life grew, a life only she and Adam knew about for the moment. But soon it would be time to share their joy. She wasn't ready to tell anyone else yet, not until the trial was over and Maya's fate decided…and she would know very soon what that fate was. Adam had been on standby all day waiting to hear the verdict. So, there she sat on the wide wraparound porch of their new home in Seaport, the home they'd moved into after getting married four months earlier.

Suddenly Adam leaned over from behind her, wrapped his arms around her, and entwined his hands with hers over their child. "I bet I know what you're thinking about."

She laughed and leaned against him, the woodsy scent of his aftershave cocooning her in comfort and a feeling of safety. Over the past year, she'd suffered nightmares and hadn't slept well, but having Adam beside her these past months had helped tremendously, and she'd begun to heal. "Have you heard anything?"

"It's over, baby."

The trial had dragged on forever, and the verdict had been slow in coming.

"And?" Jaelyn held her breath. If Maya wasn't found guilty, wasn't convicted, what would they do? She looked down at Leigha, napping peacefully on the cushion next to her. No way was she giving this child back to that monster.

"She and Josiah were both found guilty of murder. Josiah for the guy in the bed and breakfast, and Maya for the whole list of people documented in her paperwork." He rounded the swing to sit on the other side of her with Leigha between them, tucked a few strands of hair that the gentle spring breeze had blown into her face behind her ear. "They are both going away for a very long time."

He put an arm around her, stroking Leigha's cheek. "And she's ours, Jaelyn. No one can take her from us now."

She sobbed softly, the pain of not knowing if they'd get to keep Leigha finally relieved. They'd been granted emergency custody. Maya had agreed to waive her parental rights so they could adopt her only if she was convicted. "The senator?"

"Maya's testimony assured he's done," Adam said.

She nodded, wiped her eyes, and leaned against her husband. She'd given Maya and Senator Lowell all the time she'd ever give them. Now, it was time to move on, time to live her life with her husband and children.

"And now that the trial's over," Adam continued, "all the forgeries in your name will be destroyed. The ranch is to be sold. Since it's in your name, I asked that the money be donated to an organization that helps abused women and children."

"That's fine. It's good. I have all I ever want from that woman." She lifted Leigha onto her lap, cuddled her as she scooted closer to Adam.

Adam shifted so he could look into her eyes. "Are you okay?"

"I am now." And with their children between them, she pressed her lips to his, then pulled back to look at him. "Everything is perfect now."

* * * * *

Romantic Suspense

Danger. Passion. Drama.

Available Next Month

Colton At Risk Kacy Cross
Renegade Reunion Addison Fox

....

Canine Refuge Linda O. Johnston
A Dangerous Secret Sandra Owens

....

LOVE INSPIRED
Searching For Justice Connie Queen
Trained To Protect Terri Reed

....

LOVE INSPIRED
Wyoming Ranch Sabotage Kellie VanHorn
Hiding The Witness Deena Alexander

....

LOVE INSPIRED
Lethal Reunion Lacey Baker
A Dangerous Past Susan Gee Heino

Keep reading for an excerpt of a new title
from the Intrigue series,
COLD CASE DISCOVERY by Nicole Helm

Chapter One

Her phone trilled in the dark.

Chloe Brink rolled over to find the other side of the bed empty, which was good. *Best*. Considering the screen on her phone read *Do Not Answer*.

In other words, it wasn't work or something important. It was her brother calling her. At two in the morning.

She loved her baby brother and wished she could save him, but he was an addict. And until he accepted that, until *he* decided he wanted to change, her relationship with him had to be distant.

She was a sheriff's deputy. She couldn't rush in to save him from every problem. It would only get them both in trouble.

So she didn't answer.

The first time.

After the ringing paused, only to immediately begin ringing again, she sighed and did the inevitable. Maybe one of these days all the steps she'd taken to try to insulate herself from this need to be his—or anyone's—savior would actually work.

But not tonight.

She closed her eyes, let her head flop back onto the pillow and took a deep breath. "Ry, what is it?"

"I need your help."

She counted to three, inhaled deeply. Let it out. He didn't *sound* high, but that didn't mean anything. "We've been over this."

"Chloe, you don't understand. This is serious. It wasn't me. I don't know what to do. There's bones. It wasn't me. It's too old. Too deep. Chlo, I don't know what to *do*."

Panicked, clearly. But *bones* didn't make sense. She pushed up into a sitting position on the bed, tried to clear her mind. "What do you mean, Ry? I don't understand."

"By the barn. I've been digging for that new addition, right?"

She didn't say what she wanted to: *At two in the morning?* She let him blabber on only half making sense. At least it was just some jumbled talk about bones, not actual trouble with the law.

"You have to come. What am I supposed to do? I didn't do this. This isn't mine. It's *bones*."

Chloe went over everything her therapist had told her. It wasn't her job to clean up Ry's messes. He had to be responsible for his own choices.

But this wasn't the *exact* same thing. He wasn't in a fight with someone. He wasn't asking her to get him out of a ticket or an arrest. He'd just stumbled upon some bones—animal, probably—and convinced himself, perhaps with the aid of an illegal substance, it was a bigger deal than it was.

If she went over there, told him everything was fine, he'd stop bothering her for a few days. "Fine. Listen. I'll come over. But just to look at these bones, okay? But you have to stay put. And sober."

There was a pause on the other end of the line.

"I mean it, Ry. Not even a sip of beer. If I can't trust you to—"

"Okay. I promise. Nothing. Nothing else. If you just come over. Quick. I don't know what to do."

"Just don't move, and don't touch anything. Or *take* anything," she muttered, before hitting End and tossing her phone onto the empty side of the bed.

This was what her therapist didn't understand. Sometimes going over to help was the better course of action. She'd nip it in the bud and then be free of him for a few days. Best all around.

Best or easiest?

She groaned.

"Bad news?"

She didn't jolt, didn't open her eyes right away. She'd woken to an empty bed, so she figured he'd gone, because that was how this worked. Usually, that caused an ache around her heart, one she was determined to stop and never did—but tonight, him still being here was the last thing she wanted.

Just another one of her very own choices she had to face. She opened her eyes.

Jack Hudson stood, leaning his shoulder against the doorframe of her bedroom. He was dressed now, in the clothes they'd left work in: Khakis that weren't so perfectly pressed like they had been all through his workday. A Sunrise Sheriff's Department polo—untucked now.

But she knew what he looked like without all those clothes. *Hot.*

Maybe his hair was a little rumpled, but no one would think or even believe that it was *sex*-rumpled hair. Jack Hudson, the upstanding sheriff and uptight head of the

Hudson clan, engaging in a clandestine affair with one of his deputies? *Impossible*.

She still hadn't spoken, and now she watched as Tiger wound her way between Jack's long legs like she always did. Because that animal was just as foolish and weak as she was when it came to Jack.

"Chloe," he said in that half-empathetic, half-scolding tone.

He only ever used her first name *here*, what they were—and weren't—perfectly compartmentalized. Her fault as much as his, she knew, though she wished she could blame him and his rigid personality. But she'd put up walls to save herself too.

Because she was self-aware enough to know he could emotionally crush her if she didn't. She didn't think *he* knew that, and that was all that mattered.

"Just my brother. Needs me to come check something out. Typical." She slid out of bed, pulled on some sweats and put her smartwatch on her wrist. But Jack didn't leave.

She shoved her phone in her pocket. Keys and shoes were out in her living room. So she moved for the door, but Jack still stood there. Blocking her exit.

"You should head home," she told him. "A bit late for you."

He didn't say anything for a few moments as he studied her in nothing more than the glow of her smoke detector. They were shadows to each other, and yet it felt like—per usual—Jack Hudson could see *everything*.

"I'm coming with," he finally said.

Not *Would you like me to? Can I? Should I?* Not for Jack Hudson. "Not necessary, Sheriff." She threw that one at him when she wanted him to back off. Usually, it worked.

He didn't budge.

"It's two in the morning."

"Yeah."

"It's your brother."

"Yeah."

"I'm going with. We can either drive together or I can follow you, but I'm going."

"And be seen together at this hour?"

He didn't say anything. But he didn't move. Because no, Jack Hudson didn't relent. He was who he was.

Sometimes she thought she was as bad as her brother. Jack was her drug, and she couldn't give him up. Because he wasn't good for her—the secrecy; the way she couldn't get past that impenetrable, taciturn wall. But the way he made her feel when he put his hands on her was worth it.

She sighed, and she didn't relent, but Jack seemed to read the surrender in that sigh.

"I'll drive," he said, turning toward her front door.

"Of course you will," she muttered, and didn't bother to argue. She just made sure Tiger didn't bolt out the door with them in a shameless effort to follow Jack.

Chloe might be a mess, but she knew better than to throw herself against a brick wall that wasn't budging.

JACK HUDSON WAS well aware of his reputation. He knew what just about everyone thought of him. It varied a bit. To some people—particularly the law-abiding citizens of Sunrise, Wyoming—he was a saint. That was how he'd won the election for sheriff time and time again. To others—usually criminals and people related to him—he was an uptight ass.

Jack knew he was no saint, but he didn't quite agree with his siblings. Maybe he was a little strict, a little more con-

trolled than *completely* necessary. But hey, they'd all somehow made it into adulthood in one piece and were mostly
successful, and that was because of *him*.

He'd held the family together after his parents' disap-
pearance when he was eighteen. He'd created Hudson Sib-
ling Solutions to ensure his siblings always had jobs and to
help other people with unsolved cold cases—solving quite
a few, thank you.

Though never his own.

His parents—good, upstanding ranchers not involved in
anything shady, that anyone had ever found—had disappeared on a camping "date weekend" one night seventeen
years ago. Just vanished.

All these years later, hours and hours of police work,
private investigator work, research from every single member of his family, no one had ever discovered even a shred
of evidence of what had happened to Dean and Laura Hudson.

He told himself, day in and day out, that it was over.
There would never be answers, and sometimes a man just
had to accept the hard facts of life.

He was also an expert in denial.

The woman in his passenger seat, case in point. Chloe
Brink hadn't *always* been a problem. Or maybe she had
been and he'd just been younger and delusional. Hard to
say now.

They'd been engaging in this whole *thing* for a year now,
and he didn't relish the secrecy. It was an irritating neces-
sity. But one of the short list of positives was that this was
something his siblings had no idea about and, therefore, no
say in, no opinions.

Everything that happened with Chloe was *all* his.

"Don't worry," Chloe said in the dark cab of his truck as he slowed down to take the turn into the Brink Ranch entrance. "Even if Ry said something about us arriving together in the middle of the night, no one would believe him. Or at least, not believe the real reasons."

Jack didn't respond, though it required him to grind his teeth together.

He knew she didn't understand his determination to keep this a secret. He'd never tried to explain it to her because she wouldn't believe it. In her mind, he was embarrassed, and he knew her well enough—whether *she* wanted to admit it or not—that it stemmed from her own issues. It took a lot to be a cop in the same place where your last name was pretty much synonymous with *criminal*.

Hell, wasn't that part of why he liked her so much? He wouldn't say they were too alike outside their profession. Chloe was fun and friendly. No one had ever accused him of being either. Not since he was a teenager anyway.

But they both shared a dogged determination to see through whatever they thought was right.

What she would never understand—partly because of that dogged determination and a thick skull—was that people knowing about their...relationship...would cause problems for both of them.

He'd been around enough to know she'd bear the brunt of any negative reaction to their...relationship. It wasn't fair, it wasn't right, but it wouldn't matter what she did. Or what *he* did to try to protect her.

She was a woman, and she'd get the short end of the stick when it came to their work reputations. Right or not, police work—especially police work out here in rural Wyoming—

was still male dominated. Jack dealt with the public enough to know a lot of people were still stuck in the Dark Ages.

He wouldn't let Chloe get a bad rap all because he… He was weak when it came to her, and that was *his* fault. He'd be damned if he let her take the fall for that.

So it had to be a secret, but that didn't mean he didn't care or was *embarrassed* of her.

It also didn't mean he had to like it.

Jack Hudson was well-versed in all the things he didn't like but dealt with anyway.

He pulled through the open gate to the old Brink place. It was open at a crooked angle and clearly had been that way for a while, as grass and vines had grown up and twined around it.

He didn't say anything about that either. Chloe's family was her business, and *maybe* he'd on *occasion* mentioned something about her brother, this ranch and so on, but she always put him in his place.

When he pulled up to the house, Ry was standing out in front of it, pacing back and forth. Jack could see the look on his face in the harsh light of the porch—just a light bulb screwed into the wall, no cover.

Ry was all nerves. Worry. Concern. But something was missing, and he'd dealt with Ry enough in a professional capacity to find it interesting. Chloe's little brother, for once, didn't look guilty.

Yeah, interesting.

"Why'd you bring him?" Ry asked on a whisper when they got out of the truck. Not quiet enough for Jack to miss it, but he pretended he had.

"What's the emergency, Ry?" Chloe asked, sounding

less like a sister and more like a cop—but if she was thinking with her cop brain, she wouldn't be here.

"It wasn't anything to do with me. I just found it," Ry
said, louder this time, making sure Jack heard it.

Jack studied Ry Brink. No doubt he'd been high at some
point today, but whatever he'd been on was wearing off. He
was jittery, gray faced. Scared.

Chloe's expression was blank. "Show us," she said. She
switched on a flashlight Jack hadn't realized she'd grabbed
on their way out, so he figured he could turn on the one
he'd gotten out of his truck as well.

Ry leaned close; this time whatever he whispered to
Chloe was lost in the sound of insects buzzing and breezes
sliding through the dilapidated buildings.

"Show us," she repeated, whatever Ry had said clearly
not winning her over.

Ry led them away from the house, which had seen better decades. They quietly moved toward a caved-in barn.
Ry. Chloe. Jack.

It was his desire to take over, to lead the way, but he
tamped it down. Because this was Chloe's deal, no matter
how little he liked it, and he'd only come along to ensure
her brother wasn't laying some kind of trap.

Chloe might not think Ry capable, but Jack had spent his
entire adult life seeing what drugs did to seemingly reason-
able people. Part and parcel with a life in law enforcement.

They walked for a while in silence, and Jack noticed
as they came around the side of the barn that there was
a battery-powered lantern sitting in the dirt, tipped over,
like it had been dropped there.

"I had this idea that I'd dig out a new entrance to the cel-
lar," Ry said. And if he was telling the truth, it was clear

he'd been high when he'd had that idea, because that wasn't going to work.

"The first one I hit, I figured it was animal. Dad used to bury the dogs out here. You remember, Chloe?"

She didn't say anything. She pointed her flashlight beam on the unearthed dirt. A shovel lay haphazardly next to the pile.

"Then I got a few more and… It's not animal bones. I know animals. It ain't animals."

Jack didn't believe that. Lots of people mistook bigger bones for human. He approached the hole with Chloe, shined his light at the ground as well.

He sucked in a breath. Heard Chloe do the same.

Human. Definitely. A full skeleton, almost. Jack swept his flashlight beam down the bones, his mind already turning with next steps. They'd have to notify Bent County. The Brink Ranch was a little outside Sunrise's jurisdiction—and besides that, they didn't have the labs or professional capacity to deal with dead bodies.

It might not be nefarious. Ranchers back in the day buried their kin on property. There were laws against such things now, but it didn't mean people always abided by them. This could be anything. It didn't have to be criminal.

Still, Jack studied the skeletal remains with an eye toward foul play. Hard not to. He swept his beam back up and noticed that something glittered. He didn't want to touch anything, destroy the scene any more than Ry already had, but he trained his light on that glitter and crouched so he could study it closer.

And it felt like the earth turned upside down, like every atom of oxygen in his body evaporated. He saw dark spots for a moment.

Chloe crouched next to him, put her hand on his back. "Jack? Are you okay? What is it?"

He had to breathe, but it was hard to suck in air. When he spoke, he heard how strangled he sounded. But he said what needed saying: "I recognize that ring."

Chloe peered closer. "How?"

"It was my mother's."

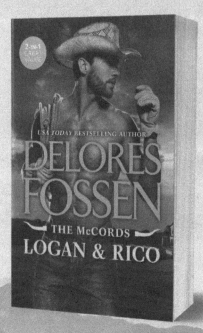